Genre 4 (Series)

D0759588

M
c.3

Thomson, June
  Portrait of Lilith.   Doubleday, 1982.
  186 p.

        I. Title
11.95   LC 82-45503

PORTRAIT
OF LILITH

PORTRAIT OF LILITH

JUNE THOMSON

PUBLISHED FOR THE CRIME CLUB BY
DOUBLEDAY & COMPANY, INC.
GARDEN CITY, NEW YORK
1983

All of the characters in this book
are fictitious, and any resemblance
to actual persons, living or dead,
is purely coincidental.

Library of Congress Cataloging in Publication Data

Thomson, June.
Portrait of Lilith.

I. Title.
PR6070.H679P6   1983   823'.914
ISBN 0-385-18335-6
Library of Congress Catalog Card Number 82–45503

First Edition in the United States of America

CHAPTER 1

Crossing the hall with Max's breakfast tray, Nina saw there were two letters lying on the doormat. One, addressed to herself, she recognised immediately by its cheap, blue envelope and overelaborate handwriting with the ridiculous flourishes on the capital letters and, balancing the tray awkwardly on one hip, she bent down, picked it up, and thrust it into the pocket of her smock.

The other lay face down, its blank reverse side giving nothing away although Nina doubted that it was from Zoe. Max's ex-wife usually wrote at the end of the month, chatty letters always addressed now to her only, containing at the end some scarcely veiled reference to the cost of living and how hard up she was, and Nina, in replying, would enclose a fiver, saying nothing to Max either about the money or the exchange of letters. However, the thick, cream envelope looked too good a quality to be Zoe's.

Picking the letter up, she scrutinised the front of it carefully but it told her nothing except it was neatly typewritten, had been posted in London and was addressed to Max Gifford Esq., Althorpe House, Althorpe, Chelmsford, Essex, and she placed it on the tray next to the big brown teapot, Max's mug with the white daisy on it (one of the few usable products to come out of her evening pottery class), and the plate of fried eggs, sausages and bacon which, with a conventionality that still surprised her, he insisted was the only breakfast worth eating, and began the long climb up the stairs towards his room.

They had never been carpeted, partly because of the cost, partly because Max insisted that the broad oak treads were too beautiful to be covered over, and they should have been polished regularly to preserve them. But the task was too much for her, as indeed was the upkeep of the whole house, and the wood was now scarred and battered. Besides, she had never much cared for the place. It was Max's choice, this great, ugly, inconvenient heap of brick and slate, with its ruined garden, its huge rooms, impossible to heat adequately in winter, its antiquated plumbing and its surprising touches of Victorian exuberance, such as the stained-glass window which faced her on the half-landing as she toiled up the stairs; large enough for a church and just as gloomy, in her opinion, depicting a girl with streaming yellow hair and eyes turned piously upward on the point of being ravished by a man with a curly beard and an off-the-shoulder tunic which revealed the right half of his chest, so extravagantly muscled that it looked like armour plate. A swan's head, peering with a black, malicious eye from the background, suggested it was meant to represent Jove's seduction of Leda. For some reason, it had appealed to Max, largely, she suspected, because he had identified himself with the lecher-god, and it had been one of the factors in his decision to buy the place; that, and the equally preposterous Victorian conservatory, like a scaled-down railway terminus, all glass and wrought iron and coloured floor tiles, tacked on to the dining room which, in the past, he had used as his studio. As far as she was concerned, she would have preferred to stay in London where there was a bit of life going on and shops just round the corner.

She paused in front of the stained-glass window to rest for a few seconds and to shift the tray to the other hip.

I'm getting old, she thought and then smiled at her own self-pity. It was becoming a habit, reminding herself of her age. She was forty-five. No longer a spring chicken, it was true, but hardly with one foot in the grave, yet there were days when she felt more like sixty-five.

She mourned the loss of her vigour more than the decline in her looks and figure although she was still an attractive woman—handsome even, as she had to admit to herself, when she took the trouble to dress herself up and arrange her hair which was still thick and dark red though not the startling colour it had once been. This morning it was bundled back and tied with a bit of string and, because she wasn't planning to go anywhere special except perhaps down to the village shop on her bike, she was wearing an old denim skirt and one of Max's smocks, nice and roomy, which she remembered him buying years before in Brittany from a shop selling fishermen's clothing. Max had liked the colour, a bright orange, faded now to an indeterminate pale red, and the huge front pocket which he could stuff with tubes of paint and brushes and other painting paraphernalia.

It now contained Danny's letter which she could feel crumple against her stomach as she moved the tray over and began to climb the next flight of stairs to the upper landing.

Outside Max's door she stood listening for a few seconds before entering. The room was in semidarkness and silent except for the sound of his heavy breathing although she guessed he was probably awake and watching her from under his eyelids as, putting down the tray on the bedside table, she crossed the room to draw back the curtains. There was a theatrical quality about the deep, regular intakes and exhalations of breath, the way children pretend sleep, and she was amused as well as exasperated by it. Why on earth did he bother with such small deceits?

To catch him unawares, she remained standing at the window, as if absorbed by the cool May morning, a light rain more like mist coating the leaves and grass, before turning unexpectedly to surprise him. He was lying, a great, grey, bull-seal of a man beached amongst the crumpled bedding, the neck of his nightshirt unbuttoned to reveal a broad chest, Jove the Ravisher's once magnificent torso grown flabby with age, and with one eye slyly open. It snapped shut immediately and she pretended not to notice.

"Breakfast, Max!" she said loudly and he grunted, yawned, and stretched, going through the pantomime of waking up.

The old fool! she thought with affectionate contempt as she helped him into a sitting position, propped up among the pillows against the massive oak headboard under the portrait of the nude that hung immediately above his bed.

It was familiar to her. In fact, it was the first thing she had noticed in Max's London studio all those years before when, as a young girl, she had run away from home to become his mistress, and yet it still possessed the power to command her attention. Firstly, its sheer size dominated the room; so did its colour. The pale body of the naked girl lay curled up asleep on a red sofa, her back, with its spine bent like a taut bow, and the buttocks presented to the viewer. Thrown over one corner of the sofa near her feet was a pink shawl, or perhaps a dressing gown—even Max couldn't remember which—it had been the colour, not the garment itself, which had attracted him and the shocking, vibrant contrast it made with the red background.

The other intriguing quality about the portrait was the anonymity of the model. There was no indication of her features at all, not even a glimpse of profile, only the back of her head being visible, propped up on one hand, her dark hair loose and flowing over one shoulder, and yet what was clearly evident was the beauty of the girl who had posed for it. That dazzling skin! That exquisite line of hip and spine! And how Max, in painting her, had luxuriated in that beauty! He had used a palette knife, laying the paint on thickly and drawing it across the pigment to emphasise the curves of the body, while in the hollows, the little cups behind the bent knees, for example, or at the ankles where the shadows were pink-tinted from the red reflected from the sofa, the skin tones had been painted in with small, rounded flakes of pure colour.

The total effect was of overwhelming sensuality and yet the girl herself remained strangely aloof, untouched by the passion of the artist who had represented her.

Max would never speak of her except once—years before, prompted by Nina's direct questioning, he had said her name was Lilith and she had acted as his model for a short time in London.

It was ridiculous, of course, to feel jealousy of someone she had never met, and yet, looking at the portrait even now as she helped Max into an upright position against the pillows, Nina was stirred by an echo of an old resentment, directed not so much at the girl as at Max for having chosen this portrait rather than one of herself to hang above his bed.

"There's a letter for you," she said, setting the tray across his knees.

"Who's it from?" he asked. He was fumbling with the mug of tea she had poured for him, his hands, swollen with arthritis, cupped carefully round its sides.

"How should I know?" she retorted. "Why don't you open it and find out?"

He peered at it suspiciously where it lay propped up against the teapot. In old age, he had assumed this habit of carefully scrutinising anything that was new or unexpected as if he had grown increasingly wary of anything that intruded into his world.

"You read it for me," he said. "I can't see properly without my glasses."

It was another small deception, like the pretence of being asleep. Although he might be crippled, his hearing and eyesight were unimpaired and, judging by the crumpled sheets of yesterday's newspaper lying discarded at the foot of the bed, he had been awake in the night reading. And smoking. The ashtray was full of stubs of the strong French cigarettes he preferred.

Nina, however, made no protest. The suggestion that she should read the letter to him suited her very well for, left to himself, he might hide it away somewhere in the room and then she might never know its contents. All the same, she put up a show of exasperation, a habit she had got into as Max grew increasingly old and dependent. He didn't seem to mind. In fact, it appeared to amuse him for she had often caught on his face an expression of pleased, secret satisfaction as if her annoyance was the very reaction he had been hoping to arouse.

Tearing the envelope open, she took out the sheet of paper, allowing herself a few seconds to scan its contents although she didn't absorb them properly until she read them aloud to Max. Her attention was mainly caught by the name at the top, the Demeter Gallery, beautifully embossed in thick, black print, as hard and as glossy as a beetle's back.

"'Dear Mr. Gifford,'" she read. "'A few weeks ago, I was fortunate enough to buy one of your paintings, "Figures on a Suffolk Shore," from a private collector. Since then, I have made inquiries regarding your work and have had the opportunity of viewing several more in provincial galleries. I have greatly admired what I have seen and I feel very strongly that your work has been seriously neglected in the past, not having been given the public attention or acclaim that it deserves. In order to rectify this, I would like to discuss with you the possibility of mounting a retrospective exhibition of your paintings and drawings at my gallery. Would it be possible for us to meet some time in the near future to talk it over? Perhaps you could telephone me to discuss the arrangements. Yours very sincerely, Eustace Quinn.'"

As she read it, Nina glanced up from time to time to Max's face. He was sitting back, his eyes closed, his expression impassive, giving nothing away, the old fox, but she noticed he had put down his knife and fork, leaving his breakfast neglected on his plate.

Confronted by his unresponsiveness, she was uncertain herself how to react. Her initial excitement was replaced by a wariness similar to that which Max often displayed. An exhibition in London! But was that, after all, a good idea? The mention in the letter of drawings, too, made her anxious. She had extracted several from Max's portfolios and she wondered if their absence would be noticed. Besides, if she showed too much enthusiasm either for or against the idea, Max could quite easily, out of sheer cussedness, decide the opposite. So she remained silent, waiting for his reaction.

"'Figures on a Suffolk Shore?'" he asked at last in an offhand voice, opening his eyes and getting on with the business of eating his breakfast as if it were the only concern that had any importance for him.

"Yes," Nina replied, glancing down again at the letter.

"Ah, of course! A woman lying among some sand dunes with a male nude standing beside her. I sold it for a hundred and fifty pounds in 1947 but who the hell bought it? I can't remember but"—pointing his fork at her—"I bet whatever-his-name-is paid a damn sight more for it than that."

"Eustace Quinn," she put in.

"Daft name," he commented. "Eustace! Makes me think of some lah-di-dah public school twit with no balls. And Quinn!" He laughed. "You could write a limerick about him. 'There once was a fellow called Quinn, Whose tool was so terribly thin . . .'"

"Oh, for God's sake, Max!" she interrupted him. "What are you going to do? Will you see him?"

"I don't know. I'll have to think about it."

And that, she knew from experience, was that. It would be useless to press the subject. Max would return to it in his own time. Meanwhile, she would have to wait, knowing that he was finding pleasure in keeping her waiting. Her only defence was to pretend she didn't care.

"What's the weather like?" he asked, through a mouthful of food.

She glanced indifferently towards the window.

"Raining."

With a little luck, Max would stay in bed for the morning, provided she didn't reveal either by her tone of voice or her expression that this was what she wanted. In that case, he'd get up and she'd have him sitting about downstairs, making it impossible for her to check the portfolios.

"Oh, hell," he said. "I think I'll stay in bed."

She got him up, however, to wash, removing the tray and helping him into a sitting position on the side of the bed. It was at times like this that she realised how helpless, in fact, he really was and her pretended exasperation was replaced by a fierce compassion for this great, ruined hulk of a man. His legs, pitifully thin under the old-fashioned nightshirt he always wore, dangled down as his feet, long, white, gnarled, and yet still incredibly elegant, felt uncertainly for the firm surface of the worn carpet. She waited with him, still holding his arm, while he recovered from the exertion and while they both gathered together their strength for the final haul that was needed in order to get him on his feet.

There was no need for her to count. With some shared instinct, they rose together, Max pressing down on the mattress with one hand while she lifted him by the other arm. Like some great sack, he was levered upward, hung perilously for a moment and then, once his balance was established, she felt some of his weight transferred as he found his feet. The rest was comparatively easy although painfully slow. Still holding his arm, she helped him out of the room and along the passage to the bathroom, Max walking with the careful, shuffling steps of an old man, his dressing gown worn loose over his shoulders, his great head with its shaggy white hair hanging low as he watched his feet, still bare as he found it easier without slippers, moving forward one in front of the other as if he were fascinated by their unaccustomed motion.

Once in the bathroom, she could seat him on the wooden kitchen chair and leave him to it. Providing he had everything within reach, he could cope. She laid the towel over the rim of the bath, found his toothbrush and made sure that the old-fashioned brass taps, their metal corroded with age, could be turned on and off easily.

In the doorway, she paused, looking round critically to make sure she had forgotten nothing, and thought suddenly, seeing it as if with Max's eyes, how the setting would make a perfect background to a portrait of him: the huge bath with its claw feet and the dark water-stain spreading down under the taps, the lavatory with its iron cistern and dangling chain, the white tiles that covered the walls, their glaze crackled, the narrow frieze of blue stylised tulip heads running along the top of them, and, placed centrally, the figure of the old man on the wooden chair, his back to her, very slowly turning on the taps with his crippled hands, his broad shoulders bowed under the striped nightshirt, and the top of his bent head reflected in the mirror above the basin.

At the same moment, she was aware that the mirror contained an image that she had not expected. Max had lifted his head and was watching her observing him, not with his usual expression of secret amusement but with a look of long, careful speculation. On catching her eyes, it was immediately veiled.

"I think I'll have a bath today," he announced unexpectedly.

"All right," she agreed, hiding her surprise. What in God's name had put that idea into his head? Could he, after all, be seriously considering Eustace Quinn's offer? With Max one never knew. "You'll have to wait, though, until Lionel can come round. I can't get you in and out of the bath on my own."

"When? This evening?" He seemed impatient at the thought of a delay.

"I don't know, Max. I'll have to ask him. He's on half-term holiday this week so it should be all right. I'll call at his house this morning, if you like."

"Good." As she turned away, he added, rubbing one hand over the harsh, grey stubble on his face, "And tell him to bring that fancy electric razor of his with him. I feel like poncing myself up."

It was one of their shared expressions and she smiled at him through the mirror before remarking over her shoulder as she left, "I've got things to do. Shout when you want me."

Closing the door behind her, she returned to the bedroom where she hastily tidied the bed before going downstairs to the hall. There she paused outside the dining room and glanced upstairs to the landing to make sure the bathroom door was still shut. Max could manage a few steps on his own if he had something to cling to and she did not want him observing her movements. Reassured, she turned the big brass handle and entered.

The air in the room, never used nowadays, struck cold and she shivered slightly and folded her arms round her body. It had always been dark and cheerless, situated as it was on the north side of the house, with the conservatory, which had once been Max's studio, cutting off most of the natural light. She glanced into it through the tall French windows as she crossed the room, abandoned now, the glass grimy, the tiled floor littered with dead leaves which had blown in through a broken pane. Only the easel, still propped up in one corner, and the big iron stove which Max had had installed, its pipe, red with rust, going up through the roof, served as reminders of his former occupation. All his other stuff, the canvases and the big portfolios of drawings, together with his artist's materials, had been moved into the dining room where they were better protected from the damp and where they now lay scattered about: shoe boxes full of half-used tubes of paint, jars of brushes, palettes still bearing the dried-up daubs of colour from the last painting he had worked on; and the paintings themselves, stacked up against the walls, showing the discoloured backs of the canvases and the wooden stretchers.

The portfolios lay on the table to keep them flat and she looked at them carefully, wondering if Max would notice they had been opened should he ever come into the room—a possibility that had seemed unlikely until Eustace Quinn's letter had arrived. Since he had given up painting, he had never shown the slightest inclination to enter the dining room or his studio nor had he expressed any concern about his past work.

The fact that she had extracted some of the drawings had not worried Nina at the time. There were hundreds of them, some finished sketches, some mere charcoal scrawls on scraps of paper—a hand, perhaps, or the outline of a head, the rough notes which Max had jotted down as he worked. It hadn't seemed likely that he would miss half a dozen out of the huge collection, especially as she had always been careful not to take any of the larger, completed drawings, only the quick sketches—a couple of nudes, she remembered, some drawings of trees, two or three seascapes washed in briefly with colour.

Now, concerned that Max might notice she had opened the portfolios, she moved the top one from which she had extracted most of the drawings, first tying up the tapes which fastened it together, and dragged another on top of it. If, for any reason, he wanted to examine them, he'd look through the first to come to hand, she told herself, and not bother with those underneath.

As she did so, she wondered how much Danny had got for the sketches. A fiver each? It was possible. They were good in their way, especially the nudes which had demonstrated Max's vigorous line, but she felt no guilt about her part in it, only anxiety to cover up her tracks and prevent Max from finding out, because then there'd be a row and, worse that that, she'd have to explain why she'd taken them, which she wanted to avoid doing at any cost. It wasn't stealing. Danny had needed the money and, as she hadn't had the cash to give him, it had seemed perfectly moral at the time since all the money she had possessed had been used up to pay off Max's debts. Therefore it was legitimate to take back from Max, in the way of a few drawings, what he owed her anyway. Nevertheless, she'd now have to stop doing it and find some other way of helping Danny out.

His letter was still lying unread in the pocket of her smock and, having satisfied herself that the dining room looked just as Max had last left it, she went into the kitchen to read it in comparative comfort, making herself a cup of coffee first before sitting down at the big, deal table that occupied the centre of the room.

She was putting off, she realised, as she finally took it out of her pocket, the moment of opening and reading it. Letters from Danny usually meant trouble and she saw, with a sense of foreboding, that there was no address at the top although it was dated Saturday. It was short and read simply:

"Dear Nina, Can you meet me at the usual place on Monday? I'll be there about half past eleven and I'll wait for an hour, hoping you can get away. If you can't, leave the signal and I'll try again on Tuesday. Love, Danny. P.S. Try to be there. It's important."

It always is, she thought grimly, tearing the paper across and dropping it into the stove. Before adding the envelope, she glanced at the frank and saw that it had been posted in Bexford, the local market town. Danny, therefore, was staying in the neighbourhood and hadn't come down for the day on one of his usual, quick forays from London.

There was only one consolation: she'd have no trouble meeting him. With Max safely in bed and the ready-made excuse of calling at Lionel's, there'd be no problem and she wouldn't have to go through the ridiculous pantomime of hanging two tea towels on the washing line, the signal Danny had devised so that she could warn him when she couldn't leave the house. It was a stupid subterfuge, anyway, which smacked to her of a third-rate thriller or some cheap, adulterous affair and she often wondered how much of Danny's life was governed by such deceits. Quite a lot, she suspected. Luckily, she had never had to make use of the signal, for God knows what Max would think if, say, she rushed out to hang up tea towels in the pouring rain. It would be enough to make him suspicious.

Max shouted for her just as she was replacing the top of the stove and she returned upstairs to help him back into bed, settling him against the pillows and making sure he had his cigarettes and matches handy. The full ashtray she emptied out of the window, watching the stubs and ash cascade down into the laurels below. It was a wonder, she thought, that over the years the damned things hadn't died of nicotine poisoning.

It had stopped raining and the sun was beginning to emerge from behind low, pale clouds, its light pearly and diffused. The garden smelt sweet after the rain, that green scent that she always associated with veridian paint, mingled with the brown odour of the earth. But the colours of the garden weren't yet heightened by the sunlight and the view had the subdued look of one of Max's sketches, washed over with a thin, grey transparency, as if it were still early morning.

Behind her, she could hear Max grunt and heave as he made himself comfortable and then she caught the surreptitious crackle of paper. Turning, she saw he was reading the letter which she had left on the bedside table as a mute reminder that sometime he'd have to come to a decision.

He gave her the cocky grin he always assumed when she had caught him out, although, on this occasion, he probably intended that she should see him reading it.

"Well, Nine," he said, using the diminutive form of her name and laying the letter down, "what do you think?"

"I don't know," she replied quickly. "It's up to you."

"Eustace Quinn." He chuckled again as if he still found the name amusing. "Ever heard of him?"

"No."

"Or his gallery? The Demeter?" He put an ironic emphasis on the name. "Goddess of corn, wasn't she?"

"I think so."

He seemed to lose interest, stuffing the letter back into its envelope and throwing it down to the bottom of the bed.

"Has the paper come?" he asked.

She brought it upstairs and left him reading it, the letter still lying discarded, although when she came back at eleven o'clock to bring him his cup of coffee, it was placed where she had originally left it on the bedside table.

"Going out?" he asked.

She had changed out of the smock into a blouse and jacket as the morning was still cool and had tied her hair back with a piece of brown ribbon. Trust Max to notice such details. She sometimes wondered if anything escaped his attention.

"Only to Lionel's," she lied.

"Why?"

"Because you said you wanted a bath."

For a moment, it occurred to her that he might have changed his mind and she'd have to make up a fresh excuse, like needing to go to the shop for bread, but he merely said, "How long will you be?"

"Not long. About half an hour, I suppose."

"A whole half hour for Lionel?"

"Well, I can't just walk in and out again, can I?" she retorted. She felt real exasperation rising. "It'd look rude. Besides, he'll ask after you; he always does."

He began to heave up and down in bed and she looked at him with alarm, wondering if he was having one of his coughing attacks. Those bloody cigarettes, she thought fiercely. They'll finish him off one of these days. But she saw he was laughing, his eyes squeezed shut and two little drops of moisture gathering in the corners above the pouches of flesh.

"Oh, for God's sake!" she cried, banging her fist down furiously on the footboard.

He recovered enough to sit up and wipe his eyes on the sheet although he was still shaken by great gusts of laughter.

"Lionel! Little lion! Nina's soft-pawed, pussy-cat pet!"

"It's not like that!" she protested.

"Oh, come off it, Nine. The minute I kick the bucket, he'll come scurrying round here, a wreath for me in one hand and a bunch of red roses for you in the other. I bet you!"

"Well, if you're right, I don't see how you'll collect your winnings," she replied coldly and marched across to the door, ready to slam it shut on him.

"Nine, wait a moment." His voice was wheedling, conciliatory.

"Yes?" She paused in the doorway.

"You've forgotten something."

"What?"

"This."

He chucked the letter towards her and it fluttered down to the floor so that she was forced to come back into the room and bend down to retrieve it.

"While you're at Lionel's, ring up this Eustace man and tell him I'll talk to him. But mind you make it clear I'm not committing myself to a decision yet. It's only a discussion."

Straightening up, she said, "You old sod."

He grinned at her, unrepentant.

"Give my love to Lionel."

She slammed the door anyway, determined to have the last word.

Downstairs, as she looked in her purse to see how much cash she had to spare for Danny, she thought about the exhibition for the first time as a real possibility. Supposing Max agreed to the suggestion, what could it mean? Money, perhaps, and they could do with some of that. If there was enough, she'd get someone in to mend the roof and she might even treat herself to a few new clothes. She needed a pair of winter boots and a decent overcoat. One thing was certain: she wouldn't let Max get his hands on it; not that he'd have much opportunity now to spend it, unlike the old days when, after a profitable sale, he'd go out and blow the lot on bottles of brandy or weekends in France—once, a whole smoked salmon from Fortnum & Mason's, decorated with leaves and flowers piped on in mayonnaise. Stupid, really; but all the same, she sighed at the memory.

Nor would she tell Danny; that would be crazy. He'd write twice as often, looking for a handout. The same applied to Zoe, although, being in London and still in touch with their old artist connections, Zoe might get to hear of it eventually. In that case, Nina thought, she'd have to play it down, pretend Max hadn't made too much out of it, and fob her off with an occasional tenner.

Anyway, wasn't she counting her chickens too soon? Max might change his mind, or Eustace Quinn his, come to that. And even if the exhibition was ever mounted, there was no guarantee it would be a success.

Art had changed since Max's time and not for the better, in her opinion. It was all this avant-garde stuff now—coloured shapes daubed onto canvases or strange symbolic paintings representing God knows what. She had no time for it.

All the same, she would like to think that fame might come to Max in his old age. He deserved it. After a lifetime of dedication, she thought bitterly, what is he left with? A room full of paintings and perhaps a two-line mention, if he's lucky, in some art history book—that's all.

She wondered how much he minded. It was difficult to tell. Although she had lived with him for nearly thirty years, there were many areas of his life that remained hidden from her, not just the time before she had met him but whole stretches of his personality as well. She might fool herself into thinking that she could read him like a book but, if she were honest with herself, she had to admit that it was only those pages which Max himself chose to disclose to her.

Glancing at the clock on the mantelpiece, she saw that it was now twenty past eleven and, shouting good-bye up the stairs to Max, she went out to the stable to collect her bike, shoving her handbag into the basket on the front. The gravel on the drive crackled under her wheels as she cycled off, turning right at the gate into the road that led to the village.

The day was warming up, she noticed with pleasure. The sun was now properly out and the metalled surface of the road steamed gently as the moisture on it dried.

At the corner of the long, overgrown hedge that bounded the garden, she dismounted and, having glanced up and down the road to make sure no one was watching, she bumped the bike across the grass verge onto a rough pathway that led between the hedge and the adjoining field towards the back of the house. At the far end where a coppice of trees extended in which the rooks had built their untidy nests, a small gate, once painted white, now stained green with damp, stood ajar, and, pushing it further open, she dragged the bike through before abandoning it behind a clump of rhododendrons.

This end of the garden was rarely visited by anyone and the shrubs, untended for years, had grown to massive size. Between them ran a whole network of narrow, moss-grown paths which occasionally opened out into a small clearing where a garden seat or a piece of statuary, strategically placed to make the most of a vista, betokened long-ago, warm, Victorian afternoons when there was time to spare for leisurely, after-luncheon walks.

At the edge of the shrubbery, where the bushes ended, stood a summerhouse of rustic wood, facing a sunken lawn intended originally as a tennis court, judging by the iron posts round its perimeter still supporting in places the rusting remnants of wire netting which had once enclosed it. The grass was now knee-high and the banks, on which the spectators had once sat and applauded, were overgrown with periwinkle and its small, blue flowers, which Nina rather liked, now starred the slopes.

Since she approached the summerhouse from the rear, it was impossible to tell, until she rounded the corner, whether or not Danny had already arrived. Nina hoped he hadn't. She would have preferred a few minutes alone to recover her breath and compose herself before facing him.

Danny heard her coming. Christ! he thought, she blunders about like some bloody elephant. If anyone should be keeping a watch, they'd hear her a mile off.

It was the same exasperation he had felt when they were children together. Nina had always been impulsive, acting first and thinking afterwards. Protecting him from Father's or Aunt Connie's wrath, she would make matters worse by losing her own temper, thereby doubling his punishment. "But it's so unfair!" had been her cry throughout their shared childhood.

As a little boy, he had felt frightened, too, at times, by her passionate involvement with him, but also horribly fascinated. She would weep over him, he remembered, holding him close and rocking him backward and forward, her hair hanging down over his face. Even now he imagined he could still feel and smell it. Cradled within her arms, he had felt suffocated, but oh God! how inexpressibly safe.

And then she had run away; with Max, as he found out later, a betrayal that he had never quite forgiven her for. Nor, he suspected, had she quite forgiven herself. It was as much her guilt as her love that made it so easy for him to keep coming back.

Rounding the corner of the summerhouse, Nina saw that he was there before her, seated on the bench and leaning forward, his expression anxious as if he were not sure who was approaching. His unnecessary fear touched off the same exasperated pity that Max often aroused in her. Who else could it be except her? This part of the garden could not be seen from the house and no one, certainly not Max, was likely to be prowling about. Besides, hadn't he arranged to meet her here?

Relief showed in his face as soon as she appeared in the open doorway and that spontaneous, almost childlike joy which was one of the reasons why she loved him and wanted so fiercely to protect him.

Jumping to his feet, he flung one arm round her, lowering his head against her shoulder so that she could feel his breath on her neck and she knew at once, as she hugged him close, that something must have gone badly wrong.

They remained in silence for several seconds, Nina still holding him, Danny passive in her embrace as if he could have remained like that for ever until she drew back and looked him in the face.

"What's happened?" she asked.

But the moment of spontaneity in which he might have told her the truth had passed and she wondered, as she often did with Danny, how far, in fact, that initial warmth of his greeting had been genuine, or if it had been merely assumed in order to disarm her subsequent disapprobation. His expression had changed and had taken on the sulky, hard-done-by look which was more characteristic of him.

She noticed, with disquiet, how ill he seemed. He had lost weight and his features looked darker and more shadowed than usual. He had always been thin even as a child, with that delicate fragility which had once been appealing. Now he looked famished and, as even she had to admit, a little weird with those high, triangular cheekbones and prominent Adam's apple sticking out above the collar of his shirt which moved convulsively up and down as he answered her. It seemed to possess a separate existence of its own and she could hardly keep her eyes off it; it fascinated her.

"I'm in a bit of a jam," he admitted.

She sat down on the bench and he took his place beside her; not facing her, however, but looking out across the garden so that she could only see his profile, the thin nose and high, bony forehead looking more exposed than ever now that his hair had begun to recede, and she realised with a shock that he was thirty-six, no longer a young man.

He'll go like Father, she thought. At forty, he had already been thin on top and stoop-shouldered. Danny had inherited his physique and his fine brown hair. As for herself, she resembled neither of their parents. Their mother, who had died shortly after Danny was born, had been much darker in colouring—a real brunette and beautiful, judging by the photographs of her. Nina, who had been nine at the time of her death, could remember only her presence and a sense of being cherished, which was probably why, she thought wryly, that she herself loved Danny with such a passionate concern. It had fulfilled in her a deep need to exercise that same quality of love because it was the only way she knew how to keep it alive. And now it had become part of her; part of him, too, she realised. She could never now withdraw it. How on earth would he manage without it?

He gave her an oblique look, slyly appealing.

"I owe someone some money," he explained.

"How much?" she demanded quickly.

"About a hundred."

It was probably a lie but whether it was a hundred or a thousand or a hundred thousand, there was no way she could possibly pay it.

"Anyway, the man I owe it to turned awkward." He was speaking more rapidly now, his Adam's apple jerking up and down frantically. "He's been causing trouble so I thought I'd better clear out of London for a bit and let things cool down. The thing is, Nine"—using the same diminutive form of her name as Max—"I thought if I could get straightened out, start fresh somewhere else . . ."

"What about your job?" she broke in.

"I had to pack that in."

God knows what it was; something to do with second-hand cars down in Kennington, she understood. Before that he had been working as a barman at a drinking club. He was never specific about what he did and she had to drag what little information she could out of him. She had the impression, too, that it was more often than not something semilegitimate if not downright illegal, and she wondered if this wasn't the cause of his present problems. It could be anything—drugs, gambling, a protection racket.

"And your flat?"

"I cleared out of that last week."

"So where are you staying?"

"In Bexford. There's a hotel that takes in commercials. Look, Nine, what I wanted to say was this—if you could see your way clear to lending me about fifty quid—only as a loan, mind—I'd pay you back once I've got things sorted . . ."

Fat chance, she thought grimly. She had some money saved up towards paying the rates but she daren't part with that. God knows how she'd ever raise it again although if the worst came to the worst, she'd have to hand it over. Not yet, though.

Out loud, she said, "I can't, Danny. I haven't got it."

"Twenty-five then."

"Not even that straight away. I'd have to raise it."

Although how she wasn't sure. There wasn't much left in the house worth selling.

"But I'll need it soon. They'll be asking me to settle the bill at the hotel by the end of the week. What about Max's drawings? There's a chap I know in London who'll buy them."

"No, I can't give you any more."

"Why not?"

"Because Max has been talking about going through his stuff. He might miss them."

It was only half a lie, she thought. If anything came of Eustace Quinn's suggestion, Max would certainly begin to show an interest in what he had available for exhibition.

"Oh, hell! I was counting on those. Can't you spare even a couple?"

"I daren't, Danny. It's too risky."

"So what the bloody hell do you suggest I do?"

Always back to me, she thought wearily, as if he isn't responsible for the mess he gets himself into.

"Look," she said, "if there's a problem about a place to stay, I can have a word with someone I know who might be able to put you up for the time being. If not, we'll have to think again."

There were plenty of spare rooms in the house where he might have slept but she didn't dare suggest it. Max would almost certainly find out and she didn't want that. For some reason which she couldn't rationally explain, Max and Danny must never meet. In fact, she wasn't even sure that Max knew of Danny's existence although in the past, when they first met, he may have been vaguely aware that she had a younger brother. Certainly his name was never mentioned and she had no wish to introduce Danny at this late stage. She knew instinctively that it wouldn't work. They'd never get on together and she loved both of them too much to run the risk. Between them, they could tear her apart.

"When can you let me know?" he asked.

"Tomorrow probably. I'll be seeing this . . . friend later today."

Knowing Danny, she was reluctant to divulge Lionel's name or address. He might turn up on Lionel's doorstep, claiming heaven knows what privileges on the basis of her friendship with him.

"I'll phone you sometime," she added. "Where are you staying?"

"The Dolphin Hotel." He parted with even this morsel of information reluctantly. "If I'm not in, leave a message for Mr. Anderson."

Christ, she thought, he really must be in a jam if he's using a false name. Or perhaps it was merely Danny's pathetic need to dramatise his very ordinary, squalid life, like the signal with the tea towels.

"What'll you do meanwhile about settling the bill if they ask?" she inquired.

"Oh, I'll get by for a couple of days," he said with pretended indifference. "There's usually a way round these things."

Like creeping out without paying, she thought. She could imagine him doing it, too, the pockets of the cheap, shabby raincoat he was wearing stuffed with a few portable belongings, the rest of them abandoned along with the second-hand fibre suitcase—a small price to pay, probably, in his estimation, for bilking the hotel. And, anyway, who was she to point a finger? There had been an occasion in London when, unable to pay the gas bill, she and Max had pawned everything of any value they possessed—her watch, his big japanned box of paints, even an overcoat belonging to God knows who which had been left behind in the studio.

"How much do you need now?" she asked, getting out her purse. "I can only spare a couple of quid."

He took the notes and thrust them away in his pocket, not bothering to look at them or even to thank her except perfunctorily.

"What I really need, Nina," he was saying before his hand had left the inside of his jacket, "is a fresh start in London—a flat or a room somewhere north of the river where I'm not known. I've still got a few business contacts I can trust. They'd set me up again, I know."

She thought immediately of Zoe. Zoe lived in Fulham; she might know of a flat going vacant.

"I'll see what I can do," she replied. "Mind, I can't promise anything. I've lost touch with a lot of my old London friends. I'll have to let you know."

"All right."

He was getting to his feet, brushing the dirt from his sleeve where it had been in contact with the damp, wooden walls of the summerhouse, and she thought sadly how typical it was of Danny to bother with such a small detail when the whole raincoat was grubby and in need of a damn good clean. It seemed to sum him up.

"Danny," she began and then stopped. What was the good of asking him anything more about himself? He wouldn't tell her and, even if he did, she couldn't be sure it was the truth.

Instead, she asked, "Why don't you go down to Heversham? Perhaps Dad would see you right, or Aunt Connie."

As she said it, she had a brief, mental image of the village, small and bright and perfect, like one of those miniature scenes inside a glass globe before it is shaken to make the snow fly; the church and the vicarage and the cluster of houses bathed in the unchanging sunshine of childhood.

He was looking at her, his upper lip lifted in a small, bitter smile.

"Christ, Nine! Have you seen them recently? Stupid of me to ask; of course you haven't. Well, Dad's practically gaga and Aunt Connie's almost as bad. Besides, they'd ask too many questions. It gets on my nerves after a few hours."

She took the hint and said no more, following him in silence to the doorway of the summerhouse and trying not to think of those two elderly people, as old now as Max. How strange, she thought. It had never occurred to her before that they were of the same generation.

Danny kissed her briefly on the cheek this time, with none of the warmth of his greeting, and she watched him walk away into the shrubbery, his hands pushed deep into his raincoat pockets, his head bent and one shoulder thrust forward with that odd, lopsided, defensive gait which was so familiar and, suddenly, so painfully poignant.

CHAPTER 2

Nina waited for ten minutes to give him time to get well clear of the place before she followed, retrieving her bike from the bushes and pushing it along the edge of the field into the road.

There was no sign of Danny and she assumed he had turned to the left, towards the Feathers, half a mile along the road, where he could have a drink while waiting for the next bus into Bexford. Thank God, with his own natural tendency towards secretiveness, he had never, as far as she knew, appeared in the village.

Remounting her bike, she turned to the right in the direction of Althorpe. On the outskirts, just within sight of the village, was Lionel's house.

It was a small, neat, detached cottage, built of brick, with a formal front garden—typical of Lionel, which was probably why he had bought it in the first place. Propping her bike up against the interwoven fencing that screened the side of the house from the adjoining sugar beet field, Nina squeezed her way past Lionel's blue Cortina which was parked in the narrow drive.

The back garden never failed to delight her. It faced south, catching all the sun, and, perhaps influenced by the light and warmth, Lionel had broken free from the prim formality of the front and had turned the area immediately behind the cottage into an Italian-style patio, with little, raised, brick-bordered flower beds and an extraordinary collection of containers for the fuchsias he specialised in growing: urns, tubs, pots of every dimension, even buckets, which Lionel, with painstaking care, had painted with those bright, formal patterns that one finds on old-fashioned barges. The total effect was strange, exotic—quite out of keeping with her accepted view of him.

Beyond lay a lawn, neatly mown, a greenhouse for the overwintering of the fuchsias, and, at the far end, under an apple tree, a small caravan.

The back of the cottage, too, was less formal than the front, its straight lines being broken by a one-storey addition containing the kitchen, the window of which was open and at which, as she rounded the corner, Nina caught a glimpse of Lionel in the act of drying his breakfast dishes, wiping the front and back of each plate and saucer with a housewifely concern that put her own slapdash methods of housekeeping to shame.

Seeing him for those few seconds before he was aware of her presence, she was able to observe him with an objective and critical eye. Until that moment, it had never crossed her mind to wonder how old he might be; she had merely accepted him for what he was—just Lionel, a middle-aged, bachelor schoolmaster, a little pedantic and overfussy—the type, she imagined, who would inspire ribald comments behind his back from irreverent pupils. Now, watching him as he pottered about in his kitchen, self-absorbed and happily occupied, she supposed he must be in his early fifties. He was slightly built and undistinguished-looking with rimless spectacles and thinning, sandy-coloured hair that was turning a yellowish grey and that had an odd, dusty look about it, as if it had been powdered all over with fine meal; mild-mannered, judging by his eyes, overenlarged by the lenses of his spectacles, but stubborn as well, from the way in which his narrow lips would sometimes press together.

Could Max possibly be right and Lionel be in love with her? Nina asked herself. The idea had never occurred to her before. She had always regarded him as Max's friend, however unlikely even that relationship might be. But Max adored admiration and it was perfectly obvious that Lionel deeply respected Max the artist. How he regarded Max the man was another matter entirely. Nina was of the opinion that Lionel disapproved but had learnt to suppress any overt signs of criticism. And the reason wasn't difficult to find. Lionel, a history master at Bexford Boys' Grammar School, was also an aspiring artist; at least, he painted pale, ladylike water-colours about which Max, with a tolerance that old age and dependence had taught him, usually found some pleasant comment to make—a tree, a cloud effect—although, as a younger man, he had been scathing in his criticism of amateur, Sunday painters. But, in those days, Max hadn't needed the assistance of one of them to hoist him out of the bath or to take him for drives in the country. So he and Lionel, in their different ways, tolerated one another and, over the years, a relationship, even a friendship, had grown up between them which Nina had believed was exclusive.

Now, remembering Max's words, she felt suddenly self-conscious at meeting Lionel face to face, an entirely new experience.

It was at this moment, as she stood hesitating, that Lionel glanced up and, seeing her, hurried to open the door. There was nothing she could do except walk forward, aware suddenly that the middle button on her blouse, too tight now that she had put on weight, had come undone and her hair was escaping from its ribbon.

God, what on earth will he think of me? she wondered. I must look like some overblown, aging artist's model, all tits and bum.

The thought made her want to giggle, more especially as Lionel was wearing, because it was half-term, a neatly pressed pair of jeans and a pale blue shirt with a darker blue silk scarf worn cravat style in the open neck—what Max had once referred to sardonically as his "doppelganger getup." But it suggested to Nina not so much an alter ego as a pathetic and quite futile attempt on Lionel's part to dress up to some romantic image of the artist, as a small boy might buckle on a toy sword and pretend to be a soldier.

"Nina!" he exclaimed, beaming delightedly as he bustled forward to greet her. "What a pleasant surprise!"

"I'm afraid I'm on the cadge again, Lionel," she replied, trying to deprecate her visit and dampen his enthusiasm. "May I use your phone? I'll pay for the call."

"Of course! Of course! You know where it is. As for paying . . ."—he waved his hand, dismissing any sordid financial consideration.

In the hall, where the telephone stood on a little oak table, Nina took Eustace Quinn's letter out of her pocket and dialled the number of the Demeter Gallery. While she waited for the call to be connected, she looked at a sample of Lionel's water-colours, expensively framed in gilt, which hung on the wall above. It was one of his sunlit landscapes of woods and cornfields, with a complicated sky and a church spire in the distance. Quite competently painted but too bland, she thought, remembering Max's sketches which, in a few rapid brushstrokes, could say more about the soul of a place than all Lionel's careful detail. Behind her in the kitchen, the door of which he had scrupulously closed, she could hear him clattering about in a subdued manner in case she should think that his silence meant he was listening to the conversation.

A woman answered the phone. A secretary, Nina guessed, from the impersonal voice. She asked to speak to Mr. Quinn and, after a few seconds' delay, a man spoke.

"Eustace Quinn. Who is calling?"

The voice was of the type Nina always classified as "posh"—educated, urbane, and slightly amused, as if he were raising a quizzical eyebrow at the telephone.

"I'm Nina Gifford, Max Gifford's wife. About your letter, Mr. Quinn . . ."

"Oh, Mrs. *Gifford!*" There was a pleased stress on the name. "I'm so delighted you've phoned. Has Mr. Gifford considered my suggestion?"

"Well, he'd like to discuss it with you," Nina replied cautiously. The voice had a confident air that was quite capable of sweeping her into admissions and decisions she might not want to make on Max's behalf.

"Of course! Any time. I'm entirely at his disposal regarding any arrangements. How soon could he come to London?"

"That's the problem. I'm afraid he couldn't. He's bedridden, you see, with arthritis."

It seemed quite the wrong thing to say. I must sound, Nina thought, like one of those awful women talking about their operations on the top of buses.

The voice was immediately vibrant with concern.

"I'm so sorry to hear that. But there's no difficulty as far as I'm concerned. I could come to Althorpe to see him. If you're agreeable, that is."

It was a suggestion which hadn't occurred to her, and in the fluster of the moment she could think of nothing more positive to say than, "Well, if it's all right with you."

"Would Thursday be convenient?"

Nina tried to think of Thursday. Today was Monday; that gave her three days in which to get the house in some sort of order to entertain a guest.

"Yes, I think so."

"Splendid! You won't mind, will you, if I bring my assistant? I like to have someone with me to take notes."

Nina agreed to that, too.

"Then Thursday it is. Shall we say at eleven o'clock?"

He sounded quite satisfied, although it seemed to Nina that the arrangements had been concluded with too few preliminaries.

"I don't know if you'll be able to find us . . ." she began.

"Oh, don't worry, Mrs. Gifford. We shan't lose our way," he assured her. "Good-bye and thank you so much for phoning me. I look forward to meeting you both very much."

And that was that. He had hung up before she even had time to ask if they would be staying for lunch.

Returning to the kitchen, she found Lionel had prepared coffee for them both, the tray already set with the flowered china and four digestive biscuits, two each, on a plate. At his suggestion, they drank it in the garden, sitting on the patio outside the back door where a table and chairs were set out for the summer. Real, percolated coffee, Nina realised, sipping hers appreciatively. She supposed she ought to buy some for Thursday to serve to the guests instead of the powdered variety she and Max always drank.

"Everything's all right?" Lionel was asking in a general way, although she was sure he was referring to the telephone call. He had, at times, an almost womanish interest in other people's affairs. She would have to explain, she thought. He'd find out anyway sooner or later and, besides, she wanted his help in other ways.

"It was about a letter Max got this morning. There's a gallery in London that's interested in putting on an exhibition of his work. They're coming down on Thursday to discuss it with him."

"Oh, Nina, how perfectly splendid!" His delight was quite genuine and yet she felt the need to deflate that also.

"Nothing may come of it," she said, shrugging. "Besides, you know Max. He may change his mind at the last moment."

"Surely not over something like this? Just think of it! An exhibition in London! Aren't you excited?"

"I will be when it happens," she replied grudgingly and then added, "Look, Lionel, there's a couple of things you could do for me, if you don't mind. Could you come round this evening? Max wants a bath and I can't manage him on my own."

"Of course," he said immediately. "What time?"

"About seven," she suggested. "And could you bring your electric razor? He can't hold his safety one now his hands are so stiff and he hates me shaving him."

"Very well," Lionel agreed less enthusiastically. "And the other thing?"

She chose her words more carefully this time.

"If you don't want to do it, you've only got to say so. I shan't mind. In fact, I think I've got a damned nerve myself asking you. The thing is there's someone I know who's in a bit of a jam and needs a place to stay for a few days. I'd put him up myself only I don't want Max to meet him." Even now, when it would have been perfectly natural to confide in Lionel, she couldn't bring herself to tell him the truth about Danny. "I can't explain why at the moment. What I thought was this—if you'd agree to him sleeping in the caravan, that's all—he won't need meals or anything like that—it'd give me time to fix him up somewhere else."

She saw Lionel hesitate. He used the caravan as his studio because the cottage was too small and she knew she was asking a lot of him. It was his little kingdom, his ivory tower to which he retreated when the real world grew too burdensome for him. All the same, for Danny's sake, she was prepared to brazen it out.

"Well, I don't really know . . ." he began uncertainly.

"It's only for a few days," she said quickly, pressing home the advantage of his doubt. A new idea suddenly struck her which she was surprised hadn't occurred to her before. "Look, Lionel, if you'll do something else for me by taking care of Max tomorrow, I could go up to London, find a flat for this friend, and, at the same time, look at the gallery where the exhibition may be put on. Then you and Max could have the day to yourselves."

It was almost a form of blackmail. She knew Lionel would agree to that. He'd take along his water-colours and, under Max's tuition, would paint some scene or other—a view in the garden, perhaps—sitting on the little, folding campstool he always brought with him on such occasions, while Max, ensconced in his basket chair, played the teacher, telling him with undisguised impatience, "For God's sake, *look*, Lionel! Use your bloody eyes!" and enjoying every minute of it. She wondered if, in fact, it wasn't the reason for Lionel's fancy dress—not so much the artist as the art student, seated at the feet of the master.

"Very well, Nina," Lionel agreed without much enthusiasm, the disadvantage of giving up the caravan almost outweighing the advantage of spending the day with Max.

"You'll have to help me persuade him," Nina said. "You know how he hates me going out and leaving him. We'll both have a go at him tonight while you're there. By the way, you won't say anything about this friend of mine, will you?"

"Not if you don't wish me to," Lionel replied. He pressed his lips primly together, expressing disapproval. "When shall I expect him?"

"I'll have to let you know. Soon, I think."

"Not tomorrow," Lionel said with unexpected firmness. "The bed in there wants airing and, besides, I shall need to put away some of my things."

"All right," Nina conceded. The delay was a nuisance but it couldn't be helped. "I'll tell him Wednesday, shall I?" It suddenly occurred to her that she hadn't thanked him. "I can't tell you how grateful I am. I don't know what Max and I would do without you."

It sounded terribly phoney to her but Lionel seemed pleased. He added, as a further example of his magnanimity, "If you like, I'll drive you to the station tomorrow. It'll save you catching the bus into Bexford."

"Oh, Lionel, how kind!"

She saw him flush with pleasure, his eyes behind his spectacles shining.

"It's nothing, Nina, nothing at all."

Yet it was true, she thought. He is kind, and it crossed her mind that being married to Lionel would have many advantages. She'd be looked after for a start and that'd be a change. And then there'd be all sorts of small comforts: fresh coffee and aired beds and help with the shopping. If Max died and she married Lionel, she supposed she'd live here, in the cottage, and, as she got to her feet, she looked at it again with new eyes. It was small, of course, but it was centrally heated and the kitchen was properly equipped with a modern cooker and those plastic-topped units which only needed a quick wipe-down.

But, God, what was she thinking of! It was almost like wishing for Max's death and, as a charm against the thought, she quickly crossed her fingers. Lionel, busy loading the tray with their used cups, was unaware of her momentary guilt and confusion. She said good-bye to him hurriedly, and it was only as she rode off down the road that she remembered she hadn't paid him for the phone call after all.

It was largely because of her guilt that, on her return, she went straight upstairs to Max's room without even stopping to take off her jacket, although she was also eager to tell him about the phone call.

"Coming on Thursday, you say?" he repeated.

He was sitting upright in bed so that he could see out over the garden through the window.

"Yes," she replied.

For a moment he was silent, his head turned away and his eyes fixed on the great cedar tree which, with its layers of dark, level branches, filled the view. His expression was quite inscrutable; Nina had no idea what he was thinking. Was he pleased at the thought of an exhibition? Or anxious about it? Or even bitter because it had come so late?

He had never been well known as an artist, even as a young man. His portraits, mainly of female models, had been too harsh and starkly honest to attract either the critics or the fashionable sitters, and he had sold his paintings mostly to a small group of private collectors who had appreciated his work or to a few provincial galleries, eking out a living by teaching part time in the London art schools. Then, during the war years, he had acted as adviser to the Admiralty on camouflage techniques, at the same time trying to continue his own work. From the little she knew of his past life, Nina gathered that he had lost touch with the new ideas so that, when the war ended and he had returned to his full-time painting career, he had discovered that styles had changed and he was now considered old-fashioned and dated. Somewhere in those years, he had missed the boat. Or perhaps he had never intended catching it. Max had always been too much of his own man to be influenced by artistic trends or schools of painting. But the blunt truth was that very few people had tried to understand or appreciate what he had been trying to say in those canvases that were lined up downstairs, their faces turned towards the dining-room wall.

Now, at last, it seemed possible that he might become well known, and she wondered if that thought was in his mind as he gazed so fixedly out of the window.

Suddenly his expression altered with one of those abrupt changes of mood that she was used to, and, bringing both hands smacking down on the bedclothes, he announced in a loud voice, "It's sunny! I think I'll get up."

It was always hard work getting him downstairs, Max clinging to the banister while she supported him at the other side. They had to take one tread at a time and rest on the half-landing under the stained-glass window. As he regained his breath, Max cocked a sardonic, lascivious glance up at it.

Downstairs in the hall, he paused outside the dining room as if about to say something and then, changing his mind, continued on into the kitchen where Nina settled him in the basket chair by the back door which, on his instructions, she opened to allow him to enjoy the sun.

There was a wheelchair, supplied by the Welfare services, but Max would rarely agree to use it and it stood abandoned in one corner of the kitchen, to Nina's exasperation although she could understand his reluctance. To use it regularly would be to admit to his handicap. There was even a wooden ramp spanning the back doorstep, for easy access. But no —he preferred, with his old man's stubbornness, to rely on her to help him about, even though the wheelchair would have given him more independence. He could, for example, have propelled himself out into the garden instead of being stuck by the back door looking into the yard, she thought as she began to prepare lunch. Of course, it was company for him to be in the kitchen near her and, as she peeled potatoes and fried onions, they talked together in that easy, desultory fashion that had become part of their shared lives.

In the afternoon, he dozed off for a couple of hours, part of his normal routine these days, still sitting in the basket chair although Nina covered his legs with a rug and stuffed a cushion behind his head. He slept simply, his hands lying flaccid on the tartan blanket, head back, mouth open, and his cheeks quivering gently, sucking in and out with each breath. As she bent down to make sure he was sound asleep, it struck her that this was what he would probably look like when he was dead, the thick white hair rumpled, the formidable nose jutting upward to show the two pits of nostrils, the flesh falling away from the skull, and she suddenly wanted to touch him, to feel the warmth of his body in contact with hers.

Lionel arrived at half past six, earlier than arranged, parking his Cortina in the yard outside the kitchen where the spaces between the old flagstones with which it was paved were roughed in with fuzzy green lines of grass and the broken windows of the semiderelict stables and outbuildings opposite caught the late afternoon sun.

Max and Nina hadn't quite finished their evening meal and he joined them, accepting a cup of the strong, brown tea that Nina always left to brew until it was the colour Max liked.

Max seemed pleased to see him and cheered up at his arrival. He had been in a subdued mood since waking up from his afternoon nap. Leaving the two men to talk, Nina loaded the tray with the dirty dishes and carried it through to the scullery to wash up, taking the radio through with her to listen to a quiz programme as she did so. The sound of the voices, turned up to full volume over the clatter of dishes, drowned all other sound and she was surprised when, on returning to the kitchen, she found Lionel sitting alone at the table.

"Where's Max?" she asked.

"He wanted me to take him through to the dining room," Lionel explained and, as Nina started towards the door, he added, "Leave him alone for a while, Nina. I think he'd prefer it."

She nodded, trying to hide her anger, which was directed partly at Lionel for daring to offer her such advice but mainly at Max for making the request, not of her, but of Lionel, an outsider.

"I think," Lionel continued uncomfortably, as if aware of her feelings, "that he wants to look at the paintings and he'd rather do it on his own."

She merely said, "He'll be chilled to the bone in there, the silly old fool."

All the same, she couldn't settle down and, after half an hour had passed in which Lionel talked and she answered abstractedly, she got to her feet and went in search of Max.

He was sitting on one of the hideous mahogany chairs which, together with the rest of the furniture in the room, they had bought cheap at an auction soon after they moved to the house because nobody else had space to house the huge monstrosities. He was leaning forward in the act of examining the paintings that he had set out in a row in front of him, their fronts exposed for the first time in years.

The sight of them startled her. It was like opening a door and finding yourself confronted by people who you thought had died years ago. There they all were, the familiar faces that had once hung in Max's London studio: the old woman who had sold newspapers outside Charing Cross station; delicate, consumptive Marjorie, once a waitress at a Lyons Corner House; the stripper—Eileen, wasn't that her name?—from some long-defunct Soho club, holding up one breast with her hand and smiling lewdly over her shoulder. And herself, at seventeen, at twenty, at twenty-six, caught in a dozen poses: reaching up to hang washing on the line that stretched across the Notting Hill studio; or, stripped to the waist, washing herself in an enamel basin; or lying naked on the same scarlet sofa on which Lilith had once posed, fondling a little black kitten which was cradled against her thigh.

She gasped and Max turned to look at her, holding out his hand. Hurrying forward to grasp it, she saw that his eyes were wet.

But all he said was, "They can exhibit any of these, Nine, but not the Lilith portrait. You understand that? Not the painting upstairs."

As she helped him out of the room, she thought, He said that as if he expected to die before Thursday.

He perked up, however, when he had his bath. Between them, she and Lionel hoisted him into it, as they had done many times before. Nina was used to his nakedness but Lionel still looked pink and flustered at the sight of the great white torso, the chest matted with grey hairs, that fell away so pathetically to the thin old man's legs and knees. Leaving him to wallow, they retreated onto the landing where Nina said in a whisper, "Don't forget to mention tomorrow's trip to London."

Lionel nodded in agreement. The steam had misted up his glasses and dampened his hair which flopped forward onto his forehead, making him appear ridiculously youthful, and she wondered, with one of her idiotic urges to giggle, what he would look like stripped of his clothes. Like a reed, she thought, all spindly and ridged, with a chicken's breastbone.

They broached the subject as they got Max out of the bath. Nina, handing Max the towel as Lionel lowered him onto the chair, nodded to him over the top of Max's head.

"Max," she began, trying not to sound too eager, "what would you think if I went up to London tomorrow? It occurred to me I could have a look at the Demeter Gallery and see what it's like. It'd give you a better idea of the setup before they come on Thursday."

And Lionel piped in, "Oh, what a good idea, Nina! I'll come over for the day, if you like. I'm free tomorrow."

Max, in the act of drying between his toes, lifted his shaggy head to look up at the two of them, as if scenting a conspiracy.

"All day?" he asked.

"Well, I thought I'd look round the West End while I'm up there,"

Nina said. "It's years since I've done any window shopping down Oxford Street."

If she made it sound frivolous, Max might agree. He was surprisingly tolerant at times towards feminine whims. They seemed to bring out the amused, benign patriarch in him.

All the same, she nudged Lionel with her elbow behind his back.

"We could go for a drive," Lionel suggested, taking his cue. "I'd like to have another attempt at that ruined church in Frendsham. My last water-colour of it didn't quite come off."

"You made a balls-up of the perspective, that's why," Max said gruffly.

They waited until, unable to bear the suspense any longer, Nina turned away and began cleaning down the bath. Behind her, she heard Max add to Lionel after a maddening silence, "All right, then. We could have a pub lunch at the Crown."

So it was decided! She tried to hide her jubilation. A whole day in London! She hadn't realised until that moment how much she needed a break from Max, the house, the whole bloody countryside. To be back in the city, among the red double-deckers, the smell of the underground, the anonymous crowds which generated their own special sense of urgency and excitement!

While Lionel helped Max into bed and fixed up the electric razor, she went into her own room, which she had occupied ever since Max had become more bedridden. It was small and cosy, facing southeast over the back of the house and giving her a view across the top of the stables and outbuildings to the coppice of trees and the shrubbery. If she stood on tiptoe, she could just see the peaked roof of the summerhouse and the little iron weather vane that surmounted it in the shape of an old man with a scythe, depicting Death. How they had loved death, those Victorians! They were as fascinated by it as today's generation was by sex.

Looking through her wardrobe, she tried to decide what to wear the following day. It would have to be the blue linen dress because there wasn't much else that was suitable. Although it could do with a press, she thought, and I ought to wash my hair.

Lionel came downstairs while she was still at the ironing board. She had already washed her hair and had swathed a towel round it like a turban which, together with the silk kimono she was wearing as a wrapper, a present from Max years before, gave her an exotic, oriental appearance. She saw Lionel look at her with shy appreciation. He was also embarrassed at finding her in such a half-dressed state but she was too happy to let it bother her.

"Is he settled?" she asked, meaning Max.

"He said he'd like a brandy," Lionel replied.

"Him and his brandy!"

She was never sure how genuinely Max needed it. It was true that getting in and out of the bath tired him but she suspected it was merely an excuse for a small tipple. All the same, she retrieved the bottle from its hiding place in the pantry and poured a glass for Max, adding to Lionel as she left the room carrying it, "Don't go yet. We'll have one ourselves in a moment."

Max was sitting up in bed, looking content and sleepy. His hair, too, had been washed and it stood out round his head in a flossy, white aureole.

He's still handsome, she thought, although that wasn't the right word to use. Max had never been good-looking. Instead, he had possessed a strong sexual magnetism and vigour which was still apparent in his eyes and mouth. Even at seventeen, when she had first met him and ought to have been too young to know about such things, she had been overwhelmed by the instinctive knowledge that he'd be a marvellous lover. And so he had.

On a sudden impulse, she dumped herself down on the bed and flung her arms round him.

"You lovely old woolly bear!"

She felt his arms clinch round her in response, hugging her so tight that her breasts hurt. Then he said, releasing her, "Brought the booze, Nine?"

While he drank it, she fussed about the room, drawing the curtains, wiping her hand across the window ledge, thinking, The whole place could do with a damn good clean, but happy just to be there looking after him.

"I think I'll sleep," he announced unexpectedly.

It was a signal for her to go. She knew why. He wanted to be alone so that, in the dark, he could go over in his mind all the old memories that the paintings had evoked, which he couldn't do while she was present in the room. Nevertheless, she lingered for a few more minutes, making sure he had everything he needed for the night: his cigarettes and matches, the newspaper in case he woke up and felt like reading, the brass bell he could ring if he needed her.

It wasn't exactly jealousy she felt; more a sense of being shut out. For all their years of intimacy, they had never been close except on a physical level; bodies not minds, she thought. Most of the time she had no idea what went on in his head. There was part of him that always remained utterly secret and private.

Take the question of children as an example. They had never had any; neither had he and Zoe. Had he minded? Would he have liked a child if that had been possible? She had no idea. Max had never talked about it and it was she who trailed round the hospitals, not saying a word to Max about it, submitting to all the humiliating tests which had finally proved that she was capable of conceiving.

So it must have been Max. Odd to think that for all his sexual vigour he was sterile.

"Go on, Nine, shove off," he was saying. His blue eyes, still bright above the pouches of flesh, were watching her with an amused tolerance and, as she bent to give him the ritual good-night kiss, one hand came slyly round to fondle her backside.

"God, you've put on weight," he said. "You've got an arse on you like . . ."

"A cow?" she suggested.

"You look at a cow's backside sometime," he told her. "It's all bone and gristle. Not like yours, my darling. I was going to say 'pig' but you might have taken it the wrong way. They've got nice bottoms, though; round and porky and worth getting hold of."

His hand fell away as he said it and, leaning back, he closed his eyes, his expression suddenly inexpressibly old and sad.

Well, she thought, sighing, it can't be helped, although when she went downstairs again to Lionel, she was still lit up with the idea of making love and she sloshed brandy into their glasses with a gaiety and abandon which alarmed him so much that he took off his spectacles to polish the lenses, always a sign of unease. Without them, his face looked exposed and vulnerable.

"About your friend," he began in his severe, schoolmaster's voice.

"Oh, God!" she cried. "Don't say you can't have him!"

Just when everything else was working out so beautifully! Surely her luck would hold for Danny?

"No, no," he said hurriedly. "Please, Nina, I didn't mean to imply that. Of course I'll put him up, providing it isn't for too long."

"Just a few days," she promised recklessly. Somehow she'd have to find Danny somewhere else, although God alone knew how.

"In that case, I'll be happy to have him. I've prepared the caravan. You said no meals, didn't you?"

He was clearly anxious to have the arrangements cut and dried.

"Yes, he'll manage those for himself."

He'd have to eat at the Feathers, she thought. Or she'd smuggle a hot meal out to him in the summerhouse.

"And you did say he'd come on Wednesday?" Lionel continued.

"If that's all right with you."

While she was in Bexford tomorrow, she added to herself, she could drop a note off for him at the Dolphin, explaining the situation.

"Very well. And tomorrow? What train did you intend catching?"

"Oh, heavens, I haven't thought!" Nina exclaimed.

"The nine-five is a fast, through train," Lionel said. Trust him to know the timetable by heart. "I could pick you up here at half past eight. Now, about coming home?"

"I'll catch the bus," Nina put in quickly. If she went to see Zoe as well as the gallery and, on top of that, tried to find a room for Danny, there was no knowing what time she'd be back. "I won't be late, though," she added, trusting to luck she could also keep that promise.

"So that's all settled," Lionel said with an air of satisfaction.

Some of her warmth still lingered when, later, Lionel rose to go. She accompanied him into the yard and, as he found his car keys, she suddenly rushed forward and kissed him on the cheek with the same impulse of affection with which she had embraced Max.

"Oh, Lionel, I'm so grateful! I don't know how I'd manage without you."

He stood silent and bewildered for a moment, then put up a hand to the place on his cheek as if her kiss was still there to be touched.

"It's nothing, Nina," he said, clearing his throat. "I'm only too happy . . ."

The rest of the sentence was lost as he ducked into the car and started the engine.

Standing in the yard watching as he drove away, she waved and waved, as if seeing him off on a long and dangerous journey, and it was only as the car finally disappeared round the corner and she lowered her arm that she remembered that she still hadn't paid him for the phone call.

CHAPTER 3

London was beautiful the following morning as Nina emerged from the underground at Green Park station. The air was sharp, dazzling, with that familiar, exciting, complex taste to it of petrol and exhaust fumes and women's scent that brought nostalgia rushing back as she savoured it on her lips. Strangely enough, the sun seemed brighter here than in the country for it winked back at her from so many glittering surfaces: shop windows, gold lettering, car windscreens and chromium fittings. Even the paving stones contained little twinkling points of light. Opposite, in the park, the leaves of the trees seemed polished by the sun, like so many small, shining mirrors, revolving as the breeze caught them. And the flowers! They were everywhere. You wouldn't have thought you were in a city. There were beds of them in the gardens backing onto the park, bright oblongs of colour in the distance, and, at closer view, as she turned to walk up Piccadilly, she passed a street barrow loaded with roses and irises, while the window boxes outside the banks and the car showrooms were crammed with geraniums, hanging lobelia and the pretty, delicate leaves of ornamental ivy.

The Demeter Gallery was in Half Moon Street, about a third of the way down on the right. Crossing to the other side of the road, Nina sauntered along, examining its exterior. It impressed her. There was an expensive simplicity about it that, under Max's tuition, she had learnt meant good taste. "Line," he always said. "That's what matters."

Well, there's line there all right, she thought.

The facia was of plain, black marble, polished to a deep gloss, and across it in flowing bronze letters, like beautiful handwriting transformed into metal, was displayed the one word "Demeter." Below it, two large, plate-glass windows stretched down almost to street level, apart from a narrow, black marble plinth running along the bottom. On a central glass door, the name of the gallery was repeated in the same bronze-coloured script.

The traffic impeded her view of the contents of the windows, forcing her to cross the road to examine them more closely. In one was an oil painting of a landscape; a bit dark and heavy in her opinion, all thunderous trees and frantic clouds, not the sort of scene she'd want hanging in her house. It reminded her of those weather forecasts predicting a deep depression moving rapidly south. But she guessed it was probably valuable. Certainly the wide, ornate gilt frame looked expensive. There was nothing else in the window apart from an artfully arranged fall of black velvet against which the painting was displayed.

The other window was more cheerful: a lot of gay, little mobiles made of thin pieces of polished metal which revolved this way and that, like children's carousels or the twinkling leaves in the park.

Beyond, she caught a glimpse of the interior—quite large and very beautiful, with thick, silvery-grey carpet on the floor and the same colour linen on the walls on which were hung rows of paintings, each one softly bathed in illumination from spotlights on the ceiling. Apart from some black leather chairs, a black marble-topped table on which stood a white telephone and a huge flower display in a white urn, the place contained no other furniture.

She would have liked to go in but dared not. There was a young girl seated at the table, white-skinned and black-haired, like the rest of the colour scheme, who glanced up as Nina lingered at the window and, fearful lest the girl might be Eustace Quinn's assistant, or that Eustace Quinn himself might appear at any moment, she walked on. It would be embarrassing if, on Thursday, they recognised her as the woman peering in like a spy.

Although I suppose I am, really, she admitted, turning right at the next intersection and making her way back to Green Park station. I'm spying out the land for Max.

The thought gave her a small thrill of excitement but otherwise the morning began to take on an air of anticlimax. The best bit was now over; what was left was mere chores. Seeing Zoe, for instance.

Seated in the tube train on her way to West Kensington, she thought about Zoe. Although her own relationship with Max had had nothing to do with the break-up of his first marriage, she still felt irrationally guilty about Max's ex-wife. It was one of the reasons why she sent her a fiver once a month. It was paying off some sort of debt, Max's more than hers.

Poor old Zoe!

She was still living in the basement flat in a turning off the North End Road. Walking towards it from the underground station, Nina stopped at every newsagents' and tabacconists' on the way to study the boards of ad-

vertisements displayed outside, reading the contents of the noticecards
through the dirty glass, several of them so faded that they were difficult
to decipher. Some offered second-hand cars, French lessons ("advanced
tuition"), rewards for lost cats and budgerigars; some requested baby-sit-
ters, domestic help, friendship ("genuine replies only"), and, depress-
ingly, furnished rooms or flats: "Young, married couple, quiet, respect-
able, no children, desperate for furnished accommodation. Anything
considered."

Oh, God! she thought. What do I do now? Poor Danny!

In two shops, she paid for a card of her own to be pinned up, printing
the words with great care as she stood at the counter: "YOUNG SINGLE
BUSINESSMAN URGENTLY REQUIRES ROOM OR FLAT. PLEASE CON-
TACT . . ."

At this point, she hesitated. No one would be likely to bother writing
to her in Essex or phoning Lionel if she gave his number. In the end, she
wrote down Zoe's address. At least it was nearby and, if she slipped Zoe a
couple of quid, she surely wouldn't mind passing on any contacts.

"Young, single businessman." Well, it wasn't exactly a lie. Danny was
certainly single and young compared to Max. As for the "businessman"
part of it, although it might be stretching the truth a little, second-hand
cars and even drinking clubs were businesses after all. The urgent part of
it was only too desperately true.

Judging by the slight sneer on the faces of the shopkeepers as she
handed over the cards and the fee for displaying them, she was wasting
her time and money.

The estate agent she tried was even less hopeful. He was a young man,
wearing a pale grey suit with a silky tie that flowed like a small, green
waterfall over the front of his shirt.

"A furnished flat or room? You must be joking!"

"No, I'm not," Nina retorted sharply. For Danny's sake, she was
prepared to take on any battle. "What have you got on your books?"

"A three-bedroomed flat at one hundred twenty pounds a week."

It was said with a take-it-or-leave-it air.

"Couldn't you take my name and address in case something cheaper
turns up?" Nina suggested, adopting the wheedling tone she used sometimes on Max, but the young man wasn't impressed.

"There's no point, madam," he said indifferently. "Anything we do
have to rent is taken the same day."

Outside on the pavement, she stood still for a few moments, trying to
readjust her thoughts, while round her people shoved and jostled their
way in front of the stalls in the North End Road market. For two pins,
she would have burst out crying. Instead, she felt suddenly angry.

It was so bloody difficult! All she wanted was a room for Danny and
nobody cared, nobody showed the slightest sympathy. Even London
seemed to turn ugly. The buildings were hideous, their brick dirty and
pocked, the posters on the hoardings discoloured and peeling into rags
while the faces that pushed past her were full of meanness and greed,
anxiety, stupidity, pettiness.

I need a drink, she thought savagely.

There was a pub on the corner and she pushed her way inside to the bar through the press of people to order a gin and tonic and some ham sandwiches. Once served, she remained at the long mahogany counter, trying to ignore the crowds and the noise behind her, concentrating instead on the rows of glasses in front of her, the vases of artificial flowers, and the fairy lights strung out along the top shelf. In the steamed-up mirror, like figures in another world, distanced and dreamlike, faces and hands were reflected back at her while, further off still, through the pub windows, more people swam past.

The gin did her good and she ordered another, remembering the old days when she and Max would spend the evening with friends at one of their favourite public houses: the White Hart in Drury Lane or the Bunch of Grapes in Shepherd Market. It had been fun then, listening to the conversation, joining in the laughter, feeling the gin gently circulating through her veins. Then back to the studio, to more laughter as Max fell up the stairs, to the big room suddenly illuminated as she switched on the light, all the objects it contained jumping out at her—the vase of dried cow parsley in the corner, the plaster sculpture of her head and shoulders that Jerry had made—little Jerry whom Max used to call Po and who was now dead—and the big, double bed with the Mexican rug over it. And, of course, the paintings hanging on the white walls.

Coming home.

I'm getting morbid, she thought, and, putting down her empty glass, shoved her way towards the sign that said "LADIES."

It smelt unpleasant in there, the sweetish scent of disinfectant mingled with the odour of urine. Paper towels littered the floor.

The first cabin she tried was dirty and she retreated to the next, squatting awkwardly above the seat so that no part of it should come into contact with her skin and reading the graffiti scrawled on the walls. Boys' names mostly—Chris and Rog and Brian—although someone had written a longer message on the door: "I love Keith but they took him away from me." It read like a cry from the heart. Above it, in lipstick in big, angry capitals were the words "Screw Sex" and she laughed out loud, thinking, I must remember to tell Max—it'll amuse him.

Rinsing her fingers at the stained basin, she looked for a paper towel and, finding the dispenser empty, shook the water from them before drying them off on the sleeve of her dress. The action and the surrounding grime reminded her of Zoe—Zoe drawing the back of her hand across her mouth or pushing soiled underwear under the bed with the toe of her shoe.

Why is it, Nina thought, that other people's dirt is so much worse than your own? There ought to be an absolute of squalor.

Before leaving, she took a last look at herself in the mirror for reassurance. Not bad, she decided, for forty-five. Blue suited her; it brought out the colour in her hair which, newly washed, hung heavy and thick again. She liked to feel the weight and bulk of it against the nape of her neck.

She was still attractive enough to draw the occasional appreciative glance, but not the heads turning as they used to or the wolf whistles. It was odd that men no longer seemed to whistle in the streets after girls. Perhaps it had gone out of fashion. A pity, though. She had enjoyed those shrill signals of admiration.

Comforted, confident, she emerged from the ladies and rejoined the tumult of the North End Road.

Zoe's house had gone down in the world in the three years since she had last visited it. There was more rubbish lying on the path and it looked shabbier, its paint peeling off in great scabs and lumps fallen from the stucco.

The area steps leading down to the basement were broken and Nina, in unaccustomed heels, trod gingerly, hanging on to the rail and wondering how the hell Zoe managed to get up and down them in the winter. At the bottom, the tiny yard was almost completely occupied by dustbins —surely not all Zoe's?—that exuded damp, evil-smelling newspaper bundles, inadequately wrapped. Averting her eyes, Nina banged on the knocker.

It took several moments for Zoe to answer the door and Nina was about to knock again when a shadow appeared behind the grubby net curtain covering the two glass panels and a voice, Zoe's, demanded huskily, "Who is it? What do you want?"

"It's me, Nina."

"Nina?"

She sounded as if she'd never heard the name before and Nina wondered if she was going a bit gaga. After all, she must be about the same age as Max.

"You know, Max's Nina."

It seemed a ridiculous way in which to describe herself, but it appeared to satisfy Zoe. There was a clatter and a rattle as bolts and chains were unfastened and finally the door was opened to reveal Zoe standing in the dark, narrow passage, blinking at the bright sunshine like a mole emerging from its tunnel.

Time had served her no better than the house. She looked shrivelled up, wasted; a tiny figure in a dingy, red Crimplene dress and a dragged-down navy cardigan, worn with men's grey socks and stained espadrilles.

Her hair, Nina thought, as Zoe rather grudgingly invited her inside, was too black and lustreless to be natural. Like Zoe herself, it had grown thin and sparse and patches of white scalp showed through.

"Well," Zoe remarked as they entered the back room, "you're a stranger."

It was said accusingly, putting Nina immediately on the defensive.

"It's not always easy to get away," she replied.

"No, I can imagine it can't be."

There was a sardonic glitter in Zoe's eyes as if she didn't consider Nina had got much of a bargain, an implication she emphasised by asking, "How is he?"

By "he" they both knew she meant Max.

"He has his ups and downs," Nina replied briefly, not wanting to discuss him with Zoe. "How are you?"

"All right, I think," Zoe said, as if not too sure herself about her state of health. "You might as well sit down."

Now you're here, was the unspoken comment but at least she made one welcoming gesture by turning on the light so that the small, dark room was illuminated.

It was a semibasement, with a sash window looking out into a tiny, concreted area, a few feet above which rose an unkempt lawn, so that not much light, even on a sunny day, penetrated the interior. The crowded furniture—for Zoe used the room to live, cook, and eat in—added to the air of gloom as did the brown paint and the patterned wallpaper, its flowers and leaves so darkened over the years that they had almost disappeared into the sepia background.

The absence of the portrait was immediately apparent, if only by reason of the paler patch on the wall where it had once hung and, caught unawares, Nina exclaimed, "Oh, Zoe! What's happened to the painting?"

Like the one hanging above Max's bed, it had been a portrait of Lilith, only this time she was seated straddle-legged on a chair, facing the viewer, her features still hidden, however, by the shower of dark hair which fell forward as, with one arm lifted, she brushed it out. The pose was more awkward and more deliberately sensual than the one in Max's painting—the right arm that held the hairbrush, for example, forming a sharp angle, the feet turned out, the breasts hanging down like ripe, pink fruit. Yet, oddly enough, it had been painted with greater tenderness, as if each delicate brushstroke had been placed there with loving care. The colour, too, had been more subdued. The figure had been posed against a plain, pale blue background, suggesting sky or sea—or perhaps Max had chosen it to convey the concept of purity and grace?—and was flooded with pearly light which fell softly from the left as if through a hidden window that was letting in a gentle, opalescent dawn.

Nina had no idea how Zoe had acquired it and, in her anxiety not to refer to Max, had never liked to ask.

Zoe glanced indifferently at the empty wall.

"I sold it."

"When? Who to?"

Zoe couldn't possibly know about Eustace Quinn's offer, Nina thought, although the sale of the portrait seemed ominously timed.

Zoe shrugged.

"Several months ago. Last February, I think. A man came round from the Council to check the loos. Doing a survey, he said. Anyway, it caught his eye and he offered to buy it. So I thought, why not? He came back that evening with a van to collect it."

Nina longed to ask how much Zoe had got for it but didn't dare. She was willing to bet, however, that she had let it go for much less than it was worth, especially now there was the possibility of a West End exhibition. It was obvious Zoe knew nothing of that and Nina could see now that it had been unlikely from the start.

Instead, she asked, "Zoe, how did you get hold of it in the first place?"

Zoe laughed, showing her teeth and looking, for a brief second, like the young girl whose portrait hung in the Blackheath gallery. Years ago, soon after she had first met Max, Nina had made the journey down there on the No. 53 bus especially to look at it, curious to see her through Max's eyes. The same smile had been on her face then—pointed, sly, feline, the way a cat would smile, a small-featured, pert, pretty cat with a sharp little chin and high cheekbones. Oh yes! Nina could well understand why Max had been fascinated by her. She had looked both innocent and corrupt; a tiny, black-haired doll of a girl with knowing, glossy eyes.

"Now that's a story worth telling," Zoe said, cocking her head on one side as if still secretly pleased with herself. "It happened like this. When I finally left Max, he told me, like a fool, I could take half of everything. So I took the painting; he'd got two. Christ, he was furious, but he couldn't go back on what he'd said, could he? So he chucked all my stuff down the stairs after me. Someone sent for the police."

Her eyes glistened at the memory.

Theirs had been a stormy relationship, or so Nina had gathered. Little Po, drunk one evening, had admitted that Zoe had once threatened Max with a revolver which, for God knows what reason, she had kept in the studio in those days. Only she hadn't known how to release the safety catch and, while she fumbled with it, Max had knocked her down, blacking her eye.

"Like cat and dog," Little Po had said, still impressed by the drama of their quarrels.

"I never liked it much, anyway," Zoe continued. "The painting, I mean. I only took it to pay him out. It was *her*, you know, who finished our marriage."

"Who? Lilith?" Nina asked, her curiosity getting the better of her. She had learnt bits and pieces from friends but it would be fascinating to hear Zoe's account.

"That's what he called her," Zoe said contemptuously. "I don't think it was her real name. It was in 1936, I think. Before the war, anyway. Max met her somewhere in London and wham! that was it. He was in love." She looked sideways at Nina. "She was the only woman he ever cared for, you know, according to him."

What a bitch she is! Nina thought, although she went on nodding encouragingly.

"I don't know where they used to meet. Max wouldn't let on. He'd got that job at the Slade and he used to go trotting off every morning, all innocent-looking, but I knew he was up to something. You could always tell with Max."

Yes, you could, Nina agreed silently. He'd done the same to her only he'd always come trotting back again pretty damn quickly.

"I tried following him once but he gave me the slip," Zoe continued.

"I think they were meeting somewhere in Bloomsbury—at least, someone saw him with a woman in Russell Square. But wherever it was, he must have done those two portraits of her there. Has he still got his?" she broke off to ask.

"I think so," Nina replied with deliberate vagueness.

"There should be some drawings, too. He had a whole caseful of them at one time."

They were still in the dining room, Nina added to herself, in the big portfolio she had hidden underneath the others. It was two of those drawings she'd given to Danny because they were initialled and dated. That made them worth a bit more.

"He smuggled them back to the studio with the portraits," Zoe was saying, "and then had the bloody nerve to pretend he'd had them for years, stored at a friend's, and Lilith was some little shopgirl who wanted to earn a few quid modelling. Anyway, I'd had about a bellyful of him by then and, as there was someone else I thought I fancied, I made damn sure I'd got the evidence for a divorce the next time he went jaunting off."

Nina made sympathetic noises, not letting on that it was Max who had gone out of his way to supply her with that evidence. "We were finished, Zoe and me," he had told her, "so there was no point in trying to keep the marriage together."

"Why didn't he marry Lilith if she meant so much to him?" she asked. It was an aspect of the relationship she had never understood. All Max had ever said was, "The woman in the portrait? It was someone called Lilith I knew years ago for a few weeks." And then he had given her one of those looks, warning her off asking any more questions.

But Zoe didn't know either.

"Perhaps she was married," she suggested vaguely. "Or she'd gone off him."

No, thought Nina, that wasn't the reason. Some instinct told her that whatever Lilith and Max had felt for one another, it hadn't merely drained away like water into the ground. Certainly Max had never quite given her up. There was part of him that Lilith still occupied, a corner of his heart that no other woman, not even herself, had been able to inhabit.

But it was time to change the subject. She was afraid she had gone too far and she felt guilty for encouraging Zoe to talk; it was disloyal to Max.

"Zoe, there was something I wanted to ask you," she said hurriedly. "Is there any chance of you hearing about a room going vacant?"

"Why?" Zoe asked promptly, scenting gossip.

"It's for a friend of mine." There was no reason why Zoe shouldn't be told that much, at least. The chances of her passing the information on to Max were nil. They hadn't met for years and Nina always intercepted her letters.

"I might."

Nina got out her purse and, producing a fiver, passed it over.

"Let me know if you do. I'll make it another tenner if you can fix something up." As Zoe shoved the note into her cardigan pocket, she added offhandedly, "By the way, I've had some cards put up outside a couple of the local shops and given your address. You don't mind, do you?"

With the fiver already pocketed, Zoe could hardly object.

"All right. And I'll keep an eye on the papers," she agreed, not very enthusiastically. "Who's it for? A man or a woman?"

"A man." Nina rose to her feet before Zoe could ask any more questions, announcing, "I ought to be going."

Now that she was on the point of leaving, Zoe suddenly seemed to want her company.

"Aren't you going to stay for a cup of tea?" she demanded.

"I'd better not," Nina replied.

She was anxious to get back to Max, and besides, she didn't fancy anything Zoe might prepare in the squalid little washroom opening off the passage which housed the lavatory as well as the sink and was her only source of water. It suddenly occurred to her that this was how Danny would probably end up, in a basement room, existing somehow among the unwashed curtains and the overflowing ashtrays, listening to other people's lives going on upstairs.

As she was showing Nina to the door, Zoe made a last reference to the missing portrait, but so obliquely that, for a moment, Nina wasn't sure what she was talking about.

"I saw him again, you know," she remarked.

"Who?" Nina asked, bewildered.

"That chap who bought the painting. He turned up at the pub one evening and we chatted."

"Oh, really?" Nina replied, at a loss to know what else to say. There was a strange expression on Zoe's face which she couldn't understand— sly, secretive, triumphant, like a child who chants provocatively, "I know something you don't know."

The next moment, Zoe was saying, "Bye then, Nina. See you again sometime," and had closed the door.

Nina considered the remark as she walked back to the underground station. Zoe had probably meant to imply nothing more than the man had bought her a few drinks—she was always adept at cadging—and Nina put it out of her mind. Her main concern now was to get home to Max as quickly as she could. She had had enough of London. The day, looked forward to with so much jubilation, had been reduced to tired feet and an increasing feeling of irritability. London wasn't the same; or perhaps she had changed; it was hard to say. It certainly seemed dirtier, noisier, and more exhausting than she had remembered.

There was one more duty, however, that she had to perform before she could catch the bus to Althorpe. Getting out of the train at Bexford, she made inquiries of passers-by and eventually found the Dolphin Hotel in a side street behind the Corn Exchange. It was an unprepossessing building converted from three terrace houses, the entrance door painted bright blue to match the large wooden cutout of the creature that had given the place its name and which was fastened above it on the brickwork.

The door opened into a passage, smelling of dust and gravy, with a small reception cubbyhole on the left that was empty. Nina had to bang on the bell several times before a man in shirtsleeves emerged from behind a curtained opening and asked in a surly voice what she wanted.

"Mr. Anderson's out," he said in answer to her query.

"I'd like to leave a message for him then," Nina retorted.

With bad grace, he produced a sheet of paper and an envelope, leaving her to plunge about in her handbag for a pen.

Finding it at last, she wrote hastily:

"Dear Danny, I was hoping to get you fixed up with somewhere in London, but so far no luck. In the meantime, you can stay for a few days with a friend of mine, Lionel Burnett at Brick House. That's the cottage on the right-hand side just past us going towards the village. It's got geraniums in the front garden. He'll put you up in the caravan but *no meals!*"

She underlined this twice before continuing.

"Eat at the Feathers or I'll arrange to get something to you. He's expecting you tomorrow (Wed.). Don't let on you're my brother. I told him a *friend.*"

She underlined this also.

"I'll try to come over to see you Wed. afternoon about 3 so try to be in. Love, Nina. P.S. Don't forget you're a friend. P.P.S. I've enclosed £2."

She added the second postscript in case the hotel proprietor should have seen her slipping the notes into the envelope before she licked the flap, stuck it down, and scrawled "Mr. Anderson" on the front. It would discourage him from trying to steal it, she thought; these days you can't be too careful. She waited to see him prop the letter up on the shelf behind the counter before she hurried away to catch her bus.

Getting off outside the Feathers and walking towards the house, she realised how good it was to be going home. It was still daylight although the sky was already taking on that predusk deepening of colour that made everything—the foliage, the grass, even the house itself—seem more rich and splendid.

Max and Lionel were in the kitchen when she entered by the back door, engrossed in a book of Constable reproductions that Lionel must have fetched from the dining room.

Looking up briefly, Max remarked, "You're back early," before turning to say to Lionel, "See what I mean about the light?"

But she didn't mind the perfunctory nature of his welcome; there had been a shine in his eyes which told her how pleased he was that she was home. She brushed the back of her hand gently across his hair as she passed behind his chair on her way upstairs to change.

Dressed once more in her comfortable, baggy skirt and old blouse and with those damned shoes off her feet at last, she returned to the top of the stairs. But, changing her mind, entered Max's room instead and stood for a few moments in silence in front of Lilith's portrait.

It was true, she thought, realising it for the first time, that none of Max's other paintings possessed quite the same passionate concern for texture and richness of colour as he had displayed in this one. He had poured into this portrait of Lilith all the sensuous nature of his love, just as the second one, which had been in Zoe's possession, had expressed his tenderness.

The two portraits should never have been separated, Nina realised. They were meant to be a pair: Sacred and Profane Love. Hadn't she heard that phrase somewhere?

Zoe had no damned right even to own one of them, let alone to sell it to some stranger who happened to arrive on her doorstep.

I bet she spent the money on booze, she thought bitterly.

One thing was quite certain, however. Not one word of any of it must get back to Max.

CHAPTER 4

On Thursday the weather was fine. Getting up at six o'clock when the alarm woke her, Nina went straight to the window and pulled aside the curtains. If it were raining, she told herself, the day wouldn't go well. If it were sunny, it meant good luck.

And evidently their luck was in. The sky was a clear blue except for a few small, puffy, white clouds—the sort, she thought, with a laugh of pure joy, Lionel might have painted with one of his fine brushes.

Everything else, too, had gone the way she wanted. Danny had moved into the caravan and both he and Lionel seemed fairly satisfied with the arrangement; at least, neither of them had openly complained so far. Lionel had even fixed up a small electric boiling ring in the caravan so that the problem of Danny's meals was partially solved. He could fry himself an egg or heat up a tin of soup on it.

She had called at the cottage on her way to the shop the previous afternoon and, by a few adroit questions, had learnt that Lionel had said nothing to Danny about the exhibition and Danny, in turn, hadn't divulged the exact nature of his relationship with her. So she had nothing to worry about there either.

In fact, the only disappointment was the house. Describing the

Demeter Gallery to Max on the evening of her return from London, she had been aware of how shabby their own surroundings would look compared to the black and white elegance of Eustace Quinn's and his assistant's, and she had spent most of Wednesday cleaning and polishing, concentrating her energies on the bits they would see. The result was an improvement, but, even so, there was nothing much she could do except try to brighten up the surfaces.

Going downstairs quietly in order not to waken Max, she glanced into the sitting room to give it a critical, early-morning examination and had to admit that it didn't look too bad after all. The sunlight was flooding in, highlighting the worn covers on the chairs, it was true, and the faded carpet, so thin that, hoovering it yesterday, she had noticed it was actually being sucked off the floor in places. But the pictures on the walls and the huge vases of leaves and flowers she had placed about the room would distract the eye.

They would eat in there, she decided, rather than in the gloomy dining room and she had already set up the gate-legged table in the window bay and placed round it four of the mahogany chairs which, removed from their normal setting, looked less hideous than usual.

So perhaps the house wasn't going to be quite the disaster she had imagined.

All that remained to do were the finishing touches, a new roll of loo paper in the downstairs cloakroom, a quick wipe over the hall floor with a damp cloth, and a rub down with polish on the first flight of treads leading up to the half-landing—all they would see of the staircase—and that ought to do it, she thought. Lunch was almost ready—stew, basically, although by serving it with rice she hoped to pass it off as goulash. She would have liked to cook something more exotic—one of her fiery curries, for example—but Max's stomach couldn't take spiced foods these days. Then there was apple snow to follow, with whipped cream, and a bottle of red wine to drink with the main course; and, last of all, real coffee. She had borrowed Lionel's percolator and four of his good glasses.

The money she had spent! Not just on the meal but on the trip up to London as well as the handouts to Zoe and Danny. Of course, it was cash well spent and she begrudged none of it except perhaps for the cream. Nearly a whole quid for a pint of double! She'd have to cut down on the housekeeping for the rest of the week to make up for it all.

At the usual time, nine o'clock, she took Max's breakfast upstairs and tried to hurry him into eating it quickly but, maddeningly, he refused to be affected by her sense of urgency.

"What's all the fuss about, Nina?" he asked her. "They're only people."

"But I want to be ready when they come."

It was no good, however, trying to explain to Max that she wasn't just in a flap. It was being in control of the situation that mattered to her; that, and making the day as perfect as she could.

Finally, she got him out of bed, washed, dressed, and downstairs. At first, he grumbled at having to sit, not in the kitchen in his comfortable, baggy wicker chair but in the sitting room, so that in the end she relented and brought the chair through for him, placing it in the sunny bay window. And then, just as it was nearly eleven o'clock, he asked to go to the lavatory. On purpose, she was sure, to be aggravating and to pay her out.

As she was lowering him back into the basket chair, he said to her in a strange voice, unusually quiet and full of meaning, "Nina, don't try to be different. I like you the way you are."

It was meant, she realised, as a warning and also, in an unexpected, backhanded way, as a compliment and she patted his arm reassuringly. There was no time, however, for her to reply because at that moment there was a splatter of gravel and, looking out of the window, she saw a large, black car turn in at the gate and approach the house.

"They're here!" she announced and hurried to let them in.

In the flurry of their arrival, the shaking of hands, and the introductions, Nina found it difficult to absorb much detail about either of them, except to notice briefly that Eustace Quinn was of medium height and wore a beard, while his assistant, whose name was Blanche Lester, was the white-skinned, black-haired girl whom she had seen on Tuesday seated in the gallery at the marble-topped table, a realisation that threw Nina into further confusion. But the girl, who Nina saw in a dazed way was very attractive without being able to say exactly how, appeared not to recognise her. So that was all right.

"Come and meet Max!" she cried, flinging open the sitting-room door.

He looked splendid, she thought, and made up for any shortcomings in the house—seated like a king in his wicker chair in the dazzle of sunlight, his great head lifted proudly and his white hair a bright coronet. Like a lion! Like an emperor!

"I'll get the coffee," she murmured and withdrew into the kitchen, glad to be on her own for she was trembling. Max was right, she thought. I am in a flap.

As she was heating up the percolator and finding the milk, the door opened and Blanche Lester unexpectedly entered.

"Anything I can do to help?" she asked.

Nina would have preferred to be left alone. For one reason, her efforts to prepare the house hadn't extended as far as the kitchen, which was untidy, the breakfast things still not put away, the table covered with plates and dishes in readiness for lunch. But Blanche appeared not to notice and began to help at once, drying up the cups that were on the draining board and placing them on the tray. People who offered to help and then just stood about doing nothing always infuriated Nina.

"The sugar's in there," she said, nodding towards a cupboard. As Blanche fetched it, Nina appraised her quickly, able at last to take in details of her appearance as if her vision had suddenly cleared.

Blanche Lester was in her early twenties and was the sort of girl whom Max would have loved to paint: not just attractive but possessing that fine bone structure that Max had taught her was more important than

mere surface prettiness. She reminded Nina of one of Shakespeare's hero-
ines dressed in boy's clothing—Viola, perhaps, or Jessica. Not just on account of the clothes she was wearing—dark red velvet trousers and a
short jacket, the colour of garnets, and a white silk shirt with ruffles at
the neck and wrists—although they added to the impression, but the
figure inside the clothes was boyish, trim, and narrow-hipped, with only
the merest suggestion of small breasts under the white silk. And her hair!
It was long, tied back very simply, and so very black and glossy. Nina
tried to think of a comparison but ridiculously, could conjure up no
closer image than the stamens of poppies. They, too, possessed the same
fine, silken, shining strands.

Blanche carried the tray, Nina going ahead to open doors, and, as they
entered the hall, the sound of voices and laughter came towards them,
not from the sitting room but from the dining room, Max's laugh rumbling out in a way Nina hadn't heard for years.

Entering, they found the two men installed in front of the paintings,
propped up in a row in front of them, Max seated on a chair, Eustace
Quinn standing beside him and both of them obviously getting on splen-
didly together.

Passing cups of coffee round, Nina had the opportunity to look at Eustace Quinn more closely, too.

Her first impression had been of a man who was elegantly dressed and
was perhaps in his thirties. She saw now that he was older than that,
nearer her own age, but his supple movements and his clothes—a lightweight beige suit, fashionably cut—gave him the illusion of youth. The
suppleness extended to his facial expressions, which changed quickly with
boyish eagerness and had left their mark, especially round the eyes where
the skin was deeply crinkled, giving him an amused, alert, Pan-like look.
She could almost imagine two little horns sprouting from the thick,
springy, brown hair. If Blanche possessed an emblematic, Renaissance
colouring—white, red, and black—his was warm, earthy tones—tawny
brown, the colour of bark or bracken.

"They're absolutely splendid, Max!" he was saying and then, turning
to accept the cup, he looked Nina full in the face and she was startled by
the immediate sexual recognition that passed between them. On her part,
it was quite involuntary. It was a long time since it had happened to her,
that sudden jolt of desire, as much a real physical sensation as an electric
shock, like picking up a wire and feeling the current leap and tingle
through the flesh, making the blood very bright and effervescent. And so
loud was the signal they exchanged, or so it seemed to her, that she
glanced fearfully at Max, half expecting him to have heard it, too.

Still clutching the tray, she stepped back deliberately out of the line of
vision of the two men.

"Do you think so?" Max asked, sounding pleased. All the same, he
cocked his head and pursed his lips doubtfully, examining the paintings
with a judicious scrutiny as if they weren't his at all and he had been
asked to pass judgement on them.

"The one of the girl with the kitten is particularly fine."

Max laughed and looked significantly over his shoulder at Nina.

"Yes, it's not bad, that one," he admitted.

Eustace Quinn followed his gaze and Nina stood blushing as she hadn't blushed since she was fourteen, feeling stripped naked under their eyes. To hide her confusion, she said quickly, addressing Blanche in order to avoid Eustace Quinn's glance, "You'll stay to lunch, of course?"

Blanche in turn looked at Eustace Quinn who replied, "That's very kind of you. Are you sure it's no trouble? We were going to lunch at the George in Bexford. As a matter of fact, we're booked in there for the night. There's an auction at Cawleigh Hall tomorrow afternoon I want to go to. Some water-colours I'm interested in are due to go under the hammer."

"It's ready. Lunch, I mean," Nina replied awkwardly, stricken by the thought of all that food going to waste. "I was expecting you to stay."

"In that case, we'd be delighted to," Eustace Quinn decided.

Suddenly everything was all right. From that moment, she was able to relax and enjoy the day as Max was doing. Even the awareness of the mutual attraction between herself and Eustace Quinn seemed part of the fun for, conscious of her embarrassment, he turned it into a game for the benefit of the others, flirting with her in a lighthearted way and paying her extravagant compliments so that she felt young and carefree again.

After lunch, Blanche offered to help her wash up and, when that was done, Nina suggested a walk in the garden in order to leave the two men alone. She felt warm towards the girl, partly because she was young and attractive and that, a gift from the gods, was to be admired, not envied. She was conscious, also, that Blanche was probably in love with Eustace Quinn—almost certainly they were lovers—and that quick glance of physical awareness that had passed between herself and him made her feel tender and protective towards the younger woman by reason of their shared femininity and her own greater sexual experience. But, most of all, it was Blanche's openly expressed admiration of Max that finally sealed her affection.

"I think he's wonderful," she had said, drying plates and stacking them on the table. She had spoken with a naïve, unashamed enthusiasm that could not be anything but genuine. "He's like somebody out of the Old Testament with that marvellous hair."

So, it was inevitable that, walking through the garden, their conversation should turn to Max. Nina felt no guilt as she had with Zoe. In fact, it was a relief to have another woman to talk to, especially one who admired Max so openly.

"It must be splendid being married to someone like him," Blanche continued as they strolled under the cedar tree towards the shrubbery.

"Yes, it is," Nina agreed. And so it was. All the day-to-day exasperation of coping with Max appeared as nothing.

"Where did you meet? In London?"

"No, it was in the country," Nina replied. She had told the story to very few people and hadn't even thought about it herself for a long time, but now, as she talked, it seemed as if the years were rolled back. They had met, she explained, in the fifties when Max was on a painting holiday. He had come to the village, Heversham in Essex, on the other side of the county, where her father was the vicar. Yes, actually the vicar! She had been a seventeen-year-old schoolgirl then, in the Lower Sixth, preparing for A-levels and a career in teaching. Max had stopped her in the village one Saturday afternoon to ask her the way and that had been it—love at first sight. Of course, he was older than she, nearly thirty years, in fact, but it hadn't seemed to matter. Her father had naturally disapproved of the relationship and so had her aunt who looked after the family, her own mother having died nine years before. So she and Max ran away together to London.

As she recounted the story, she was gratified to see the expression of astonished approval on the girl's face and, even to her own ears, the account possessed all the qualities of romance and adventure that one might read of in a novel.

Here I am, she thought, middle-aged and broadening on the hips and yet I could teach someone as young and attractive as Blanche a thing or two about passion.

"An elopement!" Blanche exclaimed.

Nina laughed, warm with the remembrance of that summer all those years ago.

"Yes! And do you know what he did then? The moment we arrived in the studio, he rushed out and bought huge bunches of roses and put them all round the place. He must have spent pounds and pounds."

Oh, the wild extravagance of it all! Rose petals everywhere! She could almost catch their scent now and feel their texture, cool and silken, against her skin.

"Max, the last of the great romantics!" she cried and Blanche, responding to her mood, laughed also.

"And when did you move down here?" she asked.

They had arrived at the summerhouse where they stopped by common consent, Blanche leaning in the doorway, wrapping a fine tendril of ivy round one finger.

How paintable she is! Nina thought. I wish I had Max's talent. I'd try to draw her just as she is now with that black and white beauty and the ambivalence of her sexuality.

"About eight years ago," she replied. Her mood began to ebb. It was not just thinking of the more recent past but the depressing effect that the summerhouse, with its melancholy air of old, forgotten pleasures and its rotting timbers, always had on her spirits. She tried not to think of Danny and their last meeting there only a few days before. "The lease on the studio ran out and Max couldn't afford to renew it. Besides, he was getting a bit arthritic then and he thought the country air would suit him. He used to work here sometimes, as a matter of fact. He'd set his easel up in the doorway and paint the view. Not that there's much to see except the lawn and the trees."

There was one portrait, however, which had come out of these sessions; the last one, in fact, that Max ever completed. At the time, it had disturbed her and since then it had disappeared, God knows where; perhaps he had burnt it or hidden it away. It had been much less positive visually than his other paintings, as if his eyesight were failing: a view across the lawn towards the surrounding trees, only everything had been diffused and vague in outline, drenched in a strange light that dissolved contours and perspective. In the background, a woman had been walking away, her back towards the onlooker—a misty, insubstantial figure in a white dress, her loose, dark hair a mere shadow, caught, as it were, a few seconds before she vanished, like an apparition on the point of melting away and merging with the foliage.

Nina had known instinctively that it was Max's final portrait of Lilith; his farewell, not to her memory—nothing could erase that—but to her inspiration of him as an artist. He never produced another painting nor even a sketch after that. A few days later, he abandoned his studio, emptying it of all his artist's materials and stacking the canvases and portfolios in the dining room.

But all of this was Max's secret, not hers, and so, while Nina was prepared to talk about her own life with him, certain aspects that touched him too closely, such as Lilith, could never be discussed. In an odd, irrational manner, she felt also that, in being frank, she was somehow making up to Blanche for that glance that had passed between herself and Eustace Quinn and, at the same time, was compensating the girl and perhaps, even in an oblique way, was instructing her in the art of relationships with men. For Eustace Quinn would be unfaithful, as Max had often been, only whereas Max's infidelities had never amounted to much more than passing whims, she wasn't so sure of Eustace Quinn's. She wanted to say, by talking about her years with Max, "You see, it's all right, really."

The two women returned to the house at half past three, the time when Max liked to have a cup of tea on being awakened from his afternoon nap which, in this instance, he hadn't had. Nina was a little afraid he would be tired. To her surprise, however, she found him alert and vigorous, holding court from his basket chair in the sitting room to which he and Eustace Quinn had removed, together with the portfolios of drawings, having found the dining room too dank and chill. At the sight of the huge folders and their contents spread out on the floor, Nina's heart gave a little squeeze of fear but one glance at Max's face reassured her. He hadn't missed the half dozen she had given to Danny and, indeed, seeing the vast collection of them displayed, she realised her fears had been groundless.

Eustace Quinn was squatting in front of them, sitting back on his heels, as he examined each one in turn, from time to time appealing to Max for details concerning a particular sketch. A pile lay beside him, presumably those which he had picked out from the general collection.

Max was in his element; expansive, witty, amusing, he held the floor.

My God! Nina thought, listening to him. He's on an outsize ego trip and good luck to him.

"That one?" he was saying. "Now there's a story behind that. I saw the woman on a tram in Clapham. Fascinating creature. Big, dark eyes; tiny waist; probably Italian in origin. Marvellous! 'Madam,' I said, raising my hat, 'I'd like to draw you.' ' 'Ow much?' she asked, quick as a flash in pure Cockney. 'Ten shillings an hour?' I suggested. 'My Gawd!' she said. 'It's more than I get up the 'Dilly. I'll even make the bed for that!' "

Laughter greeted the story as Max had intended and he leaned back, beaming. He could easily have gone on the stage, Nina thought admiringly. She could imagine him as one of those old-fashioned actor-managers, all heavy greasepaint and rich, dark vowels like fruitcake.

The rest of the afternoon passed in the same easy, pleasant manner and there was only one moment of anxiety when Eustace Quinn found one of the sketches of Lilith, done in charcoal in a few, bold strokes. Nina glanced quickly into Max's face. He was silent for what seemed like several minutes before he replied to Eustace Quinn's query.

"She was a model I used before the war," he said at last, his expression quite impassive.

"A professional?" Eustace Quinn asked.

"No. I can't remember what her job was or where I met her."

"I like the economy of line and the fluid movement. It's a pity one can't see her face."

"You're not meant to," Max replied shortly. He could have been referring to the pose, for the body was twisted from the hips to show the tense line of the backbone while one arm was curved round the head, lifting the breasts but also shielding the features. Eustace Quinn appeared to accept this explanation, for, apart from remarking "Marvellous!" as he added it to the pile of drawings he had set aside, he made no other comment.

Shortly afterwards, Nina had a further cause for concern that outweighed any other. It was now nearly half past six and Max was used to an early supper at seven. There was nothing left over from lunch and the only food in the house consisted of two small pork pies that were intended just for the pair of them. It had not occurred to her that Eustace Quinn and Blanche would stay so long.

"About supper," she began tentatively when there was a suitable gap in the conversation. She half hoped that Eustace Quinn, reminded of the time, would say they would have to leave. But Max, ignorant of the situation, remarked with infuriating generosity, "You'll stay, of course."

Eustace Quinn took one look at Nina's face and burst out laughing.

"Blanche," he said, addressing the girl who was jotting down in a notebook the details of the sketches he had set aside, "take the car and drive into Bexford. Give the chef at the George my compliments and tell him I'd like a supper hamper fit for a king."

He had taken out his wallet and there was a crisp crackle as notes were taken out and passed over. Twenties by the look of them, Nina thought, impressed by the extravagance of the gesture.

They ate the food on their laps by a log fire which Nina lit against the evening chill: cold chicken and lobster mayonnaise, little crab patties, smoked salmon, and champagne; and a whole selection board of cheeses, covered in transparent wrap, with a box of Bath Olivers to go with them. All Nina had to do was to find plates, cutlery, and glasses and make coffee.

Except for its lavishness, the improvised picnic supper reminded her of the old studio days when friends would drop in and Max would dash out to the all-night delicatessen to return with his pockets full of salami and tins of sauerkraut, bottles of cheap red wine, and long French loaves tucked under his arms, and everyone would eat sitting cross-legged on the floor, laughing and talking and passing round the opened bottles.

Oh, God! she thought. Those really were the days!

She was suddenly overwhelmed with nostalgia.

Later, after supper when she was in the kitchen with Blanche, a curious incident occurred, the full significance of which didn't strike her until much later. They had finished clearing up and were sitting talking at the table, relaxed and comfortable together, when Eustace Quinn entered and said to Blanche, "Go and talk to Max, darling. I want to chat to Nina alone."

The girl left the room without any comment, a sign of immediate, unquestioning obedience that made Nina more uneasy than ever about their relationship.

"Well?" she said sharply to show she wasn't quite so amenable. "What do you want?"

She had risen from the table in an attempt to establish that this was her little kingdom; a mistake, as she realised at once, for it gave him the opportunity to stand quite close to her. She was very conscious of his physical presence—the warm, bold, brown eyes; the way the little, glistening hairs of his beard sprang out of his skin and clustered together—and, to her anger and dismay, she found she was trembling.

"Nina," he said in a low, urgent voice, "I think you and I ought to get together some time to discuss Max's exhibition."

"That's Max's business," she retorted but not as fiercely as she had intended.

"Of course. I'm not trying to exclude him. I just feel that, as he's getting on now, he might not want to be bothered with details. I'm sure you could handle those."

A sop, she thought, although she had to admit that the compliment was subtle. Not many men would appeal to a woman's business ability in an attempt at seduction, for that's what it was.

"So there'll be an exhibition?" she asked.

"Oh, almost certainly, providing we can come to an agreement that suits everyone. The point is, if you could come to London, we could meet and sort out a lot of the groundwork over lunch one day."

And afterwards in bed, Nina added silently. She knew exactly what was in his mind, and the realisation angered and, at the same time, excited her. The bloody nerve of the man! All the same, she found herself, fascinated, watching his mouth, framed in the beard, with its full bottom lip, the flesh of which looked oddly bright and distended, as if the blood in it were very near the surface.

"What do you say? Will you come?" he persisted, placing one hand on her arm.

There was no time for her to reply or withdraw from the contact. For, at that moment, as they stood in the kitchen facing one another, Nina was aware of a face behind him at the window that looked into the yard. It hung in the darkened glass, white, disembodied, startlingly unfamiliar for a few seconds until, with a small shock of recognition, she realised it was Lionel's. The next instant, the face disappeared, there came a diffident knock at the door and Lionel appeared on the threshold, saying apologetically, "I'm so sorry, Nina. On Tuesday, when I was here, Max told me to come round about eight o'clock this evening."

She had moved quickly away from the close proximity with Eustace Quinn as soon as she had first caught sight of Lionel's face. It was quite the wrong thing to do because her action emphasised the intimacy of their former position, and she now tried to cover up her confusion by introducing the two men to one another.

Eustace Quinn immediately extended a firm, brown-skinned hand, Lionel a pale, limp one. It was embarrassingly obvious which of them had the advantage; Lionel was passive, allowing his hand to be shaken, and yet, quite irrationally, Nina felt more angry towards Eustace Quinn than Lionel. He was smiling in a superior, sardonic manner as if he found the slight figure of the wispy, flustered schoolmaster amusing. Lionel, his lips pressed together and two patches of colour burning on his cheekbones, began retreating towards the door.

"Oh, don't go," Nina protested.

She guessed why Max had asked him to come at this time. Expecting the guests would have departed, he had wanted to tell Lionel about their visit in order to impress him.

"We'll be leaving soon," Eustace Quinn put in.

"No, I think I ought to go. I shall only be in the way. Tell Max I'll call back another time," Lionel said.

There was no point in arguing with him. Lionel could be as stubborn as Max at times and Nina didn't attempt to dissuade him further. She walked to the door after him in time to catch the look of strong dislike that Lionel cast in the direction of Eustace Quinn, whose back was turned as if already dismissing him.

Oh, dear! she thought. How stupid it all is!

Out loud, she called out in too friendly a voice, "Good-bye, Lionel! Call back tomorrow."

Pretending not to hear her, he walked towards his car, his shoulders very stiff.

Nina closed the door, turning back into the kitchen where Eustace

Quinn was regarding her, eyebrows raised, his white teeth gleaming in a quizzical smile, and she realised what he reminded her of—a fox, dapper, jaunty, handsome; and yet clinging about him, an unmistakable aura of danger and freebooting self-regard.

"So I'll see you in London," he remarked, as if the arrangements were decided. And, not giving her time to reply, he added, "I'll just say good-bye to Max and then I think Blanche and I really must leave."

He was in the sitting room with Max for quite a long time. Blanche and Nina waited in the hall, expecting him to join them at any minute and chatting sporadically in the disjointed manner of women who, ready for departure, are forced to keep conversation going while they wait for their menfolk.

At last, Eustace Quinn emerged from the sitting room, looking pleased, as if he'd reached some satisfactory arrangement, and shook hands with Nina in a very special grasp, enclosing her one hand in both of his and holding it there for much longer than was necessary. She could still feel the warmth of his skin against hers when she followed them to the door and watched them get into the car. Blanche fluttered a hand, Nina waved back, and Eustace Quinn, before getting into the driver's seat, tipped her a salute as significant as the handclasp as if in recognition of something very personal between them or perhaps to signal his admiration of her as she stood in the lighted doorway. The car then disappeared down the drive.

Nina lingered on the doorstep after it had gone, looking at the evening. It was almost dark, the twilight thickening so that the shapes of trees and bushes were beginning to merge as the night closed in. A few stars were out and the evening star, which Max had told her was the planet Venus, hung low in the sky, very clear and brilliant, a drop of pure, distilled light.

It was the time of day she had loved best in London, when the streetlamps had already flowered and yet their brilliance had not quite quenched the sky so that it was still visible above the buildings, throwing into dramatic silhouette the darker outlines of chimneys, aerials, and roofs.

She would have liked to stay longer, watching the night deepen, but Max's voice called her from the sitting room and she hurried indoors to see what he wanted.

He looked exhausted, his face grey as he leaned back in the basket chair and she was suddenly furious with Eustace Quinn for reducing him to this pitiful old man.

"Bed!" she said immediately.

It took her a long time to get him upstairs. At every step, he had to rest because of the trembling in his legs, and she waited patiently, hold-ing his arm, until he had recovered sufficient strength to mount the next tread, the hand that clung to the banister so taut that the skin covering it seemed stretched to nothingness, leaving only the knuckles and tendons visible.

At last they reached the landing with its long vista of brown-painted doors, each one with its white china knob and finger plate, and she supported him into the bedroom where she finally lowered him onto the bed.

"You've done too much," she scolded him. She was out of breath herself and had to sit down beside him for a few moments to recover.

He merely nodded and sat passively while she undressed him, submitting to her hands like a child. Kneeling down in front of him, she took off his shoes and socks, exposing his long, white feet, and was suddenly overwhelmed by a great storm of pity and tenderness. If it hadn't been embarrassing for them both, she would have taken them in her hands and kissed them, washing them with her tears and drying them on her hair. Like Mary Magdalene. A comparison, she thought, that was more apt than she had intended, for hadn't Mary Magdalene been guilty of adultery? She knew then that she would not accept Eustace Quinn as her lover on even the most casual basis.

Pulling back the sheets and blankets, she managed somehow to half lift, half roll him into bed where he lay, his eyes closed, the great prow of his nose jutting up and the corners of his mouth turned down as if in massive disapproval.

She was aware that this was how he would end, totally bedridden and dependent, and the thought terrified her. How on earth would she cope?

"Nine, I'd like a brandy," he whispered.

"You're having nothing of the sort," she told him in a hectoring voice because of her love and her fear. "You're going to have your tablets and you know you're not allowed to drink spirits with them."

The tablets were in a bottle on the shelf in the bathroom. They had been prescribed months before as pain-killers when Max's arthritis had been causing him a great deal of discomfort. Since then, the pain had subsided and he had refused to see the doctor or take any more drugs. Shaking them out into the palm of her hand, she saw there were only two left and she was furious with herself for not having checked the bottle before. Supposing he needed more in the night? Should she call the doctor now or wait until the morning? What the hell ought she to do? Common sense told her to wait.

Max took the tablets without any fuss, a sign that he was far from well, but, as she stood by the bedside, she saw with relief the muscles in his face relaxing as the pain lessened.

"Nina," he said at one stage, opening his eyes, "about the exhibition . . ."

"We'll talk about it in the morning. Go to sleep now," she replied.

A few minutes later, he had fallen asleep. She softly drew the curtains and, switching off the light, tiptoed to the door, leaving it open so that she could hear him should he wake in the night and need her.

Several times she thought she heard him call and went to him, but he was still sleeping. The last occasion was at dawn and, returning to her own bed, she lay stiff and rigid, watching the grey light seeping in round the curtains, her thoughts tumbling about in her mind like bright discs spinning, too fast and too urgent for her to focus her full attention on any one of them for more than a few seconds. She felt dazzled by their flickering rapidity. Max and Danny's discs were the brightest. Then there were Zoe's, too, and Lionel's. She felt she had been unwittingly cruel to Lionel over that stupid business with Eustace Quinn. And then there was the exhibition, which took her back again to Max.

Finally, she slept uneasily, waking again at half past seven to the sunlight bright behind the curtains and Max calling her.

CHAPTER 5

He was sitting up against the pillows, looking better, not nearly so grey and drawn but Nina could tell he was still not his usual self; he was too quiet and subdued.

"How do you feel?" she asked cheerfully. She felt awful herself, weary to the bone, every muscle aching.

He merely grunted in reply.

"Shall I get your breakfast?"

"I don't think I want anything."

That wasn't like him, and she said coaxingly, "You ought to eat something, Max. Have some toast and tea."

"Later, perhaps. Are there any of those tablets left?"

She pounced on the question.

"Why? Are you in pain?"

He rolled his head about restlessly on the pillows.

"A bit."

"I've only got aspirin. You took the last two tablets yesterday."

"Oh, hell!" There was a pause and she waited for the request she knew would follow. "Do you think you could get me some more, Nine?"

The doctor's surgery was in the next village, Great Rushleigh, a three miles' cycle ride away. Still, she had only herself to blame. She should have arranged to have the prescription renewed much earlier.

"Only, you see," he continued, "I want to get up. Eustace Quinn said he might call this morning."

"If you're not well, he'll have to see you up here," she retorted. "What time is he coming?"

"I'm not sure."

"Well, if I'm not back before he comes, he'll have to come upstairs to talk to you. There'll be no one to help you out of bed."

Max pulled a face. He hated strangers seeing him helpless but he'd have to put up with it for once, Nina thought. She couldn't be in two places at once, although she relented enough to promise, "I'll get back as soon as I can. You realise the doctor will probably want to see you? And it's no good you looking like that."

"I hate being poked about," he grumbled.

She meant to make an early start so that she could arrive at the surgery as soon as it opened at nine o'clock, but there were delays. Max decided after all that he'd like some breakfast, and by the time she had prepared it and carried it upstairs and got herself ready, it was ten to nine. Besides, she wanted to find out from Max what arrangements had been made about the exhibition, but he was uncommunicative about it and it was only by a process of direct questioning that she was able to drag any information out of him. In a way, she could understand his reluctance. He had never liked talking about anything before the outcome was certain; a kind of superstition, she imagined, as if the very act of naming it brought bad luck and made it less likely to happen.

Finally, he revealed that Eustace Quinn was indeed interested, hoped to mount the exhibition in the following late spring, but had to discuss it first with a partner.

"What partner?" she asked suspiciously. It was the first time she'd heard about anyone else being involved.

"I don't know." Max sounded impatient. "There's another man, I gather, who may go halves with him on the expenses." Seeing her expression, he added, "It'll cost money, Nina. There'll be advertising and catalogues to pay for."

"What about you? Will you get a percentage?"

"We haven't discussed that yet. Perhaps he'll talk about it this morning."

"You hold out for a fair share," she warned him. She knew instinctively that Eustace Quinn would drive a hard bargain.

It must have been well past nine o'clock before she arrived at the doctor's surgery to find, as she had feared, that there were other people already waiting. Giving her name to the receptionist, she took her place at the end of the row of chairs, counting heads quickly as she did so. There were five, including an old man, a woman with a baby, and a sullen-looking youth with his foot in a cast. Knowing the doctor's methods, it was going to take nearly an hour before her turn came, and she sat there, seething with impatience, remembering suddenly that she had forgotten to pin a note on the front door telling Eustace Quinn that Max was in bed and he'd have to let himself in by the back door and find his own way upstairs.

Well, it was too late now.

Meanwhile, there was nothing to do except read the posters on the walls and the dog-eared women's magazines that littered the table.

Eventually, the sullen youth emerged from the surgery and the buzzer rang to summon the next patient, herself.

Dr. Foreman was a large, deliberate, middle-aged man, with a broad face and stomach, who took his time. Nothing would hurry him. He even drove his car in the same stately manner.

Nina described Max's symptoms which he wrote down carefully, using an old-fashioned gold-nibbed fountain pen, holding up his left hand to warn her not to go too fast.

"The thing is," Nina said, watching the gold nib scratching away before finally coming to rest, "I'd like his prescription renewed."

Dr. Foreman thought about it.

"I can't do that, lassie," he said at last, a term he applied to all his female patients whatever their age. "I'll have to see him first." He consulted his appointment book with the same deliberation. "I could fit in a visit at three o'clock this afternoon."

"All right," Nina agreed. Max would have to put up with it. "Meanwhile," she added coaxingly, "could you let me have just a few of his tablets? He's in quite a bit of pain."

The prescription cupboard had to be unlocked, the bottle carefully chosen, its label checked, and a small white envelope found before four tablets were extracted and placed inside the envelope, which was then handed over to her.

Outside, Nina retrieved her bike which she had propped up against the surgery wall and set off for home. On the way back, she passed Lionel's cottage and, had she not been so anxious about Max, she would have called to see how Danny was getting on and to try and make amends to Lionel for yesterday's misunderstanding.

There was no sign of a car parked outside the house, she noticed as she turned in at the drive, so it seemed that Eustace Quinn had not yet arrived. There might be time to give Max his tablets and help him downstairs or, at least, tidy up the bedroom and make him more presentable to receive a guest.

However, rounding the corner of the house into the yard, she saw Eustace Quinn's large, black Rover parked in front of the outbuildings. So he had arrived after all. He must, she thought, have tried the front door and, finding it locked, had driven round to the back and let himself in.

Hurriedly abandoning her bike, she entered the house and went straight upstairs.

Max was in bed, still propped up against the pillows, his eyes closed and his hands folded on top of the quilt, dozing quietly. Apart from him, the room was empty.

It gave her a small shock. She had been so sure that, on entering his room, she would find Eustace Quinn already installed there, seated by the bed and engaged in conversation with Max that his absence was totally unexpected. She had even imagined the expression that would be on his face as he rose to greet her.

Max opened his eyes as she came in and seemed as bewildered as she, only at her presence.

"Nina!" he exclaimed, and his voice sounded husky as it did sometimes when he first woke up. "You've been gone for hours."

"I had to wait. The surgery was full," Nina explained briefly. "Where's Eustace Quinn?"

She expected Max to answer that he was downstairs, looking at the paintings. Instead, to her surprise, he replied, "I don't know. He hasn't come yet."

"But his car's outside."

"Well, I haven't seen him," Max retorted as if she were accusing him of some dereliction. He tried to sit up properly and then sank back again, grimacing.

"You'd better have your tablets," Nina said, fishing the little envelope out of her cardigan pocket. There was a glass of water on the bedside table which she held out to him. Waiting while he swallowed a tablet, she gave him only half her attention. If Eustace Quinn hadn't come upstairs on his arrival to see Max, it must mean that he had gone straight into the dining room to examine the pictures and drawings. The bloody nerve of it! she thought.

Water splashing on her hand brought her back to the immediate present. Max, lifting the glass to his lips, had spilt some of its contents onto her outstretched palm on which she was holding out the second tablet in readiness for him to take. Sharpening her attention, she saw that his hand was trembling. His head, too, as if the effort of holding it erect to drink was too great, while his whole face had resumed the taut, grey look it had had last night.

She shifted position quickly, putting one arm round his shoulders, and, taking the glass from him, she held it to his lips while he put the second tablet into his mouth, blaming herself for not having noticed his condition before and thanking God that the doctor was coming to examine him.

She didn't think of Eustace Quinn again until about half an hour later when she had settled Max properly and made sure the tablets were working. He said nothing while she carried out these ministrations until, when she was on the point of leaving, he took one of her hands in his, half lifted it to his lips as if to kiss it, and then, simply holding it, murmured, his eyes closed, "Sorry, Nine."

Sorry, she supposed, for her having to wait on him, to cycle to Great Rushleigh and back, to heave him about in bed.

She was sorry, too; for herself but mostly for him. Poor Max! That he should be reduced to this. She could almost see the fire dying down in him. His hand on hers felt light and frail, the skin as insubstantial as a leaf's thin membrane. She bent and kissed him on the forehead and, as she did so, she felt his hand fall from hers.

Going downstairs, she allowed her compassion for Max to harden into the more exciting sensation of anger towards Eustace Quinn. It was quite stimulating and she was looking forward to it although part of it, she had to admit, was disappointment at her inevitable refusal to take him as a lover. If only, she thought with a momentary surge of regret . . .

The dining-room door faced her at the bottom of the staircase and, marching across the hall, she flung it open, the words she intended using already on her lips.

"I think you might bloody well have had the decency to ask Max's permission first!"

She stopped on the threshold. This room, too, was empty. Only the row of painted faces confronted her where they had been left propped against the wall. The portfolios still lay unopened on the table where they had been returned the previous evening. Without moving from the doorway, she could see through the French windows that there was no one either in Max's studio.

More mystified than anxious, she searched the rest of the house. The sitting room where the chairs were still grouped from yesterday, the curtains closed. She drew them back before continuing her tour of the house, even the unused bedrooms, the bathroom, the downstairs cloakroom, the series of little pantries and sculleries that opened off a separate passageway from the kitchen.

But nowhere could she find Eustace Quinn.

Returning to the kitchen, she stood irresolute for several minutes. It was ridiculous! He must be somewhere. He couldn't have vanished into thin air. There was his car, clearly visible through the window, glittering richly in the sunlight, its doors closed, its great, black bonnet thrusting forward.

Staring at it, she tried to imagine what sequence of actions he must have gone through after his arrival. Finding no answer when he rang the front-door bell, for the simple reason that it didn't work, he must have driven round to the back of the house, as she had first assumed, and tried the back door which had been closed but was unlocked. Getting no answer there, for Max's bedroom was on the far side of the house and he wouldn't have heard either the car arrive or anyone knocking, Eustace Quinn must have then decided, contrary to her belief that he had let himself into the house, to walk about in the garden until she returned. So she had maligned him, after all, in thinking that he had used the opportunity of finding the place empty to poke about in Max's possessions.

It was still strange, however, that he hadn't yet returned. It was nearly an hour since she herself had arrived home and she began to worry that something might have happened to him. Perhaps he had fallen—the garden was overgrown and full of hazards such as broken branches and hidden holes—or even had a heart attack. He looked healthy enough but that was no criterion.

She ought to go and look for him, she decided, even though the garden covered more than two acres and consisted mainly of undergrowth and shrubbery. It meant, too, leaving Max alone in the house, which bothered her, and she suddenly felt harassed by the situation. Hadn't she enough to do without searching for Eustace Quinn?

All the same, there seemed no other answer, and, leaving the back door propped open with the heavy flatiron that was used as a doorstop in case he should return before her, she crossed the yard, glancing into the interior of the car as she passed it and noting that a lightweight overcoat and a briefcase were lying on the back seat.

The search of the garden proved as unrewarding as her search of the house. The most likely places, the summerhouse and the seats in the shrubbery where someone might choose to wait, were empty and the entire place seemed deserted apart from birds and an occasional squirrel that darted up a tree at her approach.

From time to time, she paused to call out, feeling self-conscious and ridiculous. "Mr. Quinn" seemed too formal, "Eustace" too familiar. In the end, she merely hallooed, startling the rooks which rose from the trees, cawing bad-temperedly.

Tramping about, she was conscious, too, of the state of the garden. It was a reproach, the kitchen garden in particular. All that ground going to waste! She thought of Lionel's neat patch of vegetables where everything grew in rows. The asparagus that, when they first bought the house, Max had so enthused about—"Think of it, Nina! Fresh asparagus from the garden!"—had bolted into a jungle of tall, feathery fronds while the ground under the fruit trees was littered with last year's crop, turned brown and rotten.

Finally, she gave up and returned to the house, glancing up at Max's window as she crossed the shaggy lawn where the cedar stood.

Turning the corner into the yard, she was in time to see a Mini, with Blanche at the wheel, come to a standstill at the other end, its entrance blocked by her bike which she had left leaning against the wall.

"Hang on!" she shouted and ran forward to move it. Blanche lowered the driver's window.

"Where's Eustace?" she asked. "He was supposed to meet me in Cawleigh."

Holding her bike by the handlebars, conscious of what a sight she must look with her hair full of bits of leaf and her blouse parting company with her skirt, Nina tried to explain. Blanche looked so cool and sophisticated—in a green linen trouser suit, her hair braided up on top of her head in an elaborate knot, quite different from the young, girlish figure she had presented the day before—that Nina felt disadvantaged.

Blanche frowned.

"You mean you can't find him anywhere?" she demanded as if it were all Nina's fault.

"Well, I've looked," Nina replied defensively. She was conscious of another side to the girl's personality which hadn't been revealed yesterday, much harder and more self-confident, and this awareness added to her sense of harassment.

Blanche got out of the car.

"Oh, God!" she said. "Isn't that just typical of him? He said, 'Meet me in Cawleigh at twelve o'clock.' He wanted me to look at the preview of the sale this morning while he spoke to Max. We were supposed to have lunch at the Hollybush. I've been hanging about in the bar for nearly half an hour."

"Why, what's the time?" Nina asked. She had no idea.

Blanche looked at her watch.

"A quarter to one."

Oh, hell! thought Nina. She had done nothing towards preparing lunch which was beef that would need braising for at least two hours. Max would have to have an omelette and lump it.

"I'll just put my bike away," she said, "then we'll go indoors."

Wheeling it across the yard to the outbuildings, it occurred to her that she hadn't searched them, although why Eustace Quinn should choose to enter any of them she had no idea. It seemed quite unlikely. However, on the principle of leaving no stone unturned, she thought it best at least to look inside them.

The only usable one was the stable in which she kept her bike. The others—a coal house, a wood store, and a washhouse still containing the old-fashioned, brick-built boiler in one corner, its little fire door red with rust—were almost derelict, the ivy that scrambled thickly over them having dislodged so many slates that the roofs were open to the sky in places.

The doors to the first two had to be forced open but the washhouse door remained permanently ajar, the hinges having dropped so that it could not be properly closed. Nina swung it back and peered inside. The interior was dim, its one small window so obscured by ivy that the light could barely penetrate. It contained, too, a lot of junk, some of it belonging to the previous owners: a rotting roll of underfelt, spotted with mould and smelling strongly of must; a mangle; some pieces of decrepit furniture; a pile of old newspapers which the damp had fused together into one lump. As she entered, some small creature, probably a mouse, scuttled away behind the newspapers and, following it with her eyes, she saw something else lying beside them, a big bundle that seemed unfamiliar. Surely it hadn't been there the last time she entered the place, admittedly several years before? It looked like clothes piled up untidily under some sacks which, if she remembered correctly, had been hanging over the mangle.

Stepping forward into the dark green gloom, she felt cautiously with her feet on the uneven brick floor and, using the toe of her sandal, lifted one of the sacks aside.

Two legs clad in light grey trousers confronted her and, below them, the upturned soles of a pair of black leather shoes.

She wasn't sure afterwards if she cried out. A scream certainly started somewhere inside her, close to the pit of her stomach, but it seemed to be strangled before she could utter it.

She backed away, unable to take her eyes off it. The bundle was Eustace Quinn. She knew that without seeing the face; knew, too, that he was dead. The angle of the shoes, one turned out, the other flopping inwards, told her that.

Still backing away, she bumped into the wall, felt blindly for the doorway, fumbling with her hands stretched out behind her and, only when they came into contact with the jamb, was she finally able to turn and run away.

Blanche was waiting in the yard and called out immediately when she saw Nina stumbling towards her, "What's happened?"

Her face alone, Nina thought afterwards, must have been expressive of what she had seen.

"Don't look!" she kept repeating. "Don't look!"

"But what's happened?" Blanche insisted. And then, "Oh, my God, it's Eustace!"

"I think he's dead," Nina said and added apologetically, "I'm so dreadfully sorry," as if it were something she had broken.

She began to cry, huge tears spilling down without any apparent effort on her part.

"Brandy!" Blanche said shortly. She seemed less affected than Nina, although it was only when they had entered the kitchen and Nina, fetching the bottle, poured out two glasses that the extent of the girl's shock became evident. Sitting at the table, she lifted the glass to her lips to drink and then her head began to shake, in much the same manner as Max's had trembled earlier, the brandy running down her chin.

The sight was so grotesque that Nina was startled into composure, her own brief bout of weeping passing as suddenly as it had begun. It had been caused, she realised, not just by the discovery of Eustace Quinn's body but by a great many other factors: Max's illness, Danny's problems, exhaustion following the cycle ride to Great Rushleigh and back, the search of the garden, and also by the accumulation of years of stress and tension—running the house, getting Max in and out of bed, the shortage of money, even the bloody hot-water boiler which never lit properly the first time and had to be coaxed into burning.

The tears that had poured out of her seemed to have washed it all away, leaving her empty and curiously relaxed so that all her movements were slow and deliberate. As she comforted Blanche, making her finish the brandy and fetching a damp flannel to wipe her face, as she might have done to a child, her mind was patiently working out step by step what would have to be done next.

The police would have to be told. That was first. She would cycle down to Lionel's and use his telephone. Should she call an ambulance as well? she wondered. But the question seemed too difficult to answer.

Decide that later, she told herself. Or ask Lionel. He'll know. She was suddenly very anxious to see him. Lionel, so reliable and sensible, would take her problems onto his shoulders.

"Listen," she said to Blanche and explained what she was going to do. "Wait here. I shan't be long. And if Max calls out, just tell him there's been an accident. Do you understand?"

Blanche nodded dumbly, and Nina was struck again, as she had been at their first meeting the day before, by the girl's extraordinary and unusual beauty and, at the same time, by an overwhelming compassion towards her because of it. What was the use of it, after all? It was no guarantee against unhappiness or a lonely old age. Look at Zoe. Or even herself. Given the chance, she thought distractedly, I'd rather have been clever, but then Max wouldn't have fallen in love with me and where would I be now?

There was no answer to that question.

She got her bike from the stable, giving the washhouse a wide berth, not even looking at it. The door was still open, but luckily it faced her so that she was shielded from any view of the interior although the image of those two shoes turned up came very vividly into her mind before she was able to suppress it.

Blanche's Mini still stood in the yard entrance and she said out loud to herself, "I wonder where she got that from?" as she squeezed past it, pushing her bike. Yesterday Blanche had arrived in Eustace Quinn's car. It didn't occur to Nina even then that Blanche could have driven her down to Lionel's.

He was pottering about in the garden when she arrived, gently loosening the soil round the fuchsias with a miniature hand fork and sprinkling on white granules that she supposed was fertilizer. The box stood on the flagstones beside him together with an old kitchen spoon with which he was measuring out the contents as carefully as a woman following a cake recipe.

He put the fork and spoon down as she came puffing round the corner, his first reaction one of pleasure that was quickly tempered by a more cool distant expression.

"Oh, it's you, Nina," he said as if her arrival were embarrassingly ill-timed.

Cycling to his house, she had forgotten yesterday's incident and now, reminded of it, she was robbed of all speech and could only stand there looking at him.

"What is it?" he asked and then, with quick anxiety, "Is it Max? Is he ill?"

Then it all came tumbling out, the words strung together anyhow. She was conscious that, as she spoke, she was punching her fist into the palm of the other hand, as she had seen people with a speech impediment behave, trying to force the sounds into a more coherent form.

She had to admit he was kindness itself as she knew he would be. He made her sit down on the patio. He fetched her neat whisky which he made her drink. He even found her a cigarette, God knows from where because he was a nonsmoker, and lit it for her, making a small grimace as he drew in the smoke. And finally, he went into the house to telephone.

Nina sat in the sun. The day now began to take on a strange, distanced quality in which she participated only peripherally, like being caught up in a dream, the inconsequentiality of which only touches one indirectly. It was probably caused, she realised, by the brandy and whisky combined with the cigarette, which tasted dry and harsh, making her head swim. And exhaustion. Now that she was sitting down, she could feel the muscles in her calves leap and tremble.

Lionel returned, his eyes behind his spectacles very solemn.

"I've rung the police," he announced in that special, low-pitched voice one might use in church. "They're on their way. Would you like to stay here, Nina?"

"No," she said quickly. "There's Max. I can't leave him."

She had forgotten all about Blanche.

"Then I'll drive you home," he said with unexpected firmness, allowing no refusal.

"I'd like to see Danny first," she replied. She didn't know why it was so important.

Lionel looked fussed.

"Please," she coaxed.

"Very well," Lionel conceded and added, as he escorted her up the garden, "I don't know if he's up yet."

There was a note of faint disapproval in his voice.

Nina had never been inside the caravan. It stood on its own neat, flag-stoned patch with two little steps up to the door. The curtains were closed and a cardboard box containing empty beer bottles stood at the bottom of the steps. Lionel looked at them with distaste as he knocked at the door.

There was no answer and he knocked again, looking at Nina over his shoulder as much as to say, "You see."

"Go in," she urged.

She followed him inside. The caravan was small, containing only one room, with a bit at the far end, separated by a serving counter, which formed a tiny kitchen, and it was quite obvious even before Lionel drew the curtains that it was empty. And also very untidy. The bed, which in daytime could be folded back to form a couch, filled most of the space and was unmade, the bedding spilling down onto the floor to join Danny's clothes which were strewn about everywhere, while in the kitchen end the tap, left running, pattered into the tiny sink.

Without saying a word, Lionel clambered over the bed and turned it off. His face, as he came back, was very angry with that quiet, controlled, cold rage that frightened her far more than one of Max's roaring out-bursts of temper.

"I'll tidy it," she said and added quickly, "he'll have to go."

"Never mind that now," Lionel replied. His voice was pinched and austere and Nina realised how much she had misjudged him. He would be formidable in a classroom—that voice alone would quell even the most unruly pupil.

"But where is Danny?" she asked as they emerged into the garden.

"Gone for a walk?" Lionel suggested briefly. He didn't appear to care.

It didn't seem likely to Nina. More probably, she thought, he's at the Feathers.

Sitting in the passenger seat beside him as he drove back to the house, Nina felt oddly in awe of Lionel. Both of them were silent, Nina too wrought up to speak, Lionel too angry. At least, his profile when she peeped sideways at it looked very disapproving and magisterial.

Just as they were turning into the drive, he cleared his throat and asked in an embarrassed manner, "How did he die?"

"I don't know," Nina confessed. It hadn't occurred to her until that moment to consider this aspect of Eustace Quinn's death.

Now, faced by it, she could only suppose some accident must have happened to him although, remembering again the two legs sticking out from under the sacks, she realised that someone must have covered him up. Even then the full significance of it didn't strike her. She was merely bewildered.

Anyway, there was no time to consider it further. Lionel parked behind the Mini because there was no room to get past it into the yard and, as they walked towards the house, Blanche came running out to meet them while, through the open kitchen door, Max's voice could be heard shouting from upstairs, "Nine! *Nine!*"

CHAPTER 6

"Murder," said Pardoe succinctly.

The short, dapper figure of the police surgeon was squatting down at the side of the body, looking, Detective Chief Inspector Rudd thought, like a small, alert fox terrier at a rathole. He was watching from the doorway of the washhouse as there wasn't room for them both inside. Even with the door open, the place smelt strongly of mildew. Behind him, Detective Sergeant Boyce craned for a better look.

"How?" Rudd asked.

Pardoe sniffed disparagingly and, taking the head between the hands, rolled it to and fro like a football.

"The neck's broken," he explained snappishly, as if any fool should have seen that straight away. "I'll need to get him stripped to see exactly where the blow was struck, but my guess is"—and here he poked two fingers down the back of the expensive, polo-necked sweater the body was wearing and felt about—"that it caught him in the region of the sixth or seventh vertebra and the weapon used was heavy and probably flat-edged. It's bruised the skin but hasn't cut into it or the fabric of the clothing."

"No blood," commented Boyce, shifting his bulk from one foot to the other.

"There wouldn't be," Pardoe retorted. "The double layer of wool round the neck of the sweater would have cushioned the blow and prevented the skin from being broken. But it wasn't enough to stop the spine being snapped like a stick of celery. Well, I've finished with him for the time being," he added, getting to his feet and dusting off the knees of his trousers. "You can take him away if you like."

Rudd and Boyce exchanged a glance and the Sergeant retreated to the yard where he could be heard giving orders for the ambulance to be backed up to the washhouse door, a difficult manoeuvre as the yard was partially filled already by the dead man's Rover. McCullum, the police photographer, having finished taking shots of the body and the interior of the outbuilding, was now snapping the Rover from various angles before it was towed off for forensic examination. The Mini, belonging, Rudd understood, to the dead man's assistant, Blanche Lester, had already been moved to allow the ambulance access to the yard, while along the drive and outside the gate were parked the various cars and vehicles in which the police and their accompanying experts had arrived from head-quarters in Chelmsford.

Stepping aside, Rudd watched as the men with the stretcher stooped down to lift the dead man onto it. So far, he knew very little about him, except his name was Eustace Quinn, that he owned an art gallery, and that he had been visiting the artist and his wife, Max and Nina Gifford, who lived in the house. To judge by the body, Quinn had been in his middle forties and was of medium height and build, bearded, well-dressed in a style that managed to be informal, expensive, and what Rudd loosely described as "arty"—that is, more colourful and flamboyant than is conventionally acceptable and yet conforming to a certain stylish fashion. The smarter men's boutiques were full of his kind of clothing—well-cut denim trousers and jackets, exclusive T-shirts, sweaters bearing the name tabs of well-known designers—and of expensive price tags as well, as Rudd had once discovered to his cost, wandering into one of them in the hope of finding a cheap sports shirt.

Perhaps more significant than the clothing as indicative of Eustace Quinn's character was the thin gold chain round his neck from which was suspended the initial E, also in gold. It swung loose over the pale blue cashmere sweater as his body was lifted onto the stretcher, glinting for a few seconds before the body was covered over with a blanket and was carried away to the waiting ambulance.

"And," Pardoe added, at Rudd's elbow, before he could open his mouth, "don't ask me for the time of death, Jack. Let me have him on the slab first. Although I'll tell you this—he's been dead for at least three hours."

With that, he turned on his heel and followed the stretcher party into the yard.

Rudd lingered in the doorway. The scenes-of-crime officer had already examined the interior of the washhouse and had reported that there was nothing in the way of evidence in the immediate vicinity of the body, nor were there any tracks or footprints on the floor, apart from Nina Gifford's, to suggest how the body had been transported there, if that is what had happened, although the bricks were covered with a thin layer of dust and mould. Someone, as Rudd himself had realised when he first arrived, had backed out of the doorway, dragging some object across the floor between the body and the entrance, thus obliterating any foot-prints; one of the sacks, Rudd suspected. The one covering the lower half of the body had been smeared with brick dust on its upper surface.

From where he stood, Rudd measured the distance with his eye. The chalk outline marking where the body had lain was about four feet in from the door. It would have been possible for the murderer, having wiped away his tracks, to throw the sack that far onto the body. Certainly, the arc-shaped markings on the floor suggested he had used some kind of coarse material in a wide, sweeping motion."

But why had the killer bothered? The dust was too thin and granular to take anything more than an indistinct print that would be too vague to preserve the details of a pattern on a shoe sole, say, or individual signs of wear. It seemed an unnecessarily careful action when all the indications pointed to the body having been hastily dumped down and minimally hidden.

What struck him more forcibly, however, was the choice of hiding place. Why here? True, the outbuilding wasn't used much, judging by the state of its interior and the old junk and rubbish that filled it. On the other hand, it was very close to the house. In fact, it was directly overlooked by windows. Whoever had hidden the body had been taking a hell of a risk.

Or had the place been chosen because it was where Eustace Quinn had been killed and the murderer had simply left the body where it lay, merely throwing a couple of sacks over it and wiping out the footprints on the floor?

It was a possibility although it seemed unlikely that Eustace Quinn, dressed in an expensive, pale blue cashmere sweater and light grey trousers, would have chosen of his own free will to enter the washhouse. Nor was there any object lying about with which he might have been killed. As Pardoe had pointed out, it was something heavy but not sharp-edged —the classic blunt instrument, in other words. Although, of course, the murderer might have removed it from the scene of the crime.

On balance, however, Rudd's instinct told him that the murder had taken place elsewhere. The problem was, as Boyce's brief comment had emphasised, the absence of blood would make the exact site difficult to establish.

Boyce came up behind him at that moment and, tapping him on the shoulder, brought him out of his reverie.

"The ambulance's gone," he reported, "and McCullum's finished. Do you want the Rover shifted? The breakdown van's ready to be backed in."

"Right!" Rudd said briskly. "I'll leave you to organise that, Tom. I want to find out a bit more from the people in the house exactly what was going on this morning. Join me when you've finished."

All the same, Rudd took his time, lingering in the yard for several minutes, hands in pockets, surveying the back of Althorpe House with a speculative eye. It was a large, Victorian building of ugly, yellowish grey brick and, viewed from the rear, had a grim, institutional air about it, emphasised by the crisscrossing pattern of black-painted downpipes and the rusty bars that covered some of the ground-floor windows. The front was more attractive, although still plain and serviceable with its sash windows and heavy front door. But there, at least, its severe lines were softened by creepers and shrubbery. Here, at the back, it rose straight out of the yard with no benefit of vegetation except for the grass growing between the stones which only served to underline the atmosphere of neglect. The paintwork was shabby; the interior, or what he had seen of it, was also in need of decoration although the big, square kitchen, despite its worn, untidy appearance, had seemed homely and inviting. Money, though, was evidently short and he wondered why the Giffords had chosen to go on living in this huge, run-down place.

In the kitchen Nina glanced up from her seat at the table and saw him standing in the yard. She was not sure what to make of him. Her experience of policemen was limited to the village bobby, a pleasant enough young man whom she had seen driving about the neighbourhood, and a uniformed sergeant who had once arrived at the studio to take a statement from Max as witness to a drunken brawl at a Chelsea party in which windows had been broken and a fistfight had spilled out into the street. The Sergeant, intrigued it seemed by their life-style, had called several times on other occasions and stayed talking into the small hours with Max.

Rudd fitted into neither of these categories and her first reaction to him had been one of relief. He looked so very *ordinary* in his rumpled jacket and unpolished shoes—the sort of person you might see standing in a bus queue. His expression was bland, his features undistinguished, more like a farmer's in their fresh-complexioned, open-air bluffness, his whole attitude relaxed and casual.

But now, catching sight of him as he surveyed the exterior of the house, she was aware of another side of him: watchful, alert, perceptive. And she was afraid.

It was the first release of any sensation resembling strong emotion she had felt since she had found Eustace Quinn's body. The horror of that discovery seemed to blunt all other feelings and, since her return to the house with Lionel, she had remained in a suspended state of bewilderment and disbelief.

Besides, practical matters had taken over and she had willingly submitted to them as a barrier to thought. Max had to be seen to, some sort of lunch prepared, Blanche comforted.

She thanked God for Lionel's presence. He had helped her get Max out of bed to go to the lavatory, been present with her in the bedroom while she told Max of Eustace Quinn's death. To her dying day, she thought, she would remember the expression on his face as he heard the news. He had looked from one to the other of them as they stood at the bedside and, for an awful moment, she thought he was going to weep. The whole surface of his face had trembled—like a pool ruffled by a sudden gust of wind. By that time, however, she had given him the last two tablets and they were beginning to take effect. Whatever drug was in them, it made him sleepy as well as easing the pain, and, within a short time, they were able to leave him drowsing against the pillows.

There was nothing she could give Blanche apart from brandy. The girl's silence worried her. She seemed to have retreated to some secret place behind that extraordinary face where neither she nor Lionel could reach her.

Finally, Nina persuaded her to lie down on the sofa in the sitting room and it was only as she escorted her out of the kitchen that Nina realised Blanche was suffering from the effects of shock combined with several stiff brandies. She spoke for the first time as Nina lifted her legs onto the couch.

"I didn't *love* him, you know," Blanche said with careful emphasis and then turned away to face the back of the sofa, closing her eyes, although Nina doubted if she were asleep.

Lionel was beating up eggs in a bowl, she discovered when she returned to the kitchen.

"Scrambled eggs on toast?" he suggested brightly. He was too perky by half, in Nina's opinion, as if he were secretly enjoying the drama. She also resented his bustling efficiency and the way in which he had taken over her kitchen to the extent of tying one of her aprons round his waist to protect his beautifully creased jeans. All the same, she was grateful. It was good to have one task taken off her hands.

The two of them had been in the middle of eating the improvised lunch when the police arrived and the first interview had taken place as she and Lionel sat at the table. It hadn't alarmed her in the least. Rudd had been sympathetic, accepting a cup of tea as he seated himself at the table with them, asking the minimum of questions and listening quietly as she gave her account of Eustace Quinn's visit the previous day, his subsequent return that morning and disappearance until, searching for him, she had found his body.

Since then, forced to remain in the kitchen because Blanche occupied the sitting room and Nina could not bring herself to retreat to the gloomy dining room, she had been a reluctant witness to the activities going on in the yard and had been aware of the quiet authority this short, stocky Chief Inspector wielded over his men.

Now, watching him walk towards the house, she knew instinctively that the first interview had merely been a preliminary. The serious business of cross-examination was about to begin.

Rudd knocked and entered, taking in the scene with one swift but apparently casual glance as he stepped over the threshold.

The middle-aged man in glasses, whom Nina Gifford had introduced as Lionel Burnett, a neighbour and a friend of her husband and from whose house, Rudd gathered, the telephone call to the police had been made, was making tea and busying himself while he waited for the kettle to boil by putting various things away in cupboards. Under his ministrations, the kitchen already looked much tidier. Rudd guessed he was the type of man who liked order and mentally classified him, correctly, as a bachelor and, incorrectly, as a civil servant.

Nina Gifford, in a desultory manner as if she had only half her mind on the task, was folding up clean washing which, as he entered, she bundled away onto a wheelchair that stood in the far corner of the kitchen. She was a handsome woman, strongly built, robust, with the fine skin and high colour which often goes with red hair and with a superb negligence about her appearance which suggested a total disregard for conventionality. She was wearing a red-spotted handkerchief tied gypsy-fashion over her hair, a red and white gingham blouse with the sleeves rolled up and the neck open, and a blue denim skirt. Her colourful appearance was diminished by her quite obvious exhaustion and anxiety—but not entirely. Rudd was aware of a latent energy which, under normal circumstances, would dominate her personality and, he suspected, other people's, too, given half a chance. It was apparent in the way she moved, the lift and turn of her head, the quick, dipping swing of her skirt as she bent towards the wheelchair, the shift of tension from her knees to her hips as she straightend up again, as if her body remained unhampered by the clothes that covered it. More than that, her physical presence seemed to overflow into the space about her, disturbing it with a careless, unconscious animation that was almost palpable as little, bright, excited currents of air.

Beside her, Lionel Burnett appeared very squeezed-in and deficient.

She had turned towards the door in readiness for his entrance and her eyes were fixed on his face as he stepped inside the kitchen.

"There are a few more questions I'd like to ask you, Mrs. Gifford," he said pleasantly. "Is there somewhere you and I can talk?"

"I can leave if you'd prefer it," Lionel Burnett put in.

"I'd rather you didn't," Rudd replied. "There may be one or two details you can help me with, Mr. Burnett, if you don't mind staying."

Nina looked at Lionel doubtfully. She would have preferred him to leave. Danny would probably be back by now and must be wondering where Lionel was. She wanted, without quite knowing why, Danny to learn as quickly as possible what had happened so that he could be forewarned, although she ascribed her anxiety over this to a reluctance to explain the situation to him herself.

In the face of the Chief Inspector's request, there was nothing she could do, however, but suggest they go into the dining room. As she led the way, she added over her shoulder to Lionel, "Listen out for Max, will you, in case he calls?"

She might as well make use of him, she thought, since he was going to stay.

"Well?" she continued as she closed the dining-room door. Rudd appeared in no hurry and was wandering about the room, his hands clasped behind his back, examining Max's paintings which were still lined up against the wall.

"Mr. Gifford's work?" he asked in an interested voice.

"Yes," she said shortly, impatient to get on with the interview now that it had become inevitable. "What did you want to know?"

He returned to the matter in hand, drawing out two chairs at the far end of the table where there was a small space left unoccupied by the portfolios and, seating himself on one, indicated that she should take the other. Nina sat down reluctantly.

"Now, Mrs. Gifford," Rudd began with a comfortable air, "I'd just like to check briefly the account you gave me earlier, just so that I know I've got it straight. Mr. Quinn and his assistant, Miss Lester, spent the day with you yesterday looking at Mr. Gifford's work and discussing the possibility of mounting an exhibition. Am I right?"

Nina nodded.

"By the way," Rudd added unexpectedly, "where is Miss Lester?"

"She's lying down," Nina explained. "She's a bit in shock."

"Of course," Rudd agreed as if he understood perfectly. "Now to get back to what happened this morning. Would you mind going over again exactly what occurred?"

He hasn't forgotten, Nina thought. That's not the reason; he's no fool. He's checking up that I'll tell him the same story I did the first time.

Out loud, she said, "As I've already explained, Max wasn't feeling very well and, as he'd taken the last two of his tablets last night, I cycled into Great Rushleigh to the doctor's."

"What time did you leave?"

"I'm not sure exactly. About ten to nine, I think. I'd meant to set off earlier but what with seeing to Max and getting his breakfast, I was held up."

"And what time did you arrive at the surgery?"

Nina looked flustered.

"I can't tell you that. I haven't got a watch. It takes about half an hour to get there, I suppose. There's a long hill I have to push the bike up. I think it must have been about twenty past nine."

"And the time you left?"

Nina made rapid, confused mental calculations.

"There were five people in front of me in the waiting room. I must have waited about an hour for my turn, although I wasn't all that long seeing the doctor. About ten minutes, I think."

Rudd appeared to have worked the figures out for himself.

"So you must have left about half past ten?" he suggested. It was obvious to him from her expression that, although she agreed with his estimation, she had no clear idea what the exact time had been. "And therefore," he continued, "you must have arrived home at roughly eleven o'clock?"

"I suppose so."

"You didn't stop anywhere on the way?"

There was a disconcerting exactitude this time about the questions which distressed her. The Chief Inspector was evidently going to inquire very precisely into her movements.

"No."

"What happened then?"

"I went upstairs to see Max."

"I believe," Rudd put in, "that you'd already noticed Mr. Quinn's car parked in the yard?"

"Oh, yes, of course," she said quickly. She had forgotten to mention it this second time. "I simply thought he'd arrived while I was out and had let himself into the house. In fact, I imagined I'd find him upstairs with Max."

"Was Mr. Quinn expected?"

Rudd hadn't established this fact in their first interview, his main concern then having been to let her talk freely.

"I think he must have been," she replied. "At least, before I left Max said something about Eustace Quinn calling later this morning. Nobody had said anything about it to me yesterday."

"Were you surprised?"

Nina tried to think back to the conversation and her reaction to it.

"No, not really," she said at last. "I was a little annoyed, I think, that there'd only be Max in the house and, as he can't get out of bed on his own, Eustace Quinn would have to let himself in." As she spoke, she realised it hadn't been exactly annoyance she had felt, more a mild exasperation that the morning's arrangements were becoming more complex than she had imagined. "I meant to leave a note pinned on the front door for him but I forgot."

"So you weren't present when Mr. Quinn made the arrangements?"

"Oh, no." She seemed surprised at the question. "Max and Eustace were alone for a lot of the time, talking about the exhibition and Max's paintings. In fact, in the afternoon, Blanche and I went for a walk in the garden in order to leave the two men together."

"Was any time mentioned when Mr. Quinn would arrive?"

"No, I don't think so. As far as I can remember, all Max said was he'd be coming sometime in the morning."

"I see," Rudd said and returned to the main business under review. "Now, Mrs. Gifford, what happened next? You went upstairs?"

"Yes, and found Max alone." Nina felt more sure of herself as far as this part of the morning was concerned. "Max was surprised when I told him Eustace Quinn's car was outside. He hadn't seen or heard him. You see," she added in a little rush of explanation, "the front-door bell doesn't work and even if he'd knocked, Max wouldn't have heard anything. His bedroom's at the back of the house and on the other side. Anyway, I assumed Eustace Quinn had let himself in and, finding I wasn't there, had gone into the dining room to look through Max's work."

"A bit cheeky of him," Rudd suggested, as if this was, in fact, what had happened.

"That's what I thought," Nina agreed, "although I wouldn't have put it past him."

Rudd made no comment but he stored the small, revealing remark away in his mind for future reexamination.

"Anyway," Nina continued, oblivious of the effect of what she had said, "he wasn't in the dining room. By that time, I was getting worried —well, not exactly worried," she corrected herself, "more surprised as to what had happened to him. I checked the whole house, then the garden, in case he'd had an accident and, as I was coming back, Blanche arrived. She'd been waiting for him, she said, at Cawleigh."

"What was the time by now?"

"God knows," Nina confessed. "Blanche said it was a quarter to one. I'd no idea myself. I went to put my bike away in the stable because it was blocking up the entrance to the yard and Blanche couldn't get her car in, when it suddenly struck me that I hadn't looked in the outbuildings."

She stopped abruptly, overwhelmed by the recurring image of those legs and shoes sticking out from under the sacks.

Rudd, aware of her distress, completed the account for her by direct questioning.

"You noticed the bundle lying on the floor and went inside the washhouse to look at it more closely, moving one of the sacks to one side? Is that right?"

"Yes," she said quietly.

"You said, I believe, that the sacks had been hanging over the mangle the last time you went into the outbuildings? How long ago was that?"

"Oh, God, ages ago. Two years, at least."

"And then you saw the legs and realised it was Eustace Quinn's body?"

Again she repeated the single word of assent.

"Did you touch the body in any other way, apart from moving the one sack?"

"No, I backed away as soon as I realised what it was."

The next question had to be asked.

"Mrs. Gifford, how did you know it was Eustace Quinn's body if you didn't uncover the head?"

Her distress increased.

"I don't know! I just guessed! He was missing. How could it be anybody else? Just as I knew he was dead."

Rudd let it go. It was possible that she was speaking the truth, but he still found it strange that she hadn't examined the body further to find out if Eustace Quinn was still alive. Panic, though, made people react in different ways.

"And then you cycled down to Mr. Burnett's house and telephoned us?" he asked, resuming the account.

"Lionel phoned. And I didn't start off straight away," she corrected him, as if these small matters were important. "Blanche and I had a brandy first. Then Lionel brought me back in his car."

The rest you know, her expression implied.

Her account tallied, except for the greater detail he had drawn out of her on this second occasion, with the brief statement she had given him on his arrival. Two new, interesting points, however, had emerged. The first was the timing. The telephone call that Lionel Burnett had put through had been made at 1307 and it seemed the only exact time that had so far been established. The other interesting aspect of the case, which would need further investigation, was Eustace Quinn's relationship with the Giffords.

Rudd, however, was prepared to leave both these points until later. Nina Gifford was clearly distressed and exhausted, a condition the Inspector could understand. Her morning appeared to have been tiring enough without submitting her to a long cross-examination. He could return to her later. Meanwhile, there were two other people to be questioned: Blanche Lester and Lionel Burnett.

"Could I speak to Miss Lester?" he asked, rising to his feet.

"She isn't well," Nina replied, immediately on the defensive for the girl's sake, a fact which Rudd noted.

"I won't keep her long," he promised.

"Perhaps you'd better speak to her in the sitting room," Nina suggested. "She's lying down."

Boyce was discovered hanging about in the hall, unsure whether or not to break in on the interview, and he tagged along as they entered the sitting room where Blanche Lester was lying down on the sofa, her face still hidden although she turned listlessly towards them as the door opened.

Rudd was struck immediately by two things: the girl's beauty and the appearance of the room. Blanche Lester was young and quite dazzling with her black hair and fine-drawn features. She was also, Rudd suspected, fairly drunk. She had the stupid, unfocused look and uncoordinated movements of someone who wasn't quite sober. Nina Gifford, murmuring in his ear, explained apologetically, "I'm afraid I've given her several brandies."

Well, it couldn't be helped, Rudd thought, although he realised that, in her present condition, he was unlikely to get a coherent statement out of her.

The room seemed a strange background for her. It was large, shabby, and full of objects that caught the eye: pieces of sculpture in stone and wood, pictures everywhere on the faded wallpaper, some framed, some merely pinned up with thumbtacks, and huge bunches of leaves and flowers stuffed into containers with a careless lavishness in which Rudd detected Nina Gifford's hand. Pulled forward, as if still in tête à tête, presumably from yesterday's meeting with Eustace Quinn, were several armchairs covered in worn chintz.

"Just a few questions, Miss Lester," Rudd began, drawing one of the chairs up to the sofa. Behind him he was aware that Nina Gifford, after a few seconds' hesitation, had left the room while Boyce, in an attempt to make himself scarce, a difficult task because of his bulk, had retired to another chair at the far side of the room.

The girl struggled to sit up and then sank back, saying, "Sorry. I'm afraid I'm a bit whooshed."

It was one way of putting it, Rudd thought, but whooshed or not, she'd have to make some kind of statement.

The account she finally gave, or what he was able to piece together from her dazed answers to his questions, amounted to this: she and Eustace Quinn had left the hotel, the George in Bexford, at approximately five minutes to nine, Eustace Quinn intending to call on Max Gifford to continue the discussion about the exhibition, although she seemed vague about his exact purpose. On the way out of the town, he had dropped her off at a car-hire firm, the idea being that she would hire a Mini for the day and drive herself over to Cawleigh Hall where an auction sale was to take place that afternoon. Eustace Quinn was interested in some water-colours by a late Victorian artist called Roland Cutler which were due to come under the hammer when the sale began at two o'clock. Her job was to look at the paintings and, by lingering among the presale crowd, to estimate the extent of the interest in them, so that Eustace Quinn would have some idea, before the bidding began, what kind of opposition he was likely to meet in the saleroom. They had arranged to meet at the Hollybush in Cawleigh at twelve o'clock for prelunch drinks. She had waited until nearly half past and then, growing impatient, had driven to Althorpe to find out what was keeping him. She couldn't get in touch with him in any other way; the Giffords weren't on the phone. She had arrived just as Nina was entering the yard, a piece of information which corroborated Nina Gifford's statement. Nina explained that she had no idea where Eustace Quinn was and, in fact, had been looking for him. She, Blanche, had waited near the back door while Nina put her bicycle away. The next thing she knew, Nina had come running across the yard to tell her Eustace was dead.

No, she said in reply to Rudd's question, she hadn't seen the body.

Nina had then poured them both a brandy and had left to phone the police. She, Blanche, had remained in the kitchen for about a quarter of an hour, she thought. Then Max had started calling from upstairs and, as she was wondering whether she ought to go up to him, Nina had returned in a car with a friend. That's all she knew. After that, she'd had several more brandies and Nina had helped her into the sitting room to lie down.

"Can I go now?" she asked, looking at Rudd with glazed appeal.

She was incapable of driving herself, he decided, and sent Boyce to find Kyle, one of the plain-clothes detective constables, to take her back to the George in Bexford before returning the Mini to the car-hire firm.

"And while you're at it," he added, "get him to check with the hotel staff what time she and Quinn left this morning and with the car-hire firm the time she booked the car out. He's to find out the mileage it's done as well, if he can."

Cawleigh, as Boyce pointed out as they conferred together briefly in the hall, was only about three miles from Althorpe. Boyce himself then departed for Cawleigh to check the girl's statement at the Hollybush and the saleroom. Rudd watched through the kitchen window as Kyle drove Blanche Lester away, the girl having been assisted out of the house by Nina Gifford who, on her return, excused herself and went upstairs to see if Max was still asleep. Which left Rudd and Lionel Burnett alone in the kitchen, making it, Rudd thought, a good opportunity for him to question Burnett about his involvement, if any, in the case and his relationship with the Giffords.

Lionel Burnett seemed prepared to talk, more especially as Rudd began in an easy, conversational manner, commiserating with him on having been kept waiting about for so long.

PORTRAIT OF LILITH

"I don't really mind," Lionel Burnett assured him. "I'm on half-term holiday this week so my time's my own."

"So you teach?" Rudd asked, looking interested. He had sat down at the table where Burnett joined him.

"History, at Bexford Boys' Grammar school."

"Indeed?" Rudd's interest appeared to deepen. "And have you known the Giffords for long?"

Lionel Burnett thought for a moment, working out the years. He was one of those men who was scrupulous about facts, which should make him a reliable witness.

"Let me see. I must have met them a few months after they moved here which would make it just over seven years. Max was still able to get about then. As a matter of fact, I was making a sketch of the church one afternoon when he happened to walk past. He stopped and we got into conversation. That's how the friendship started."

It was obvious from the tone of his voice and the shine in his eyes behind his spectacles that he had a deep admiration for Max Gifford.

"So you paint, too?" Rudd asked.

"Only water-colours, Chief Inspector, and on a very amateur basis. I can't paint like Max. I wish I could."

"He's a good artist?" Rudd inquired. He was genuinely curious to know. Having no knowledge of art himself and only a limited interest in it, which didn't extend further than the better-known paintings of some of the acknowledged Old Masters, he had no means of judging Max Gifford's work. The paintings in the dining room had struck him as powerful, bold in outline and colour, but that was as far as he could go in assessing them.

"In my opinion, yes, he's a good artist," Lionel Burnett said, after giving Rudd's question due consideration.

"Good enough, presumably, for Mr. Quinn to think of mounting an exhibition of his work," Rudd continued, turning the conversation neatly. "Did you meet Eustace Quinn?"

For the first time during the interview, Lionel Burnett seemed to lose his composure.

"Only very briefly last night. I'd called, you see, at Max's invitation—I assume because he wanted to tell me how the discussion had gone after Mr. Quinn and his assistant had left. Unfortunately, they were still here so I went straight home."

"But you met him?" Rudd persisted. Lionel Burnett's use of the word "unfortunately" seemed significant.

Lionel Burnett looked harassed, two patches of dull red appearing high on his cheekbones.

"Yes, I did. I came into the kitchen for a few moments. He was in here talking to Nina—Mrs. Gifford. I was introduced to him and we exchanged a few words, that's all."

If that were all, Rudd thought, why was Lionel Burnett so clearly distressed by the memory of that meeting? He settled back in his chair, crossing his legs comfortably, his expression bland.

"What was your impression of him?" he asked, his voice suggesting he would value Lionel Burnett's judgement.

"I didn't like the man," Lionel Burnett said promptly. "I thought him conceited, vain, and far too familiar."

With him? Rudd thought. It hardly seemed likely on so short an acquaintance. With Nina Gifford then? It was a possibility which opened up a whole new area concerning Burnett's relationship with the Giffords, especially Nina, and which would be worth pursuing at a later stage in the investigation.

Now he merely remarked, "About this morning, Mr. Burnett. I believe Mrs. Gifford came to your house to telephone. What time was this?"

"Just after one o'clock, I think. I poured Nina a whisky, as she was obviously in shock, and then made the call myself."

Which fitted in with the time the call had been made.

"Then I drove Mrs. Gifford home," Lionel Burnett concluded.

At this moment, Nina Gifford herself entered the kitchen, her appearance so neatly timed that Rudd suspected that she had been listening outside the door for the right moment to interrupt them. Lionel Burnett turned to her.

"By the way, Nina, I'll bring your bicycle back myself later."

"Oh, don't bother," she replied carelessly.

"It's no bother. Besides, you may need it."

Rudd observed this small exchange with disguised interest. Burnett's eagerness to serve her was significant; so, too, was her indifference, although that could have been assumed or merely caused by tiredness. She looked exhausted as she walked heavily forward into the room.

"Max is awake," she informed Rudd. "I suppose you'll want to talk to him."

"Yes, indeed," he replied, getting up from the table.

In the event, however, the interview had to be postponed, for at that moment a car drove into the yard, its horn sounding a warning to the group of policemen who were completing the search of the outbuildings, and a large, paunchy, dishevelled man climbed out, clutching a black bag.

"Oh, my God!" cried Nina. "The doctor! I'd completely forgotten he was coming to see Max."

CHAPTER 7

Feeling his presence would be unwanted under the circumstances, Rudd took the opportunity offered by the doctor's arrival and Nina Gifford's confused attempts to explain the situation to slip away and find Stapleton, the tall, slow-moving Inspector under whose command the uniformed men were making a search of the yard and its adjacent outbuildings.

As Stapleton explained, a great number of objects had been found which might have been used to murder Eustace Quinn, especially in the outbuildings, which contained an astonishing variety of rubbish and junk, some of which, judging by its condition, had been lying about for years.

Rudd took a look at Stapleton's discoveries, which ranged from a collection of bricks through to iron bars of various sizes, an old spade, a couple of sash weights, a heavy curtain pole to which the rings were still attached, and what appeared to be part of a small, stone garden statue, broken off at the knees and presenting the bizarre appearance of two naked legs and feet standing on a square plinth. In the Chief Inspector's opinion, none of them was likely to be the murder weapon, as the surfaces of all of them were dirty and would have marked the neck of the dead man's sweater which, from his own examination of the body, hadn't been the case. Nevertheless they would all have to be submitted to forensic examination and he nodded encouragingly at the young constable who was wrapping them up in plastic as carefully as if they had been priceless works of art, before strolling on, in an apparently casual manner, to the far end of the yard where it narrowed to an opening between two crumbling brick buttresses, beyond which stretched the garden.

Here he paused and looked back. Anyone approaching the yard had the choice of two entrances: this one, where he was now standing, which had evidently once been enclosed by a pair of gates, judging by the buttresses and heavy iron pivots still attached to the brickwork; or the one at the other end, where the drive, after leading up to the front door, swung round the side of the house to the yard at the back. This entrance was also restricted by the corner of the house on one side and the walls of the outbuildings on the other, the yard thus forming a narrow oblong, open at both ends with the lines of the buildings acting as its sides.

Having satisfied himself about the layout of this part of the house and its grounds, Rudd moved on, crossing a large, unkempt lawn in the centre of which stood a cedar tree. At the far side ran a wide, herbaceous border, long since gone wild, backed by shrubs and trees, with a grass path leading under a wrought-iron archway, covered with climbing roses, the long, untended strands of which plucked at his sleeves as he passed under it. Beyond, he found himself approaching another lawn, sunken this time, and surrounded by banks; a tennis court at one time, he guessed. Facing it, on his right, was a small, rustic summerhouse with a thatched roof.

As he walked along the bank towards it, he glanced back over his shoulder. Apart from its roof and chimneys, Althorpe House was now out of sight behind the trees.

Reaching the summerhouse and looking briefly inside it, he sauntered on. Beyond and behind it, the garden became more enclosed and overgrown. A large shrubbery extended for about half an acre, composed mostly of laurels and rhododendrons, the massive bulk of which spilled over the tiny paths that threaded tortuously through the dense leaves. At the far side, he came to a gate that opened into a field where young wheat was growing. Once again, Rudd paused, getting his bearings. The village of Althorpe lay straight ahead across the open farmland. To his left, he could see the line of telegraph poles that marked the road leading into the village.

Giving a small nod, as if satisfied with that too, he turned back towards the shrubbery, choosing a different path this time—one that circled back towards the house, taking him past a neglected kitchen garden, edged with fruit trees and partially walled against which a lean-to conservatory had been built, full of an unpruned vine, its leaves pressing close against the glass as if trying to burst free. The whole edifice seemed in imminent danger of collapse. The ground itself was thick with weeds amongst which an occasional rogue potato or cabbage plant, grown tall and spindly with neglect, thrust itself upward.

The back of Althorpe House now faced him and he strolled towards it, checking his watch as he did so. He had been gone for half an hour; time enough, he felt, for the doctor to have completed his visit and left.

In fact, he was just departing as Rudd reentered the yard, his old black Morris slowly reversing out of the entrance at the far end while Nina stood on the doorstep to see him leave.

"You'd like to see Max, I suppose?" she asked as Rudd approached.

"If it's possible."

"He's still not well. The doctor said he's to rest as much as possible. You'll probably find him a bit dopey, too, from the tablets," she replied. There was a fierce, protective air about her that was also apologetic and, as he followed her into the house, he wondered why.

"I'll try not to tire him too much," he promised.

They crossed the hall and mounted the stairs, passing under a large stained-glass window that threw coloured blobs and lozenges of light across the battered treads. Rudd glanced up at it curiously, amused by its inappropriateness and its odd amalgam of piety and lust.

At the top, Nina turned right along the landing and knocked at a door at the far end before opening it and putting her head inside the room.

"It's the police, Max. Detective Chief Inspector Rudd," she announced briefly, adding over her shoulder to Rudd, "You can go in. Don't keep him too long. And leave the door open when you've finished so I can hear him when he calls."

Then she went away, leaving him to make his entrance alone.

Walking into the room, Rudd was immediately struck by two impressions, so contradictory that it took him a few seconds to reconcile them. One was the old man in the bed; the other was the painting of the nude that hung above it. Both seemed larger than life, both were quite immobile, but there the comparison ended.

The girl's body was beautiful against its vibrant setting—almost alive, it seemed, full of light and colour and the supple gracefulness of youth, the curve of hip and spine flowing across the dark red background, the black hair showering down.

Below it, Max Gifford was propped up against a pile of pillows, like an elder statesman laid out on his bier, his crippled hands, freckled with the brown patches of age, resting side by side on top of the bedclothes, which were smoothed down across his chest; his head, with its great mane of white hair, tipped slightly backward. He was like a stone figure on a tomb, the only colour the red stripe in his nightshirt and the faded blue of the counterpane.

And the brighter blue of his eyes.

As he approached the bed, Rudd was conscious of their scrutiny, very alive and bright and intelligent. He realised, too, the reason for Nina Gifford's concern. It was immediately apparent that Max Gifford was a sick man. His skin had a grey, unhealthy pallor and he struggled unsuccessfully to pull himself into a more upright position.

"Don't trouble to sit up on my account," Rudd advised him and, fetching a chair from the other side of the room, he placed it at the bedside. "I shan't keep you long."

He sat down, feeling at a loss to know how to begin. Despite Max Gifford's age and infirmity there was a presence and majesty about him that made it impossible to treat him merely as an elderly invalid.

Feeling his way, Rudd began the interview quietly, concentrating on routine questions regarding the circumstances of Eustace Quinn's visit, the details of which he had already obtained from Nina Gifford but which needed corroboration.

The two accounts tallied: Eustace Quinn had written to suggest an interview and, because Max couldn't make the journey to London, Nina had telephoned the gallery and arranged for Quinn and his assistant to call at the house the previous day.

"He wrote out of the blue?" Rudd asked. "You'd had no previous contact with him?"

"Never heard of him or his gallery," Max Gifford replied. "You can read the letter if you like."

It was lying on the bedside table among a clutter of other objects including a bottle of tablets and an ashtray full of dark, strong-smelling cigarette stubs. Max Gifford tossed the envelope towards Rudd who opened it and read the letter it contained.

"Seems he'd bought one of my paintings," Max continued, "got interested and fancied the idea of putting on an exhibition, which was the reason why he came yesterday."

"Yes, I see. Was any decision reached?"

"Not cut and dried, although he talked about a possible date next spring. That's down the drain now, of course." The corners of his mouth turned down. "Unless his partner decides to go ahead on his own."

"Partner?" Rudd asked quickly. "You mean Blanche Lester?"

"No, of course not!" Max Gifford sounded impatient at Rudd's ignorance. "She's only his assistant, a bit of decorative crumpet for the front office, to draw in the trade. You've seen her?" When Rudd nodded, he continued, his voice growing more vigorous, "Incredible bone structure! And that hair! I'd've painted her twenty years ago. Now . . ." Raising his swollen hands, he gave Rudd an amused, rueful look as much as to say, "Look at them! What good are they?"

"But his partner?" Rudd persisted.

Max shrugged and appeared indifferent.

"I don't know his name or anything about him. Eustace Quinn only mentioned him last thing yesterday, just as he was about to leave. He was going to put up some of the money to mount the exhibition. A businessman, I think. At least, that's the impression I got from Quinn. I don't suppose he'll be interested now."

He broke off, the corners of his mouth resuming the turned-down expression of deep disapproval, and Rudd realised how much he had counted on the exhibition. Its loss had caused him more than mere disappointment; it had shattered his hopes.

The last remark gave him his own cue into the main topic of the interview.

"About Mr. Quinn's death," he began.

"I don't know anything about it," Max Gifford interrupted. He was suddenly an old man again as he had appeared to Rudd when he first entered the room, his moment of brief animation extinguished.

"I'm sorry, Mr. Gifford," Rudd continued, "but I must try to establish what happened."

He got there eventually although Max Gifford gave him little assistance. The facts had to be drawn out of him in a question-and-answer session that was exhausting for them both and, at times for Rudd, exasperating. There was a stubbornness in the man, so that on occasions Rudd felt it was like trying to shove a rock uphill. In between the questions, Max Gifford lay back against the pillows, his eyes closed, resembling an effigy on a tomb, although the Chief Inspector noticed that his hands plucked restlessly at the sheets.

Stubborn, yes; but there was more to it than that. Rudd had the distinct impression that Max Gifford was refusing to face up to the unpleasant reality of sudden death, which at his age was understandable. It was much too close; it touched him too personally so he refused to think about it. He was like a child who, confronted by something frightening, covers its eyes with its hands in the belief that, no longer seen, the apparition ceases to exist.

Although Rudd could sympathise with his reluctance to talk, nevertheless he had to pursue the interview to its end.

The sequence of events, pieced slowly together, amounted to little that was new, especially those regarding the earlier part of the morning which was largely a reiteration of what Nina Gifford had already told him. Max had been unwell, an admission he seemed unwilling to make, almost as if he regarded his infirmity as shameful. All his tablets had been used up and Nina had gone to the doctor's for more. No, he didn't know what time she left. There was no clock in the room and, anyway, time was something he no longer bothered with. He had dozed while she was away. Yes, he was expecting Eustace Quinn to call, but no precise appointment had been fixed, Quinn merely saying that he'd drop by sometime during the morning.

Nina had arrived back, although at what time Max again had no idea, and had asked where Quinn was. Evidently his car was parked in the yard.

"Did you hear it arrive?" Rudd asked.

The simple negative was repeated: "No."

"Isn't it likely he came first to the front door?"

"I don't know."

"He was a guest. Wouldn't that seem the most obvious choice?"

Max Gifford shrugged, jutting out his bottom lip indifferently as if other people's habits neither concerned nor interested him.

"You'd've heard him if he knocked?"

"Possibly. It would depend how loud it was."

"But he didn't?"

"He may have done. If he did, I didn't hear him. I told you, I was dozing for much of the time."

"I understand the bell doesn't work?"

The great, shaggy head moved in assent.

"What about the back door?"

"I heard nothing."

Rudd got to his feet and wandered, as if aimlessly, across the room, like a man restless after being seated for too long. At the window, he turned back to face the bed but not before he had checked the view that lay outside: the unkempt lawn with the central cedar tree that lay on the far side of the house from the kitchen and where, a little earlier, he had strolled on his way to the shrubbery and the further boundary of the garden. Given the layout of the house and the position of Max Gifford's bedroom, it was perfectly feasible that he'd heard nothing of either Quinn's arrival by car or his subsequent attempts to rouse someone's attention in the house. It seemed likely, therefore, that Nina Gifford's reconstruction of the man's movements was correct. He had driven up to the

front door where he had tried ringing the bell and, getting no answer for
the simple reason that the bell didn't work, had got back into the car and
followed the driveway round to the back yard where he must have
knocked on the kitchen door and again received no answer because Max
Gifford, in his bedroom on the far side of the house, hadn't heard him.

What had he done then? Entered the house? It was possible, although
he hadn't, according to Gifford's evidence, gone upstairs to find him or
even called out to make his presence known. Had he, therefore, sauntered about the garden, as Nina had supposed? Then, had Quinn been
murdered in the garden? That, too, was possible although Rudd was inclined to dismiss this theory on the grounds that the murderer would
have left the body lying where it fell or concealed it somewhere near at
hand and would not have gone to the trouble of carrying it back to the
yard to hide it in the washhouse.

Given the evidence, it consequently seemed more likely that Quinn
had been killed shortly after his arrival by someone whom he had en-
countered in the yard and before he had time to acquaint Max Gifford
of his arrival—by someone who was already lying in wait for him or who
arrived at roughly the same time.

So far, Rudd had three possible suspects: Nina Gifford, Blanche
Lester, and Lionel Burnett, although the latter's motive seemed pretty
thin. Certainly, Nina Gifford could have had the opportunity. Her timetable was vague enough to allow her the twenty minutes, possibly even
less, which would have been needed to kill Quinn, hide his body in the
washhouse and then disappear from the scene, having obliterated her
first set of footprints from the floor. He would have to check the time of
her visit to the doctor's at the earliest opportunity. Lionel Burnett's and
Blanche Lester's movements during the crucial times still had to be
investigated too.

He tried to picture the scene: Eustace Quinn drawing up in his car
and getting out, a slightly built man, dapper in pale grey trousers and
powder blue sweater, slamming the driver's door behind him before
approaching the house, a little impatient, perhaps, because no one appeared to be there to let him in.

It was all conjecture, of course, but it was possible that at the very moment he crossed the yard, his killer appeared—Nina Gifford or Blanche
Lester in the rented Mini or someone else on foot, who called out his
name and as he turned . . .

"Have you finished?"

The question startled Rudd out of his reverie. Turning from the window, he saw that Max Gifford was regarding him from the bed, his eyes
hooded with fatigue, his great body slumped back against the pillows.
Even his voice sounded exhausted, struggling up from his chest in a
husky whisper as if it were too much effort for him to draw breath.

"I'm sorry," Rudd apologised, referring not only to his temporary
lapse of attention but also to the whole business of the interview.

"Because I am. Finished, I mean," Gifford continued.

Under the lowered lids, there was a faint, ironic glitter and his mouth curved briefly in a small, bitter smile, expressive of the absurdity of the situation: Eustace Quinn's death, his own infirmity, Rudd's presence in the room.

"I've overtired you," Rudd said, crossing back to the bedside.

Max Gifford did not bother to deny it.

"Ask Nina to come," was all he said.

In the bedroom next door, Nina lay staring at the ceiling, trying to hear what was going on in Max's room. She had taken off her shoes only and climbed onto the bed, covering herself with the eiderdown because she felt cold. A symptom of tiredness, she decided, for the day was quite warm. However, she had found it impossible to sleep and was lying rigid, her eyes fixed on the pattern of stains and cracks in the ceiling above her, her ears straining to catch the slightest sound that would indicate what was happening next door between Max and Rudd. But she could hear nothing for, although she had purposely left her door open, Rudd must have closed Max's and the intervening wall was too thick to allow voices to penetrate.

At one point, the floor vibrated gently, causing the objects on top of the chest of drawers to tremble, a sign that someone had crossed the room. Rudd, she supposed; Max would hardly be walking about. But that was the only sound to come out of the room.

In comparison, she could hear too distinctly the noises outside where the police were still conducting the search of the outbuildings. She had closed the window and drawn the curtains, but the yard lay directly beneath her room and the sounds carried clearly upward.

"Have you finished in there, Johnson?"

"Not quite, sir."

"Then tell Fletcher to take over this area."

"What the hell's this?"

"Don't ask me. Stick it with the rest of the stuff."

The snatches of conversation, the sound of feet moving to and fro, at one point the grate of something heavy being dragged across stone seemed to fill the room.

Although she knew Eustace Quinn's body had been taken away, for she had seen the ambulance depart, she wished absurdly for his sake that they would be quiet. It seemed disrespectful of them to talk in such normal voices, to carry on as if everything were quite ordinary, and she pictured him still lying in the washhouse, his shoes turned out at that pathetic angle.

Someone must have killed him. Now that Lionel and the doctor had left and she was alone, she began to consider for the first time how he had died. It would be comforting to think it had been an accident, but she knew this wasn't so. He had been covered with sacks and that was deliberate. But who could have done it? Someone who had called at the house, perhaps—a stranger? She grasped at the possibility wildly, fleshing it out with detail to make it seem more real. Of course! That was it! Why hadn't she thought of it before? A man had been planning to rob the house, only Eustace Quinn had arrived just as he was about to push open the back door. She preferred not to think too closely of what had happened next, picturing only a vague image of a sudden attack, the body bundled away in the washhouse, the killer, no longer interested in burglary, running from the scene—she could imagine the crunch of gravel under his flying feet. Or had he made off across the garden, crashing through the bushes in his panic-stricken flight?

It seemed so realistic that she sat up and began scrambling off the bed in her haste to tell Rudd, realising, as she did so, that the theory would clear her of any implication in Eustace Quinn's death.

Which was crazy, anyway, she told herself, finding her discarded sandals and thrusting her feet into them. Why on earth should she want to kill him?

Hurrying onto the landing, she almost collided with Rudd who was emerging from Max's room and shutting the door behind him with a solicitude that immediately alarmed her.

"What's the matter?" she demanded. "Is Max ill?"

"Only very tired," Rudd replied. "He'd like to see you."

She didn't even stop to give him an I-told-you-so look as she pushed past him. The bloody police! she thought furiously.

Rudd continued down the stairs, feeling a little guilty at his own part in Max Gifford's relapse, although he had only been doing his job. Besides, with Nina now occupied upstairs, it gave him the chance to reexamine the main rooms leading off the hall and, entering them in turn, he wandered about in the same casual manner with which he had earlier strolled about the garden, getting the feel of the place and snuffing up the atmosphere, but keeping one ear cocked all the time for Nina's return.

He stayed longest in the dining room, lingering in front of the line of paintings, hands in pockets, like an interested tourist in an art gallery, before turning away to glance through the French windows into the abandoned studio, noting, as if in passing the rusty stove, the dirty glass, the scattered, withered leaves. He then crossed to the table where he opened, with the same air of idle curiosity, the top portfolio, leafing through some of the drawings before retying the tapes. Having done that, he took a last look round before leaving the room.

Nina found him in the kitchen when, having settled Max and given him two more of the tablets, she came downstairs. Rudd was sitting at the table, hands clasped on the top, and looking, she thought with the same amused exasperation she often felt towards Max, completely at home.

"Is he all right?" he asked in the manner of a family friend.

"Dozing off," Nina replied briefly.

It was strange how easily she accepted his presence and felt relaxed with him; even more so than with Lionel. In Lionel's company, she always felt the need to react in some way, to laugh or talk or smile. Silence seemed an unnatural void which she had to fill. Rudd, on the other hand, possessed a stillness that was comfortable. Odd, when she considered the reason why he was there, sitting in her kitchen, looking as if he belonged in the place.

"Tea?" she offered, acknowledging his right to be there.

She felt more at ease herself. Max was resting and, while she had been upstairs, she had washed her face and done her hair, which had given her confidence. Even Eustace Quinn's death seemed more acceptable, now that she had settled in her mind how it had happened. And the whole place, too, seemed quieter.

Passing the window to put the kettle on to boil, she noticed the yard was empty except for a police van that was drawn up close to the outbuildings.

"They've gone," she said in surprise.

"They're searching the garden," Rudd replied. He had followed her across the kitchen and was taking cups and saucers from the draining board to place on the table. In her absence, he had spoken briefly to Stapleton who had reported that, since the search of the outbuildings was completed, it would now be widened to include the grounds.

"What are they looking for?" she asked, pausing with the tea caddy in her hands.

"Evidence." Rudd sounded vague.

She was about to ask more and then changed her mind. It was better to know as little as possible about the inquiries. Instead, she opened the back door, propping it in position with the flatiron. Now that the yard was empty, she no longer felt the need to barricade herself inside the house.

Rudd noted the action. He was also aware of her greater ease of manner and wondered what had given rise to it. The reason was not long in making itself apparent.

"I've been thinking," Nina Gifford announced, carrying the teapot over to the table and sitting down.

"Yes?" Rudd said encouragingly.

"Suppose someone was trying to break into the house and Eustace Quinn surprised him. It would explain everything."

She still couldn't bring herself to put into precise words what had happened, certainly not to voice the word "murder" out loud.

Rudd nodded as if he found the idea interesting.

"Go on."

"Well, that's about it," she admitted. "Max wouldn't have heard anything. His bedroom's too far away."

That part of the theory, at least, made sense.

"Of course," Rudd agreed. "By the way, is Max totally bedridden?"

It seemed natural for him to use his Christian name and the question itself appeared perfectly innocuous to Nina, leading, as it did, from her own remark.

"Not completely," she confessed. "I mean, he can't get out of bed or down the stairs on his own, but he can manage a few steps on his own if he's got something to hold on to." Seeing him glance towards the wheelchair, its seat piled high with washing, she added, "He won't use that, although it'd help him to move about more. He won't admit he's crippled, you see. It takes two of us to get him out of the bath."

"Two of you?"

Rudd sounded sympathetic, a friend who was interested to know how she managed.

"Lionel comes over to help."

"That's Mr. Burnett?"

"That's right. You met him when he was here earlier."

"A neighbour, you said."

"Yes, he lives a little way up the road."

"Wasn't it from his house that the phone call was made?"

It seemed to Nina, as she nodded agreement, that the Chief Inspector was merely making conversation as he drank his tea, enjoying a little interlude of chat and the chance to relax.

"A schoolmaster, isn't he?" Rudd continued. "On half-term holiday, I suppose. Well he's got nice weather for it." He gestured towards the open door to where the thin sunlight poured across the yard, cut into sharply by the hard, angular, black shadow cast by the house. "Married, is he?"

"No, he's a bachelor." Nina Gifford suddenly appeared flustered and she added quickly, "He's Max's friend really."

"Yes, I see." Rudd's face was perfectly bland.

He saw a great deal more than either his voice or expression revealed. The relationship between Nina Gifford and Lionel Burnett evidently caused her embarrassment, even guilt, and suggested that she was perfectly aware of Burnett's feeling towards her, although how far those feelings went and whether she returned them had still to be established. She had also unwittingly supplied him with a piece of information he had been seeking. If Burnett was unmarried, he probably lived alone and could therefore have had the opportunity to murder Eustace Quinn.

"They met years ago," Nina continued, anxious to establish the fact that the friendship was between the two men. "Lionel paints, too, you see. Water-colours but only as an amateur. Max gives him advice."

"I was going to ask about Max's work," Rudd remarked in the same easy manner and saw her relief at the change of subject. "How well known is he as an artist?"

"Not as famous as he should be," Nina replied, promptly loyal and partisan. "He's sold paintings in the past, mostly to the smaller galleries and a few private buyers but he's never made a lot of money. We've got by, though. Max did other things when we were short—commercial work, posters, and book-jacket designs mostly. Teaching as well although he didn't like it; he's too impatient. He's had the occasional exhibition but not for years now."

"So Eustace Quinn's offer was important to him?"

He was surprised to see her hesitate.

"Yes, I suppose it was. He's never shown his feelings about his work. At least, not to me. In some ways, I think it's come too late. It should have happened thirty, forty years ago. But underneath, I think he was excited about it although he didn't like to show it. It's a West End gallery, after all. He's never been asked to exhibit in the centre of London before."

"He seemed disappointed that the exhibition might be called off."

"It's a bloody shame!" Nina cried passionately. "He should have had the chance!"

"Perhaps Mr. Quinn's partner will carry on with the arrangements," Rudd suggested.

"I don't know anything about that," Nina replied. "Max mentioned a partner only this morning. It was the first I'd heard of one. Nothing was said yesterday. I shouldn't imagine he's a proper partner. In the gallery, I mean. Otherwise he'd've come with Eustace Quinn and Blanche yesterday. Max seemed to think he was a businessman who was going to help finance the exhibition."

"What would Max have made out of it?"

"God knows. I don't think they'd got round to discussing the money side of it. What usually happens is the gallery takes a percentage of sales to pay for overheads and make a profit. It used to be ten percent but I don't know what it would be nowadays or what a gallery like the Demeter might charge."

"And how much would his paintings sell for?"

Nina looked doubtful.

"I don't think even that had been worked out. Max got three hundred pounds for the last one he sold back in the fifties. In fact, he said himself he'd be interested to know how much Eustace Quinn paid for the picture he bought recently. You know about it?"

"Yes, Max showed me the letter."

"It was sold originally for one hundred and fifty pounds, but that was years ago, before the war. A great deal would depend, of course, on how much publicity the exhibition was given. A lot of it's fashion. An artist's name suddenly becomes news and the prices can shoot up overnight. Max never had that sort of luck."

She sounded bitter as if she despised the whole business of art dealing.

Rudd was about to reply when, through the window, he caught a flicker of movement in the corner of his eyes and, turning his head, noticed a man approaching the yard from the driveway entrance, where he paused, keeping to the shadow, from which vantage point he surveyed the house. He was thin and dark-haired, with stooping shoulders and a pale, narrow face, too high in the forehead, making the face disproportionately long. There was a furtive air about him, too, the lurking manner of the car thief or pickpocket, that made Rudd sharpen his attention on the figure.

Danny approached the house warily, realising it was stupid to take the risk of being seen but unable to keep away. Lionel had told him enough of what had happened to rouse his fear, but too little to convince him that his own connection with the dead man had not been uncovered. He had to know more if only to prepare himself for possible questioning should the whole story come out. The only alternative was to do a bolt, but with less than three quid in his pocket that wasn't going to be easy.

He comforted himself with the thought that if anyone stopped him, he'd got some sort of story ready. He would simply say that he'd heard there'd been an accident and he was worried about Nina. If the worst came to the worst, he'd even be willing to admit his relationship with her but that was as far as he would go. As for Eustace Quinn, he'd plead ignorance. There were only the sketches to link him with the murder and Quinn had given his word that nothing about the deal would be mentioned. It was unlikely, anyway, that Max knew about the sketches at all. Nina would have seen to that—right from the beginning, Danny had realised that she had taken the drawings without Max's knowledge; he knew enough about her to be convinced of that. The capacity for secretiveness was one of the few qualities they had in common, for hadn't they practised it enough as children, the pair of them together against the authority of father and Aunt Connie?

He doubted either if Nina herself had made the connection. She hadn't the type of mind that could work things out rationally—not that she was stupid, but she could be naïve at times. Gullible where he himself was concerned; probably also with Max although that wasn't his affair. But anyone she loved could always twist her round his little finger. He had proved it time and time again, despising her for letting herself be fooled so easily, himself for having to turn to her so often for help. If only he'd had a bit more luck, he'd've cut loose from her years ago.

The police cars were in evidence all along the drive but the house itself seemed quiet. Skirting the front, he looked up at it curiously. It was the nearest he had ever been to it and he was impressed by its size.

Max must have made money at some point in his career even though Nina was always complaining how hard up they were, and he suddenly wondered if she had been stringing him along all this time.

The bloody cow! he thought. If he couldn't trust her, who the hell could he rely on? When you came down to it, there was no one in the whole sodding world you could depend on, except yourself. It crossed his mind that perhaps she had also deceived him over Lionel and the caravan and that the whole setup had been planned so that she could keep an eye on him. It would account for that pratt Lionel always snooping about. He was probably on the watch so that he could report back to Nina.

I'll have to clear out, Danny thought. The only problem is where to?

He came to the corner of the house and halted. The yard in front of him was empty—that much was obvious. Standing close to the wall in the shadow cast by the house, he surveyed it carefully. A van was standing near some outbuildings, its back door open. Inside were boxes and bundles wrapped in plastic sheeting. He knew enough about police procedure to guess it was probably stuff they'd collected in the search. But there was no sign of the fuzz itself although voices carrying faintly from behind the buildings suggested they were searching the grounds.

So far so good, he thought.

The back door of the house was also open, indicating someone was at home. Nina, of course. Given what had happened, she'd hardly have gone out. Whether or not Max was in the kitchen with her, he couldn't tell. Nina had told him enough for him to realise that, although Max was partially crippled, she still got him downstairs most days. Certainly someone was in the kitchen. He could see the side of a head but, at that distance, wasn't sure if it was Max's or Nina's. It was as he was contemplating it, wondering whether he'd do better to clear off and return after dark, that the head turned in his direction and a man's face looked directly at him.

At the same moment that their eyes met, Nina, aware of Rudd's distraction, followed the direction of his gaze and saw the man, too.

Rudd heard her give a little gasp of shocked surprise as she jumped to her feet. The sudden movement must have been discernible through the window for the man seemed to be on the point of bolting, but the Chief Inspector forestalled him by striding rapidly to the door and calling out, "Do you want something?"

"It's all right, I know him," Nina assured Rudd hurriedly and, pushing past him, ran out into the yard. Rudd heard her say, "Danny, what on earth are you doing here?"

Danny came forward reluctantly to meet her. He was stuck now, thanks to her, but at least, now he was here, he might as well find out more about what had happened.

Nina, on her part, was aware of his tension. She had linked her arm in his and tried to draw him towards the house, but he remained fixed, refusing to come any further.

"Is it okay?" he asked, jerking his head towards the windows. She took him to mean, Is Max up? and she said reassuringly, "Max is in bed. He won't be coming downstairs."

"Who's with you then?"

"A police inspector." It occurred to her that Lionel might not have told him about Eustace Quinn's death, out of pique or, more charitably, because he hadn't yet had the opportunity to do so, and she added quickly, "Someone's been killed. A man called Eustace Quinn. He'd come to see Max about his paintings . . ."

"Yes, I know. That friend of yours, Burnett, told me."

He sounded indifferent but Nina knew him too well to be deceived. She could feel the muscles in his arm were rigid under her hand as if he resented the contact and the expression on his face was familiar, that closed look of sullen withdrawal that, as a child, he had always assumed when he knew he was in trouble.

But what trouble? Any connection with Eustace Quinn seemed so outlandish that she discounted it immediately, although the idea left a residue of doubt, not entirely dismissed when Danny added, "I was worried about you. I wanted to make sure you were all right."

She believed it because she wanted to believe it and hugged his arm in gratitude.

"So what happened?" Danny asked.

It was clear to him that nothing was suspected. Nina would have warned him if the police wanted to question him. Come to that, the Inspector, who had retreated from the doorstep, would have come forward; not that he wasn't interested in what was going on. Flickering a quick glance in the man's direction, Danny could see him standing just inside the door, quietly observing the encounter.

"God knows!" Nina was saying. "I found him dead this morning. I was out when it happened and Max was in bed. He didn't hear a thing. I think someone was trying to break in when Eustace Quinn arrived and that's why he was killed."

It sounded possible but Danny wasn't interested in her theories. All he wanted now was to be gone. He had found out what he wanted to know and there was no point in hanging about any longer.

"Look, I'll see you later," he said, trying to disengage his arm. If I'm still around, he added silently. Perhaps it would be better to clear out straight away while the going was good.

Rudd watched the exchange from the doorway. He was too far away to hear what was being said, but it was clear from Nina's gestures that she was telling the man, whoever he was, what had happened that morning. At one stage in the account, Rudd saw him glance furtively in his direction. Nina had succeeded in drawing him a step or two nearer the house and they were now standing in a patch of sunlight so that the Inspector had a better view of his face. Its length, he could see, was caused by a receding hairline beneath which the features were tightly bunched together, very sharp and knowing and yet curiously unformed although the man must have been in his thirties. It was the face of a city adolescent, wise in street law and not much else.

He obviously hadn't been fooled by Rudd's apparent withdrawal and had turned himself deliberately so that he no longer presented a full-face view of himself, shoving one hand into his pocket and bringing the shoulder forward in a defensive gesture against authority that Rudd had seen many times before and all the time edging little by little towards the yard entrance. As soon as Nina finished speaking, he would be off. Curious to meet him, Rudd strolled forward in time to catch Nina's last remark.

"So God knows what's going to happen now, Danny, but I suppose the police . . ."

She broke off as Rudd approached and, dropping her hand from the man's arm, introduced him awkwardly.

"This is Detective Chief Inspector Rudd, Danny. He's in charge of the case. Danny Webb, a friend of the family. He's staying with Lionel Burnett for a few days."

Rudd nodded a greeting but, seeing Danny Webb thrust his right hand further into his pocket, made no attempt to shake hands. There was a wary insolence about his manner which suggested to Rudd that he'd probably had some brush with the police before. He also doubted if Webb's relationship with Nina Gifford was quite as she described it. The warmth of her greeting, the eagerness with which she had clasped his arm, and the undisguised anxious affection in her face as she watched his minimal acknowledgement of the introduction suggested a closer connection. The scene also stirred in him some faint memory of his own which he couldn't remember in detail except that it evoked a sense of shame and guilt that was still painful even in vague recollection.

On his part, Webb seemed impatient of her concern, and as soon as she had finished speaking he said, addressing her and ignoring Rudd, "Since you're all right, I'll clear off."

"I'll try to come round to see you later this evening, if you like, Danny," she replied, "once Max is settled for the night."

Rudd doubted if the man heard the last part of her remark for he had gone before she completed it, walking rapidly away round the corner of the house without so much as a backward glance.

Her disappointment was obvious. All her animation seemed to go with him, and as she turned to reenter the house her movements were heavy and listless.

"He's staying with Mr. Burnett?" Rudd asked as if making conversation.

"Yes, just for a few days until he can find another flat."

"In the house?"

"No. Lionel's got a caravan in the garden. You see, I can't put him up here . . ."

She stopped suddenly, aware of the drift of the questions and the possible areas of danger into which her replies might lead her. Halting on the doorstep, she said rapidly, "He's got nothing to do with Eustace Quinn. He wasn't even here yesterday so he didn't meet him. And he was out this morning, down at the Feathers, I expect. You ask. He wasn't anywhere near the house."

"Yes, of course," Rudd agreed.

Two facts, however, were immediately apparent. Firstly, she was much too anxious to discount Danny Webb's possible part in Eustace Quinn's murder and, secondly, he had lost her trust.

She was standing in the middle of the doorway, barring his entrance, whether deliberately or not Rudd couldn't decide. But it was quite clear that his presence was no longer welcome and, rather than arouse her further hostility, he said good-bye and walked away to where his car was parked in the drive.

There would be time enough to question both her and Danny Webb again when he was more sure himself of the facts concerning the pair of them.

CHAPTER 8

He found Boyce and Kyle waiting for him when he returned to his office at headquarters.

Kyle's report, which he heard first, was short and straightforward. He had driven Blanche Lester back to the George Hotel in Bexford and waited while she booked in—a single room this time, as the double room she and Quinn had occupied the night before had already been relet to other guests.

"A double room?" Rudd repeated.

Kyle, a married man with a child and six years' service in the force, looked embarrassed, his face and neck, from its pleasant, nondescript features down to the collar of his shirt, flushing red.

"Yes, sir. They'd registered as Mr. and Mrs. Quinn. She was quite open about it, too. I'm afraid I put my foot in it when I explained that Miss Lester wasn't feeling very well and wanted to stay another night."

Rudd could understand the reason for the Detective Constable's confusion. The situation must have caused him a few moments of public discomfiture. It also opened up a new and interesting area of speculation regarding Blanche Lester's relationship with Eustace Quinn.

"She said she'd probably return to London by train early tomorrow," Kyle continued. "I then went to the car-hire firm to inquire about the Mini." He produced his notebook and turned over the pages. "It was booked out just after nine o'clock, at nine-oh-three to be exact. The mileage was read before it was brought round to the front for Miss Lester to drive away. It was 10,648. When I returned it, it was 10,693. I was with the man when he checked it."

Rudd jotted the figures down, exchanging a glance with Boyce as he did so.

"Interesting," he remarked as the door closed behind the young Detective Constable. "We'll have to check the figures, of course, but with 10,693 on the clock, she must have done about fifteen miles more than she had to if the story she gave this afternoon is true. What did you find out about her at Cawleigh?"

"The sale was just finishing when I got there," Boyce replied. "I had a word with two or three of the officials, including a couple of security men who were mingling with the crowd at the preview to make sure nothing got nicked. There were quite a few valuable pieces on show, small enough to put in a pocket or a briefcase. The really pricey stuff was under lock and key in showcases and was only brought out if someone asked especially to see it. Both the security men noticed her but not until at least half past ten when the place began to get really full. The point is, if they picked her out from a crowd, they'd've certainly spotted her when there was less of a crush. She's striking-looking enough." Rudd nodded in agreement with this argument and Boyce continued, "There was an elderly bloke on the gate directing traffic who remembers her arriving, again he thinks about half past ten because by ten o'clock the main drive had to be closed to cars. There wasn't any more room. Anyone who arrived after that was directed to a small paddock at the back of the house, used for extra parking space, which is where he sent her. But none of them could give an exact time and nobody noticed her leave."

"So she started out from Bexford soon after nine o'clock but didn't arrive at Cawleigh Hall until around half past ten, an hour and a half later," Rudd remarked, summing up the gist of Boyce's report. "And if we allow her half an hour to get there, that still leaves roughly an hour unaccounted for."

"It seems that way," Boyce agreed. "Alternatively, she could have left Cawleigh Hall some time after she arrived. There was a one-way traffic system in operation for vehicles: in at the front gate, up the drive, and out by another gate in the paddock. The man on duty was only interested in the cars arriving, not leaving. So she could have slipped out at any time. The last sighting I could establish for her in the house itself was about quarter past eleven when one of the security men saw her leaving the main room where most of the furniture and paintings were on view. The next timing we have"—and here Boyce, like Kyle, referred to his notebook—"is approximately five to twelve when she turned up at the Hollybush in Cawleigh village and checked with the headwaiter about a table that had been booked for her and Quinn for a quarter past twelve."

"Quinn had booked?" Rudd interrupted. He was beginning to feel that the visit to the Giffords coincided just a little too conveniently with the sale at Cawleigh Hall and he wondered if the two events hadn't been planned.

"Yes, he had. According to the manager, Quinn phoned up yesterday evening and asked for a reservation for twelve-fifteen, which would give them plenty of time to eat and be back at Cawleigh Hall for the auction which was due to start at two o'clock. It's about a ten minutes' drive from the Hollybush. Anyway, to get back to Blanche Lester. She made some comment to the manager about being early and went into the bar where she had a sherry. The barman noticed her particularly, partly because of her looks, partly because she was a woman on her own. At a quarter past twelve she had another sherry and about ten minutes later the manager went over to her and asked if she was going to have lunch or not. The place was pretty full by then with people coming from the preview and he needed the table. She seemed annoyed that she'd been kept waiting, the manager said, and told him to cancel the reservation as Mr. Quinn must have got held up. She then left."

"Presumably to drive over to Althorpe," Rudd put in. "Nina Gifford said she turned up about a quarter to one, just before she found Quinn's body."

"It would seem so," Boyce agreed. "All of which gives her plenty of opportunity to murder Quinn."

"And she's not the only one. There's Nina Gifford whose timetable is just as vague as Blanche Lester's. Then there's Lionel Burnett. As far as I can make out, he was alone this morning in his house, which is only a short distance from the Giffords' place."

Boyce looked surprised.

"You mean that little, wispy bloke who was at the house when we got there? Did he know Eustace Quinn?"

"Evidently he called on the Giffords yesterday evening and was introduced to him."

"A bit of a short acquaintance for murder, isn't it?" Boyce asked disparagingly.

"It could be jealousy," Rudd explained. "There's quite a complex little web of relationships going on there, Tom. It only takes half an eye to see that Burnett is very strongly attracted to Nina Gifford and, if I've read the signs correctly, Eustace Quinn also made it clear he fancied her. At least, Burnett spoke of Quinn's familiarity, which he took more than ordinary exception to. I admit it's a bit thin as a theory but we can't rule it out of court yet. He might have had as much opportunity as the two women. Supposing he called at the house this morning, not knowing that Nina Gifford was at the doctor's or that Eustace Quinn was due to arrive? If we're to believe Nina Gifford, she didn't know herself until about half past eight this morning. Anyway, Burnett drops by, hoping to see her, meets Quinn just as he arrives, there's a quarrel during which Quinn gets clumped with the classic blunt instrument, whereupon Burnett panics and hides his body in the washhouse. Not keen on it?" he added, seeing the sergeant's doubtful expression.

"Not much," Boyce admitted. "I'm not even sold on the Nina Gifford theory. I admit she had the opportunity but where's the motive? At least the case against Blanche Lester seems pretty straightforward."

"You mean she killed Quinn because they were lovers?"

"Well, not exactly." Boyce had the grace to look a little shamefaced. "But you must agree it places her a damn sight closer to him than either Nina Gifford or Burnett."

"Fair enough. But it could also give her just as much reason for not wanting him dead. But we still haven't exhausted our list of suspects."

"Who else is there?"

"Danny Webb for a start."

"Danny Webb? Who the hell's he?"

"A family friend according to Nina Gifford, although I suspect it's a closer relationship than that, judging by the way she greeted him when he turned up at Althorpe House this afternoon."

"Boyfriend?" suggested Boyce, brightening up.

"No. Too young."

"That doesn't mean a thing these days."

"I agree, but she didn't quite treat him as a lover."

As he said it, Rudd tried to recall the scene as she ran towards Webb, her hands held out in greeting. It had stirred some memory of his own past that he hadn't been able to place although he had been aware that it had caused him pain. A yard. A young man just entering it. A woman running to greet him. And then recollection returned and he realised that he had been that young man, the woman his mother. There had been about her the same air of awkward eagerness, the same embarrassing warmth as she had clutched his arm with both her hands and, like Danny Webb, he, too, had tried to move away from the embrace because it had represented an emotional bond that had become too overpowering and too restrictive in its intensity.

"If they're not lovers, what are they then?" Boyce put in, impatient at Rudd's hesitation.

"I'm not sure," Rudd replied, rousing himself. "Not mother and son either. There's not enough age difference. But whatever he is, he's closer than a friend. And the odd thing is, Tom, he's not staying at Althorpe House, even though there must be plenty of empty bedrooms. He's at Lionel Burnett's, in his caravan. He seemed anxious, too, not to meet Max Gifford, God knows why. It may be nothing at all, but it's worth inquiring into if only to satisfy my curiosity. I'm damned sure, as well, that he's been involved with the police at some stage in his life. I'll check with the Yard as soon as I get the chance."

"So we add Danny Hebb as a possible suspect," Boyce conceded. "Is that the lot?"

"Not quite. There's Max Gifford."

"God Almighty, you really are scraping the barrel! I thought he was bedridden."

"Yes, he is, to all intents and purposes, although Nina Gifford said he can manage a few steps alone. Not enough to get down the stairs, though. But he was in the house when the murder took place so we can't discount him yet. I agree he's the least likely of the lot and I can't see, either, what motive he could have. Now that Quinn's dead, he'll probably lose the chance of the exhibition in London, so he's not likely to clobber the one man who might have made his name for him as an artist. Then there's Nina Gifford's theory of an intruder."

"Do you go along with it?" Boyce asked, not sure what to make of it from the Chief Inspector's tone.

"No, I don't," Rudd replied without any hesitation, "although I pretended it was a possibility. She was very eager to tell me about it. But it won't stand up to examination, Tom. Her theory is that someone was trying to break into the house through the back door when Quinn drove up and, as he went to see what the man was up to, he was attacked. Now, no sneak thief is going to hang about waiting for a car to arrive round the corner. He'd be off like a shot the minute he heard it coming up the drive. And there's no evidence to suggest Eustace Quinn surprised him inside the house before the man could make a bolt for it. Max Gifford would have heard their voices or at least something of the encounter. But he didn't even know Quinn had come, so my bet is Quinn was killed in the yard within a short time of his arrival, which must have been around half past nine, assuming he set off for Bexford shortly after he took Blanche Lester to the car-hire firm. Max Gifford wouldn't have heard his car draw up—his bedroom's too far away. But he can't have failed to hear a murder taking place inside the house.

"Besides, I can't see a burglar bothering to move the body into the washhouse or stopping to wipe his prints off the floor. So I think we can throw that theory overboard. In fact, that part of the case still doesn't make sense. Why should any of them bother to remove their footprints?"

"Distinctive soles on the shoes?" Boyce suggested without much enthusiasm.

"No, that won't wash. The prints Nina Gifford left when she found the body showed no detail at all. The dust's too thin for that and the bricks on the floor are too uneven. They were nothing more than smudges. In fact, we'd've been hard put to it to come up with a correct shoe measurement, let alone pick out any individual markings."

"It could be someone who's extra careful," Boyce put in.

"Could be," Rudd agreed and thought immediately of Lionel Burnett. Remembering the obsessive manner in which he had been tidying up Nina Gifford's kitchen, Rudd realised he possessed that pernickity attention to detail that the removal of the marks suggested.

"Or someone who's already had a brush with the law and fancies he knows something about evidence," the Sergeant continued and added, before Rudd could voice the name himself, "Danny Webb, for instance. If you're right and he's been in trouble with the police, it's the kind of thing he might think of—getting rid of telltale signs at the scene of the crime. The trouble with that sort is they usually forget the obvious. Remember Billy Barnes? He went round that office where he'd done the safe, wiping every surface he could think of even though he'd worn gloves and then forgot he'd needed a pee halfway through the job and left his dabs on the lid of the lavatory next door, the only time he'd taken the bloody things off."

Rudd was about to reply when there was a knock at the door and he called out, "Come in." A young, uniformed police constable entered, carrying a suitcase, an overcoat, and a briefcase.

"I've been told to bring these up to you, sir," he announced. "They were found in Quinn's car. Wylie thought you'd like to have a look at them."

"He's finished with them?" Rudd asked.

"Yes, sir. The cases have been tested for prints."

"Put them down on the desk," Rudd told him and, when the Constable left, Rudd moved across the room with Boyce to look the articles over, handing the overcoat, which was of good-quality, lightweight wool, to the Sergeant who began frisking the pockets while Rudd himself turned his attention to the briefcase. It too was expensive—leather bound with polished metal with Quinn's initial stamped in gold on the top. Finding it unlocked, he laid it flat on the desk and, clicking open the fastenings, tipped back the lid. Its contents were few. A road map of the area was tucked into one of the upper compartments while the base contained a copy of the *Times*, folded back to the financial page, and a catalogue of the auction sale at Cawleigh Hall. One item in it had been marked with a star, as Rudd discovered, flicking over the pages: the entry describing the water-colours by Roland Cutler which Rudd remembered Blanche Lester telling him Quinn intended bidding for.

The only other object was a large, manila envelope, its flap unsealed. Thrusting his hand into it, Rudd drew out several sheets of paper and laid them on the desk alongside the objects that Boyce had already removed from the overcoat pockets: a handkerchief, car keys, a gold cigarette lighter, and a wallet.

"What have you got there?" Boyce asked nosily, coming closer to get a better look.

Rudd spread the sheets out individually, turning over two that were lying face down.

"See for yourself," he said briefly.

There were six of them, all sketches done on thick artist's paper, some of them jagged along one edge as if torn from a drawing pad. Two were seascapes, mere hasty washes of blue, green, and brown, indicating with minimum detail the sky, sea, and beach and yet, even to Rudd's untutored eye, they contained a quality of light and space that he would not have thought possible to convey with so few brush strokes.

Next were a pair of pencil drawings of trees, showing more detail—the leaves and bark hatched in with tiny, dark lines—while the last two, which were initialled and dated "M.G. Sept. '36," were charcoal studies of nudes. Both of the same woman, Rudd guessed, for although they were simple outlines, the figure with its long, dark hair was clearly reproduced in both. In one, she was standing with her back to the viewer; in the other, she was lying curled up, possibly against a cushion, one arm bent across her face as if in sleep.

"Max Gifford's work," Rudd commented, indicating the pencilled initials, although even if they had not been there, he would have recognised the style. The sketches of the nudes, especially the last one in which the figure was lying down, reminded him strongly of the portrait that hung over Max Gifford's bed.

Boyce looked at them grudgingly and with an air of faint disapproval. Rudd suspected that, as far as art was concerned, the Sergeant was even less educated than himself, an ignorance that was further compounded by the belief that art was unmasculine and that, in some subtle and subversive way, he would be unmanned if he showed too much interest.

"Not bad," Boyce commented and turned his glance away. "I suppose Gifford must have given them to Quinn last night."

"As samples?" Rudd suggested.

"Could be. Or a present."

"I'll check with Blanche Lester," Rudd replied and began sliding the sketches back into the envelope before picking up the wallet. "Anything interesting in this?"

"Only the usual stuff—cheque book, credit cards, about fifty quid in cash, and some cards for his gallery." As Rudd extracted one of these cards and glanced at it briefly before putting it into his own wallet, Boyce added, "Nothing much in the suitcase either. Just clothes and toilet things. You're going to see Blanche Lester?"

He posed the question as Rudd was shrugging his way into his old raincoat, at the same time slipping the envelope of sketches into his pocket.

"Yes. If, as Kyle said, she's thinking of returning to London tomorrow, I'd like to question her again before she goes. By now, with a bit of luck, she should have sobered up and I'll get a more coherent story out of her."

"Anything I can do?"

The tone of voice implied a negative answer and Boyce looked disappointed when Rudd replied, "Yes, there is, Tom. Check the mileage from Bexford to Cawleigh, starting off outside the car-hire firm and ending up at Cawleigh Hall. From there, do the trip to Althorpe and back. There's no need to go right up to the Giffords' place. Just make a note of the mileage at the gate. And while you're in Althorpe, you can call in at the Feathers and ask the landlord if Danny Webb was in the pub this morning. If he doesn't know the name, then tell him he's in his mid-thirties, thin-faced, clean-shaven with receding brown hair. He's new to the district and is staying at Lionel Burnett's."

"Clothing?" Boyce asked.

"When I saw him this afternoon, he was wearing jeans and a navy blue windcheater. And report back here when you've finished," Rudd added, raising his voice as Boyce let himself out of the door.

The George Hotel dominated the centre of the market town of Bexford, its classical eighteenth-century facade and heavy, pillared portico making the surrounding buildings look mean and dwarfish.

Its interior was even older or perhaps had been faked up to appear so. The beams and panelling in the main rooms could easily have been a modern addition to satisfy a clientele who associated the Tudor period with the good life of barons of beef and tankards of real ale but without the concomitant miseries of draughty rooms and rush-strewn floors. The whole place had a warm, overdense atmosphere which greeted the Chief Inspector as soon as he entered the foyer, as if the air had been reduced, like soup stock, by being heated up too many times. The foyer was curiously noiseless as well, the thick carpets, low ceilings, and heavy panelling appearing to absorb sound.

The rooms were large and open, but even so Rudd had the impression of entering a series of dark boxes, each intricately lined and decorated and yet quite separated in their claustrophobic self-containment from the world outside the revolving doors. There it was evening; here it was already night and lamps and sconces shed little areas of soft radiance, strategically placed to highlight a bowl of flowers or a collection of hunting prints on a wall.

The manager's office was the only brightly lit area in the middle of this rich gloom. Situated behind the reception desk, it was like an empty fish tank, brilliantly illuminated with strip lighting, an impression that was heightened by the glass door and the upper walls facing the main entrance which were also glazed. Standing in the office, Rudd could see across the foyer and into both the bar and the dining room, a vantage point from which the manager, Mr. Hesketh, could keep an eye on his staff although it was not the surroundings Rudd would have chosen in which to interview Blanche Lester. Hesketh, however, took the matter into his own hands by telephoning upstairs to her bedroom and passing on the message that Miss Lester would rather come downstairs than have the Chief Inspector go up to her.

"I expect you'd like to speak to her in here," Hesketh had added. "It's more private than the lounge and you won't be disturbed."

Rudd had to agree. It was a damned nuisance all the same. He could hardly expect her to relax and talk freely among Hesketh's filing cabinets and functional furniture. There was not even a proper armchair, only a pair of contraptions consisting of metal frames and leather-covered slabs of foam rubber—mere seating units, in his opinion.

Hesketh showed Blanche Lester into the office and then departed, carefully closing the door after him, leaving Rudd to wave her towards one of these units while he perched himself on the edge of the desk and tried to look friendly and relaxed.

She sat down quietly, her hands clasped in her lap, her legs together and curved to one side, the only posture, he imagined, one could assume with any elegance on such a low-slung and uncompromising piece of furniture. She had changed her appearance, too, he noticed, since he had seen her earlier. The smartly cut trouser suit had been replaced by a dress of fine, green wool and her hair was worn loose, caught back by a large tortoiseshell clasp from which it hung halfway down her back in what Rudd, whose knowledge of women's hair styles was vague, believed was called a ponytail. The total impression was much more youthful and he wondered how far the transformation was deliberate in order to create an air of innocence.

To be fair to her, her pallor and listlessness were less easy to fake. She had a naturally clear, pale skin, but no amount of makeup could have produced the wan transparency of her face under which the delicate bone structure seemed too close to the surface. All the same, he was aware of an ambivalence about her personality and that she might very well have consciously preserved the childlike side to her nature, finding it had its uses. It was certainly appealing—mostly to men, Rudd imagined, although in some women, too, like Nina Gifford, it would arouse a protective, maternal instinct.

He said, "I'm sorry to have to worry you again, Miss Lester, but one or two points have come up that need clarifying. Firstly, these." Taking the envelope of sketches, he rose to his feet to pass them to her, as he did so catching a glimpse, through the upper glass panels of the wall, of a man standing at the entrance of the dining room to his left. The room was empty since it was too early yet for dinner to be served, and it presented an oblique view of white-covered tables, each bearing a small lamp already lit, retreating in a series of diminishing circles of light into the shadows at the far end. The man, dressed in a waiter's white jacket and black trousers, was standing just inside the doorway, looking towards the manager's office. When Rudd got to his feet, the movement must have been visible to him for he turned his back and began to straighten the cutlery on one of the nearest tables with the overzealous care of someone anxious to appear occupied with other things. Rudd noted his presence but made no sign of being aware of it, not even giving the man a second glance as he handed the envelope to Blanche Lester.

"We found these in Mr. Quinn's briefcase. I wondered if Max Gifford had given them to him."

She looked at the sketches briefly before passing them back to him.

"No, Eustace didn't get them from Max. He bought them several months ago."

"Do you know where?"

"From a dealer called Askew. He sells art books and prints, that sort of thing. Eustace has been buying stuff off him for several years. He owns a shop off the Charing Cross Road but I'm not sure of the exact address."

Taking the envelope from her and replacing it in his pocket, Rudd returned to his perch on the desk, glancing again, as if casually, towards the dining room.

The waiter was back in the doorway, but turned away as he had done before, occupying himself this time by flapping with his napkin at the seat of one of the chairs.

His pretended preoccupation amused Rudd. If ever he had seen a potential informer, then this man was certainly one.

Well, he'd wait and see what information he had to sell when the time came. Meanwhile, he gave his attention to the next question he had planned to ask Blanche Lester and which needed more careful framing than the first.

"I'd like to check over your statement you made this morning," he began. "I believe you left the hotel just before nine o'clock?"

"Yes, about ten to, I suppose. Eustace paid the bill and we went straight from here to the car-hire firm."

Which corroborated the time of 9:03 which, as Kyle had established, was when Blanche Lester had booked out the Mini.

"And then you drove to Cawleigh Hall for the preview?" Rudd asked, his expression bland.

He saw her falter and it was several seconds before she replied. Time enough, he thought, for her to work out that he probably had evidence to the contrary and it would be better to admit the truth. She was by no means unintelligent, although the candour with which she met his eyes was intended to disarm him with its childlike ingenuousness.

"No, as a matter of fact, I didn't," she confessed and drew in her bottom lip in an expression of innocent appeal. "The preview wasn't due to start until half past nine and I didn't want to arrive too early and have to wander about on my own until twelve when I was due to meet Eustace. Besides, the whole purpose of my going there was to find out what interest the rest of the buyers were showing in the Cutler water-colours. I thought there'd hardly be enough people there at half past nine to make it worthwhile."

It was a plausible enough explanation and Rudd nodded as if in agreement before asking, "So what did you do instead?" in a tone that expressed friendly interest.

"I—I drove about for a while." Her voice had grown more breathless with a little husky gasp in it as if the muscles in her throat had closed over. "It was a lovely morning and I don't know this part of the countryside very well so I—I went exploring. Don't ask me where because I have no idea. I remember going through a village called Medlow or something like that. Eventually I saw a turning signposted to Cawleigh so I took it and drove to the house where the auction was being held."

"What time did you arrive?"

Again she drew in her bottom lip and widened her eyes.

"I'm not sure. About half past ten, I think. I know by then there were quite a lot of people there. I had to park in a field at the back of the house."

That, too, corroborated the evidence Boyce had discovered at Cawleigh Hall but gave her no alibi to cover the intervening hour and a half between the time she had set off from Bexford and her arrival at the preview—enough of a time gap for her to murder Eustace Quinn and dispose of his body, a realisation that seemed to occur to her for she added quickly, "It's quite true, you know. I did go for a drive."

"Yes, of course, Miss Lester. I don't doubt it for a moment," Rudd said, lying agreeably. "Now, concerning the auction, did Mr. Quinn know about it when he decided to visit Mr. Gifford?"

She smiled for the first time during the interview, a strange smile which touched only one side of her mouth and gave her face a sudden, unexpectedly knowing look, quite out of keeping with the girlish dress and hair.

"Of course. Eustace never did anything without having it planned out first. When he wrote to Max, he knew there was no likelihood of his coming to London so, when Nina phoned, he suggested Thursday. That way, he could fit in the auction in the same trip."

This piece of information and her manner of relaying it suggested there was a quality of ruthlessness and the ability to manipulate others in Eustace Quinn's personality which she had been aware of and perhaps even admired. Her smile indicated a mixture of emotions—a certain wry amusement that was, at the same time, touched with a faintly contemptuous indulgence in much the same manner as some women, when describing their husband's shortcomings, end with the words, "Isn't he dreadful?" but, all the same, smiling as they say it.

It seemed a good opportunity to Rudd to ask the next question.

"You knew Mr. Quinn quite well, I believe?"

"We were lovers, if that's what you mean," she replied. The smile had vanished and her face again wore the expression of wide-eyed candour that seemed particularly ill-suited to the remark. "It was not a regular affair. Neither of us wanted to marry. It wouldn't have worked out. But he was fun to be with and I enjoyed his company."

Nowhere in the statement had she referred to any affection for Quinn nor even a liking for him as a person, but Rudd supposed that this was the way girls regarded love affairs these days, as a source of amusement or diversion or as an extension of friendship that included sex. He didn't know. He only felt that, while such relationships might be more honest, some important quality was missing; not just romance, although he was old-fashioned enough to consider this important, but also commitment and the sense of belonging. But perhaps that was what girls had rebelled against. They wanted to belong only to themselves, and certainly there was about Blanche Lester, for all her childlike innocence, an air of self-sufficiency and an aloofness from contact which hung like a thin veil between her and others.

"I see," he said noncommittally and left it at that. "Before you go, Miss Lester, there are just two more questions I'd like to ask. Firstly, do you know anything about Mr. Quinn's partner who was going to help finance the Gifford exhibition?"

She looked genuinely surprised.

"No, I'm sorry I can't help you. Eustace never mentioned any partner to me but he never told me much about his business affairs. Perhaps Miss Martin, his secretary, could help you. What was the other question?"

"Only this. I believe you're thinking of returning to London tomorrow morning?"

He had meant to ask for her address, but she replied before he could complete the query.

"No, I've decided to go back this evening. I share a flat with a friend and she's coming down by car to pick me up. You see, the gallery's open on Saturdays and I ought to be there. Miss Martin doesn't deal with the showroom side of the business."

"Better than going back on your own," Rudd agreed. Despite his doubts about her, he was genuinely relieved that there was someone to take care of her. He thought she looked too fragile to cope alone even while admitting that this could very well be the impression she intended to convey.

It also settled the question of how he would get in touch with her if he needed to. He could call in at the gallery the following day, which might be worthwhile doing anyway. He could then interview Miss Martin who, as Blanche Lester had pointed out, might know about the partner that Max Gifford had mentioned.

He saw her out, catching a glimpse again of the waiter who was now standing outside the dining room, studying with apparent absorption the gilt-framed menu that was hanging by the door.

Rudd deliberately lingered for a few moments, giving Blanche Lester time to go upstairs, before he, too, left the office, pausing outside the door to button up his coat.

The waiter turned. Rudd raised his eyebrows. The man gave a tiny backward jerk of his head, indicating the rear of the hotel, and then walked away. The exchange was over in a couple of seconds and would have been imperceptible to the casual onlooker.

Hesketh certainly seemed unaware of it. Turning from the reception desk where he had been talking with some guests, he shook the Chief Inspector's hand.

"Everything all right?" he asked. He was young for the job; smart, well-groomed and already possessing that air of urbanity that hotel managers exude but which was not yet quite perfected. He was anxious about possible scandal.

Rudd said with reassuring heartiness, "Perfectly, Mr. Hesketh," and saw the man's face clear.

Outside, in the gravelled area behind the hotel, Rudd slowly fitted his key into the driver's door, watching over the car roof the tall line of white-painted ranch fencing that separated the car park from the service yard. Presently, a door in it opened, allowing the Chief Inspector a brief glimpse of a row of dustbins and the barred downstairs windows of the rear of the hotel, and the waiter came slipping out.

Rudd joined him, strolling across unhurriedly. Seen at close quarters, the man was short, middle-aged and pale-faced, with a forward slant to the upper part of his body as if he had become permanently fixed in the attitude of service.

"You've got something to tell me?" Rudd asked. He had already put his hand into his inside pocket, a gesture which the man followed with his eyes. The five-pound note was transferred as quickly as their original signal, disappearing into the waiter's trouser pocket with the alacrity of a playing card being palmed by a stage magician.

"I might have," the man replied. He spoke softly in the long-practised murmur of the trained servant. "It's about the girl."

"The one I was talking to?"

"That's right. The man she was with is dead, isn't he?" Without waiting for Rudd to reply as if he were already well aware of this fact, he continued, "They were quarrelling at breakfast this morning. Bloody angry she was, too."

"You heard them?" Rudd asked with a faint note of disbelief.

A small, jeering smile lifted one corner of the man's mouth. "What do you know about anything?" it seemed to imply. It expressed as much contempt for Blanche Lester and Eustace Quinn as for Rudd, the scorn mixed with envy that those who wait on others feel towards those they serve.

"I was behind the service screen, filling up their coffeepot. They didn't know I was there. Mind you, they were quiet about it. No raised voices; nothing like that. But I heard her say to him, 'One of these days you'll come a hell of a cropper and I hope to God I'm there to see it.'"

" 'A hell of a cropper'?" Rudd repeated. It didn't sound like the sort of remark Blanche Lester was likely to make. But the man had already gone, slipping back through the gate with the same silent swiftness with which he had appeared.

Rudd walked back to the car. There was no point in following the man to question him further. That would only arouse suspicions and, besides, he doubted if he had any more to tell him. If he had, he'd've played it for another fiver.

Two things, however, were clear. Firstly, the waiter knew who he was and why he was there. Not all that surprising. Gossip spreads quickly in an enclosed world such as an hotel.

Secondly, he'd definitely make that trip to London tomorrow to check out the waiter's story and to question Blanche Lester more closely about her exact relationship with Eustace Quinn.

It was a point he put to Boyce when he returned to headquarters. Boyce arrived shortly after him, bustling in with his notebook already in his hand as if eager to get his report over and done with and shove off home. Rudd let him speak first.

"For a start, Danny Webb," Boyce said, briskly flicking over the pages. "The landlord at the Feathers knows him, although he hadn't heard about the connection with Nina Gifford or the fact that Webb was staying in Burnett's caravan. Evidently Webb was fairly tight-lipped about himself and used his mouth mainly for drinking with. He's been in the Feathers quite a few times. In the past, only on the odd occasion, but on Wednesday and Thursday he was there lunchtimes as well as the evenings. On beer mostly, although he splashed out on the odd whisky. And the landlord's quite positive Webb didn't arrive in the bar until half past eleven this morning, well after opening time."

"He's sure about that?" Rudd asked.

"There's no doubt in his mind. Someone missed a cigarette lighter off the counter yesterday evening and the landlord's pretty certain Webb nicked it. For that reason, he kept a watch on him on the quiet."

"So his evidence puts Webb on our list of murder suspects. I can't see much motive but it's early days yet. We may turn one up. What about Blanche Lester's car?"

Boyce turned back a page.

"It's 11.27 miles from Bexford to Cawleigh and 3.56 miles from Cawleigh to Althorpe. Adding it all up, it means she did more than enough extra mileage to get from Bexford to Althorpe and back again to Cawleigh with about another fifteen miles on the clock. Which I would have thought put her on the list of runners, too."

"It looks like it," Rudd agreed. "She says she went for a drive round the countryside because she didn't want to arrive at the preview too early, which would tie in with the extra miles she did and would be in her favour. On the other hand, she could have a motive for killing Quinn. One of the waiters claims he heard them quarrelling at breakfast this morning."

"There you are then," Boyce said, as if that put an end to any further argument. "She drives to Althorpe, kills Quinn, and then goes on to Cawleigh in time to put in an appearance at the preview at ten-thirty. I don't see what more you need."

"The answers to a couple of questions, Tom. Firstly, how did she get the body into the washhouse?"

"Dragged it," Boyce said without any hesitation. "Quinn wasn't a big-built man. She could have managed it. Just." He added the rider grudgingly. "Or she lured him into the washhouse and killed him there."

Rudd let it pass although the theory seemed unlikely and continued, "The other point is why, having killed him, she didn't drive straight to Cawleigh? If your figures are correct, she drove another fifteen miles."

"Perhaps she wanted to drive round for a bit to give herself time to recover."

It was a more plausible explanation than Boyce's earlier one and Rudd accepted it.

"So what happens now?" the Sergeant asked.

"I'm going to London tomorrow," Rudd replied. "According to Blanche Lester, Quinn bought those sketches from a dealer called Askew. He's got a shop in Bucks Lane, off Charing Cross Road." While waiting for Boyce to arrive, Rudd had looked Askew up in the London telephone directory and found the address. "I want to check with him. From there, I'll go on to the Demeter Gallery and have another word with Blanche Lester and also with Quinn's secretary. She may know something about Quinn's partner. No one else seems to, except Max Gifford. If there's time, I'll also check with our liaison officer at the Yard in case they've got Danny Webb on their files."

"What about me?" Boyce asked. "Do you want me to come with you?"

"No, Tom. I'll go alone. I want to make it look as casual as I can at this stage, as if I've just dropped in for a chat." He saw Boyce drawing in his breath ready to point out that, in that case, he'd be free, wouldn't he? and Rudd added quickly, "There's just one thing you can do. Blanche Lester mentioned a village she drove through, a place called Medlow, she thought. I've checked the map and the only name that's at all like it is Medlave. Take Kyle with you and drive over there tomorrow. Ask around if anyone saw a green Mini passing through the village this morning between half past nine and half past ten." As a sop, he added, "It should only take the pair of you a few hours. Once you've done that, you're off duty, although stay near a phone so I can ring you if I need you."

"I'll be watching sport on the telly," Boyce replied. "You won't find me shifting far tomorrow afternoon, especially as there's wrestling on the box."

"Fair enough," Rudd replied. He half envied the Sergeant's pleasure at the anticipation of a few hours' leisure even though he did not share his enthusiasm for the manner in which it would be spent.

As for himself, he'd be lucky if he got home in time to watch the nine o'clock news. And even if he allowed himself that short diversion, there would be the unpleasant prospect of the reports he would soon have to begin writing hanging like a dark cloud over even those few, snatched minutes of relaxation.

CHAPTER 9

Bucks Lane was a tiny side street off Charing Cross Road, one of those narrow, crooked turnings, buttressed with tall, thin buildings of dingy brick whose appearance seemed not to have changed since the nineteenth century. The shop was single-fronted, squeezed in between a truss wholesaler's, its drab merchandise displayed with a defiant, take-it-or-leave-it bravado, and an anonymous doorway, standing ajar, revealing a flight of dirty, precipitous stairs leading up to God knows where.

The shop's one window was crammed with books, old, shabby volumes with worn gilt edges, arranged on a series of dusty display steps with no apparent plan except size, although, studying its contents briefly, Rudd gathered that Askew specialised in art history and archeology. These were not his only interests, however. A brass telescope lying among the books and some faded postcards and photographs propped up negligently in the front of the window base suggested he dealt also in other objects which could be loosely described as coming under the general heading of art.

Pushing open the door above which a bell on a spring jangled frenetically, Rudd saw that the interior was as crowded and as haphazardly arranged as the window. It was narrow but deep, running back to a dim recess at the far end, occupied by a rolltop desk that evidently served Askew as an office for it was piled with files and papers, some impaled on vicious-looking spikes.

Of Askew himself there was no sign although the ceiling-high shelves, which divided up the space into narrow, claustrophobic aisles barely wide enough to accommodate one customer at a time, made it impossible to see who else might be in the place. Dangling from the ceiling and further obscuring the view were long festoons of prints, clipped together with clothes-pegs, like washing hung up to dry.

The pungent smell of cigarette smoke and the gentle vibration of the worn, bare floorboards under someone's weight suggested another's presence. Before Rudd had time to accustom himself to the dim lighting, a few more low-powered, unshaded bulbs were switched on, lifting the gloom a little, and a short, stout man with pale, pendulous cheeks squeezed himself round the end of one of the bookcases and came towards him, his high paunch thrust forward and straining apart the lower edges of a brown tweed waistcoat liberally sprinkled with cigarette ash.

The cigarette in question hung from the corner of his mouth, an habitual position, Rudd imagined, for the muscles in that side of his face were contracted with the effort of keeping it in place and the eye was permanently half closed against the smoke.

"Yes?" he asked. Despite his crumpled suit and general air of unkempt shabbiness, his voice was disconcertingly educated, with an old-fashioned roundness and plumpness about the vowel sounds to which nicotine had added its own liquid richness; disinterested, too, as if Rudd's presence were an irrelevance.

"Mr. Askew?" Rudd asked, and, producing the manila envelope of sketches and his own identity card, he handed them over together.

Their effect was less dramatic than Rudd had hoped although Askew went as far as to remove the cigarette from his mouth and drop it onto the floor where he neatly extinguished it with a quick, shuffling movement of his right foot, not unlike a little dance step, and where it lay, flattened and disembowelled, among the many others littering the boards.

He returned Rudd's card without any comment apart from a slight lifting of his shoulders as much as to say, "So what?" But the sketches caught his attention and he examined them carefully, tipping each one in turn towards the nearest light in order to study it in detail. Rudd waited without speaking.

At last, Askew spoke.

"Where did you get these from?"

He still held the drawings and Rudd had to extend his hand before Askew relinquished them.

"Eustace Quinn," Rudd replied, replacing them in the envelope and tucking it under his arm. He saw Askew's eyes shift towards it, an expression on his face that was difficult to read. It was partly wariness mixed with a glint of covetousness, the kind of look a dealer might give towards some desirable object that he had parted with reluctantly.

"You know Mr. Quinn?" Rudd continued.

Askew lit another cigarette, mumbling a reply as he struck the match and drew in the smoke. As far as Rudd could ascertain, he was admitting the acquaintanceship.

"In fact, I believe you sold him the sketches."

"What if I did? It was a legitimate sale. No funny business involved," Askew replied, the cigarette bobbing indignantly up and down.

"I never suggested there was," Rudd said coolly. Askew's immediate defensiveness suggested to him, however, that not all of the man's business was as innocent as might first appear. What else might he deal in? Dirty books? It was possible. Despite the ubiquity of soft porn magazines and paperbacks freely on sale all over London, there was still a market for illegal, hard pornography, especially the more expensive and outré erotica that a man like Askew might very well be peddling from the back room of his shop. But that wasn't Rudd's immediate concern.

"So what's your business here?" Askew demanded.

"A murder investigation," Rudd told him and was gratified to see that at last the man was shaken.

"My God, whose?"

"Eustace Quinn's."

"My God," Askew repeated, and, taking the cigarette from his mouth, he turned hurriedly and began to shoulder his way through the hanging streamers of prints towards the back of the shop where he flung open the lid of the desk and scrabbled about inside. His broad shoulders blocked the view but Rudd could guess what he was up to by the chink of glass and the smell of whisky.

"Join me?" Askew asked, half turning towards the Chief Inspector, and seemed relieved when Rudd declined the invitation.

"Shock," he explained, laying a plump hand on his waistcoat before knocking back the contents of the glass. He came up like a man renewed, shaking his head so that his cheeks trembled and reminding Rudd of some shabby, rough-haired dog emerging from a pond.

"Take a pew," he said, putting down the empty glass and indicating the swivel chair by the desk with a sudden, welcoming expansiveness. "How can I help you?"

Rudd sat, waiting until Askew had dragged another chair round to face him, so close together in the confined space that their knees almost touched. He was not fooled by Askew's apparent change in attitude, taking it as proof that the man's business was almost certainly on the windy side of the law and that his cooperation was motivated as much by a desire to keep on good terms with the police as by a wish to assist in any inquiry in which Rudd was involved. Not that it mattered. As long as he was prepared to talk, Rudd wasn't bothered with his motives. Fear was as good a tongue-loosener as any other higher-minded emotion. At the same time, he was aware that Askew would only tell him what he wanted him to know.

"How long have you known Mr. Quinn?" he began.

"Quite a long time," Askew replied and, as Rudd cocked his head interrogatively, he continued, "He's been buying stuff off me for the past five years. Not on a regular basis, but he'd drop in when I happened to have anything in stock that I thought might interest him. I could look up the sales book if you like."

"No need to bother," Rudd replied. Seated only a few feet away from the man, he could hear his heavy, sibilant breathing, as if the air was being sucked up through a long, antiquated tube, and he was aware also of the false geniality of the half smile that quirked up his lips but had no effect on the slablike flesh of the rest of his face. A cigarette was again in his mouth and the half-closed eyes peered out at Rudd through the smoke with a cold, fixed droop. "Tell me about the sketches."

"Oh, *those!*" Askew's tone was dismissive as if they hardly entered into the inquiry. "I acquired them a few months ago. Mr. Quinn came into the shop a couple of weeks later, liked the look of them, and bought them. That's all."

" 'Acquired them'?" Rudd repeated. "How?"

There was a small silence and then Askew said carefully, "From a man. He brought them in one day." He added with an unconvincing attempt at joviality, "My God, don't tell me they were stolen!"

Ignoring the exclamation, Rudd merely said, "Describe the man."

"Mid-thirties, dark-haired."

It was not enough and Rudd suspected that Askew was being deliberately vague. As a dealer, he'd have a more astute knowledge of human nature and a much keener memory for faces.

"Go on."

Askew flung out a hand in protest.

"Oh, come on, Inspector! You really can't expect me to remember some nondescript little chap who comes in here hawking a few drawings . . ."

Rudd got to his feet, making a great show of buttoning up his raincoat.

"Right! Then if you'll lock up the shop, Mr. Askew, I'll arrange for you to look through some photographs at Scotland Yard."

Askew stared at him for a few seconds before admitting defeat.

"All right. His name's Danny Webb and he's been in here on three different occasions, the first time about four months ago. January, I think. He brought along the couple of seascapes. Just rough sketches but they were good and I bought them with Quinn in mind. I was right, too. He was interested and asked me to get hold of more if I could. He also asked me to find out about the artist who drew them. A few weeks later, Danny Webb came back with the drawings of the nudes. I got chatting to him and found out the artist was someone called Max Gifford. Quinn had asked me to try and fix up an appointment with Danny, so while Danny was in the shop, I rang him. Danny spoke to him and they arranged to meet."

"Where?" Rudd asked. The information that Quinn's purchase of the sketches had been made through Danny Webb didn't entirely surprise him. It fitted. Nor was it difficult to guess from whom Danny Webb had acquired them in the first place—Nina Gifford. But whether Nina had given them to Danny Webb or he had stolen them hadn't yet been established.

"Here, of course," Askew said promptly. And that fitted, too. Rudd couldn't imagine Askew passing up the chance to act as go-between in a deal he himself had set up. "They met one evening about a week later. Danny Webb brought a couple more sketches with him which Quinn arranged to buy. I heard Webb promising he'd get hold of more if he could."

"Did he say how?"

"Not exactly. He just said he knew Max Gifford's wife so he shouldn't have too much trouble. There were plenty more where those came from."

"And that was all?"

Askew looked uneasy.

"They talked for a bit longer," he admitted.

"What about?"

"I didn't hear it all. Quinn asked me to make some coffee and I was busy in the back room getting it, but I heard enough to guess Quinn was pumping him about Gifford: where did he live? was he still painting? That sort of thing. Webb didn't seem to know much about him, though. I heard him telling Quinn that he'd never met Gifford, only his wife."

He seemed about to say something else and then changed his mind, covering up the hesitation by lighting another cigarette and blowing the smoke in Rudd's direction.

"And what about you, Mr. Askew?" Rudd asked, flapping it away with one hand. "What other special favour were you able to do for Mr. Quinn? Apart from selling him the sketches, of course, and introducing him to Danny Webb."

It wasn't entirely a shot in the dark. Askew's hesitation had suggested that there was more to the story than he had so far divulged, and besides, his earlier remark that the deal had been legitimate made Rudd suspect that something a little more shady had been going on than the mere buying and selling of half a dozen sketches. The whole situation smelt to him of a setup in which Danny Webb had played only a small, insignificant part.

Askew's smile vanished and he sat quite still for several seconds with the immobility of a small, rotund, pagan idol, his thighs set wide apart beneath the paunch to reveal a plump, straining crotch, both eyes closed now, while the cigarette smoke spiralled gently upward above his head like incense.

"Ah!" he said at last. "The deal."

"That's what I wanted to hear about," Rudd said comfortably.

"Well, it was hardly what you'd term illegal. Less so than an auction ring," Askew began. His voice was more hurried now, the breath wheezing in his lungs. "Quinn wanted me to get hold of as much of Gifford's work as I could, only to keep it under my hat who I was buying for. It took time, of course. There's not a lot of it in private hands and even less that's likely to come up in the saleroom, but I managed to round up quite a few for him. Luckily, there were some of Gifford's old cronies still knocking about who'd got paintings, which I was able to persuade them to part with, including his ex-wife. Times are hard and a couple of hundred in ready cash . . ."

"Whose ex-wife?" Rudd interrupted. Askew's vague use of pronouns hadn't made it clear. "Max Gifford's?"

Askew's eyelids lifted momentarily and he looked at Rudd with an expression of cold dislike, aware that he had been tricked into the admission, the Chief Inspector's knowledge of the background of the deal being a lot less precise than he had been led to believe.

"Haven't you come across Zoe Hamilton yet in your inquiries?" he asked.

"You tell me what you know," Rudd replied, brushing aside the question.

Askew shrugged as if conceding that, having come so far, there was no point in holding back.

"I asked here and there," he continued. "There's always someone in the trade who knows someone else who'll come up with the information you want. For a price, of course, but, then, Quinn was paying and he didn't seem short of the odd fiver. Even the occasional tenner, if need be. Zoe was married to Max Gifford in the thirties and divorced him in thirty-seven, I think. Before the war, anyway. She married again but that went down the drain shortly afterwards. Anyhow, I got hold of her address and passed it on to Quinn."

Also for a price, Rudd added to himself. How much had Askew managed to net out of the various deals he had set up for Quinn? A few hundred quid possibly, made up over the months in the small cuts he'd taken on each transaction. Not a lot compared to what Quinn had probably hoped to make once he had cornered the market in Gifford's work. Bought at rock-bottom prices, the paintings could have been worth how much? Anything from five to fifty times more, once Gifford's name had been established? Although exactly how Quinn had intended doing this wasn't yet clear, unless he counted on the exhibition to promote Gifford's reputation. Remembering the copy of the *Times* in Quinn's briefcase, folded back to the financial page, Rudd realised that art was as much a commodity as diamonds or coffee beans. On Quinn's part, his purchase of Gifford's pictures could have been nothing more than a gamble in the same way that speculators with a nose for the stock market will buy up shares, trusting to their instinct that their value will increase and they'll make a killing.

A killing. The phrase seemed ominously apt. Was that, in fact, what had been behind Quinn's death? A murder planned by one of his business rivals who had got to hear of his undercover dealings and had killed him in order to put a stop to it? The world of art dealers could be as cutthroat as that of drug traffickers, and even Rudd knew enough about forgeries, thefts, and the international smuggling of art treasures to realise that murder, too, couldn't be discounted.

If that were so in Quinn's case, Rudd realised he'd have to bow out and hand the investigation over to Scotland Yard. He possessed neither the facilities nor the specialised knowledge for handling it.

But not yet. Because he wasn't entirely convinced that this had been the motive behind Quinn's murder and, until he had more evidence to the contrary, he intended keeping the inquiry in his own hands.

"I'd like Mrs. Hamilton's address," he told Askew.

The street where she lived was evidently coming up in the world. Several of the terrace houses were in the process of being refurbished and builders' and decorators' sign-boards hung on the front railings. Not hers, though. A row of bells beside the front door suggested multioccupancy.

So did the cluster of dustbins in the area round which Rudd had to pick his way as Nina Gifford had done a few days earlier.

There was a long delay before anyone answered his knock and even then the door wasn't opened to him. Instead, the letter box rattled and a woman's voice demanded hoarsely, "Who is it?"

"The police," Rudd replied, bending down to the slot in the door. He would have preferred a less public announcement but it was obvious Zoe Hamilton wasn't going to let him past the doorstep unless he first stated his business.

All the same, she wasn't entirely convinced. The door partly opened but remained on the chain, the woman staying out of sight.

"Let's see your card then," she told him, "*if* you're a copper."

Her tone implied she doubted even this fact and, exasperated as well as amused by the situation, Rudd produced his official identification and proffered it in the gap where it was immediately whisked away by a not too clean hand before being returned to him. There followed a rattle as the chain was removed and the door finally opened sufficiently wide to allow him to sidle into a dark, narrow passage smelling of stale cooking and sweetish odour of old, quiet decay.

"If you've come about that row upstairs last night, I don't know anything about it," Zoe Hamilton announced.

"I haven't," Rudd replied.

"Then you bloody should!" she countered with a swift change of tactics. "Shouting and carrying on to all hours! And playing that steel-band music. One of these days, they'll come through the bloody floor. I've been up there enough times to complain and banged on the ceiling with the broom."

Rudd could well imagine her doing it, too—clambering onto a chair and thumping vigorously on the stained plaster. Despite her age, for she must have been over seventy, and her diminutive size, there was a fierce, battling quality about her that would enjoy a damn good blazing row.

"So what do you want?" she asked. "Only I was just going out."

While they had been talking, she had led the way into a back room in which the electric light was burning even though the sunlight outside was flooding a tiny strip of neglected garden visible through the dingy net curtains over the window. Rudd glanced about him briefly as he entered, taking in, without apparently showing the slightest interest in his surroundings, the shabby, crowded furniture, the bottle of gin on the mantelpiece, and, above it, a large rectangle of lighter wallpaper where a picture had once hung and which he had no doubt was now in Quinn's possession. Or rather his trustees', whoever they might be.

Zoe Hamilton herself had also been included in that first, swift glance and it occurred to Rudd that her announcement that she had been about to go out probably accounted for her bizarre appearance. Seeing her properly for the first time in full light, he saw she was wearing a black cocktail dress of the forties era, with a crossover, gathered bodice and a low, V-shaped neckline revealing the withered skin of her throat, its padded shoulders giving the upper part of her body a curiously square, top-heavy appearance. A grubby pink silk rose, its stiffening gone limp, hung at the waist. Her makeup had the same dated look: dark red lipstick and black mascara that seemed to have been daubed on at some distance from a mirror for, like an Impressionist painting, it was not meant to be seen at close quarters, composed as it was of quick, little dabs and dashes. Rudd concluded she was probably longsighted but was too vain to wear glasses.

He was also aware of her curiosity. She was regarding him, head tilted to one side, her bright little black eyes lively with interest. He would be stupid, he realised, to tell her more than he had to.

"It's a case of possible theft," he explained, which was partly true. After all, he wasn't yet sure how Danny Webb had acquired the drawings. "We're trying to check the ownership of some paintings and sketches."

He saw her curiosity quicken at the word "painting" and her glance went immediately to the blank space on the wall, although she said nothing, leaving him to supply further details. Shrewd of her, he thought. Unlike Askew, she wasn't going to blurt out anything until she knew exactly what information he had in his possession. Forced to continue, he added, "I believe you sold a painting some time ago."

"That's right," Zoe replied, bristling up at once. "But it was mine and I don't see it's any of your damned business what I did with it."

There was nothing for it but to produce a photograph of Quinn which McCullum had prepared for him that morning and the envelope of sketches which he passed to her first.

"Do you recognise these by any chance?"

"Good God!" she said, going through them like a hand of cards. "I haven't seen these for years. They're Max's. What's he been up to?"

"Nothing that I know of. It's this man we're interested in," Rudd replied, handing her one of McCullum's photographs of the body, a close-up taken in the mortuary in which Quinn, despite McCullum's skilful touching up, still looked very dead.

Zoe Hamilton studied it at arm's length, confirming Rudd's suspicion about her eyesight, and when she finally handed it back, her expression was wary.

"Do you know him?" Rudd asked.

"I might," she replied. "But I want to know what the hell's going on first. You don't fool me. You're a Chief Inspector from Chelmsford CID. I saw it on your card. You wouldn't come chasing up here just for a few sketches and a painting. Not Max's, anyway. You'd've sent a Sergeant. And that man's dead."

"Murdered," Rudd told her.

"Oh, Christ!" said Zoe but her concern wasn't for Quinn. "I suppose this is going to take bloody hours and I'm dying for a drink. I was on my way to the pub when you came."

"Then allow me to treat you," Rudd suggested, taking the hint which was exactly what she had been angling for, judging by the alacrity with which she accepted his invitation.

"You're on, dear, but let me find my coat first," she told him and, scrabbling about in a mound of clothes on the sofa, came up with a bright red jacket which Rudd gallantly held out for her while she thrust her arms into the sleeves, smiling with oblique flirtatiousness over her shoulder at him as she remarked, "It's years since I had a gentleman friend take me out."

"Well," she continued later when he had settled her in a corner of the saloon bar of a pub in the North End Road and carried over to the table his own pint of bitter and her gin and orange, "what do you want to know?"

"The man in the photograph," Rudd prompted her.

"Mr. Johnson? He turned up about three months ago. Said he was from the Council, checking the loos. He showed me a card with 'Borough Surveyor' on it so I let him in."

Clever of him, Rudd commented silently to himself. God knows where Quinn had got the card from, although it wouldn't be too difficult to acquire it. He might even have had it specially printed.

"Anyway," Zoe was saying, "he had a look at the loo and the sink and wrote something down in a notebook. Then he came into the living room to ask a few more questions and saw the painting."

"Can you describe it?" Rudd asked.

"Of course I can!" Zoe retorted promptly. "The bloody thing's been hanging up there for years. It was a portrait of a woman. A nude. Max did it ages ago, before the war, when we were still married. Lilith, he called her. She was some little shopgirl or other he fancied. There was a pair of portraits originally. Max kept the other one. I don't know if he's still got it."

It was hanging over his bed, although Rudd did not tell her this. He merely nodded, encouraging her to continue. Zoe, who had finished her drink, replaced the glass on the table, pushing it towards him and looking at him from under her mascaraed lashes. Rudd, guessing her meaning, got up and ordered her another one at the bar. At this rate, he thought wryly, returning with it to the table, it was going to cost him the best part of a tenner before she reached the end of her story.

Zoe sipped it appreciatively before resuming.

"As I was telling you, this Mr. Johnson noticed the painting and asked if I'd be interested in selling it. I said I might if the price was right."

"How much?" Rudd interrupted.

Zoe looked at him speculatively.

"Five hundred quid."

Enough to be tempting but probably nowhere near the price Quinn must have hoped to get for it.

"Well, I ask you," Zoe appealed to him. "It was a hell of a lot of money and I didn't particularly want the damned thing, so I said all right and he said he'd come back that evening with a van to collect it. Which he did."

"Alone?"

"No, there was another man with him."

"What did he look like?" Rudd asked, wondering if the second man had been Danny.

"A short, fat chap." Zoe sketched in the air with the hand not holding the glass, making rotund gestures. "Got a fag stuck in his mouth most of the time."

Askew. Well, that followed.

"Was anybody else mentioned?"

Zoe finished her drink and considered, head to one side, smiling at Rudd as she dabbed the corners of her mouth with a handkerchief.

"There might have been," she hinted.

When Rudd returned from the bar once again, she continued, "They were talking as they carried the painting up the basement steps. It's quite heavy and they'd got it wedged against the railings. I was standing in the passage and I heard Mr. Johnson say to the other man, 'For God's sake, be careful. I don't want it damaged.' And he said, 'Why didn't you let me send Danny?' And Mr. Johnson said, 'I've told you, I don't want to get more involved with him than I have to.' Christ! I don't know how I kept my face straight. The little fat bloke was huffing and blowing so much I thought he'd have a heart attack."

"Danny?" Rudd repeated to check he'd heard the name correctly. "Are you sure?"

"That's what he said. I'm not deaf yet," Zoe snapped.

Or losing interest, Rudd added to himself. He could picture her following the two men to the door, determined to get her money's worth and finding malicious amusement in the sight of them manhandling the painting up from the basement, the five hundred pounds already tucked away somewhere safe.

"By the way, how did Mr. Johnson pay you?" he asked.

"Cash, of course. I wasn't messing about with a cheque." She paused and then added without any prompting, "He came back a few days later."

"Mr. Johnson?"

"That's right. Turned up here in the pub one evening. Bought me a few drinks and we chatted."

"What about?"

It was obvious she was enticing him on and Rudd was perfectly amenable although quite where it was leading he wasn't certain.

"About Max mainly."

"Oh, yes?"

He looked suitably interested.

"Wanted to know all about him—what sort of person he was, that sort of thing." She stopped briefly before adding, "He was curious, too, about his marriage. He asked especially about Nina."

The throw-away casualness of the remark didn't fool the Chief Inspector. So that's what it had all been leading up to—a spiteful little dig at Nina Gifford. How long had Zoe Hamilton been divorced from Max? Over forty years. And yet it seemed the bitterness towards his second wife still rankled. Nor had her interest in Max diminished, for she continued.

"How is he? Max, I mean. You've seen him?"

"Yes, I met him recently."

"He's crippled, isn't he? At least, that's what Nina told me."

"You know her?" Rudd asked. It was news to him.

"We've kept in touch." Zoe sounded offhand. "Not Max, though. I haven't heard a word from him for years, the old goat. As a matter of fact, I saw Nina only a few days ago."

"When exactly?" Rudd asked, more sharply than he had intended and he saw her give a small, pleased smile at having stirred up possible trouble.

She took her time to reply, teasing him deliberately.

"Let's see. It was last Tuesday, I think. Yes, that's right. Tuesday. She called round in the afternoon, asking me to look out for a flat for a friend of hers. Or so she said."

Probably for Danny Webb, Rudd thought. The timing of her visit, only a few days before Quinn's murder, seemed significant and he wondered if the two events were connected.

"Come to think of it," Zoe continued, "she seemed interested in that portrait I'd sold, the one of Lilith." She laughed, showing her teeth, and her tongue flickered in her mouth. "Not that it was any of her damned business. She seems to think she owns Max but, as I pointed out to her, no woman's ever meant much to him since *her.*"

Rudd assumed she meant the woman in the portrait and he realised for the first time the full poignancy of its position over Max's bed. What Nina thought, he could only guess, but it was clear Zoe knew nothing about it or she would have seized the opportunity to make malicious capital out of it.

He said, "Let me get you another drink."

It would be the last one. The interview was over as far as he was concerned, Zoe Hamilton having nothing more to tell him except to make more innuendoes against Nina Gifford, which hardly added to the evidence regarding Quinn's murder.

At the bar, he glanced back at her, touched with a sudden and curious mixture of pity and revulsion. What an absurd creature she was! She put him in mind of the Wicked Fairy at the princess's christening party in that children's story—malignant, evil, full of revenge, and yet not entirely unsympathetic. After all, she hadn't been invited, a tactless omission which had excused her in his mind when, as a child, he had listened to the story being read aloud in school.

Sitting perched on the edge of the bench seat in the window embrasure, her thin, little legs crossed at the knee to reveal shrivelled calves, she had taken the opportunity of his absence to touch up her makeup and was peering with intense concentration at her own reflection in the mirror of a powder compact she had produced from the shabby, patent-leather handbag at her side. Unaware of his scrutiny, she was wiping the puff over her nose and cheeks, stretching and relaxing her mouth as she checked her lipstick, fiddling with a strand of hair, totally self-absorbed.

An aging, bedraggled flapper, left over from her heyday of the twenties, as dated as Turkish cigarettes or the Charleston.

"Cheers, darling!" she said when he put the glass down in front of her. Raising it and winking at him over its rim, she added, "Bottoms up!"

"Bottoms up!" he echoed with only mild amusement, raising his own glass in salutation.

CHAPTER 10

There was nothing old-fashioned about the Demeter Gallery. Rudd strolled past it on the far side of the street, noting its glossy, contemporary facade. At the end, in front of a white, ornate church, oddly truncated like the top tier of a wedding cake abandoned on the pavement, he crossed the road and walked back, stopping outside the gallery to peer in through the window. Inside, he could see Blanche Lester seated at an enormous black desk, her chin resting on her clasped hands as she viewed the passers-by. She seemed bored and listless, but the sudden stiffening of her posture warned him that she had noticed his presence so, smiling and nodding to her across the painting on display, he pushed open the door and entered.

She came forward to meet him, her anxiety immediately apparent and also a childlike wistfulness emphasised by the white dress she was wearing. Made of some light, fine fabric, high-necked and long-skirted, it was a frock out of a Victorian schoolroom, its waist tightly belted with a blue sash. A band of the same-coloured silk held back her hair, which she wore loose this morning over her shoulders—a black-haired Alice in Wonderland, with dark smudges under her eyes and little high-heeled sandals of white kid.

"I can't talk to you now," she explained hurriedly. "I'm expecting some clients at any moment. They've made an appointment. Can you come back later?"

"In that case, I'd like to see Miss Martin," Rudd replied. "Is she in?"

Face to face with Miss Martin, Rudd could appreciate Max Gifford's comment that Blanche Lester had been chosen as decorative crumpet for the front office. Quinn had obviously employed Miss Martin for more serviceable and practical qualities. She was small, brisk, and plain, wearing an enormous pair of round horn-rimmed spectacles through which she eyed him with some disfavour. It was true, as Rudd himself would have admitted, that his appearance was hardly in keeping with the immaculate and elegant decor of Eustace Quinn's office—beige and brown this time instead of the black and white of the gallery, but just as expensive judging by the buttoned leather, thick velvet, and raw silk of its furnishings.

"I suppose you've come about Mr. Quinn's murder," Miss Martin stated bluntly, getting straight to the point as she waved him into a chair. Across the desk—Quinn's, Rudd assumed, its leather top empty apart from a blotter and a heavy silver desk set, but then, with a secretary like Miss Martin he'd hardly need to bother himself with papers—she regarded him with a headmistress's quiet speculation, as if running an eye over him with the intention of writing some comment at the end of his school report.

Rudd admitted that Quinn's murder was indeed the purpose of his visit and hurried into his next remark before she had time to assume control of the interview which, given half a chance, she would do.

"I understand Mr. Quinn was thinking of mounting an exhibition of Max Gifford's work."

"That's right. Why do you ask? Does it have any bearing on Mr. Quinn's death?" she demanded as if he were under interrogation.

"If you'd just answer my question," Rudd replied pleasantly.

He won that round but not without one of those ridiculous confrontations in which he and his antagonist stare at each other for several seconds before the latter concedes defeat. Miss Martin conceded hers when she signalled . . . by removing her spectacles, without which her face looked naked and much more vulnerable.

"He discussed it with me, of course. He'd arranged to see Mr. Gifford on Thursday and I entered the meeting in his appointments book. I left Friday free as well as I understood there was an auction in the same area which he wanted to attend. The two dates coincided quite satisfactorily."

But not entirely coincidentally as Blanche Lester had made clear.

"When he discussed the exhibition with you, was any date mentioned?"

"No, although Mr. Quinn said that if the meeting with Mr. Gifford went as well as he hoped, he'd aim for a date in late spring next year."

Which corroborated Max Gifford's statement, Rudd thought, and also brought him to the main purpose of the interview.

"Did he mention a business partner?"

Her response was immediate.

"What partner? Mr. Quinn has no partner. The gallery is owned, or rather leased, in Mr. Quinn's name only. As far as I am aware, he never considered taking anyone else into the business."

"He spoke of a partner to Max Gifford. Someone who was going to help finance the exhibition."

"But Mr. Quinn had no need to ask for outside financial backing. The gallery is perfectly able to cover the costs of any exhibition we might choose to mount."

She seemed to be taking it personally, as if any suggestion of financial dependence on outsiders somehow reflected on her own efficiency. Judging by his surroundings, Rudd could well believe her denial. Quinn hadn't been short of money. Why then the talk of a partner? And why only to Max Gifford and not to his own secretary who appeared to know about all other aspects of his business affairs?

"Perhaps Miss Lester could help you," Miss Martin continued. "Have you asked her? She may be more intimate with Mr. Quinn's arrangements."

The significance of the word occurred to her too late and Rudd saw her colour rise. For a moment, she looked uncharacteristically flustered and Rudd wondered what she thought of the relationship between Quinn and Blanche Lester. No doubt she disapproved. She might even feel a little resentful.

"I have asked her," he replied, pretending not to have noticed her momentary confusion. "Miss Lester knows nothing about it either."

"Then I'm afraid I can't help you," she stated flatly.

"There is one thing you can do for me. You spoke of Mr. Quinn's appointments book. I'd like a list of the names and addresses of all the people he had any contact with since January."

He chose the date deliberately because, according to Askew, this was about the time when Quinn had bought the first of Max Gifford's sketches and was the earliest date, he calculated, that the idea of acquiring more of Gifford's work and of mounting the exhibition must have occurred to him.

"All of them?" Miss Martin protested. "But there must be dozens!"

"I'd like the list all the same," Rudd countered firmly. "While you're preparing it, perhaps I could take a look at the other paintings by Max Gifford which Mr. Quinn bought. I assume they're kept in the gallery?"

"They're downstairs in the basement. If you'll come this way."

Miss Martin rose to her feet and conducted him into the passage from which a flight of steps led down into a large cellar, protected by a heavy steel door which she unlocked before swinging it open and switching on the lights to reveal the storage space beyond.

It was large, extending under both the office and the gallery, and was lined with vertical metal racks, stretching from floor to ceiling, in which canvases of all sizes were stacked behind curtains of white sheeting. The faint whirring of a motor and the freshness of the atmosphere suggested that some form of air conditioning was in operation. A series of fluorescent tubes along the ceiling cast a hard, white, almost shadowless glare.

Miss Martin appeared to know exactly where Gifford's work was stored for she went without hesitation to one of the sections and drew out seven canvases, the last of which Rudd had to help her lift forward and lean against the wall.

"I'll leave you to examine them while I type the list," she told him. "When you've finished, I'll put them away myself and lock up."

Not trusting him evidently even with so simple a task. He waited until she had departed before turning his attention to the paintings. They were propped up in a row, reminding him of the pictures he had seen ranged

in a similar fashion in Max Gifford's dining room and, remembering
those, he had no difficulty in recognising Gifford's style. Like the others,
they were portraits, mostly of women, one of which he realised was of Zoe
Hamilton when young, standing naked in front of a mirror and admiring, with the same expression of narcissistic absorption he had seen on
her face in the pub, the contours of her own body; but, in all other re-
spects, how different! The flesh was youthful, the breasts high and
pointed, the black, sleek hair, cut close to her head in the twenties style,
forming a cap that curled round in two small semicircles to frame the
cheekbones.

"Figure on a Suffolk Shore," the only painting which, to his knowledge, Quinn had admitted owning in his letter to Gifford, was recognisable from its subject matter: a woman lying naked among sand dunes, a
man, also nude, standing beside her.

The largest canvas, which Rudd left to the last, was without a doubt
the portrait of Lilith for which Quinn had given Zoe Hamilton five hundred in cash. There was no mistaking the fact that it made a pair with
the one hanging in Max Gifford's bedroom. Like that one, the woman's
face was hidden but the body had the same fluid beauty and cascade of
dark, flowing hair.

Moved by a sudden desire to touch it, he leaned forward and ran the
tip of one finger over the canvas. It seemed to come alive under his touch
as he felt the texture of the paint, rough and sensual where the marks of
brush and palette knife were petrified in the pigment, a mute and static
token of the passion with which they had first been applied.

Miss Martin was still typing out the list when he returned to the office
and, when she had completed it and handed it to him, he glanced
quickly down it. She hadn't been exaggerating; there were over forty
names on it, together with addresses, telephone numbers, and the dates
on which Quinn had been in contact with each individual. Alongside
some of them, she had also typed in their business or personal status
where it was known to her—accountant, bank manager, fellow club
member. Some were not listed in this manner and Rudd assumed that, in
these cases, she had no record of their exact relationship with Quinn.
Only one of the names rang a bell in his mind, that of Bruce Lawford,
which seemed faintly familiar although Rudd could not remember where
he had heard it. Or rather, read it, for he associated it vaguely with the
printed word—possibly a newspaper report he had read, the details of
which he had now forgotten. There was no indication of what Bruce
Lawford did for a living or why Quinn should have had lunch with him,
which, according to the date, he had done on February 14. St. Valen-
tine's Day, Rudd realised, another familiar detail which fixed both the
time and the name in his mind.

Pocketing the sheet of paper, he thanked her before adding casually,
"by the way, what would a portrait by a modern painter fetch these
days?"

"It depends who the artist is," Miss Martin replied in a voice that was
intended to put him in his place for displaying such ignorance. "If you're

talking of Picasso, then you're in the several hundred thousand pound bracket, perhaps even a quarter of a million or more. Work by a less well-known but collectable artist, an Augustus John for example, might fetch anything up to twenty thousand. But those figures are only approximate. There are so many other factors to take into consideration—the quality of the painting, for example, or the competition to buy. Picasso or Matisse are still much sought after, of course. Augustus John less so than before, although his sister, Gwen John, is now highly desirable."

An interesting point, Rudd thought, as he left the office. So it was possible that, working on a conservative estimate of five thousand pounds a painting, Quinn could have made a profit of thirty thousand or more from the seven Gifford paintings he had in his possession, assuming the exhibition had established Gifford's reputation. Not bad when his initial investment must have been a mere couple of thousand pounds.

Returning along the passage to the gallery, he found Blanche Lester displaying a large oil painting, a seascape, on an easel to three neatly tailored Japanese, probably businessmen, who were standing in a semicircle in front of it, regarding it with unsmiling attention.

They were unaware of his presence and Rudd was able to watch from the doorway the little scene that was being enacted. Blanche Lester, in her white dress, looked like a small girl playing at school, the three men her pupils, standing obediently before her, grouped politely, all with their hands clasped behind their backs as if assuming a regulation pose set down in some manual of etiquette on the correct stance to adopt when viewing a painting.

The painting in question, huge and ornately framed, depicted a stormy sea with a ship in full sail leaning to the wind and was full of frantic movement—spray flying, clouds racing, flags streaming, immobilised on the canvas and symbolising, for Rudd, at least, that very English sea-dog attitude epitomised in such heroes as Drake or Nelson.

Heaven knows what the Japanese businessmen made of it, and he tried to imagine it hanging in one of their elegant, flimsy houses of oiled paper and bamboo. An absurd conception, of course, one of those conditioned images from childhood that would never be entirely superseded, despite television and the cinema, by pictures of present-day Japan with its skyscrapers and modern office blocks. On the same basis, he would always think of Eskimos in igloos and Red Indians in tepees, so firmly had the illustrations in his primary school geography book impressed themselves on his imagination.

The group seemed absorbed, but some sixth sense must have warned Blanche Lester of his presence for she glanced in his direction and, having murmured an excuse to her clients, crossed the gallery towards him, the three men all bowing in unison at her departure and following her with their eyes.

"I'm afraid this is going to take longer than I thought. Can you come back later?" she asked in a low voice.

"What time do you close?" Rudd inquired.

"Six o'clock."

He glanced at his watch. It was nearly a quarter past five, time to get himself tea, and he nodded in agreement before turning, on a sudden inexplicable whim, to bow his apologies to the Japanese whose private view he had interrupted and who, surprised and gratified by this courtesy, bowed deeply back. As he left, he could feel their ripple of astonishment follow him in almost audible, tinkling waves.

They were gone when he returned and Blanche Lester was alone, in the act of spreading a dust sheet over the desk. Seeing him through the window, she gestured that she would join him outside and, pausing to turn off the spotlights only and close the door behind her, she came out into the street.

"Is that all?" Rudd asked, the policeman in him outraged by her perfunctory preparations for securing the place for the night. "Don't you have grilles to pull down over the windows?"

"Miss Martin supervises the locking-up," she explained. "There's a caretaker who does it but she goes round with him. She holds all the keys, you see."

It was a piece of information that didn't entirely surprise him, remembering Miss Martin's insistence that she herself would lock up the basement storeroom after him. All the same, he wondered a little at the arrangement. Although Blanche Lester had been Eustace Quinn's lover, Quinn evidently hadn't entrusted her to the extent of giving her keys to the gallery, an ambivalent situation to find herself in, he would have imagined, although she seemed to accept it.

By common, unspoken consent, they walked towards Piccadilly, crossing over it and entering Green Park where they turned in the direction of the underground station. Her habitual route home, he supposed.

The noise of the traffic made conversation impossible and, even when they reached the comparative peace of the park, Rudd seemed in no hurry to begin the interview. Content to remain silent, he strolled along beside her, conscious that she was matching her pace to his and that normally she would have hurried, anxious to catch her train home.

"It's very beautiful here," he said at last and indeed it was. Behind the plane trees, their piebald bark reminding him of small jigsaw pieces of different shades of brown, intricately pieced together, the traffic went roaring up Piccadilly, sounding at that distance like the low growling of some restless animal, while above the trees, the pale stone facades of the buildings with their many windows caught the late afternoon sun. But here, in the park, was a very different world to the throngs of people passing to and fro in front of glittering car showrooms and the international airline offices, although some home-going commuters, hurrying along the paths to the tube station or the bus stops, introduced some of that frenetic activity even here.

Otherwise there was only sky, trees, and grass. And lovers. They lay in attitudes of slumber, face to face, oblivious of the passers-by. In the distance, a woman threw a stick for a dog again and again. It was too far away to hear its barking, only its leaping form was apparent, paws and head uplifted in joyful, heraldic gestures.

Blanche Lester did not reply to his remark and he hadn't expected an answer although he glanced sideways at her as if anticipating one. Her profile was serene but blank, unaware of anything about her, even the admiring glances of the men who, passing her, looked directly into her face, caught by her beauty, and Rudd was again reminded of the children's story, first evoked by Zoe Hamilton, which was now projected onto Blanche Lester. Extending the comparison, she could be likened to the Sleeping Beauty herself, the princess from the same fairy story whom the prince awakened with a kiss, a thought that might have been partly induced by the sight of the couples lying in the grass in one another's arms.

But who would awaken her? Certainly not the men who glanced at her as they passed. Nor, apparently, had Eustace Quinn succeeded in arousing her. She seemed as untouched by that affair as if it had never happened.

With this thought in his mind, it seemed quite natural to ask the question which, after all, was the reason for his being there.

"Why did you and Eustace Quinn quarrel on Friday morning?"

Its effect on her was more dramatic than he had foreseen. She stopped abruptly and, turning to face him, forced him also to halt in his tracks. He saw that she was at last awakened.

"Who told you that?" she demanded, her voice imperious. "Oh, I can guess! Someone at the hotel, I expect. A snooper, listening in to other people's conversations. Does that please you, picking up that sort of tittle-tattle? Do you get job satisfaction from it?"

"It's certainly part of my work, listening to gossip," Rudd admitted, more mildly than he felt. In fact, he was acutely embarrassed by her outburst and conscious of the stares of the passers-by amused at the sight of the shabby, middle-aged man and the beautiful, young girl quarrelling in public, or so it must have seemed to them. A lovers' tiff? their expressions seemed to be asking. Oh, hardly! I mean, he must be years older than she.

As abruptly and unexpectedly, her mood changed.

"Oh, I'm sorry, so sorry!" she cried, like a child close to tears, and, partly to comfort her and partly to break up the confrontation, he drew her arm through his, where he could feel it trembling against his side.

"You know, you'll have to tell what happened," he explained, gently avuncular.

With subdued obedience, she replied, "Of course. I understand you have to know."

Rudd was struck again, as he had been the previous day, by her apparent candour and ingenuousness which he felt he was at last beginning to understand a little better. It was, or rather had been, a natural part of her personality which, when confronted by Quinn's aggression and deviousness, she had been forced to exaggerate in much the same way as shy people will increase their diffidence in the company of an extrovert. It was a defensive pose, assumed in an attempt to protect her own individuality against the pressure of a stronger and more ruthless character and, once having found its uses, she could no longer return to the guileless innocence of its original form. The artlessness was now touched up by art and the ingenuousness had become self-conscious.

They had begun walking again, still arm in arm, pacing slowly along the path. After a silence, in which he refrained from pressing her for an answer, she started speaking in a hesitant, tentative manner.

"It was about Nina. The quarrel, I mean. Eustace had been flirting with her on Thursday. Oh, please, don't misunderstand me; I didn't really mind. It was the sort of thing he was always doing, only this time it was different. I can't explain it properly but I felt he was using her and somehow it all seemed so stupid and so mixed up with everything else—not just Eustace and me but Max and Nina as well. It made me think about couples—men and women being together, I mean. Not about marriage so much as the way they see each other in relation to themselves. It occurred to me on Thursday, for example, when I first met Max and Nina, how incredibly selfish, in fact, Max was. I suppose that sounds an awful thing to say? I mean, he's a marvellous person in so many ways—talented and charming and terribly amusing, but that's *him*. Do you understand? Him, by himself. Nothing to do with Nina."

Rudd nodded, encouraging her to continue, although he was not sure where this disjointed account was leading to, and thinking, at the same time, that the Max she was describing was nothing like the old, sick man he had interviewed on Friday afternoon after Eustace Quinn's murder.

"The point is," she continued, "he's not a different person with Nina. He's still Max. Himself. Nothing's been altered."

"Should it be?" Rudd asked.

"I'm not sure. It's one of the things I've been trying to decide. I felt he ought to change. Nina does. She's quite different when she's alone to when she's with him. Then she just seems to be Max's woman, as if she switches off most of herself and is absorbed into him. I know he's old now and needs looking after, but it's really got nothing to do with that. I feel it's always been the same between them, Max taking and Nina giving, and the worst part is I don't think it's ever occurred to him what's happening or that there might be anything wrong in it."

"Perhaps Nina accepts the situation," Rudd suggested.

She flashed up again at once, her mood changing so rapidly that Rudd wondered if she were not unbalanced in some way. Neurotic, possibly, although her behaviour could have been caused by the shock of Quinn's death. All the same, it occurred to him that a girl with hysterical tendencies and what appeared to be a deep-seated resentment against her former lover made a good candidate for a murder suspect. Pushed that little bit too far, she could easily go over the edge into a full-blown psychosis in which there was no guarantee she would act rationally. He could see, however, how this conflict in her personality could have been caused by her own uncertainty about what role she was to assume, child or woman. He was also willing to bet that when Quinn became her lover, she had been a virgin and that he had been almost entirely to blame for the corruption of her innocence, not the mere physical deflowering but the despoliation of her own clear self-image.

"Then she shouldn't accept it!" she cried. "She ought to set a higher value on herself. Besides, it's so unfair!"

It was the protest a child might have uttered, confronted by the injustice of life and aware that there was nothing to be done about it.

"Max may not see it like that," Rudd pointed out reasonably.

"Of course he doesn't! Why should he? That way he gets the cake *and* the icing."

"And is that how you saw your relationship with Eustace Quinn?" Rudd asked, deftly turning the subject back to its main point.

"Oh, Eustace!" she said disparagingly, as if he were still alive. "Eustace is far worse than Max. At least Max doesn't really know he's doing it."

"But Eustace does?" Rudd prompted, using the present tense as she had done.

"I told you yesterday, he's never done anything without thinking it out first."

"Like flirting with Nina?"

"He was attracted. He probably really wanted to make love to her. But it was all carefully planned."

"And that's why you quarrelled?"

"Yes," she admitted simply. "How stupid it all seems now he's dead! But it was important at the time. You see, I suddenly realised that I was like Nina—someone to be used in a relationship, never really allowed to be myself. It was the reason why I drove round yesterday morning instead of going straight to the preview as he wanted me to. I thought, Why should I always do exactly what he tells me? Childish, wasn't it? But he always expected me to fit in with his plans. That's why I was taken down to Althorpe in the first place."

"I don't understand," Rudd told her. He had genuinely lost the thread of her reasoning and, surprised by his honesty, she looked at him directly, a curious expression lifting the corners of her mouth—hardly a smile, more like a wry twisting of the lips.

"Didn't you know? My job was to pump Nina about herself."

"Why was that?" Rudd asked as casually as he could. Her remark, however, had shaken him. Zoe Hamilton had made almost the same comment concerning Eustace Quinn's interest in Nina Gifford, which, at the time, he had dismissed as mere spitefulness. Now, it would appear that Quinn had been following a deliberate, planned inquiry.

"I don't know. He just said, 'Find out as much as you can about her.'"

"And did you?"

"Yes, on Thursday. It didn't occur to me then that there was anything wrong in what I was doing. Nina asked me to walk in the garden after lunch and I got her to talk about herself. It wasn't difficult."

Again he saw her lips lift and twist with that strangely bitter, ashamed wryness, as if there were a faintly unpleasant flavour in her mouth.

"What did she tell you?"

"All about her marriage to Max. She was seventeen when she met him and still at school. She ran away from home to join him in London. To listen to her, you'd've thought she was describing some wonderful romance, the sort of story you read in women's magazines—love at first sight and happy ever after," she said, with the same tone of disparaging mockery she had spoken Eustace Quinn's name.

Romance. For some reason, the word stuck in Rudd's mind although he couldn't think why. It became mixed up with other images: Alice in Wonderland and the fairy-story princess, tales from his childhood and the sweet innocence of their illustrations which, in turn, were overlaid by the more recent images of Zoe's and Lilith's naked bodies seen through Max Gifford's eyes.

Suddenly, without any warning and taking him totally by surprise, his thoughts occupied elsewhere, Blanche Lester began running, her white dress and black hair streaming out behind her like a maenad's as she fled towards the ramped path that led up to the entrance to the underground station. Rudd set off in pursuit but, after a short distance, abandoned the idea. It was hopeless attempting to catch up with her. The last glimpse he caught of her before she disappeared into the home-going crowds was the pale flicker of her dress against the railings.

Well, it couldn't be helped. If necessary, he could always interview her again, although he suspected she had told him all she knew and that her sudden flight had been caused by a desire to escape not so much from him and his questions as from herself.

He strolled towards the exit, taking his time. Tomorrow was Sunday so there was no chance of interviewing any of the people on Miss Martin's list; not even Bruce Lawford whose name, with its maddening but unidentified familiarity, occurred to him again. Never mind. On Monday, he'd get Boyce and Kyle, possibly Marsh as well, to come up to town and see each individual in turn. That way the man's identity ought to be discovered. He'd also ask Boyce to set in motion an inquiry into Nina Gifford's past, for, as he'd already be in London, the Sergeant could start at the Records Office on a simple check of a few basic facts about her, such as the exact date of Max Gifford's divorce from Zoe Hamilton and his subsequent marriage to her.

As for himself, he'd drop in at Althorpe House, making the visit look casual, and show Nina Max's sketches in order to see just what her reaction would be. With any luck, he might even get to the bottom of her relationship with Danny Webb at the same time.

Which reminded him that, while he was in London, there was one more move he could make regarding Danny Webb and that was to call in at Scotland Yard and check if Webb had a police record, a possibility which had first occurred to him when he had seen him and Nina together in the yard at Althorpe House but which would need verification before he confronted both Danny and Nina with a few uncomfortable facts about themselves and the murder of Eustace Quinn.

CHAPTER 11

Danny woke early, aware that it was Sunday morning. A hangover from childhood, he decided. There had been a special quality then about Sunday mornings, an extra, anticipatory hush about the house as if its atmosphere had thickened and grown more dense during the night. He could always sense it even before the bells began ringing for Communion.

This morning there were no bells; it was too early. All the same, reaching up to pull aside one of the little curtains over the caravan window above the bed he sensed that the garden was holding itself motionless with that familiar, awed expectancy.

Checking his watch, he saw that it was half past six.

Shit! He had meant to be off before there was any chance of Lionel being awake. He was usually up and about by seven, a routine that probably extended into the weekend as well. Lionel was a man of regular habits. He had been out cutting the bloody lawn at quarter to eight one morning, on purpose, Danny suspected, to put to shame his own preference for a lie-in until the pub was open.

Flinging aside the bedclothes, he dressed hurriedly and then began collecting up his scattered possessions, stuffing them into a suitcase and snapping it shut. There was not even bloody time to shave or make coffee.

At the door, he paused and then, smiling to himself, tramped across the bed, deliberately grinding his feet into the sheets, and switched on the boiling ring. With any luck it would be hours before Lionel discovered it had been left burning.

Outside, he eyed the back of the cottage speculatively. To reach the road, he'd have to crunch his way along the shingled drive. The bedroom curtains were still drawn, which probably meant Lionel wasn't yet up although Danny wasn't prepared to risk it. Better to make off across the fields, he decided. He could get to Nina's through the shrubbery gate and sit it out in the summerhouse until he could contact her. He might even shove a note through the letter box telling her where he was so he wouldn't be kept hanging about for too long. He was down to his last three cigarettes and he didn't relish having to wait without fags indefinitely.

In the event, he couldn't send the note. He had no bloody pen or pencil on him, he discovered when he reached the summerhouse. Going through his pockets, he laid the contents out on the bench. Cigarette packet and lighter—the one he'd nicked from the bar of the Feathers; well, people ought to take more care of their belongings—the key to his room at the Dolphin which he hadn't bothered to return, a crumpled handkerchief, a letter from some woman in Clapham, and two pounds and forty-nine pence.

He tore the letter into pieces, carrying them outside in the cupped palms of his hands before tossing them into the air to let the upward draught carry them away—little white scraps of paper that fluttered for a few moments and then sank to the damp grass like broken-winged butterflies. The money he doled out along the wooden slats of the bench seat, weighting the notes down with the key and piling up the silver and copper coins into two little stacks. But no sodding pen. Flinging himself back against the rough timber wall, he folded his arms moodily and settled down to wait.

Nina got up at eight o'clock, her thoughts on Danny but unaware of his proximity. After all, she hadn't been able, as she had intended, to see him on Friday after Rudd had left. That evening Max had claimed all her attention, calling her upstairs on various pretexts, like a child who, unable to sleep, doesn't see why the grown-ups shouldn't be equally discommoded. By the time she had finally settled him down, it was too late to set off for Lionel's and, besides, she had felt too tired to make the effort.

She had dropped by instead on Saturday morning, telling Max that she was going to the village shop, but Danny had been out. Lionel had met her in the garden, bustling out of the house to waylay her the moment she turned the corner but with none of his usual signs of pleasure. In fact, he had been quite cool and offhand towards her. Probably the memory of that stupid business between herself and Eustace Quinn still rankled even though Quinn was now dead. Or he was annoyed with Danny and was punishing him through her, an interpretation that seemed justified by the air of quiet triumph with which Lionel announced that Danny was out and he, Lionel, had no idea when he would be back.

As far as he was concerned, the later the better, his tone implied.

Oh, sod you, then, Nina had thought, cycling home. Who cares anyway?

But she was more distressed than she had at first cared to admit. Lionel's defection was added to her general disquiet, augmenting it and at the same time distracting it towards yet another source of worry without diminishing its other causes: Eustace Quinn's murder, of course, and Max, but mainly Danny.

Danny was up to something. Nina had been aware of that as she had talked to him in the yard on Friday. Trouble had been written all over him. In a confused way, she had tried to get to the bottom of it but, exhausted mentally and psychologically by the events of the past few days, she had been unable to think it through properly or put her finger on its exact cause. Danny had been uneasy and tense, that much was certain, and the reason wasn't difficult to find: it had been Rudd's presence. Which was perfectly understandable. She had long ago realised that Danny had probably got on the wrong side of the law at some stage in his life and, besides, he had always, even as a young child, resented authority of any kind. So when it came down to it, she was worrying unnecessarily, she told herself.

All the same, her fears had been only partially quietened and she had brooded for the rest of the day, although she had made no further attempt to get in touch with Danny. It would only give Lionel another opportunity for showing his disapproval and she was damned if she was going to allow him that satisfaction.

In his turn, Lionel thought of Nina as he did most of the time, her presence so real in his mind on occasion that, opening a door or turning a corner, he was surprised not to find her actually there. She seemed to overflow her own immediate environment into his, taking up residence in a manner so pervasive that even the most ordinary, everyday objects seemed to be impregnated with her aura.

His Sunday breakfast egg was a trivial and slightly ridiculous example. Cracking it delicately on the rim of the frying pan before sliding it into the hot fat, Lionel remembered whisking up eggs for Nina on Friday, the day Eustace Quinn's body was discovered, and how, as he stood at the table, she had brushed past him on her way to the sink. Her arms were the colour of the shell, brown and faintly speckled, with the same light sheen polishing the porous surface.

It is all quite absurd! he thought, gently transferring the egg to the center of his plate between the crisply curled slices of bacon and the two halves of grilled tomato. The egg seemed to stare back at him, a round, yellow eye into which he dug his fork with sudden savagery.

I am obsessed by her. And then, It's got to stop.

It was no use telling himself that he must keep aloof from her. He had tried that yesterday, in an attempt to distance her, but misunderstanding his reasons, she had been hurt and finally angry, leaving him with a careless I-don't-give-a-damn fling of her shoulders, dismissive and contemptuous. She hadn't been near the cottage since, not even to call on Danny, an omission for which Lionel was profoundly grateful. He really didn't want to see either of them again. Certainly not Danny; the sooner he left the better. Nina, too, although her absence would be a bereavement as well as a relief.

A lot of the trouble was, he admitted, carrying his plate over to the sink where he left it to soak in hot water, bacon and eggs stains being a nuisance to remove once they had gone cold, that he no longer trusted her. She had come down to earth with a wallop in his estimation—no less desirable but a lot less admirable. Her deviousness distressed him.

Danny was no good. Surely Nina could see that? Whatever their relationship was, and Lionel was beginning to doubt he was the family friend as Nina pretended, Danny's true character must be obvious to her. Absolutely No Good. To emphasise the words, Lionel sent three little jets of washing-up liquid squirting into the bowl of hot, clean water before un-buttoning his cuffs and folding back his shirt sleeves.

As for Eustace Quinn . . .   And here Lionel rested his hands on the bottom of the bowl and stared bleakly out through the window over the sink, remembering with a deep sense of shame that brief glimpse through another kitchen window when he had witnessed them standing together in such close intimacy; shame for his own sake at finding himself in the role of Peeping Tom but shame mostly for her.

She had been sexually aroused. Lionel had been perfectly well aware of that. There had been a strange, glistening quality about her eyes and mouth and her body had been soft and slack as if ready to yield itself to Eustace Quinn's embrace.

The memory dirtied his own fantasies about her—vague dreams of lying with Nina in his arms, never clearly imagined because that would presuppose Max's death and Lionel did not wish for that. But there had been many nights when, half waking, half sleeping, he had turned in bed to imagine Nina beside him and had sought her mouth in the darkness.

Quinn's death had done nothing to erase the memory of Nina's be-trayal, not just of Max, although that was bad enough, but of his own longings for her.

About the same time, Nina carried Max's breakfast tray upstairs. Like Danny, she had never cared for Sundays. Her memories were of going to church twice during the day and the aching boredom of sitting on a hard, polished pew or kneeling on a hassock that appeared to be stuffed with sawdust. Aunt Connie had insisted on her wearing hat, gloves, and stockings even in the hottest weather.

"You behave and dress like a hoyden for the rest of the week," she used to say. "At least look like a lady on Sundays."

As if God cared! Nina had imagined Him, lolling somewhere above their heads, elbow resting on a cloud, as He looked down on them sar-donically, amused by her own po-shaped velour hat and Aunt Connie's black felt one skewered viciously to her head with a long pin, and winc-ing as their voices wavered uncertainly upward, slightly out of tempo with the asthmatic organ pumping along half a beat behind.

"O worship the King, all glorious above!"

It had seemed to Nina that God would much prefer them to fling off all their clothes and dance joyously round the church. He would want them to be happy, not stiff and unforgiving like Aunt Connie or serious like father, climbing up into the pulpit and peering at them over the rims of his spectacles with an expression of sad, tried patience as they coughed and rustled before settling down to listen to his sermon.

Nina hadn't given God much thought for years but Sundays still bore a special quality for her. In the old days, when she and Max lived in London, they had always gone out somewhere different on a Sunday, ei-ther to the country or to some pub in an unexplored part of the city, Wapping or Ealing or Crouch End, where she had been noisier than usual, laughing and talking too much because the Sabbath streets had reminded her of home. Max had never guessed or asked the reason although she had seen him looking at her curiously at times, amused by her animation.

Today, it was like a real Sunday, quiet, subdued, with nothing much to look forward to. She hadn't the energy to sparkle and Max was equally apathetic. It seemed as if he had suddenly grown old, the process of senescence accelerated like one of those speeded-up films so that she could almost witness the decay taking place before her eyes. Today he no longer seemed to have the interest even to maintain his old, maddening pretences. Entering his bedroom, she saw he was lying awake, his hands resting listlessly on top of the bedclothes, his eyes open and staring at the opposite wall.

Overwhelmed by his sadness, which seemed to surround him like a palisade through which she could no longer penetrate and conscious of how alone, in fact, she was, she thought of all those huge, empty rooms stretching out beneath her with no one to keep her company. It was a foretaste of what it would be like when he was dead, although she couldn't express it in so many words. She just thought of it as "when Max is gone."

Longing suddenly for his company, she said coaxingly, "Come downstairs this morning, Max. You could sit in the garden. Look, it's lovely out!"

Going over to the window, she flung out an arm, as if introducing him, for the first time, to the view: the clear, early sunlight reflecting glassily on leaves and blades of grass, the soaring blue sky, very far away this morning, a bowl of pale, fragile porcelain.

Max stopped chewing and, bending his head, looked at her from under his eyebrows with the same sad, peering intensity with which her father had surveyed his congregation and she couldn't bear it. Letting her arm drop, she turned away.

"No, I don't think I'll bother," he replied. "I'm better off in bed. And I don't want any more of this breakfast. Why do you always make the fried bread so bloody hard? It's like eating charcoal."

There was a petulance in his voice and she took the tray without comment, noticing with a little surge of anger that he had nevertheless managed to spoil all the food on his plate. Everything would have to be thrown away for she didn't fancy eating his leftovers; odd, she thought, when she considered the other things she did for him without the slightest sense of revulsion.

Later, when she had got him washed and settled down again in bed, she carried the plate into the kitchen and, as she scraped the food into the bin, her exasperation returned.

All that waste! she thought furiously. But then, *he* doesn't have to worry about making ends meet.

If only something wonderful would happen!

At that exact moment, as if in answer to her wish, a car turned into the yard. Then she saw, with a sense of foreboding, Rudd in his old, crumpled macintosh clamber out of the driving seat and approach the house.

Danny saw the car, too. He had come to the edge of the lawn on several occasions to survey the house but each time the curtains at the upstairs window facing him had been drawn. Although he wasn't sure whose bedroom it was, Nina's or Max's, it was obvious that it was still too early to risk going up to the house and trying to attract Nina's attention. Retreating to the summerhouse, he had prepared himself for a longer wait. If only she'd bloody hurry up! he thought. He was down to his last cigarette which he took several times out of the packet before reluctantly returning it.

On the last occasion, the curtains had been open and he saw Nina at the window, talking to someone inside the room; Max, he assumed. She was standing in half-profile, looking back over her shoulder, one arm extended, but she had turned away and was gone before he could attract her attention. At least, he now knew that she was up. Give her a quarter of an hour, he decided, and he'd stroll round to the back of the house where he'd probably find her in the kitchen.

While he waited, he smoked his last cigarette, pitching the stub out onto the grass where it lay smouldering, a thin line of smoke going straight up into the windless air.

The sight of the car in the yard stopped him in his tracks just as he reached the corner and he backed away hurriedly, checking the facade of the house to make sure no one had seen him. This side, thank God, appeared uninhabited. On the ground floor, a series of heavily barred windows, some of them with frosted glass in their lower panes, suggested little-used pantries and storerooms. The windows above were blank.

Christ! What the hell do I do now? he thought furiously. He didn't dare hang about. Although the arrival of the car might be perfectly harmless, a Sunday visitor calling on Nina, he couldn't guarantee it. Nor could he be sure that more vehicles might not arrive at any moment, bringing back the police to resume their search of the grounds.

Get out while the going's good, he told himself. It had been bad enough coming face to face with that Inspector, Rudd or whatever his name was, on Friday. Since then they'd had another whole day in which to turn up God knows what evidence.

Turning away from the yard, he walked rapidly across the lawn, keeping well out of sight of the house and, crossing an overgrown vegetable garden, he found a gap in the hedge through which he squeezed before setting off across the fields.

The back door was open and Rudd knocked at it briefly before entering the kitchen, which, he noticed, had reverted to its normal state of untidiness, the various packets and pieces of cooking equipment that Lionel Burnett had so painstakingly put away on Friday again littering the table and work tops.

Nina Gifford, too, looked more unkempt. She was dressed in an old denim skirt gone baggy at the knees and backside, the gingham blouse, which he remembered her wearing on Friday, hanging loose outside it, its neck open and the sleeves rolled up to reveal the firm, brown flesh of her throat and arms. He was struck again by her physical magnificence, the wealth of dark red hair, bundled back anyhow but possessing its own life and vigour. He could see why Eustace Quinn had been attracted; possibly Lionel Burnett as well—Rudd hadn't yet had the chance to inquire into that relationship.

How many other men had been drawn to her? Rudd wondered. Perhaps this was the secret that Blanche Lester was meant to discover. Although she had spoken of Nina as "Max's woman," it did not necessarily imply that the Giffords' marriage had been exclusive. But so far, Rudd hadn't been able to establish exactly why Quinn had been so interested in Nina's past.

Was it blackmail? Looking round the shabby kitchen, it was difficult to believe that this had been his motive. But perhaps his reasoning had been more subtle. Judging by the evidence that Rudd had so far uncovered, Quinn had intended making himself a sizeable profit from Max Gifford's exhibition. Supposing he had planned to use Nina's influence over Max to persuade him to sell the pictures still in his possession at a deflated price or to accept a lower percentage on the sale of them?

That made better sense, he thought. Nina, then, under Quinn's threat of revealing something about her past that she didn't want Max to know about, might have killed him rather than submit to his pressure. He had already proved she could have had the opportunity. That line of reasoning would give her a motive as well.

"What do you want?" Nina asked. She was still standing by the waste-bin, holding Max's plate, and, with a gesture of impatience, she rattled it down on the draining board among yesterday's unwashed supper things. In the few moments in which Rudd had got out of the car and entered the house, she had regained some of her composure. He was alone, which seemed to suggest it wasn't an official visit and that in itself was a relief, a lowering of tension that allowed her anxiety to turn to anger, the exasperation she had felt towards Max projecting itself against the stocky, round-shouldered figure of the Chief Inspector who came ambling into her kitchen as if he were one of the family.

The bloody nerve of it!

"Sorry to bother you on a Sunday but I was passing and I thought I'd drop in," Rudd explained, his excuse ready. "How's Max?"

"A bit better but I don't want you worrying him," Nina retorted, springing immediately to Max's defence.

Oh, yes, Rudd thought, she'd be quite capable of clobbering someone if she lost her temper. There was fire there all right. And the physical strength as well.

"I don't intend to," he assured her, smiling and indicating a chair as much as to say, Do you mind if I sit down?—an unspoken appeal to which Nina acquiesced grudgingly. But I'm damned if I'm going to offer him tea, she added to herself.

Once seated at the table, Rudd seemed to settle himself down for a chat, nodding towards the window and commenting on the weather, at the same time feeling slowly through the pockets of his raincoat as if looking for some mislaid but not very important object. When he finally found it and laid it on the table in front of him, it turned out to be nothing more than a plain, square, manila envelope.

As he opened it, he continued in the same gossipy style, "By the way, we found these in Mr. Quinn's briefcase. I wonder if you could help me identify them."

The casualness of the remark left Nina totally unprepared for the sudden appearance of the sketches that she had given to Danny and that Rudd now placed on the table before her among the homely muddle of trivial, domestic objects: the bowl of sugar, a jar of coffee granules, and Max's empty tray still speckled with his breakfast crumbs.

She stared down at the top drawing, a sketch of Lilith, aware that her colour was rising and that her silence had stretched beyond normal hesitation.

"They're Max's," she said at last. What else could she say? She couldn't deny knowledge of that obvious fact.

"Do you know how Eustace Quinn might have got hold of them?"

"I've no idea," she replied, too quickly this time and, feeling this was inadequate, continued, "Perhaps Max gave them to him. Or he took them without asking."

She added the rider deliberately, aware of the pitfalls her first explanation led her into. Rudd might insist on questioning Max, which would, of course, reveal that he knew nothing about them. At least, there was no way Rudd could check on Eustace Quinn's actions.

To her relief, Rudd appeared satisfied with this response for, gathering up the sketches, he returned them to the envelope which he replaced in his pocket. His expression as he got to his feet was bland, giving nothing away.

"That's all then, Mrs. Gifford, for the moment," he remarked pleasantly. "I'm sorry I had to call on a Sunday. I'll leave you in peace now."

Peace! Nina thought as she watched his car reverse and drive out of the yard. Now he had gone, she had the opportunity to consider more carefully the implications behind his visit. Danny and Eustace Quinn were connected in some way. That much was obvious. If Rudd had found the sketches in Eustace Quinn's possession, then it could only mean that, directly or indirectly, he had acquired them from Danny. And once that link was made, it opened up all kinds of other terrifying possibilities she hardly dared think about rationally and which only expressed themselves in sudden, quick fears, darting through her mind like the shadows of fish seen at the bottom of a dark pond.

First there was Danny's anxiety and tension on Friday—in fact, the whole reason behind his visit, for she no longer believed that he had come to the house on her account. Then there was his absence from the caravan on Friday morning when she had gone to Lionel's to telephone the police after discovering Eustace Quinn's body. Added to this was

Danny's chronic shortage of money, his leaving London, her feeling that he was in some kind of trouble . . .

Oh, God! There seemed no end to it. But out of all the confusion, one thought stood out clearly. She'd have to warn him. So far, it seemed unlikely that Rudd knew how Eustace Quinn had got hold of the drawings but he might not remain in ignorance for long. She must get to Danny before he did.

Running into the hall, intending to call up the stairs to Max, she changed her mind. He would only delay her and, with a little luck, she'd be back before he missed her. Instead, she fetched her bike from the stable and, without even stopping to close the back door behind her, she cycled off down the drive.

While the interview with Nina was still proceeding, Lionel came out of the cottage carrying a full watering can, which he held awkwardly away from himself so that it wouldn't come into contact with the trousers of his best suit. He was dressed for church but, since changing his clothes, he had noticed the fuchsias were flagging in their pots and had decided to water them. Later, the sun would be on them and to water then would risk causing leaf scorch.

Tipping the can carefully so as not to swamp them, he watched the water soak down into the soil and imagined, with a small, wry smile at his own fanciful extravagance, that he could hear the little, fibrous roots sucking it in. From them, it would be siphoned upward, circulating gently like clear plasma through the complex, upright tubes of the stems and into the narrow veins in the leaves. Squatting down beside the last tub, he fondled one of the shoots gently, feeling the thin, green flesh cool under his fingertips.

As he straightened up, he glanced towards the end of the garden, wondering if Danny was awake yet and noticed the half-drawn curtain, although its significance did not strike him particularly. What caught his attention was the sun shining on some broken glass at the foot of the steps where a beer bottle, rolling off the top of the box crammed with empties, had smashed on the flagstones. Its dark shards glittered wickedly.

It's really too bad, Lionel thought, and, compressing his lips angrily, he set off up the garden, determined to have it out with Danny. This time, Nina or no, he would make it clear that the arrangement would have to come to an end. Danny must go by next Saturday at the latest.

He stooped to pick up the broken glass, placing it in the carton, before mounting the steps and knocking at the caravan door. Getting no answer, he pushed it open and entered, fully expecting to find Danny still in bed.

The interior was in semidarkness and smelt quite dreadful, an odour of stale bedding mingled with sour milk and rotting food. It was also stifling hot, a condition he couldn't account for until he saw the bright orange coil of the electric boiling ring glowing fiercely at the far end. Nostrils pinched together, he swept aside the curtains to reveal the full extent of Danny's depredations.

For a moment, he couldn't absorb it all and he was aware only of a general confusion and squalor, bedclothes flung about, dirty plates and cups everywhere, the tiny kitchen littered with God knows what filth.

His sense of shock and outrage was similar, he imagined, to that which victims of a burglary must experience, not just against their possessions but against their own persons. It was a kind of rape.

As the shock passed, it was replaced by anger. How dare he? How bloody well dare he?

Lips trembling, Lionel clambered across the bed to switch off the electric ring, aware for the first time of the details of Danny's pillage: the ground-in dirt and grit on the sheets, the long, brown scars on the edges of the furniture where cigarettes had been left burning, the ash and stains fouling the carpet. Where the boiling ring had been standing, the plastic-coated counter top had buckled with the heat and the sink was filthy with grease and scraps of food, while the smell emanated, he discovered, from a small regiment of empty tins and unwashed milk bottles clustered together on the draining board.

It could all be put back in order, of course, the carpet shampooed, the rubbish thrown away, the burn scars sanded out and varnished over, but that wasn't the point. It would be a long time before he could feel at ease in the place again. Mere scrubbing and repainting wouldn't erase Danny's presence. Nor did he have any intention of beginning on it today. There was something else he had to do first; another and more important exorcism.

Returning to the house, he spread out his portfolio on the floor of his bedroom where his art materials were temporarily housed and, from the back of it, removed a small collection of drawings from their separate paper folder. They were all of Nina, quick sketches made when she was unaware of what he was doing although some he had worked up later into proper portraits, tinted in with water-colours—Nina laughing, head flung back; Nina pensive, resting her chin on one hand. Shuffling quickly through them, he could remember each occasion when he had made them. In this one, Nina had been asleep in a deck chair in the garden, high summer with the leaves forming a dense, green background. In the next, she had been bending down to talk to Max one evening, although Max wasn't present in the drawing—just her, with her hair slipping loose and catching the light in fiery points of colour.

None of them were very good. Lionel had seen more of Max's sketches of her and had realised that, compared to those, his own were amateurish. But they were all he had; these and the notes that, over the years, she had pushed through his letter box, finding him out when she called. Scrawled on any scrap of paper she happened to have on her, they could hardly be called love letters. He glanced at them again. Requests to come round to help Max out of the bath; she'd borrowed the shears to cut the hedge but she'd bring them back tomorrow; the boiler was leaking, did he know anything about plumbing? All signed, "Love, Nina."

Putting them with the sketches, he tore the lot across the middle and, clutching the pieces in one hand, returned to the garden where, just as he was about to consign them to the incinerator, he heard the crackle of cycle wheels on the drive and had only time to fling them inside, bang the lid on top and scuttle back to the house before Nina came hurrying round the corner and, without so much as a glance at his window, went running up the lawn towards the caravan.

After he left Althorpe House, Rudd turned right at the gate in the direction of the village and drove a little distance along the road before reversing the car into a narrow lane which, according to the fingerpost at its entrance, led to Upfield Farm. A few yards in, he braked and turned off the engine.

The lane opening was obscured by trees but the boundary hedge was low enough to give him an unrestricted view of any traffic passing along the road. After a short wait, he saw what he had been expecting: the head and shoulders of Nina Gifford sailing past with the effortless ease and speed of someone on an unseen bicycle. Allowing her a few minutes' start, he bumped the car slowly down the lane and followed her.

Even if he had not guessed her destination, her bicycle was easily spotted, flung negligently up against the interwoven fence that ran along the side of Lionel Burnett's driveway where, in her haste to get to Danny, she had abandoned it. Burnett's car was standing in the drive, suggesting he was at home, and, as Rudd edged sideways past it, he could only hope to God that Burnett would have the sense to make himself scarce.

Lionel, who was keeping well back out of sight behind the kitchen window, had no intention of interfering. First Nina's arrival, followed so quickly by the Chief Inspector's, indicated that something was afoot in which he had no doubt Danny was also implicated and Lionel had no wish to be drawn into it.

Let them sort it out among themselves, he told himself, although he grieved for Nina's sake.

All the same, his concern for her did not prevent him from putting on his jacket and, as soon as the coast was clear, letting himself out quietly by the front door; too early by nearly three quarters of an hour for matins but he preferred to sit in the porch outside the church to remaining in the cottage and risk a confrontation with either Nina or Rudd.

CHAPTER 12

Entering the caravan and finding Danny was not there, Nina was more concerned with the absence of his possessions about the place than its state of confusion, to which, in the first frantic moments after her arrival, she added by flinging aside the already tumbled bedclothes and opening cupboards and drawers in the built-in units in an attempt to find something belonging to him.

Nothing. Not even a pair of shoes or his razor.

It was at this point that Rudd arrived, mounting the steps to stand in the open doorway, blocking the light, and she turned quickly towards him, her face distraught, momentarily forgetting who he was in her need to confide in someone.

"Danny's gone!" she announced.

"Has he now?" Rudd said and stepped inside.

Suddenly aware of the significance of his arrival, Nina plumped down onto the bed and burst into tears.

Rudd kept his distance, waiting for the storm of emotion to wear itself out and looking about him at the squalor. Danny had certainly left his mark on the place. From time to time, he allowed his gaze to rest on her with a professional objectivity, like a doctor observing a patient's symptoms. She was crouching on the low bed, her hands over her face so that only the top of her head was visible, her knees spread out in order to take the weight of her elbows, in the awkward, clumsy posture of a woman who, given over entirely to grief, no longer cares what she looks like.

Rudd's cool gaze, however, disguised more emotion than he cared to show. Never at ease with other people's tears, especially a woman's, he felt totally inadequate, a reluctant voyeur of emotions he knew he was partly responsible for but which, as a professional policeman, he had to learn to observe impassively.

Presently, her grief subsided into little gasping sobs and she lifted her face.

"I haven't got a hanky," she confessed, wiping the back of her hand under her eyes and sniffing deeply.

Rudd passed her his as he took a seat beside her on the bed, still taking care to leave plenty of room between them. She rubbed it harshly over her face as if scrubbing away the last dregs of emotion as well as the tears and then sat quietly, waiting for him to begin, the crumpled hand-kerchief in her lap.

"The sketches," Rudd said simply.

"I gave them to Danny," she admitted. "He was hard up and I thought he could sell them and raise a bit of cash for himself. I hadn't any money to give him."

"Did Max know?"

"No, I took them without asking. I didn't think he'd miss them. He's got hundreds and he hadn't looked at them for months."

"When was this?"

"Just after Christmas. Danny turned up one day and I gave him four. A few weeks later, he wrote asking if I'd got any others and I posted a couple more to him."

"I see. Go on."

She was silent for a few seconds before replying ingenuously, "I can't think of anything else."

"Can't you, Mrs. Gifford?"

"Only that Danny had nothing to do with Eustace Quinn's death, if that's what you're thinking. He can't have done!"

She seemed close to tears again and Rudd replied with deliberate brusqueness, the verbal equivalent of the slap round the face recommended in cases of hysteria, "He knew Eustace Quinn."

It was her worst fear and, now that it was out in the open, she was able to confront it with more courage than she had thought possible.

"I don't care. It doesn't make any difference. I know Danny didn't do it."

There was a stubborn, unyielding quality about her which, although Rudd had grudgingly to admire, he had somehow to break down.

"You realise Eustace Quinn wanted to meet Max because of the sketches?"

"Yes, I know that now."

"Which he'd bought from Danny?"

She admitted that, too. His questions bore down on her like stones, each one adding its own weight so that she felt suffocated by their burden.

"And did you also know that Danny had a police record?"

Rudd threw that in for good measure although, in fact, the sum total of this evidence was a charge of careless driving for which he had been fined and the suspicion only that he had been involved in a used-car fraud in which nothing had been proved, but Rudd had no intention of telling her this.

"I'd guessed," she replied humbly and seemed oddly grateful that this, too, could now be admitted.

"And you still think he had nothing to do with Quinn's death?"

"Yes!" she cried passionately. "Because I know him!"

"Ah." Rudd sounded satisfied as if he had at last reached the point he wanted. "How well do you know him, Mrs. Gifford? A little better than a family friend, I think. Am I right?"

"He's my brother."

The information should not have surprised him although it did. It was the one relationship that hadn't occurred to him when he had discussed the matter with Boyce.

Now that she had confessed it, she seemed eager to explain, to excuse, perhaps even to talk her way out of it for Danny's sake.

"He's much younger than me and I suppose he's always been difficult, even as a child, but never really wicked. You must believe that. You see, my mother died when he was born and he was brought up by an aunt, my father's sister. She'd never married and I don't think she understood young children. Besides, she had to give up her job—she was a maths teacher in a girls' school—to look after us and she resented it."

"Couldn't your father afford a housekeeper?" Rudd asked.

"God, no! He's a country parson. Or rather he was—he's retired now. And anyway, Aunt Connie looked on it as her duty. At least, that's what she was always telling us. 'I've tried to do my duty by you children.'"

And probably enjoyed the martyrdom, Rudd commented silently. He had known women like her who never allowed the obligation owing to them to be forgotten and who spent their lives eaten up by bitterness and resentment.

"Part of the trouble was she disapproved of my father's marriage," Nina continued. "You see, my mother was years younger than him, a local girl he'd met when he was vicar of another parish and Aunt Connie thought he'd been a fool to marry her."

Like mother, like daughter? Rudd wondered. It was strange that, in speaking of her mother's marriage to a man older than herself, Nina Gifford did not appear to make any comparison with her own.

Lifting her shoulders as if expressing the inevitability of it all, she added, "So Danny grew up without any real love except what I could give him and perhaps"—and here she looked down into her lap at the wet handkerchief which she was turning over and over in her hands—"it wasn't the sort of love he really needed."

"How old were you?"

"When my mother died? Nine. As long as I can remember, I always wanted to be like her—a mother to Danny, I mean. But I don't think I was very good at it."

"It wasn't an easy role for a child to play," Rudd pointed out in her defence.

She shrugged again with that hopeless gesture but didn't answer him.

"What about your father?"

"Oh, Dad! I suppose he did his best but he was over forty when Danny was born and he didn't want to be bothered. We were left to our own devices a lot of the time." Smiling at the memory of it, she looked Rudd in the face as if challenging him with their old, childhood misdemeanours. "It was Danny and me against Dad and Aunt Connie. I don't think they knew half of what we got up to when we were on our own."

Under the circumstances it was understandable, even forgivable behaviour, but a dangerous path, all the same, for Danny, and perhaps even Nina Gifford herself, to have started out on all those years before. No wonder Danny Webb had turned out to be the man he was—immature, resentful of authority, and yet too weak to stand on his own feet for long, still relying, like a child, on his elder sister to help him out of his difficulties. Whether or not his criminal tendencies had led him as far as murder remained to be proved and, with this in mind, Rudd decided not to tell her that Danny's alibi did not cover the time of Eustace Quinn's death. He hardly needed to rub her nose in the fact that the evidence against Webb was mounting up, quite satisfactorily from his point of view. Instead, he remarked as he rose to go,

"I suppose you have no idea where he is?"

"I wouldn't be here now if I did!" she flashed back at him.

Which was exactly Rudd's own assumption.

"By the way," he added at the door, "if Danny should turn up, tell him to be sensible and come along to talk to me. Don't try to hide him. If necessary, I could always get a search warrant, you know."

The warning, casually stated, was nevertheless not lost on her, for Rudd saw her look of alarm as he turned and walked down the steps.

She'd be a fool if she did give him shelter; not that Rudd would put it past her. Her kind of loyalty would stop at nothing, and he was prepared, if need be, to carry out his threat and turn Althorpe House over from attic to cellar. He'd certainly arrange for a panda car to patrol up and down the road in front of the house as a warning to her and her brother, should he still be hanging about the neighbourhood, that he meant business.

At the foot of the steps he paused to button up his coat, for the morning, despite the sunshine, had a late spring chill in it. As he stood there, a flicker of white on the far side of the garden caught his attention—a piece of paper trapped under the rim of the lid covering an incinerator which stood, decently hidden from the house behind a trellis, on a little flagstoned patch. His curiosity aroused by its frantic waving which seemed to be signalling to him, Rudd walked across and released it. The right half of Nina Gifford's face looked back at him from the torn sheet. With a rapid backward glance at the caravan to make sure he wasn't being observed, he took off the lid and plunged in his hand, coming up with a fistful of scraps which he transferred surreptitiously to his pocket before continuing on his way to his car.

Seated inside it, he examined them. They were all drawings of Nina, torn across the middle, some halves of which fitted together to make up the whole portrait. Lionel Burnett's work, Rudd decided. Even he could tell they were amateurish. Mixed up with them were pieces of letters, or rather rough, scribbled notes, sent, he assumed, by Nina to Lionel, judging by the names on the bits he had salvaged.

Interesting, Rudd thought as he smoothed out the creases before putting the fragments into his wallet for safekeeping. They suggested that Lionel Burnett's feeling for Nina Gifford extended far beyond normal attraction. There was something obsessional about them, especially the preserved notes. Would any ordinary lover bother to keep a woman's scrawled messages, particularly on such mundane subjects? The words "boiler" and "plumbing" featured on one; another seemed to be concerned with a pair of shears.

And why, having preserved them, had Lionel Burnett decided to destroy them? Unless, of course, he had finished with Nina Gifford and, in that case, the reason wasn't difficult to find. Burnett himself had let part of that particular cat out of the bag when he had spoken of Eustace Quinn's familiarity, presumably with Nina Gifford, and it again crossed the Chief Inspector's mind that Burnett had witnessed something of Quinn's deliberate flirtation with Nina when he had called at Althorpe House on Thursday evening. It made sense and it added up also to a possible motive for murder, farfetched though it might seem. But a man who made drawings of the woman he loved and hoarded up any scrap of her writing could hardly be judged as normal.

He'd discuss it with Boyce later, Rudd decided, starting up the car and driving away, although he could imagine the Sergeant's reaction. As far as love was concerned, Boyce's attitude was of the earth, earthly: regular meals and clean shirts in exchange for the housekeeping money with an occasional bunch of flowers awkwardly proffered, and sex twice a week with the light off. There was nothing as highfalutin as the word "romance" in his entire vocabulary.

Nina heard the sound of his car retreating and it brought a little relief. At least he'd gone. She was still seated on the bed, nursing his handkerchief in her lap, thinking about Danny and what on earth she could do for him now. The answer was nothing. Danny had passed out of the range of both her love and her assistance. All that remained was the squalor he had created.

And God, what a mess he had left behind him! Lionel would be furious if he saw it and would blame her for having introduced Danny in the first place. She'd have to do something about clearing it up, which was better, anyway, than simply sitting there brooding.

She began by stripping the bed of its sheets and rolling them up into a bundle, finding one of Danny's dirty socks mixed up with them which she stuffed into her skirt pocket along with Rudd's handkerchief before shaking out the blankets and folding back the bed into the sofa shape it assumed for daytime use.

The floor underneath was filthy with spent cigarette ends and old fluff, and, suddenly defeated by it all, she couldn't bring herself to make any further attempt at coping. Besides, to do the job properly, she'd need hot water and a scrubbing brush as well as detergents, scouring powder, and plastic sacks for collecting up the rubbish.

Searching among the confusion, she found a pen—Danny's, in fact—and a reasonably clean brown paper bag, which she tore open before writing a letter to Lionel on its inner surface, forming the words neatly and legibly instead of dashing off her normal scrawl in the first, small gesture of reconciliation.

"Dear Lionel, I'm so sorry about the mess Danny has made of the caravan but I'll come back this afternoon and clean it all up. Please forgive both of us. Danny has run away because the police are looking for him but don't say anything to Max as it would upset him. I'm very worried about him. Sorry again abaout everything but I promise to put it right. Love Nina. P.S. Could I borrow a bucket? I don't think I explained, by the way, that Danny is my brother."

Taking the note with her, she pushed it through Lionel's letter box before cramming the bed sheets into the basket on the front of her bicycle and setting off for home.

Max didn't seem to have missed her, thank God. At least, he made no comment when she took up his midmorning cup of coffee. As for the rest of the morning, she passed it as best she could, putting the sheets in to soak while she cooked luncheon, trying to keep at bay her concern for Danny, although there were occasions when it overwhelmed her. The only comfort she could find was in the thought that he had gone—to London, she hoped, where there would be little chance of Rudd finding him. What he'd do for money she had no idea. He'd probably write to her eventually. And perhaps, by then, Eustace Quinn's murderer would be found and Danny would be all right. "All right"—it seemed an absurdly inadequate phrase and, deep down, she realised that Danny would never really be all right.

She longed to talk about it with someone. Max, of course, was out of the question, but perhaps this afternoon when she saw Lionel that, too, would be "all right" and Lionel would listen as he used to do in the past, nodding his head judiciously from time to time and finding something comfortable and comforting to say to her.

But when she returned to the cottage after lunch, she found Lionel was out and both the house and the caravan were locked against her. The barring of the caravan was meant to be a deliberate snub, she realised. Lionel wanted nothing to do with her or her peace offering.

In fact, had she known it, Lionel, returning home from matins and finding her note on the doormat, had decided there and then to absent himself for the whole afternoon and, as a final gesture, had carried her note to the incinerator where he had added it to the other torn-up mementos before setting light to the lot of them.

The fact that Danny was her brother made no difference to his own attitude towards her. She still expected him to join with her in a conspiracy to keep the truth from Max and even her sentence, "I'm very worried about him" contained a characteristic ambivalence for she hadn't made it clear on whose behalf she was concerned, Max's or Danny's. Not that this mattered either. As for Danny's involvement with the police, Lionel could only comment silently to himself that it didn't surprise him in the least.

Having satisfied himself that the flames had done their work, he returned to the house and, after washing his hands thoroughly, got back into his car and drove into Bexford where he treated himself to Sunday lunch and a half bottle of claret at the George Hotel.

Lionel's absence, which Nina realised was as deliberate as his locking of the caravan, grieved her almost as much as Danny's disappearance. It was another form of running away, this time from her, a double loss that she felt with keen bitterness, and, cycling home, it was as much as she could do to hold back the tears.

Everything seemed to be falling to pieces around her; all the old, safe friendships and relationships, which she had imagined would remain immutable for ever, were breaking up. Even the house, as she reentered it, seemed subject to the same decay and she was aware, as she hadn't been since Eustace Quinn's arrival, of the shabbiness of her surroundings.

She heard Max shouting her name as she entered the kitchen, his voice echoing down into the hall with the peremptory abruptness of someone who has been calling for attention for some time. She shouted back, "All right! I'm coming!" with weary exasperation as she toiled up the stairs to his room.

"Where have you been?" he demanded as soon as she entered.

"To Lionel's."

"You might have told me where you were going."

"How the hell could I?" she cried, suddenly furiously angry. "You were bloody well asleep! I left you a note."

It was still propped up, unread, on his bedside table.

She thought he was going to return the anger. His eyes went very bright as they always did just before he lost his temper but instead he held out his arms to her and said in a voice more tender than she had heard him use for years, "What's the matter, Nine?"

She fell onto the bed on top of him, making him grunt as she knocked the breath out of his body and, as he put his arms round her and cradled her close, she could hear him making little crooning noises; like some bloody pigeon, she thought ridiculously and didn't know whether to laugh or cry. In the end, she did both while Max rocked her, stroking back her hair with one of his huge hands—a navvy's not an artist's, as she'd often told him—and finally, when the storm was over, he wiped her face for her on the edge of the sheet.

"Tell me," he coaxed her when she sat upright again but she could only shake her head and answer, "Nothing."

"It's not nothing, Nine."

"I'm tired, that's all."

"Of me?"

"No, of course not."

"Of looking after me, then?"

"Sometimes," she admitted. At least she owed him that piece of honesty. "And the house and the boiler. Don't worry. I'll get over it."

"But it's not been all bad, has it, Nina? Not all the time?"

He was looking, she realised, for assurance of her love, something he had never done before, and she said quickly, "Oh, Max, how could you even ask?"

"There have been good times?"

"Marvellous times."

One in particular came into her mind, so bright and intense that it seemed to be stamped in some glittering substance on her memory: a summer Sunday afternoon years ago when five of them had crammed into someone's Baby Austin and had driven out to the Sussex Downs for a picnic lunch. Afterwards, surfeited with sun and wine, she had fallen asleep on the grass to be awakened by the sound of laughter and had opened her eyes to find Max kneeling in front of her, holding a crown of flowers in his hands. It must have taken him hours to thread the delicate stems together. His thumbnail was stained green with the juices. She had knelt, too, she remembered, at his request, unfastening the ribbon that held her hair back so that it came tumbling loose, and then, the others silent now, Max had placed the crown on her head. It had been a supreme moment for her, the apex of their relationship, as if, in crowning her, Max had also crowned their love for each other.

"Do you remember?" she began and then fell silent. Max had withdrawn again into himself. While she had been kneeling on the grass, wearing her coronet of flowers, where had he been? Not with her, she realised, but somewhere of his own, apart.

He was still holding one of her hands and, as she faltered, he lifted it between both of his and placed it against his chest, but whether to bless or heal some hidden hurt or in unspoken tribute she couldn't decide. His eyes were closed and his face wore that look of exhausted sadness which had become his habitual expression.

She wanted to say something comforting to him about the loss of the exhibition but, feeling it would be an intrusion, she bent instead and kissed his forehead. And as she turned at the door to look back at him, she saw he was lying back against the pillows, his eyes shut and no sign that he was aware either of her presence or of her imminent departure from the room.

The rest of the day dwindled and died. At dusk, she remembered the sheets were still on the line, and as she unpegged them and folded them down into her arms, a rustle in the bushes behind her startled her and she spun round.

And suddenly there was Danny running across the lawn towards her, dropping his suitcase as he ran, and the next moment she was hugging him close to her, the sheets crumpled up between them.

"But where have you been all day?" she asked a little later when they were together in the kitchen. She had closed the door into the hall so that Max couldn't hear them talking and had bundled the creased sheets away on the wheelchair.

"I holed up in some barn across the fields. I was coming here to you when that bloody Inspector turned up. Christ, Nine, I'm famished! Have you got something to eat?"

"There's some meat left over from the joint and some cold potatoes I could fry up."

"Anything'll do. Got any fags as well? I haven't had a cigarette since this morning."

She broke off her preparations for the meal to find the spare packet of

Max's that she kept in the dresser drawer in case he ran out of them when the shop was closed.

"Is this all you've got?" Danny demanded. "Haven't you any decent ones?"

"Sorry, that's all there is, Danny," she replied, stricken by the thought of his disappointment.

"Oh, hell, I suppose they'll have to do then. I was going to the Feathers to buy some only there was a bloody police car patrolling up and down the road."

Nina made no comment, pretending to be busy with the meal, but she felt a surge of anger and fear at the news. Damn Rudd! He certainly hadn't wasted any time in putting on the pressure. One thing was clear: she dare not risk hiding Danny indefinitely. Rudd would almost certainly make good his threat of searching the house. Danny would have to leave, but when or where to she had no idea.

Decide later, she told herself. Get him fed first; that's the most important thing. I'll worry about the rest afterwards.

He ate ravenously, the cigarette he had lit earlier and hadn't had time to finish smouldering in an ashtray at the side of his plate.

She watched him in silence and only when he had finished and pushed the empty plate away from him did she venture to broach the subject.

"About Rudd," she began tentatively.

"What about him?"

"Danny, he's looking for you!"

There was no other way she could think of saying it. However much she wrapped it up in words, the truth would have to come out eventually. Besides, for Danny's sake, it was better that he knew exactly where he stood.

She saw his face go very still and quiet as it always used to when, as a child, he had been faced with irrefutable evidence of some misdemeanour.

"He knows I've cleared out?" he asked.

"Yes."

"Oh, bloody hell!"

"It was my fault, Danny!" she cried. "You see, he came here with those sketches. You know the ones I mean? I thought I'd better warn you he'd got them."

"Don't tell me," Danny interrupted with a little, sneering laugh. "He followed you. For Christ's sake, Nine, it's the oldest bloody trick in the book and you fell for it!"

"I'm sorry," she said humbly. "I just didn't think."

"Well, the harm's done now. What else does he know?"

"He knows you sold Eustace Quinn the sketches and that it was because of them that Quinn wanted to meet Max. Oh, Danny, I think Rudd suspects you might have killed him! You didn't, did you? I know you weren't in the caravan that morning . . ."

"How do you know that?"

"I went to the cottage to phone the police and . . ."

"Does anyone else know?"

"Yes. Lionel."

"That nurk!"

"It was Lionel who told me you weren't there when I called. Danny, where were you?"

"I was down at the Feathers."

"All morning?"

"Yes, of course. I was there when the landlord opened the bloody place up."

It sounded genuine but she had never been able to tell when he was lying or telling the truth.

Before she had time to question him further, he added, "Does Rudd know? About me not being in the caravan, I mean?"

"Yes. He wanted to know about you on Friday afternoon when you came to the house. I said you were down at the pub . . ."

"Shit!" Danny got up violently from the table and began to prowl up and down the kitchen, lighting a new cigarette from the butt of the old one which he pitched at the boiler. "Shut up, Nina," he told her as she started to speak. "I've got to think this out."

But she couldn't remain silent.

"Danny, I've been so terribly worried! Why did you leave London? Has that got anything to do with Eustace Quinn?"

He looked at her with genuine astonishment.

"I told you, I owed some blokes some money."

"Is that true?"

"Yes, for God's sake! What do you want—a bloody signed statement? I got into a poker game and lost more than I meant to. They threatened to send the mob round if I didn't pay up so I cleared out."

"How much?" she asked to check the truth of what he was telling her.

"Three hundred quid."

"But you told me one!" This minor point seemed ridiculously important.

"One! Three! What the hell difference does it make? I still bloody owe it."

Chastened, she sat quietly for a few moments, following him with her eyes as he paced up and down, knowing that the question she had already asked once and which he hadn't answered would have to be repeated.

"Did you, Danny?"

"Did I what?"

She lost her temper as she had done earlier with Max but this time there was no question of her bursting into tears. Inside, she felt quite dry and rigid.

"You know damn well what I mean! Did you kill Eustace Quinn? And don't lie to me. I must know the truth. If you did it, it won't make any difference but, in God's name, I have to know!"

He came immediately across the kitchen to her, squatting down in front of her and placing his hands on her knees to keep his balance as he tipped back his head to look her in the face.

"Oh, Nina, what a question! Of course I didn't!"

His eyes were stretched wide, showing a rim of white round the irises, and she searched them for any sign of falsehood. But she still wasn't sure.

"Honest Injun?" she asked, using the childhood formula which he remembered and completed.

"Cross my heart and hope to die."

And with that she had to be satisfied.

"So what about a last cup of tea then?" he asked, springing to his feet, quite sure he had convinced her and nothing more need be said. "Only, I was up at some Godawful hour this morning and I could do with an early night."

The mention of tea reminded her of Max, and she made a big potful, enough for the three of them, before carrying Max's supper upstairs—a boiled egg and bread and butter; since he had taken to his bed, he seemed not to want much to eat.

"Is anyone downstairs with you?" he asked suspiciously as she laid the tray across his knees.

"No," she lied quickly.

"I thought I heard voices earlier."

"I had the radio on, that's all."

It seemed to satisfy him for he turned to his supper, cracking the top of the egg with a whack from the back of the spoon.

Ordinarily, she would have stayed while he ate, sitting on the bed while she waited to take the tray away. They would talk together, although even at the best of times Max had never had the patience for desultory chat and it was usually she who provided most of the conversation.

This evening, maddeningly, when she wanted to get back to Danny, it was he who wanted to keep her. And how slowly he ate! Each spoonful of egg was carefully scooped from the shell. Between mouthfuls, he asked a question or made some remark with the same slow deliberation. Did she feel better now? Really? Was she sure? Perhaps she ought to see that old quack Foreman and get a tonic, although, in his opinion, there was nothing to beat a drop of champagne.

"Treat yourself to a bottle, Nine," he told her, wagging his egg spoon at her.

And where the hell did he imagine the money was coming from to pay for it? she thought impatiently.

"I've got to fetch something, Max," she said, finding it impossible to sit there any longer. "I'll only be five minutes. Finish your supper."

As she grabbed up blankets and a pillow from one of the spare beds, it suddenly occurred to her what to do about Danny. She could send him to Zoe's! Zoe knew nothing about Eustace Quinn's murder and surely she'd be willing to put Danny up for a few days. It was safer than a hotel, too. It was the last place that Rudd would think of looking for

him and she'd know herself where he was, at least for the time being. But
he'd have to leave early, before there was any chance of Rudd turning up
to make good his threat to search the house.

Dumping the bedding in the hall, she hurried back upstairs to Max,
who had finished his supper and was waiting for her.

Getting him to the bathroom and back seemed to take hours. Then she
had to settle him into bed, give him his pills, and plump up his pillows
before she could finally leave him for the night. Bending down to kiss
him, she was overcome with a pang of guilt. Poor Max! Her haste to
leave him was almost like a betrayal.

Downstairs, she forgot him in her concern for Danny. Knowing him,
everything would have to be cut and dried otherwise he'd argue, but
once presented with a complete plan of action, he'd fall in with her
wishes. It had been the same when they were children. She had only to
say, "Listen, this is what we'll do," giving him no option, and he would
agree.

First there was the rate money to find which she kept hidden in a vase
in the sitting room; sixty-five pounds altogether, although she thought
fifty should be enough. Returning fifteen to the vase, she wondered what
the hell she would do when the rates fell due. But that seemed unimpor-
tant. Something would turn up. If the worst came to the worst, she'd do
as Danny had done and sell some of Max's sketches in London.

If only that damned exhibition had come off, they'd all be sitting
pretty. There'd be money coming in, Max would be happy, and Danny
wouldn't be in this Godawful mess. But it couldn't be helped.

Shrugging, she found paper and pen and scribbled the letter to Zoe,
stuffing it hurriedly into an envelope. She looked up the local bus timetable and made up Danny's bed on the sofa—safer then letting him sleep
upstairs where Max might hear him. As a final, welcoming gesture, she
turned on the electric fire so that the sitting room would be warm for
him before returning to the kitchen.

"Christ, Nina," Danny said as she entered. "You've been gone for
bloody ages."

"I've had things to do," she told him. She felt strong and confident as
she placed glasses on the table.

"What are those for?" he asked.

"What do you think, you idiot? We're going to have a little celebration," she replied, fetching the bottle of brandy and pouring drinks for
them both. "While I've been gone, I've been thinking about what you
can do and I've got it all beautifully worked out, so listen. You stay here
tonight and then, in the morning, I'll wake you up early and we'll walk
across the fields to the Millstead road. There's a bus at five past seven
that'll take you into Millstead in time to catch the eight fifty-five Green
Line coach to London." He began to demur at the early start but she
overrode his protestations. "Don't be a fool, Danny. You've got to be out
of the house in case the police come. And don't you see? They'll be
watching this road and the buses into Bexford, expecting you to catch a
train to London from there."

"Yes, I can see that," he admitted grudgingly. "But what the hell do I do when I get to London?"

"It's all organised. You go to Zoe's, Max's ex-wife. In fact, I've already asked her to look out for a flat for you so she knows a bit about you. But never mind that now. The point is she's got a sofa in her living room you could sleep on for a few days until you can get yourself a job and somewhere else to live. Look, I've written her a letter and I'm putting twenty-five pounds in it. That's for her. The other twenty-five's for you. I know it isn't much but it'll keep you going for the time being." Before handing it over to him, she licked the flap of the envelope and stuck it down, not so much because she didn't trust him as to reassure Zoe that the money was intact. "Her address is on the front. And for God's sake, don't lose it!"

"I won't," he promised, putting both the envelope and the money into his wallet. "Thanks, Nine."

"And don't tell her more than you have to," Nina added. "She's a nosey old bitch so watch out. I told her, by the way, that you're a friend, so don't let on, will you?"

"Are you sure she'll have me?" he asked.

"Oh, yes." Nina sounded quite confident. "For twenty-five quid, Zoe'd let Dracula sleep on her sofa."

The absurdity of the idea struck them at the same time and they burst out laughing together, Danny gripping her wrist in the pleasure of their shared amusement.

"God, Nina, you're a bloody marvel!" he told her. "You could always fix things."

"Like the old days?" she asked. "Remember the time we put that balloon in with the fruit at the Harvest Festival?"

"And the bloody thing came loose during the blessing and floated down from the edge of the pulpit?"

"Dad's face!"

"And Aunt Connie's!"

"Sh! Sh!" she warned him, still laughing and pointing up towards the ceiling to remind him of Max's presence in the house. As they muffled their laughter, she felt again that sharp pang of guilt which had touched her earlier.

As in the past when they were children, it was still she and Danny in league against authority, only this time they were joining hands together against Max, forming their own circle to exclude him and from the centre of which he was banished.

CHAPTER 13

The alarm clock woke Nina at five the following morning and she got out of bed and dressed, making as little noise as possible so as not to disturb Max. Closing his door as she passed it on the landing, she could hear, inside the room, his deep, rumbling breathing.

Downstairs, she made Danny's breakfast and carried the tray into the sitting room. He slept more quietly than Max, lying in the same position she remembered he had always assumed as a child, curled up like a foetus under the bedclothes, one hand stuffed beneath the pillow. He woke in the same manner as he used to, opening his eyes as she gently shook his shoulder and staring straight ahead for a few seconds without moving, as if accustoming himself to the sensation of wakefulness.

"Breakfast, Danny," she said in a low voice.

They set off at six, leaving by the shrubbery gate and striking off across the fields, Nina in front, Danny behind.

The sun had risen but had not yet dispersed the early morning mist, which was looped between the trees in nets of gauzy light, reducing perspective and distance so that they seemed to be walking through a tent of golden muslin spun from airy filaments. A rich bloom of dew was lying on the grass and the leaves were matt with moisture.

How silent it is! Nina thought. Their footsteps were absorbed into the wet grass so that they themselves became part of the stillness. She was awed by the silence and the luminous beauty of the morning.

At the far side of the field, she turned and waited for Danny to catch up with her. He walked awkwardly in his city shoes, lugging his suitcase, his features bunched up tightly with misery and discomfort.

Why wasn't he moved by the same delight? Nina wondered, although her heart went out to him.

Behind him, until lost in the hazy dazzle, stretched a line of dark prints where their feet had smudged the dew.

"How much further is it?" he asked as he drew alongside her.

"About another mile and a half," she replied. Not even his bad mood could entirely destroy her own sense of peace and serenity.

"Christ! That far? My bloody feet are soaking wet already."

Without replying, she turned and began to walk on again. The moisture had coated her eyelashes so that, looking through them, the mist seemed doubly diaphanous, and everything around her—the outlines of the trees, the distant hedges—appeared to be dissolving and melting away. It was like Max's last painting, she realised, the one in which Lilith had been on the point of vanishing, and for a rare instant Nina felt that she could see with Max's eyes, a sensation she had never experienced before.

But not for long, for as they walked on, the sunlight strengthened and the mist gradually disappeared, licked away, it seemed, by the warmth. Little by little, outlines grew stronger, distances reasserted themselves, shapes moved forward, so that by the time they reached the Millstead road, all that was left were small pockets of white vapour clinging in hollows and a vague, watery aura along the horizon. The sun was now so bright that it hurt their eyes.

There was only ten minutes to wait before the bus was due, and as they climbed over the gate into the road Nina had ready in her mind half a dozen last-minute things that she wanted to say to Danny. But he didn't give her time for any of them, not even to repeat the warning about Zoe. As they neared the bus stop, he said, "Don't come any further, Nina," in a voice that couldn't be ignored. He gave her his cheek to kiss, the rest of his face being turned deliberately away from her. His skin was cold to her lips.

"Write to me," she begged and that was all she had the chance to say. He had walked off before she could add anything else and there was nothing she could do except retrace her steps to the gate where she paused to look back at him, even though she knew he would not turn to wave.

He was standing with his back to her, looking up the road in the direction from which the bus would come, one hand in his pocket, the other still holding onto his shabby suitcase, hunching his shoulders forward in his familiar, defensive stance which gave his figure, outlined against the sun, the silhouette of hopeless dejection, like a man in a dole queue or a refugee waiting for a cattle truck that was to take him into exile.

Rudd also watched the mist disperse. He had stayed late in the office the previous evening, organising the search for Danny Webb before catching up with the paper work involved in the case, and at three o'clock in the morning had decided it was not worth going home. Anyway, there was no one to go home to. His widowed sister, Dorothy, who kept house for him, had gone to visit Barbara, an old school friend, also widowed, in Cambridge, and he wondered again as he had many times in the past if, without him to take care of, Dorothy might not have made a better life for herself with Barbara. She liked Cambridge; and the two women appeared to enjoy each other's company. Dorothy was certainly a different person when she returned home from these visits, more animated, but also anxious in case, in her absence, he hadn't been looking after himself properly. Nina's remarks about her aunt had reawakened his own feelings of guilt about his sister. Did she, too, only stay out of a sense of duty? There was no way of finding out, for he could hardly ask her. Their relationship was based almost entirely on what was not said between them.

At times like this, he half regretted never having married even though he realised it was too late to make the commitment. The passion that might once have swept him into it had been channelled into his work and now he was not sure that he was capable of redirecting it. Like storm water, it had been caught and tamed before it could overwhelm him and the runnels he had dug for it were too deep and too intrenched by custom for it ever to break their banks. And yet, he was not quite without susceptibilities. He remembered Blanche Lester's arm trembling in his as they walked together in Green Park, the dip and sway of Nina Gifford's skirt as she bent to fold the washing and the firm, brown flesh of her hands.

There was room in his heart for someone like Nina, he acknowledged. But not for her. There were too many qualities in her, and in him, that he saw with an objective eye, which, like the Cyclops', never seemed to sleep and would lead inevitably to the nagging itch of mutual exasperation. Although it would have to be someone like her, who could, as she did, shower a radiance about her and disturb the air with the living vitality of her presence.

Meanwhile, this night, in the absence of all feminine influence in his life, including his sister's, he settled down with a blanket on the shabby armchair he kept in the office for such occasions. He slept only fitfully, waking at intervals to hear the distant echoes of a building only partly occupied: voices in a corridor, a door shutting, the ringing of a telephone that went on and on until it was silenced in mid-peal like a scream suddenly cut short.

At six o'clock, he gave up the pretence of sleeping any longer and made himself coffee, which he drank standing at the window. The sun was emerging from behind the mist, giving the rooftops opposite a dull, metallic sheen like gunmetal, and behind the haze there was the feeling of the town coming awake. Unseen traffic moved along the streets. People were up and about. He felt that if he listened hard enough he might hear their footsteps on the pavements.

Boyce arrived at eight o'clock and, by that time, Rudd had washed and shaved in the men's cloakroom and was sitting at his desk, ready for the day's work to begin, the first half hour of which was taken up with giving the Sergeant a brief summary of what had happened over the weekend.

"So you think Danny Webb might have murdered Quinn?" Boyce asked when Rudd had finished his account.

"I don't know," Rudd confessed. "He certainly had opportunity. As we know, he didn't arrive at the Feathers until half past eleven, which would have given him plenty of time to slip into the grounds of Althorpe House through the shrubbery, clobber Quinn, and clear off again before Nina Gifford came home. But I can't see he had much of a motive. Admittedly he knew Quinn. In fact, he sold him Max Gifford's sketches.

But, by my reckoning, that's not sufficient reason for wanting him dead. We'll have to pick him up, of course, if we can, although my bet is he's cleared off back to London so it's not going to be easy. By the way, I've arranged for a couple of plainclothes men to watch the London trains out of Bexford and I'm sending Marsh and Simpson over to Althorpe to find out from Lionel Burnett if he knows exactly when Webb did his bunk and to make a few inquiries locally in case anyone saw him."

"What about his sister?" Boyce asked. "Any chance she might be hiding him?"

"I doubt it. I warned her yesterday that I'd get a search warrant and, unless she's a damned sight more stupid than I think she is, she won't risk it. We may still have to search the place, but I'm inclined to play that down for a day or two. Let her start feeling secure and then we'll move in. If we haven't found Webb by then, he may have doubled back to Althorpe House, thinking the coast's clear."

"Clever," Boyce commented.

"Not particularly. Just common sense. Besides, if we put it off for the time being, we may even have turned up enough new evidence to pin the murder on him as well."

"And the others?"

"You mean Burnett and the two women? Well, the same applies to them—opportunity but not much in the way of motive. Lionel Burnett is clearly obsessed by Nina Gifford. We've only to take a look at those torn-up drawings and notes he dumped in the incinerator to see that. We also know from Blanche Lester's evidence that Quinn was deliberately flirting with Nina Gifford on Thursday, which I suspect Burnett witnessed or, at least, part of it. I know jealousy can be a strong motive for murder but, as you pointed out, the timing's a bit short for a homicidal passion to work itself up. Still, it's possible so we can't rule him out. As for Blanche Lester, she admits she quarrelled with Quinn on Friday morning about their relationship not long before he was found dead, but unless she's a lot more round the bend than she actually appears, I can't see that giving her enough reason for wanting him dead. Not to plan it in cold blood, anyhow, which is what she must have done if we go by the evidence we have against her. We'll have to keep her in mind, of course. And the same goes for Nina Gifford. According to both Blanche and Zoe Hamilton, Quinn was curious about her past and we may find a motive there if we dig about a bit. Which is what I want you to do today, Tom. Go to the Registry of Births and Marriages at St. Catherine's House in Kingsway and turn up the records on her. For a start, you can check the date she married Gifford and how old she was at the time."

"You're thinking it was possibly an illegal marriage?"

"I don't know but until I've collected a few facts together I've got nothing to go on. So, as far as she's concerned, we'll start from square one and work from there. From what she told Blanche Lester, she was seventeen when she met Max Gifford and ran away with him, so start by checking the entries for the early fifties. As she must be in her forties, it's the earliest date she and Gifford could have married, according to my calculations."

"Is that all you want me to cover?"

"No, it isn't," Rudd replied, handing Boyce two copies of Miss Martin's list which he had laboriously retyped the evening before, placing half the names on one sheet, half on the other. "While you're in London, I want you to go down these names individually. They're all people Quinn was in touch with since January when he bought the first of the Gifford drawings. Basically, there's one question you need to ask each of them in turn and it's this: Did Quinn ever suggest a partnership to mount Gifford's exhibition or any kind of deal connected with it? I've got a hunch it could be important. Quinn mentioned a partner only to Max Gifford—not to Blanche Lester or Miss Martin, his secretary, and I want to find out why."

"Right," Boyce said absentmindedly. As Rudd was speaking, the Sergeant had begun to scan the list and now he looked up, his expression incredulous.

"Just a minute!" he protested. "Am I supposed to see every jack one of them you've written down here?"

"That's the idea."

"On my tod? But there's nearly forty of them!"

"Take Kyle with you. He can cover one of the lists."

"Is that all? What about Marsh?"

"I was planning on sending him along with you, but I can't now. He's involved with the inquiries in Althorpe."

"Oh, hell, yes. I'd forgotten. Then what about Harding or Barney?"

"They're on surveillance at Bexford station. And before you try any more names, Grainger's off sick, Johnson's on leave, Cunningham hasn't had enough experience yet for this type of work, and Meredith and that other DC who's just transferred from Thames force, the tall chap with the sideburns . . ."

"Bannister?"

"Yes, well, he's gone with Meredith and the others on that burglary case over at High Watton. Which leaves you and Kyle, I'm afraid, Tom."

"You realise it's going to take us a couple of days to get through this lot?"

"So I would imagine," Rudd replied equably. "So you'd better get started. Round Kyle up and, listen, before you go, I want you to phone me every hour, on the hour, do you understand? Kyle can do the same at ten past. But I want to know as soon as possible when you turn up Quinn's partner. I'll be here in the office all day, waiting for the various reports to come in. If I get called out, leave a message with the Desk Sergeant. I'll phone in myself every hour."

Boyce departed, sighing gustily, and, as the door was about to close behind him, Rudd nearly called him back to add a rider instructing him to start his inquiries with Bruce Lawford and then changed his mind. If

Bruce Lawford was to have any significance in the inquiry then he must be arrived at through the due process of the investigation.

The first call came at ten o'clock from Boyce who merely gave the information that, so far, he had been to the Records Office in Kingsway where the staff had undertaken to check through the records for him. Apart from that, there had only been enough time to call on two people on the list and neither of these knew anything about a partnership with Quinn. Kyle telephoned ten minutes later to report the same negative result. So, too, did their next calls at eleven and ten past. By this time, they had between them visited eight people.

Replacing the receiver after talking to Kyle, Rudd took a surreptitious peep at the original list which he had kept by him on the desk. At the rate they were going, it was going to take at least another two hours before Boyce, on whose copy Bruce Lawford's name appeared, had worked his way down to him.

With a gesture of impatience, Rudd turned the list face down and fed another sheet of paper into the typewriter, shooting back the sleeves of his jacket before picking out, letter by letter, the words "but when I arrived at the caravan, Danny Webb had already gone . . ."

"Fancy another?" Danny asked.

"Thanks, dear, I'd love one," Zoe replied, as she pushed her empty glass in his direction. She had seen his full wallet and didn't see why she should offer to fork out.

It was just after twelve o'clock and they were seated together in the saloon bar of the Lamb, near Fulham Broadway, a public house which Zoe did not normally frequent but to which she had chosen to take Danny for a snack lunch and a drink shortly after his arrival. As he stood at the bar, waiting to order the second round, she watched his back speculatively.

His arrival a short time earlier had been totally unexpected and her first reaction, until she read Nina's letter with the twenty-five quid in it, had been to say no. She didn't want anyone moving in with her; certainly not someone like him. She knew his type. He'd lounge about the place all day and it'd be a hell of a job ever getting rid of him. Besides, why should she do Nina a good turn? She'd got a bloody nerve to expect any favours in the first place.

But as she stood reading the letter, two sentences had made her change her mind. Nina had written, "If you could put Danny up for a few days, I'd be very grateful. As I explained to you when I saw you last, he's a friend and he's looking for a flat."

Nina's gratitude hadn't meant a thing to Zoe but the name had. Danny. It was the same name that the little fat bloke, the man who'd come with Mr. Johnson to collect the painting, had mentioned and which Rudd had seemed interested in when he was nosing round asking questions on Saturday.

Even then Zoe might have let it pass. She had no particular wish to become involved. The police could do their own dirty work.

It was something that Danny let slip which finally decided her. As she stood there with the letter in her hand, he had remarked, "My sister seemed to think you wouldn't mind if I kipped down on your sofa."

"All right then, dear. You can stay," Zoe had told him, stuffing the letter and the money into her handbag.

Even now, watching him return from the bar with his whisky and her gin and orange, Nina's deception still rankled. Her bloody brother! And she hadn't let on, pretending he was a friend, the lying cow!

"Cheers!" Zoe said, raising her glass.

"Here's mud in your eye," Danny replied. It was meant as a joke, an awkward attempt to lighten the situation. Zoe knew he was embarrassed to be seen sitting there drinking with her. All the time, he was taking little furtive glances round the place, wondering if anyone was commenting on the pair of them—the old woman with the much younger man, and she laughed with deliberate shrillness and laid a hand on his arm. Heads turned and she saw his face darken.

Draining her glass, she gathered up her handbag.

"Shan't be long dear," she said, bending down to put her mouth close to his ear in a conspiratorial whisper. "I've got to go to the you-know-where. I'll be back in a minute."

The public telephone was in the passage leading to the toilets. With her bag clutched tightly under her arm, Zoe dialled the number and, having given her message, replaced the receiver and went on down the passage, leaving by the emergency door at the far end which led into the yard.

The message was passed on to Rudd at a quarter to one but he waited until Boyce had phoned through before taking any action.

"Listen," the Sergeant began. "They've turned up something interesting at Records . . ."

"Tell me later," Rudd interrupted. "I'm coming up to London myself. Fulham police have just phoned me. They've got Danny Webb. I want you to meet me outside Fulham police station at half past two. I ought to be there by then."

"*Fulham* police? How the hell did they get hold of him?"

"I'll explain when I see you," Rudd said and rang off.

Boyce was waiting for him on the pavement and they entered the building together.

"So?" Boyce asked as if their previous conversation had only just taken place. "How was it they managed to nab him?"

"Zoe Hamilton, Max Gifford's ex-wife, must have turned him in," Rudd explained. "It seems Nina Gifford sent Danny to her. Chief Superintendent Blakeny who's in charge said it was an anonymous tip-off but it can't be anyone else except her. She lives in the area, she knows Nina, and the name Danny cropped up when Quinn bought that picture off her. She must have put two and two together. A very shrewd old bird is Zoe."

"It's saved us a lot of sweat," Boyce pointed out.

"Knowing her, I doubt if her reasons were that public spirited. She was simply grabbing the chance to pay off an old score," Rudd replied. The irony of the situation had already occurred to him. For Danny's sake, Nina had turned in desperation for help to the one person she could think of who might shelter him, not realising that Zoe, already apprised of some of the facts of the case through his own interview with her, would turn him over to the police. He added, "Any luck yet with Quinn's partner?"

"Not so far, but Records have come up with something interesting," Boyce said, eager to get his oar in. "There's no entry for Nina Gifford's marriage."

He looked gratified when Rudd stopped in his tracks.

"None? Are you sure?"

"Positive. They checked back to the late forties, further back even than the date you suggested, and there's nothing. Gifford was divorced in thirty-seven all right but there's no record of his remarriage. You realise, of course, that it could give Nina Gifford a motive for murdering Quinn? I mean, supposing he threatened her with something in her past that she didn't want Max Gifford to know about. A lover, say. You said Quinn had been asking questions about her. She might have been afraid that, if Gifford knew, he'd change his will and she'd get nothing, not even the house . . ."

"But even a common-law wife would be legally entitled to inherit. After all, they've been living together for nearly thirty years, longer than a lot of marriages."

"Did she know that, though?" Boyce asked.

It was a reasonable point that Rudd had to concede for it did indeed give Nina Gifford a very good motive for murder. Faced with the fear that after a lifetime of caring for Max she might, at his death, be virtually homeless and penniless, she could very well have decided to silence Quinn. There was, however, still one point that didn't make sense which he voiced aloud to Boyce.

"But why the hell didn't they get married? Max Gifford was free—you said yourself the records show he divorced Zoe so there was nothing to stop him."

Boyce shrugged.

"Don't ask me. Perhaps he'd had a bellyful the first time round and didn't fancy a repeat performance. Besides, he's an artist, isn't he? You know what they're like. They shack up with the latest girl friend for a few months and then move out again when it suits them."

It was a gross distortion of what, in fact, had happened in Max Gifford's case, although Rudd didn't bother to point out to the Sergeant that, contrary to his description, the Giffords had remained together for over a quarter of a century. He had long ago realised that Boyce was in the habit of making certain snap judgements which nothing would change. Mention the word "artist" and he'd come up, like a cash register, with an automatic response: long hair, sandals, and an irregular sex life.

There wasn't time, anyway, to defend the Giffords. He and Boyce had reached the door of the interview room where Danny Webb was waiting for them.

He was sitting dejectedly on one of the regulation chairs with which the room was furnished, a full ashtray on the table in front of him. A police constable, standing just inside the door, came to attention as the two men entered and Rudd dismissed him with a nod.

"Well, Mr. Webb, you've led us a bit of a dance," the Chief Inspector remarked pleasantly, drawing up a chair as Boyce, seating himself beside him, ostentatiously took out his notebook and pen which he placed on the scarred tabletop. Years of working together had polished their performance to a perfectly synchronised double act in which their roles were clearly defined, Rudd playing the friendly, neighbourhood copper, anxious to see justice done, while Boyce assumed the part of the heavy, a mute but massive reminder of the full weight of the law.

"Who shopped me?" Danny demanded furiously. "It was that bloody old bitch, wasn't it?"

"It was an anonymous tip-off," Rudd replied, showing no reaction to Danny's anger. It was as much an act as their own, a defensive pose to hide his fear. Rudd had smelt it as soon as he entered the room, a faint aroma that was impossible to describe but which to him, as to any creature with a hunter's instinct, was distinct and instantly recognisable: a slightly sour, rancid odour compounded of human sweat and the sharper, more feral secretion of the fear itself. "But since you're here, by whatever means, I'd like a statement from you."

"Are you going to charge me?"

"Not yet. I'd like to hear what you've got to say for yourself first. Let's start with these, shall we?" Rudd laid the sketches out in front of Webb who looked at them but didn't touch them. Anxious not to leave his prints on them, Rudd assumed, although that wasn't going to help him much when his own sister's evidence as well as Askew's had already established that they had been in his possession.

"Well?" he continued, as Danny did not answer. "Come on, Mr. Webb. You're not doing your own case any good. Do you want me to start the ball rolling for you? Your sister, Mrs. Gifford, gave them to you a few months ago. Am I right?"

"All right, then, she did," Danny conceded reluctantly and stopped again, watching the Sergeant's pen also come to a halt as if its tip was connected to his own tongue and the one set the other in motion. Unsure of exactly how much Rudd knew, he was unwilling to say too much. His first instinct had been to deny everything, even his acquaintanceship with Quinn, but it was obvious that Rudd had picked up some information from Nina and he felt his fear turn to anger, not so much against the Chief Inspector, although he would have liked to wipe that stupid bloody smile off his face, but against his sister. She'd bleeding well fixed things properly for him, hadn't she! Sending him off to that sodding old cow who'd only waited long enough to pocket the money before turning him in.

"And then you took them along to Mr. Askew's where you later met Mr. Quinn," Rudd continued.

Now it was out in the open, Danny saw no point in holding back. He'd do better to talk, to minimise his own part in the whole bloody business. That way, he'd show he was willing to cooperate, which mightn't be a bad thing.

"That's right, but I only met him once," he admitted. "Askew fixed up the meeting. I went round to his shop one evening. Quinn said he was interested in the sketches and he was keen to find out about Max."

"But you'd never, in fact, met him?"

"Max? No. Nina did a bolt with him when I was about eight. Cleared off to London, or so I understood from the odds and sods of gossip I picked up in the village. It was never discussed at home. My father told me not to mention her name again."

"But she kept in touch with you?"

"Through one of the boys I knew at school. She used to write to his house. Later, when I came up to London, we'd meet from time to time, but she never took me back with her."

"Do you know why?"

Danny shrugged.

"She said it was better that way. Max wasn't the sort who wanted to be mixed up with other people's relations. Besides, she liked keeping things secret. Dad and Aunt Connie didn't know half the things she got up to on the quiet."

This sly dig at Nina, his own sister, reminded Rudd of Zoe Hamilton's smear tactics and he would have preferred to ignore it but he couldn't.

"What sort of things?"

"Seeing boys in the evenings without them knowing. She used to say she was going to the Youth Club and then slip out and meet the boys round the back of the church."

If that was all, then a great number of teenage girls were equally as guilty, Rudd thought. From the little he knew of her home background, he could imagine that such deceit would have been a necessary subterfuge, especially for someone like Nina Gifford who, even when young, must have had a normal, healthy interest in the opposite sex.

"And you kept in touch with her after she and Max moved to Althorpe?"

"On and off," Danny replied. "I'd write and we'd meet in the summerhouse at a prearranged time or she'd come up to London occasionally."

"I see. Now let's get back to Eustace Quinn, shall we?"

"I've told you all I know. Like I said, I only met him the once."

"But you gave him Max Gifford's address?"

"Yes. Why not?"

"And talked about Max?"

"A bit. There wasn't much I could tell him."

"What about your sister? Did you discuss her?"

"Quinn seemed interested so I told him what I knew."

"What sort of things?"

"About her running away from home with Max when she was still at school and Dad being a country vicar."

"Where was his parish?"

Rudd asked the question casually although he was curious to find out where Nina had lived as a girl. If Quinn had been interested in her past, then it might be worthwhile to go back there himself and make a few inquiries in the place where she had grown up.

"Heversham. It's near the Herts-Essex border, a few miles east of Bishops Stortford. Dad's retired now but he and Aunt Connie are still living in the village."

"Go on. What else did you tell Eustace Quinn?"

"That she'd only known him three days before she ran off with him and that she was under age. There didn't seem any harm in telling him. Besides, I thought it might do her a bit of good."

Quite how he had reached the conclusion wasn't clear, and Rudd suspected that he had talked from the much less altruistic motive of making sure that whatever good Quinn had to offer would be coming his way rather than hers.

"Did Quinn mention a possible exhibition of Gifford's work?"

"No, I didn't know anything about that. He didn't tell me," Danny protested, and here, at least, Rudd believed he was telling the truth. Danny's voice had the tone of authentic outrage. In order to keep prices low, Quinn had obviously informed none of the people from whom he had bought Gifford's paintings that an exhibition was planned. If he had, Danny, and Zoe also, would have asked for much more money than they had, in fact, been given.

Rudd couldn't resist asking, "What did you get for the sketches?"

His suspicions were confirmed when Danny answered sulkily, "A fiver each except for the signed ones. I got a tenner for those."

From what Danny had already said, the next question would be superfluous but Rudd asked it all the same.

"Did Quinn mention a partner to you?"

"No. No one else was in on the deal as far as I knew except Askew."

"Right, Mr. Webb. Now, I'd like to come to the more recent events of this week. Tell me exactly what happened and what you were doing in Althorpe."

"I wrote to Nina and told her I was coming down to see her. I'd got into a bit of trouble over a gambling debt so I thought I'd better clear out of London for the time being. I put up at the Dolphin in Bexford for a few days and then went to see Nina."

"When?"

"Monday morning. We met in the summerhouse and she said she'd try to find me another flat in London. Meanwhile she fixed it up for me to stay in Lionel Burnett's caravan."

"When did you move in?"

"Wednesday. She left a note for me at the Dolphin. Honest to God, I had no idea Quinn was going to turn up the next day. Nina said nothing to me about it. In fact, until Lionel told me someone called Quinn had been murdered, I didn't even know he'd been to see Max."

"When did Mr. Burnett tell you?"

"Friday afternoon. He came back from Nina's just as I turned up from the Feathers and described what had happened. Well, Christ! you can imagine what I felt like when I heard."

He looked at Rudd with shamefaced appeal, his reluctance to entreat the Chief Inspector's sympathy overcome by his desperation to be believed. Rudd could see why Nina went on supporting him. There was the hopelessness of the born loser about him which would arouse her protective instinct. Unlike her, Danny would never survive on his own, although he'd probably not need to. There would always be someone, usually a woman, who would undertake to look after him.

"So you decided to come to the house?" Rudd asked, leaving the appeal unanswered.

"I had to risk it. Lionel hadn't told me much, just the bare facts, and I didn't like to question him too far in case he got suspicious. I had to find out more from Nina, to know if I was in the clear or not. I walked past the house and couldn't see much sign of anything going on, so I came up the drive to the yard, hoping to attract her attention . . ."

"Instead of which you attracted mine," Rudd completed the sentence for him in his blandest manner. Beside him, Boyce turned a page of his notebook and waited for Webb's reply, but Danny only shrugged as if admitting that piece of bad luck.

"And that made you decide to clear out?" Rudd continued. "When exactly did you make a run for it?"

"Early Sunday morning. It seemed better than going Saturday night. I'd only got a couple of quid on me and I thought there'd be less chance of you lot hanging about Nina's first thing on a Sunday morning. I was going to borrow some money off her. Anyway, you turned up so I had to leave. I spent the day in an empty barn and went back after dark. It was Nina's idea I stayed the night and left this morning. She said if I caught the bus to Millstead, I could pick up the London coach from there. Before I left, she gave me a letter for Zoe Hamilton, Max's ex-wife." His face darkened, the expression changing from adolescent appeal to childish outrage and fury. "Nina said she'd put me up for a few days but instead the bloody bitch turned me in."

Rudd ignored both the outburst and Danny's insistence on the part Nina had played in helping him escape to London, a quite deliberate attempt to exonerate himself and lay as much of the blame on her as he could.

His face expressionless, Rudd merely said, "I'd like to return to Friday morning, Mr. Webb. We shall need a full account of your movements between nine o'clock and twelve-thirty."

Webb replied quickly, "I stayed in bed until about ten o'clock."

"Any witnesses?" Rudd asked.

"I didn't have a woman shacked up with me, if that's what you mean."

Danny spoke with something of his old swagger in an attempt to brazen it out.

"I wasn't thinking of that," Rudd replied equably. "I meant Mr. Burnett."

"No, I don't think Lionel saw me. When I left, I walked down the drive past the cottage but he didn't come out. I wasn't all that keen, anyway, on seeing him. I knew bloody well he'd stop me and make a fuss about the caravan. He'd already had a moan about the rubbish I'd left at the bottom of the steps."

"Mr. Burnett was at home?" Rudd slipped the question in casually.

"I suppose so," Danny said indifferently. "His car was in the drive."

"I see. And where did you go when you left the caravan?"

"I went to the Feathers for a drink."

"No, you didn't, Mr. Webb. Or, at least, not until half past eleven. We've already checked that with the landlord."

"Oh, Christ," Danny said softly. He was silent for several seconds, his head lowered so that Rudd could see only the top of his head with its thinning, fine, brown hair. When he raised it, his face had again assumed the expression of ashamed entreaty and he sought for Rudd's eyes, looking straight into them and confirming the Inspector's suspicion of Danny's dependence on Nina. Even if one discounted the blood tie between them, Danny had the gift of appealing to one's sympathy, of creating the image of the innocent whom no one understood and whom life had treated unfairly. With his thin, boyish features and air of hurt, bewildered honesty, he looked the part.

"You're not going to believe this," he began.

"Try me," Rudd suggested cheerfully.

"I went to look round the church in the village. God knows why. I can't explain. I haven't been in a church for years—not since I left home. But I suddenly wanted to have a look inside one again. For old times' sake, perhaps."

He gave Rudd a small, lopsided smile, inviting his amusement and his credence.

"Did anyone see you?" Rudd asked, his own face expressionless.

"No, I don't think so. If you've been down to the village, you'll know it's not in the centre. It's between Lionel's house and the others. There's a couple of cottages opposite but that's all. I didn't see anyone about and the church itself was empty."

It was a perfectly accurate description of the siting of the church in Althorpe but one which Danny could have discovered at almost any time during his stay in the village.

"And how long were you there?" Rudd asked.

"About an hour, I suppose. I wandered about for a while and then sat in the porch while I had a cigarette. Then I walked back to the Feathers."

The timing fitted, too, but also proved nothing. Danny could have easily worked out how long it would take him to walk from the cottage to the church and back to the Feathers, allowing roughly the right length of time he had stayed in the building.

Rudd rose to his feet, Danny following him with his eyes.

"What's happening now?" he asked, his voice sharp with anxiety.

"You'll be held," Rudd said simply and saw the innocent, hard-done-by expression turn to one of fear.

"On what grounds, for Christ's sake? You're not going to charge me, are you? I've told you, I had nothing to do with Quinn's murder! Why the hell should I want to kill him? I'd only met him once . . ."

"You'll be held pending further inquiries," Rudd continued, raising his voice, and, nodding to Boyce, who put away his notebook, the two men left the room, the Constable, who had been waiting outside, resuming his position just inside the door.

"We'll get him back to headquarters," Rudd told the Sergeant as they stood outside in the corridor. "I'll have a word with Blakeny and arrange for Webb to be kept here until Marsh and one of the others can be sent over to pick him up. Now we've found Webb, we shan't need them on the search."

"What about getting him to make a statement?"

"We'll do that later when he's back on our patch."

"Do you reckon he's guilty?"

"I don't know," Rudd confessed. "He's got no alibi, or at least not one that any witnesses can verify, so he could have killed Quinn. It wouldn't have taken him long to get from the caravan to the Giffords' place, especially if he cut across the fields. But, as he himself said—and quite rightly, too, in my opinion—why should he want to kill Quinn?"

"Unless Nina Gifford was right," Boyce put in.

"How?" Rudd asked sharply.

"Don't you remember her theory that Quinn was killed by an intruder? We discussed it at the time and didn't think it was very likely. But suppose Webb got into the house and Quinn found him in the act of helping himself to some of Max Gifford's sketches? Quinn may have threatened to tell Nina so Webb clobbered him."

As a theory, it had a certain appeal, which Rudd couldn't deny. It fitted in neatly with what they already knew of Webb's past dealings with Quinn over Gifford's drawings, with the added motivation that if Danny Webb had learned from Lionel Burnett of the proposed exhibition, anything by Gifford would have increased in value and would therefore be worth getting hold of by almost any means. But, all the same, it was flawed.

"Max Gifford would have heard them quarrelling," Rudd pointed out. "His portfolios of drawings are kept in the dining room and that opens off the hall. Any noise would have gone straight up the stairs."

"All right, then. So Webb suggests to Quinn they go somewhere else to discuss it and he either kills him in the kitchen or in the yard."

"Could be," Rudd agreed doubtfully. He still wasn't convinced. "All the same, I can't see Webb being sufficiently frightened by Quinn's threat to tell his sister that he'd murder him."

"Why not?"

"Because as far as she was concerned, it wouldn't have made any difference."

"But did Webb know that?"

"Oh, yes." Rudd was quite positive. "Webb knows it. And she knows it. Don't you see, Tom, it's what keeps them together? It's a conspiracy of dependence. Take Nina Gifford away and Webb would collapse like a heap of old clothes. But the reverse is also true. Without him, she's just as lost."

He might have added but didn't that, as a relationship, it was even more binding than that between Nina and Max. The loss of Max would leave a huge gap in her life that time would slowly fill. But nothing would bridge the chasm that Danny would leave behind.

As they talked, they had been walking towards the entrance where they both paused.

"So what happens now?" Boyce asked although Rudd could tell by his hangdog look that the Sergeant was very well aware what the answer would be.

"You go on checking down those lists for Quinn's partner," Rudd said, pretending as he looked at his watch not to see the Sergeant's long-suffering expression.

"And you?"

"I'll phone headquarters from here and get Marsh and Simpson organised to pick up Danny Webb. After that, there should be just about enough time to drive over to Heversham and interview Danny's father and aunt. Old Mr. Webb's retired now, so I'll have to get his exact address from Danny before I go. It's worth the trip, I think. There may be some old gossip worth raking up over there." He said it wryly, remembering Blanche Lester's comment on his methods of investigation. "First of all, though, I'll have a word with Blakeny."

"See you then," Boyce replied, setting off down the steps.

As he reached the bottom, Rudd called after him on a sudden impulse.

"Yes, what is it?" Boyce asked, turning to look back.

"Check Bruce Lawford this afternoon, will you? He's on your list."

The Sergeant seemed about to query the request, but Rudd, anticipating his curiosity, had already retreated inside the building. It might be tempting fate to pick out that one particular name from among the others, but the Chief Inspector had no intention of provoking it still further by trying to explain his reasons.

CHAPTER 14

Rudd left London just after half past three, taking the M11 towards Cambridge and turning off at Bishop's Stortford. Once clear of the city, he was able to make good time and it was getting on for five o'clock when he approached the outskirts of Heversham down a minor road that dipped and swung through the scattered villages of rural Essex.

Its centre was small and nuclear, a collection of houses and cottages grouped round the church beside which stood the rectory, Nina Gifford's former home, not dissimilar to Althorpe House in its heavy Victorian solidity and dense shrubbery isolating it from the surrounding buildings. Even the church stood aloof, as if keeping itself apart from the everyday life of the people it served.

The dependence of the place on agriculture was everywhere apparent. The farmland crowded down to the backs of the houses so that, beyond them and their little garden plots, hedged in with quickthorn, one could see the cultivated fields of sugar beet, wheat, and potatoes and, beyond those on the left, the barns and silos of a farm which stood out above the level view. Between some of the houses, five-barred gates gave access to the land and, as Rudd entered the village, he was forced to slow down behind a tractor that occupied the width of the road until it turned off through an open gateway beside the parish hall.

Opposite was the house for which he was looking—Ivy Place, a small, detached, brick and slate building, its front facade entirely covered by the creeper from which it had doubtlessly derived its name and through which four sash windows and a central door appeared to have been cut out. The effect was oddly sinister, for across the windows and door frame, little, unpruned tendrils were beginning to creep as if the ivy were only waiting its opportunity to take the house over completely, winding its way into rooms and up the staircase until the whole building was occupied with leaves. The twisted trunks from which the ivy grew, close to the front wall, were as thick as Rudd's arm and covered with a coarse, hairy growth that seemed to emphasise its crudely vigorous vegetable life. As he walked up the path to the front door, he imagined the roots spreading with the same insidious energy beneath the foundations as its branches scrambled up the brickwork.

There was a black iron ring which he banged. Presently the door was opened by a tall, thin, elderly woman, dressed in a black skirt and dark-patterned blouse, her grey hair scraped back into a small bun, who demanded abruptly to know what his business was. Rudd produced his card, explaining that he was making official police inquiries and he was somewhat grudgingly invited to step inside the hall although he was allowed no further than the coconut-fibre doormat.

"Inquiries into what?" she demanded.

"Your nephew, Daniel Webb," Rudd replied. She reminded him of the formidable primary school teacher in whose class he had once spent a terrified year at the age of eight and who had cracked him over the knuckles with a ruler for not knowing his nine-times table. "I believe I'm right in thinking you're his aunt, Miss Webb?"

"I am." Miss Webb acknowledged the relationship as reluctantly as she had invited him into the house. "Is Daniel in some trouble with the police?"

"I'm afraid so."

She made no comment as she returned his card to him, as if his announcement came as no surprise to her, merely remarking, "Then you'd better come this way," before leading him down the passage to a door at the far end which she opened, adding over her shoulder, "My brother is very deaf. I would prefer you discussed this matter with me."

The room that they entered was small and crowded with dark, heavy furniture which Rudd assumed they had brought with them from the more spacious rectory on the Reverend Webb's retirement. It was good, solid, well-made stuff, polished to a high gloss, but much too over-powering for the limited accommodation. The patterned carpet and dark red wallpaper added their own claustrophobic atmosphere, so that the air itself appeared squeezed out and there seemed no space for mere people. Certainly not for the frail, elderly man who was seated by the window in a high-backed armchair, a rug over his knees on which two fragile hands, trembling continuously, lay like pale leaves blown in from some forlorn, winter garden. He seemed barricaded in with furniture, the long, heavy curtains forming a palisade on one side, a table containing medicine bottles on the other, while in front of him stood a footstool on which rested two long, thin feet clad in carpet slippers.

Max Gifford, too, was an old man but, compared to Mr. Webb, he was alive and vigorous. He had preserved his intelligence and personality, a sense of presence. Nina Gifford's father seemed no more than a bundle of clothes propped up in a corner, surmounted by a head from which most of the flesh had shrunk away leaving only the bony protuberances of nose, chin, and forehead and the dark, fallen orifices of eyes and mouth. The eyes turned to Rudd as he entered the room but showed no sign of curiosity. They were merely registering his presence.

"It's someone called about Daniel," Miss Webb announced, leaning over him and raising her voice.

"Daniel?" the old man repeated.

"He doesn't remember," she continued, turning to Rudd. "Sit down."

She indicated the other high-backed armchair which stood on the far side of the window, drawing up for herself a straight chair from the central table and turning it round to face him.

"Well?" she said, taking her own seat.

Rudd lowered himself into the armchair. Now that he had both the Webbs in view, brother and sister, he could see a family likeness. They were out of the same mould—tall, thin, long-faced, humourless, with too much forehead and a sparsity of flesh and hair as if these were extravagances of nature that one could well do without. He could see also that Danny had inherited their physical features; their stubbornness and lack of humour, too. It was probably these shared characteristics that had caused friction in his childhood and had finally driven him away. But it must have been the dissimilarities that had forced Nina to leave home. Stifled by its atmosphere, she would have welcomed the chance to escape which Max Gifford with his vigour and his relaxed life-style had offered her.

"I'm investigating a case of possible fraud in which your nephew might be implicated," Rudd explained. The word "murder" seemed too shocking to use in front of these two elderly people.

"I see," said Miss Webb grimly, folding her lips.

"I came to see you because I need to know a little more about Daniel's background. A report has to be made, you see."

To his relief, she seemed to accept this inadequate and deliberately vague explanation, for she remarked disapprovingly, "I suppose it's become fashionable these days for social factors to be taken into consideration. A great mistake, in my opinion, and a contributory factor in the increasing crime rate. Anyone who breaks the law should be made to face up to the consequences of their behaviour, not excused. I am surprised the police have become party to it." Rudd made a deprecatory gesture with his hand which she ignored. "As far as Daniel is concerned, there is very little I can say in his defence. He was brought up in a Christian household in which strict standards were always maintained. My brother and I both did our best to instil in him a correct moral attitude but it wasn't easy. He was always wilful and disobedient, even as a small child, with very little sense of responsibility. At school it was exactly the same. He was always in trouble. In fact, the headmaster refused to allow him to stay on into the sixth form as he felt Daniel's academic record was too poor and he would be an undesirable influence on the other boys."

She spoke without emotion as if the condemnation had been rehearsed, and Rudd suspected that over the years it had become a set speech that she repeated whenever Daniel's character was called into question.

"What did he do when he left school?" Rudd asked.

"He had several jobs, none of which lasted very long. He also made some quite unsuitable friends whom he used to bring home. In the end, his father and I refused to tolerate it any longer and he was told to choose. After all, my brother was at the time still rector of the parish and had his own position and standing to consider. Neither could I be expected to have young men and women arriving at all hours, sometimes the worse for drink, and turning the house into a beer garden."

Remembering the state of Lionel Burnett's caravan, Rudd could almost sympathise with her. The choice that Danny had made was inevitable but all the same he wanted to hear her reply.

"And he chose to go?"

"He was eighteen." Miss Webb sounded defensive and Rudd wondered if, in her more honest moments, she might not have considered how far she herself was responsible for what Danny had become. "He was legally of age. One of his friends had just obtained a job in London and Daniel went with him. I believe there was talk of sharing a flat but I don't think the arrangement lasted very long."

"Did he keep in touch?"

"Very infrequently and only then when he was short of money. After his father retired, I wrote to Daniel explaining that as we were now living on his pension, it would no longer be possible for us to support him if he got into financial difficulties. After that, the letters and visits virtually stopped."

At this point, old Mr. Webb, who had appeared not to be taking any notice of either Rudd or the conversation but had remained silent, staring out through the window at a small, enclosed back garden, turned towards them and asked in a high, trembling voice, "Daniel? Has Daniel come?"

Miss Webb rose from her chair to bend over him.

"No, Henry," she said loudly. "It's someone asking about Daniel, that's all."

The old man appeared not to understand what she was saying for he continued, "He ought to be home soon."

"One of these days, perhaps, Henry. But he went away to London. Don't you remember?"

Miss Webb's tone became more insistent with the edge of some other quality about it that Rudd could not quite define. It was not exactly triumph—for all her faults, she had too much Christian charity for that —but it was the voice of a woman who believed the truth must always be spoken, whatever the circumstances, and who found a self-righteous satisfaction in doing so.

Mr. Webb fell silent and his sister tidied him up before returning to her chair, rearranging the rug over his knees and placing his hands side by side on top of it in much the same manner, Rudd imagined, that she would move the ornaments along the mantelshelf into their precise positions.

"He kept in touch with his sister, Nina," Rudd remarked when she had resumed her seat. He made the comment casually but watched her face closely as he said it and saw two patches of dull red appear on her cheekbones. Although she might be capable of discussing Danny almost neutrally as if she had learned to come to terms with his shortcomings and misdemeanours, it was quite clear that Nina could still arouse some old, emotional response.

"That doesn't surprise me in the least," she replied, a harder snap in her voice. "That girl always had the worst possible influence over Daniel. I blame her for much that went wrong. She seemed to go out of her way to undermine my authority over him. Being older than he was, she should have known better. Half of the mischief he was involved in was instigated by her. In fact, I'm not sure that Daniel's decision to leave home wasn't largely her fault. After he left, we found some letters she had sent him through a school friend, full of descriptions of parties she had been to and public houses she had visited—what she called 'having a good time.' She was quite lacking in any sense of responsibility."

"Her running away from home must have had some effect on Daniel," Rudd said with an innocent expression.

"We tried to keep the truth from him, of course, but there was so much gossip in the village that I'm afraid he found out what had happened from other people. It broke Henry's heart. She simply walked out early one morning with a suitcase, leaving a note on the dining-room table."

It was a small point but interesting all the same, and Rudd wondered if Danny hadn't been subconsciously following her example when he, too, chose to clear out of the caravan in the early hours of the morning.

"Wasn't she under age?" Rudd asked. They had at last got to the subject of Nina Gifford, a topic he intended following through as far as Miss Webb would allow him.

"She was seventeen. I felt the police should have been informed. After all, the man was years older than her and a total stranger."

"You never met him?"

"No. I believe he was from London. An artist, or so she said in her letter. The whole business was a madness! Total folly!"

"And were the police called in?"

"No. Henry refused to allow it. 'Let her go,' he said. 'But I never want her name mentioned in this house again.'"

It was an embargo that still seemed to be in operation, for Rudd realised that Miss Webb had never once referred to her niece by name. Nor did she, even when speaking of her own brother, so much as glance in his direction, as if the senile old man occupying the chair by the window had no connection with the Reverend Henry Webb who had been involved in that family drama all those years before.

"The fact was," Miss Webb continued, "we had already had dealings with the police only a short time before and Henry felt there had been enough trouble in the village without stirring up another scandal."

"Scandal?" Rudd picked the word up eagerly, wondering if this might not concern the facts about Nina's past about which Quinn had been so curious. "To do with your niece?"

"Oh, no!" Miss Webb was quick to put him right. "The church was broken into and the altar desecrated. Of course, the police had to be informed and inquiries were made round the village which caused a lot of ill feeling. Henry had his suspicions, you see, of the people who were involved although he didn't like to name them."

She broke off and got to her feet once again, this time to go to the side-board, a drawer of which she opened and from which she took a small, black-painted, metal cashbox, shielding it from old Mr. Webb's sight as she carried it back to her chair, although her caution seemed unneces-sary. He had withdrawn once more into indifference and was staring out again through the window.

Rudd watched her curiously as she lifted the lid of the box. It was full of papers—letters mostly, still in their original envelopes, and Rudd sus-pected that they were those sent by Danny over the years. Possibly Nina's farewell message was also among them, preserved not as a love keepsake as Lionel Burnett had saved the scrawled notes she had sent him but as proof of betrayal and disaffection, a black museum of the emotions. Among the papers were several newspaper cuttings, one of which Miss Webb, with another of her surreptitious glances at her brother, passed to Rudd. It was from the *Daily Telegraph* for June 8, 1953, and had as its headline, "VICAR'S PULPIT APPEAL." The story itself was short and factual, merely stating that, following the desecration of his church, St. Michael's in Heversham, Essex, the Reverend Henry Webb had appealed to his pa-rishioners to assist the police in their inquiries. "You must not allow fam-ily loyalties to protect those guilty of the sin of sacrilege," he had said. The report concluded with the statement that two youths were helping the police with their inquiries.

Rudd returned the cutting, at a loss to know why Miss Webb had shown it to him. Her motive was not long in making itself clear.

"Henry already had this trouble on his hands," she said, pinching in her lips. "The village was full of journalists, taking photographs—even reports in some of the less reputable newspapers of black magic rites. Ab-solute nonsense, of course. The two boys concerned were simply local de-linquents who knew no better than to break into the church and vandalise the altar. Naturally, it caused a great number of problems for Henry: meetings with the parish council and the bishop, who had to reconsecrate the church, discussions with the boys' parents and probation officers. I'm afraid neither Henry nor I had time to notice what *she* was up to. It was only afterwards that we realised she had been slipping away to meet that man."

"Max Gifford?" Rudd suggested in his blandest tone. It seemed time that his name, at least, should be mentioned.

Miss Webb carefully refolded the cutting and returned it to the box which she replaced in the drawer.

"I don't know his name," she replied, her back to him, "and I have no desire to know it. I hold him responsible for what happened. He was staying in the next village, it seems, at the Rose and Crown and had walked over here one Saturday afternoon to sketch the church. They met. At least, I am repeating hearsay which was told to me later by local people who, under the guise of being helpful, took pleasure in passing on the gossip to Henry and myself. Several of Henry's parishioners saw them together but didn't think it important enough at the time to mention the fact either to me or her father until it was too late. She had evidently been meeting him halfway between the two villages, going off on her bicycle and making the excuse that she was spending the evening with a school friend. Her deception was quite cleverly planned. She even asked the friend to come to the house to collect her on one or two occasions so that we wouldn't be suspicious. She is totally amoral."

It was no doubt part of her self-protection which she had built up over the years that made her unaware of the implied hostility of the local people that lay behind much of what she had told him. Even the incident of the desecration of the church, seized on so eagerly by the newspapers, especially with its undercurrent of possible black magic ritual, could have been motivated as much by a desire to get back at the vicar and his sister as by a simple urge to vandalise. And yet this possibility appeared not to have crossed her mind any more than the thought that she and her brother might have been in some way to blame for what Nina and Danny had done. Her self-righteousness was like armour.

"'Amoral'?" Rudd picked up the word. It was an aspect of Nina Gifford which he himself had been aware of but not in the sense in which Miss Webb was using the term. Nina Gifford had her own set of moral values, which an older generation of people, certainly her aunt and her father, would discount as unworthy by normal codes of behaviour. But Nina's were not circumscribed by accepted mores. Hers were based on the needs of those she loved. So she would lie and cheat and possibly steal—perhaps even commit murder—not out of confirmed wickedness but only when survival, hers or those she cared for, depended on it.

"Like her mother!" Miss Webb said, her voice so loud that it penetrated even old Mr. Webb's consciousness, for he turned from his vacant survey of the garden to look at her, his face troubled. But Miss Webb had gone beyond the point of caring. The bitterness which she had carried for nearly fifty years had, at last, found expression. "God knows why he married her. She was a farmer's daughter, years younger than him. Not even properly educated. Certainly not suitable for a vicar's wife. They'd been married for less than a year when she ran off and left him."

"But she came back?"

"Oh, yes, but only because her mother was dying. Henry forgave her and the marriage was patched up somehow. It meant moving to another parish, of course. He could hardly remain in the same district with everyone gossiping behind his back. But that's the kind of blood that Nina and Danny inherited. It's no wonder, with her as an example, that they turned out the way they did."

To Rudd's relief, the outburst was cut short by a little cry from old Mr. Webb who had been watching their faces with the staring intensity of the deaf. It was unlikely that he had followed their conversation. His expression suggested that, like a child, he had grasped only the emotions and these had frightened him. He was struggling to rise from his chair, pushing back the folds of the blanket with his frail hands.

"Where are they, Connie?" he was asking. "They should be home by now. Where have they gone to?"

Miss Webb went to him immediately, soothing, tucking, tidying, her rigid back bent solicitously over him.

Rudd rose to his feet.

"I'll let myself out," he said quietly but he doubted if she heard him. As he left the room, he could hear her voice raised in explanation although perhaps admonition might have better described it.

"They've left home, Henry. They went away a long time ago. They won't be coming back."

She might, he thought savagely, as he shut the front door behind him and walked away from the house, have found it in her heart to spare the old man that final truth.

Boyce was waiting for him when he returned to the office.

"Webb's downstairs," he announced as soon as Rudd entered the room. "Marsh and Simpson brought him back a couple of hours ago. I suppose you'll want me to hang on here while you get a statement out of him."

He seemed filled with gloom at the prospect that had obviously occupied his mind since his return from London, for, until Rudd reminded him, he appeared to have forgotten the purpose of his trip.

"That can wait," Rudd told him. "How did you get on this afternoon? Did you see Bruce Lawford?"

"Oh, him. No, as a matter of fact, I didn't. He's out of the country, filming. I had a word with his secretary but she wasn't much help. All she could tell me was Lawford and Quinn met for lunch sometime in February at Quinn's suggestion. She didn't know what about and she hadn't heard anything about a partnership. Nor had any of the others I talked to, come to that."

"Filming?" Rudd repeated.

"That's right. He's a television producer. He's working on some serial at the moment, set partly in Spain, so he's over in Madrid. Nice work if you can get it, eh? I wouldn't mind a few weeks in the sun, all expenses paid, too. The most I'll manage this year is a couple of weeks in Cornwall if I'm lucky."

Rudd hardly heard him. The familiarity of the name now made sense to him. When he had first seen it on Miss Martin's list, he had associated it with the printed word and had made the assumption that he must have read it in a newspaper. Now he could see that he had been wrong in that conclusion. He had seen it on the credit titles of a television play that he had watched a couple of months before. Its title now escaped him and all that remained in his mind were images of the sea, beautifully photographed, and a death by drowning so powerful in its realism that he had looked out for the name of the producer at the end.

He was not normally a television enthusiast, rarely having time to watch and only then when he was too tired to do anything more demanding than sit in front of the screen. Quite frequently, he fell asleep in the middle of a programme, waking to find that the news had been re-placed by some imported American detective serial, so that, for a few be-wildered seconds, it appeared that a high-speed car chase or a rooftop shoot-out were occupying the main nine o'clock headlines. Not that it would have been all that surprising if it had. Quite often the real world had the unpleasant and disturbing tendency to reflect the imagined, so that one was not sure which mirror it was that, with the ugly, distorting twist of violence running across its surface, was being held up to the world.

"That programme a few weeks ago," he began.

"What programme?" Boyce demanded. He had been in the middle of complaining that even Cornwall might be out of the question next sum-mer as the gearbox on the car would probably need replacing and there was no way he could afford both.

"At the end of March. Bruce Lawford produced it."

"Who was in it?" Boyce asked, which was no help at all.

"That tall actor with the moustache."

"Do you mean Maurice Davies? He's in 'Shades of Night' on ATV on a Thursday evening."

"How should I know?" Rudd demanded irritably. It was like trying to explain a complicated route to someone who was a stranger in the dis-trict, when familiar landmarks become totally meaningless and one is forced to describe features of an area one hadn't oneself looked at prop-erly for years. "All I know is it was set on an island off the coast of Scotland and the man was drowned trying to get back."

"Oh, I know which one you mean." Boyce sounded relieved at having got there at last. "It was called something like 'Farewell to Summer.' The chap was a game warden, wasn't he? Something to do with wildlife, anyway. Then his wife decided she'd had enough and caught the steamer back to civilisation. He had a few drinks in the meantime, realised a woman was better than an island full of bloody gannets, and tried to join her. His boat went arse over tip halfway across."

It was a travesty of the plot but it hardly mattered. They were clearly talking about the same play.

"As a matter of fact," Boyce continued, "wasn't it one of those semidocumentaries based on a real-life story? I seem to remember there was a bit of a fuss in the *Express* the next day, saying if the writer and producer wanted to make a programme about the bloke, they should stick to the facts and not muck about with them."

"My God!" Rudd said softly. "That's the answer."

Boyce looked at him.

"What answer?"

"To Quinn's murder. The facts, Tom! You know, like in the play? They've been staring me in the face, some of them for the past few days, and I haven't had the gumption to put them together to make the right story."

As he said it, he remembered the feeling he had experienced when talking to Blanche Lester in the park about Nina Gifford's relationship with Max and how the details had become connected in his mind with memories of the fairy story he had heard in school of the princess and the Wicked Fairy.

"What facts are you talking about?" Boyce was asking. "If you mean evidence, we've gone over that enough times, God help us. I don't see how you can rearrange any of it. And what's this about a story, anyway? We're not dealing with a television plot, you know."

"Of course we're not and that's the whole point. It's real. There's nothing fictional about it. So let's take another look at that real evidence which we haven't so far been able to fit into a theory. Fact number one: someone, presumably the murderer, wiped the floor with a sack after Quinn's body had been dumped in the outbuilding. Fact number two: Gifford divorced his first wife in 1937 but he and Nina never married. Fact number three, and I've only discovered this piece of evidence this afternoon and it didn't mean anything to me at the time: the church at Heversham was broken into in 1953 and the altar was desecrated. It made quite a stir at the time, enough to get into some of the London dailies."

"I don't get the connection," Boyce said heavily.

"No?" said Rudd. "Then I'll tell you."

He made the account as brief as he could, aware that time was passing and that, before the arrest could be made, there were still a few facts he had to check with Danny Webb.

Webb parted with the information reluctantly. He had been brought up from the cells into an interview room and entered with the same look of eager appeal that now seemed his habitual expression rather than the air of surly insolence with which he had first greeted the Chief Inspector. A few hours in custody had cut him down to size. In his time, Rudd had known hundreds of Danny Webbs. Small-time crooks and petty thieves, they usually ended up at the bottom of the heap—lost, pathetic, lonely men, beaten by the system they had once, with the arrogance of youth, imagined they could manipulate. Danny Webb was already halfway down that road.

He answered Rudd's questions with an air of bewilderment.

"What the hell's it all about?" he asked when the Chief Inspector had finished.

Rudd didn't even bother to reply. He grasped Boyce's shoulder as they made for the door, half pushing him through it, at the same time thrusting his other arm into the sleeve of his raincoat. He was still putting it on when they emerged from the building into the car park.

Waiting while Boyce unlocked the car, he allowed himself a few moments' grace to look up at the sky.

It was already twilight although a dull ember of light still faintly flecked the darkness to the west where the sun, slipping down beyond the horizon's rim, cast up a cindery incandescence.

By the time they reached Althorpe House, the glimmer had vanished and night had taken over; proper darkness, not the bastard city dusk which is never entirely complete but always tinged with the red glow of lights shining upward and tinselled with the cheap jewellery of the street lamps. The stars were out and the sky was vast, against which the bulk of Althorpe House seemed larger than usual—square, massive, safe, its chimney stacks blocks of solid blackness. There was no light showing in the front windows, only a dark sheen on glass.

At Rudd's instructions, Boyce parked just inside the gate and they approached the house on foot, following the pale curve of the gravelled drive round to the back.

At the yard entrance, Rudd stopped abruptly, overwhelmed by a feeling of déjà vu which, with its sudden, unexpected jarring of all normal responses, heightens awareness and sharpens the senses to a pitch beyond common, everyday perception.

The yard stretched out in front of him, enclosed on two sides by buildings—on his left, the house itself, soaring upward like a cliff of brick; to his right, the lower escarpment of the outbuildings, the irregular peak of their roofs cutting the sky into a triangle. Between them, the floor of the yard had vanished into the darkness so that he had the impression of standing on the edge of a huge, rectangular tank filled with black water across which he must plunge towards the square of lighted window which, with its curtains drawn, glowed with a subdued, yellowish gleam and seemed to symbolise old, half-forgotten pleasures: firelight and lamplight shining down onto a white tablecloth set with cups and plates.

While his attention was centred on the window and the black gulf which separated him from it, he was aware at the same time of the night noises that surrounded him: the furtive shuffling of some creature in the bushes, the tinkling rustle of the ivy that grew up the wall at his side, the rasp of branch on branch, and further away still, the subdued tumult of a light wind in the trees, sounding like some distant, landlocked sea beating on a distant shore.

And beyond that, silence and darkness that only the stars inhabited.

Coming home. The phrase came into his mind simultaneously with all the other sensations and, in the same split second of time, banished them. The connection had been made and his rational mind took over. He was no longer the child pausing in the backyard to savour the moment of homecoming. There was no table laid for tea or "Children's Hour" on the wireless; no fire banked so high in the kitchen range that it stung the skin to sit near it; no oil lamp, although conscious memory could re-create its milky glass globe and polished brass base, the circular pool of light it cast on the white tablecloth, and his scattered schoolbooks.

He was a middle-aged Chief Inspector of police, halting momentarily at the entrance to the yard of Althorpe House as if accustoming his eyes to the darkness and, behind the lighted window, the only person who waited for him was Nina Gifford.

CHAPTER 15

After leaving Danny at the bus stop that same morning, Nina walked home across the fields. The countryside had lost its early morning beauty and had settled down into the mere ordinariness of the familiar landscape, untransformed, unglorified. Without Danny, the rest of the day also assumed the same humdrum monotony. She woke Max and gave him his breakfast, got him washed, and settled back into bed. He seemed disinclined to talk and she made no efforts herself to force conversation.

Downstairs, she cleared the bedding from the sofa and put it away, unable to bear this reminder of Danny's presence. Once she had washed up his breakfast things, there was nothing left of him except her own sense of bereavement, although she tried to follow him in her imagination, checking the kitchen clock every so often to relate his time to hers. Ten forty-five, and he'd be arriving at Victoria. Eleven-twenty and he should be on his way to Zoe's, if not actually there. She tried to picture him walking along the North End Road to Zoe's turning, finding the number of the house, and descending the basement steps.

Her imagination broke down after that. She couldn't envisage what sort of welcome Zoe would give him or how Danny would behave in that dark, little underground room, and she wished to hell Zoe was on the phone so that she could ring up and talk to him, if only to reiterate the warning that he had not given her time to repeat before they parted that morning.

At lunchtime, however, the pattern was broken. Max suddenly announced that he wanted to get up.

"Now?" she asked, astonished, her attention focusing on him properly for the first time that day. She saw at once that he looked better; still not quite his former self but at least not the grey-faced, exhausted old man who had lain so listlessly in bed for the past few days.

"Yes, I'm fed up with lying here, Nine. That bloody cedar tree is getting on my nerves. If it isn't staring in at me through the window during the day, it's fidgeting about muttering to itself half the night. I want a change of scene."

"All right," she conceded. "But eat your lunch first."

He insisted on dressing himself or at least putting on as many of his clothes as he could manage alone. Sent outside to wait on the landing, Nina watched him through the crack of the door which she had deliberately left ajar, marvelling at his persistence as he struggled into his shirt and hoisted himself painfully up from the bed to drag his trousers over his backside. It was as much as she could do not to burst in and help him. Finally, when he had transferred his cigarettes and matches from the bedside table to his pocket, he called out to her, his face proud at his achievement, while she knelt, like a disciple at his feet, she thought with a mixture of genuine admiration and amused irreverence, to put on his socks and shoes.

"There!" she said, patting his ankle as she tied the last lace.

Getting him downstairs took all of ten minutes. They halted at every tread, Max carefully realigning his feet before tentatively feeling for the next one. At the bottom, he paused, clinging to the newel-post, a curious, faraway expression on his face as if all his concentration were turned inwards in the effort of gathering up sufficient strength for the final trek into the kitchen. They made it at last and she lowered him into the basket chair which she placed in its habitual position near the back door.

"Brandy?" she asked him. He oughtn't to drink, of course, but it would be hours before he took his tablets and she felt some celebration was called for. Fetching the bottle, she realised how little was left. She and Danny had almost finished it the previous evening.

He sipped it leisurely, holding the glass between both his hands as if drawing up the essence of the spirit through its sides, his face turned towards the sun to absorb its warmth with the same, slow, pleasurable indulgence of the senses.

Later, he slept, waking when she walked past him to close the back door, the sun having moved down behind the house, leaving the yard in shadow.

"What's the time, Nina?" he asked.

"Nearly quarter past seven."

He had slept longer than usual, exhausted, no doubt, by the exertion of dressing and coming downstairs.

"I can smell something cooking."

"It's supper."

While he had been asleep, she had prepared the evening meal—kidneys in gravy because that was all the village shop had to offer in the way of meat that had looked at all appetizing. Besides, she had an almost superstitious belief in the efficacy of offal as nourishment for the body. Liver, brains, heart, kidneys—they did you more good than the usual stewing steak or chops. They were cheaper, too, which was another consideration almost as important.

She took the casserole dish out of the oven to show him, lifting the lid to reveal them sizzling in their rich juices, the slices of onion reduced to a glorious, pulpy mass of pure flavour.

"It looks good," he said appreciatively.

"It is good," she retorted.

She was suddenly happy that he was at last showing an interest in food. He was her old Max again. The intervening days were like a dark valley out of which they had both begun slowly to climb.

"Tell you what," Max was saying. "What about a bottle of something to go with it? Like the old times in the studio, eh, Nine?"

She knew what he meant. In fact, for a few seconds, she felt they shared the same memory: the big, upper room with the scarred, circular table they had bought in a second-hand shop in Pimlico standing under the window, half-laid for supper with the long French loaf and the bottle of wine. Max had painted it once, one of the few still lifes he had ever attempted. It was still hanging in the sitting room because no one had wanted to buy it, and even she had to admit that it wasn't his best work; he had never been inspired by mere objects. Even so, he had caught something of their amplitude and their promise of good living in the rough, crisp crust of the bread and the light glistening richly on the shoulders of the dark wine bottle.

All the same, she hesitated, thinking about the cost. But Max, as if anticipating her doubt, was fumbling in his pocket and producing a five pound note. God knows where he had got it from. Judging by its crumpled condition, he must have been hanging on to it for months.

"Go on, Nine," he coaxed. "Even the Feathers ought to be able to rustle up a bottle of plonk."

She got her bike out of the stable and set off down the drive. The sun was setting but she thought she ought to be back before dark; a minor consideration but one that worried her slightly nevertheless. Since Max had become crippled, she so rarely went out in the evenings that the batteries in the lamps must have long since corroded.

All the lights were on in the Feathers, including the red-shaded wall lamps in the shape of candles and the pink strip light over the bar. It seemed strange to plunge into that pink and red glow when outside the sky was still on fire with the real scarlet and gold of the setting sun. She could see it through one of the tiny casement windows, like a bonfire on the far side of the wheat field across the road, and, in the distance, a line of trees cut out in dark silhouette against it. It was the sort of view she liked, dramatic and colourful. Not to Max's taste, though. That's chocolate-box stuff, he would have said. He hated snow for the same reason. Christmas cards had ruined it for him.

The bar was almost empty; it was still too early for the real evening trade. There were only two men at the counter, farmhands having a pint on their way home, she imagined. Their bikes had been propped up outside. She knew only one of the men by sight. He'd called at the house once for water when his tractor had boiled over and they had stood talking in the yard for a while about the previous owners. Nina had listened reluctantly. She had preferred not to know who had inhabited the place before she and Max moved in. Now, not remembering his name, she nodded to him and he nodded back, having also forgotten hers, and, moving his beer mug along the counter to make room for her, began talking in a low voice to his companion, half turning his back to her. She guessed he was explaining who she was because she could see the other man's eyes look towards her from time to time over his friend's shoulder.

She didn't mind their lack of overt friendliness, having long ago grown accustomed to country people's reserve, although she missed the old, easy companions in London who had dropped in at the studio at any time and stayed talking half the night. Apart from Lionel, she knew no one in the village really well and now even he had withdrawn his friendship.

The landlord remembered her, though, and asked after Max. Before Max had become crippled, they had frequently spent the evening at the Feathers where Max had built up a small circle of drinking companions. But even with them, she had never felt totally at ease and none of them had bothered to call at the house since Max's illness. She realised there were too many differences dividing them from the villagers: their own London background, Max's profession of artist, the isolation of the house from the main village, her own disinclination to join in village activities, such as the Women's Institute or the Church Fellowship. It was largely their own fault that they had remained cut off from the local people.

"Max?" she replied. "Oh, he's a bit better today."

"Glad to hear it," the landlord said. "And what can I get you?"

"I'd like a bottle of red wine, please, if you've got one."

It took time. The keys to the cellar had to be detached from their hook, the cellar unlocked and the bottle found. Carrying it back into the bar, the landlord noticed it was dusty and took it away again to wipe it.

Nina didn't mind. She was used to slow service in the village shop. While she waited, she studied the collection of beer mats pinned up on the wall behind the counter and patted the head of the landlord's Labrador which came from behind the bar to examine her, turning its ears inside out to expose the pinkish inner skin and the delicate whorls of the openings, fringed with fine, pale hairs. She thought of Danny, too, who must have become accustomed to the place during the few days he had stayed in the village and she wondered what he was doing at that moment. Probably, like her, he was standing at the bar of some pub, only in London, perhaps the one in which she had treated herself to a lunch-time sandwich and a drink on her way to Zoe's that Tuesday. It seemed a lifetime away.

The sun had sunk by the time she had paid for the bottle and could leave. Propping it up carefully in the basket, she looked up at the sky. Strictly speaking, it was after lighting-up time but she didn't want to walk home. It would take nearly a quarter of an hour.

In the end, she compromised by scooting the bike along the edge of the road, keeping one foot on the grass verge so that if the local bobby happened to pass, she could argue with some justification that she hadn't actually been riding. The bottle wobbled about in the basket, its head nodding this way and that. It had come up ice cold from the cellar, too chilled to drink straight away, but, if she drew the cork and stood it on top of the boiler, it ought to be warmed through by the time they were ready to eat. The price had been exorbitant, too, far more than an ordinary off-licence would charge, and she decided that if Max asked for the change, she'd tell him she'd treated herself to a gin and tonic. That way, she'd avoid any fuss.

"Max!" she called out when, having put her bike away, she entered the kitchen. "Max, I've got a bottle but it's . . ."

She stopped in the doorway. The kitchen was empty. The basket chair still stood where she had last seen it, facing the door, but Max wasn't seated in it. There was only his cushion lying on the seat.

Her first reaction was exasperation. The old fool! He must have been taken short and tried to go to the lavatory on his own. Dumping down the bottle on the table, she started towards the door that led into the hall but halted before she had taken more than a pace. There were unfamiliar objects on the table which had not been there when she had left for the Feathers. In the space where she had left the chopping board and pushed aside to make room for it was Max's big, japanned box of paints which she had last seen in the sideboard cupboard in the dining room. Its top tray full of squeezed-out tubes of paint was lifted out and lying separately to expose the bottom section in which was a muddle of brushes, broken sticks of charcoal, and paint-smeared rags. Beside it was a heap of washing, including the sheets from the caravan which she had intended ironing but hadn't yet got round to and had been bundled away on Max's wheelchair. The chair itself had gone from its accustomed corner.

But neither the presence of the box nor the absence of the chair alarmed her as much as the sight of the envelope, addressed to her in Max's handwriting, that was propped up against the box. It had been folded in half and was badly creased as if it had been kept in his trouser pocket.

Even before she tore it open and read it, she knew where she would find him and, throwing aside the two sheets of paper, she set off at a stumbling run across the lawn where the cedar tree stood muttering to itself just as Max had described it, its layered branches keeping up a harsh, whispered conversation.

He was sitting in the wheelchair in the summerhouse, facing out towards the darkening lawn where Lilith had last appeared to him, the gun lying on the wooden boards below his right hand, which hung down over the arm of the chair, the index finger extended as if pointed out to her.

Thank God, she thought absurdly, his head's undamaged.

It was tipped back as if in slumber, thick, white hair a little rumpled, the formidable nose jutting upward but the expression on his face serene. He might have fallen asleep in the middle of some pleasant reverie.

She did not touch him, apart from pulling up the rug to cover the wound in his chest and, when she had completed that ministration, she took his hand and laid it against her lips.

It was the kind of farewell Max would have preferred, without any fuss or histrionics; just a simple parting with the briefest physical contact between them and no words spoken as, in the same manner the day before, he had taken her hand and laid it against his heart. His own gesture of farewell, as she now realised.

Rudd found her sitting in the kitchen when, having knocked and received no answer, he let himself in, Boyce at his heels.

One look at her face was enough to tell him what had happened.

"Where is he?" he asked.

She gestured towards the garden.

"In the summerhouse."

Boyce nodded in answer to Rudd's unspoken instruction and left the room, while the Chief Inspector drew up a chair beside her.

"He left a letter explaining everything," Nina said and passed a sheet of paper to him.

"You had no idea?" Rudd asked gently, taking it from her but making no attempt to read it.

She shook her head.

"None. I was afraid it was Danny. When did you realise the truth?"

"Only a short while ago." He got up from the table and began preparing tea, putting the kettle on to boil and finding cups and saucers. Their conversation assumed an almost laconic quality, he pottering about with the slightly disengaged air of a man occupied with a simple, domestic task, Nina listening and following his movements with her eyes, occasionally indicating where he could find the things he needed. "I went to see your father and aunt this afternoon."

"How were they?" she asked with an automatic response.

"Quite well. Your father's getting old, of course. It was your aunt who told me about your mother running away from home soon after she was married. At the time, I didn't make the connection."

"With Lilith?"

"No."

"Neither did I until I read Max's letter. It seems unbelievable and yet I suppose once you realise they'd met, the rest had to follow. Like Max's exhibition."

She was speaking in the kind of conversational shorthand which only people who have known each other for years normally use, in which superfluous explanation is omitted, but Rudd could follow exactly what she meant. Once you accepted the basic premise of Max's affair with Nina's mother, her own meeting with Max and their subsequent relationship became inevitable because he had sought her out in the same way as Eustace Quinn, having acquired some of Max Gifford's sketches, came looking for him.

"Where did they meet?" he asked. "London?"

He had been forced to make that assumption as Danny had been uncertain where his mother had gone during that brief separation, although he had been able to supply the date, September 1936.

"Yes. Max explains in his letter. She went to a hotel in Gower Place, quite close to the art school where Max was teaching at the time. They met in the street one afternoon. Max stopped her and asked if she'd act as his model. It was the sort of thing he often did. They fell in love with each other almost at once. Max had a friend who rented a studio in Bloomsbury and they used to go there. She was afraid, if Max ever exhibited the portraits, that someone might recognize her, which was why he always painted her with her face hidden although, knowing him, I don't think that was the only reason. She was Lilith, his secret love, and he didn't want to share her with anyone. And then she left him to go back to my father. Max didn't say why."

"Her own mother was dying," Rudd explained.

"Who told you that?"

"Your aunt."

"How strange! She never spoke to me about my mother except to make little, hurtful remarks about her. I wonder why she told you."

Rudd carried the teapot over to the table, using this as an excuse not to reply. He did not want to have to explain that it had slipped out during an outburst directed against Nina herself, the outpourings of a lonely, embittered woman who could no longer hold back the dislike she had nurtured for so long against her niece.

"There's something else I don't understand," Nina continued. "How did Max find out our address? My parents had moved parishes, you see, shortly before I was born and Max can't have had any idea where we were living. He says in his letter that she went away and he didn't know where she had gone."

"The church was vandalised. Do you remember? There were reports in some of the London papers. I assume Max read one of them and recognised the surname. He must have known enough of Lilith's background to realise she was the wife of a country vicar, so he made the connection. The newspaper reports came out in June and shortly afterwards he arrived in the next village."

"And he came looking for her?"

"Yes. So when you met it wasn't entirely coincidental. He found out that Lilith had died several years before, which must have shocked him. But what he really hadn't bargained for was the fact that he would fall in love with her daughter."

It was Nina, thank God, who put into words the next part of the story.

"It wasn't true he was my father. That part of the letter is crazy!"

"But that's what he thought," Rudd said quietly. "He worked out the dates and it must have seemed possible that Lilith was carrying his child when she left him."

"The silly old fool!" Nina's voice was full of exasperated tenderness. "Even though neither Zoe nor I had children, it never seemed to occur to him that he was sterile. I suppose it would have hurt his pride to admit it. He was Max, the great lover, the great painter. He had to be able to create life as well as pictures. I could have told him the truth if he'd asked, but we never spoke about it. There was a lot of things we never discussed. It's too late now."

"Didn't it occur to you to ask why he would never agree to marry you, which, of course, given the relationship he thought there was between you, he couldn't do?"

She looked at him with the same baffled exasperation, surprised at his obtuseness.

"No. Max said he didn't want to and that was that. I just accepted it. Anyway, it didn't seem important. We were as good as legally married and I knew he'd never leave me."

She smiled with secret satisfaction, remembering the day when Max had placed the crown of flowers on her head, a ceremony performed in front of witnesses that had been infinitely more hallowed and binding than any words mumbled over them in some London Registry Office. Not understanding the reason, Rudd wondered at the strength of her conviction.

"And that's why Quinn had to die," he continued in the same conversational voice. "He was asking too many questions and Max was afraid he'd find out the truth. Did he explain that part to you?"

"Yes. Evidently Eustace Quinn spoke to Max about it on Thursday evening. They were talking alone in the sitting room. He told Max that he'd found out a bit about his life and it was his relationship with me that had first given him the idea. He told Max it was a good story and he knew a television producer who was interested in making a play out of it. It was to be broadcast at the same time as the exhibition was put on. That way, they'd get maximum publicity and Max's work would fetch top prices." She made a little grimace of disgust. "He told Max he'd wake up and find he was famous overnight. 'Instant success' was the way he put it. God! It makes me angry enough to want to kill Eustace Quinn myself when I think of the years Max struggled to make a name for himself and yet only a handful of people have ever heard of him."

"Did you know Quinn had already bought up quite a few of Max's paintings on the quiet?"

"No, but it doesn't surprise me," she replied, her voice hard. "I warned him that Eustace Quinn would drive a hard bargain. It was part of the deal, of course. No television play, no exhibition. Max had to choose. On Thursday evening Max decided instead to kill him. He was afraid, if I found out the truth about Lilith, I'd leave him. But even if I'd known, it wouldn't have made any difference. Max should have realised that."

"So you don't think that was the real motive?" Rudd asked.

"It was a large part of it. Max was growing old, you see, and was losing his self-confidence. Perhaps I was to blame for that. I let him see that there were days when I was tired of looking after him. But, for God's sake, he should have known me better than to believe I would ever leave him."

Her anger flashed up briefly, directed partly at Max but mostly against herself. But she did not add, as she might have done, that Max's motive for murdering Quinn must have stemmed also from his own deeply felt bitterness and resentment that after a lifetime of devotion to his art, he would be recognised, not so much as a painter but as a character from a television play designed to fictionalise his love affair with a schoolgirl.

Rudd had finished his own tea. Nina's was only half drunk and the rest was going cold. He refilled their cups before asking the next question in a voice that was almost casual.

"How did he do it, Nina?"

Neither of them found his use of her Christian name in any way un-usual. Seated with her at the table, he had again assumed the role of family friend, only this time there was nothing unnatural about it and she accepted it as real.

"He shot himself."

"Do you know where he got the gun from?"

"It belonged to Zoe. God knows how she got hold of it, but before she met Max she used to have a lot of lovers. Perhaps one of them gave it to her. All I know is she threatened Max with it once years ago and he took it off her. He must have kept it hidden in here." She indicated the lower section of the paint box with its jumble of rags and brushes. "I don't know why he hung onto it but Max was always secretive about some things. Perhaps he liked it because it was a symbol of male power. He sometimes said a paintbrush was feminine. It was the equivalent of a woman's embroidery needle."

A gun was also a phallic symbol, Rudd thought although he said noth-ing, merely nodding encouragingly to her to continue.

"He must have fetched the box when I was at the Feathers buying a bottle of wine. It was Max's idea I should go. I can see now that he had it all planned out. It was the first day he felt strong enough to get up, you see, after . . ."

For a moment, her voice faltered and she didn't finish the sentence. Rudd completed the phrase "after the murder" silently to himself as Nina added, "He must have got himself into the wheelchair and pushed himself into the dining room. God knows when he wrote the letter. This morning, perhaps, or last night. It would have taken him ages because he could hardly hold a pen. He insisted on getting himself dressed so it must have been then when he put it in his pocket. I didn't see him do it. I'm still not sure how he managed to get to the summerhouse across the grass."

Rudd had his own theory about this, which he had no intention of explaining to her. Instead, he finished his tea and got to his feet.

"I'm going to have a word with my Sergeant. I shan't be long. Among other things, I want to arrange to have your brother brought over here."

Her face immediately became full of eagerness as well as anxiety.

"Danny! You've found him in London? Oh, God, is he all right?"

"Yes, perfectly. We brought him back to headquarters for questioning, but I'll see now that he's released and I'll order a car to drive him straight here."

He left it at that. Danny himself could explain exactly what had hap-pened.

"I'll have to get a bed and a meal ready for him!" she cried.

As he left, she was already on her feet, clearing the table of their used cups.

Outside, Rudd stood in the yard and, taking Max Gifford's letter from his pocket, he tipped it towards the light which fell through the cur-tained kitchen window. It was a single sheet of paper, carrying that day's date but no other superscription, an omission which made him suspect that there had been another letter addressed to Nina that she had not shown him. If he asked, she would no doubt deny its existence. Besides, what was the point? What he had in his hands was sufficient.

It read, in an awkward, painful handwriting as if Max Gifford had found difficulty in holding the pen:

"I killed Eustace Quinn because I was afraid he was going to find out the truth about Nina's mother. I called her Lilith but her real name was Margaret Webb. I met her in London in 1936 when she had run away from her husband. We became lovers but, after a few weeks, she left me to return home, I didn't know where.

"In 1953, I discovered her address and went to find her, only to learn she had died about eight years before. While in the village, I met her daughter who, I had reason to believe, was also my child, a secret I have told no one.

"Eustace Quinn wanted to make the story of my relationship with Nina into a television play which would be broadcast at the same time as the exhibition. He made it clear that one would depend on the other and that I would have to sign a contract permitting the facts to be used as a basis for the plot. It seemed possible that, in researching the story, he might stumble on the truth about Lilith, a risk I dare not take.

"He told me this on Thursday evening when we were alone together and I decided then that I would have to kill him. He came the following morning after I had arranged for Nina to be out of the house. I was genuinely in pain but I also knew that there were only a few tablets left. At my request, Quinn helped me downstairs to the kitchen where I struck him with the flatiron which was used to prop open the door. I then lifted his body into the wheelchair and moved it to the washhouse before returning to bed.

"I have decided to kill myself rather than face old age in prison. It is the cleanest way out. Nina knows nothing either of Quinn's murder or of my intention to commit suicide. She is entirely innocent of both."

It was signed "M.G." in the same manner in which he had initialled the sketches of Lilith, the tail of the letter G curling back to encompass the M.

Having read it, Rudd replaced it in his pocket. He was more than ever convinced that Max had written another letter, intended only for Nina, for she had referred to details of Max's relationship with Lilith which were not included in this account.

This one, his official statement, was short and factual, unemotional in its stark language which did not attempt to excuse or even to explain more than the barest outline of what had happened. What agony Gifford had experienced in deciding on that double killing, Rudd could only guess. But the memory of his face with its expression of utter exhaustion returned to the Chief Inspector's mind. Max Gifford had looked into the abyss of a personal hell and had been unable to contemplate its horrors any longer. At least, as he himself had stated, the alternative had the merit of a clean quietus which he had been able to control and in which some degree of self-respect had been possible.

Rudd would not have wished it otherwise, a sentiment he did not express to Boyce whom he found pacing up and down the sunken lawn that faced the summerhouse.

"I thought you were never coming," he said, as he clambered up the bank to meet the Chief Inspector.

"You've had a look at him?" Rudd asked, ignoring the complaint.

"Yes. He's been dead about an hour, I'd say. Shot through the heart so he didn't stand any chance of surviving it. He'd undone his shirt to get to the right place, I assume."

"Don't forget he was an artist. He'd know quite a lot about human anatomy," Rudd pointed out. "Got a torch?"

"I fetched it from the car. Do you want to have a look at him?"

The beam caught the seated figure in its spotlight and illuminated also a restricted circle of rough planks, some still retaining the bark, of which the summerhouse was made.

"Someone must have pulled the rug up over the wound," Boyce added. "I had to fold it back."

Nina, Rudd guessed. The rug was now lying across the lap, exposing the broad chest with the wound, dark with blood, on the left-hand side, like a mouth set agape.

Moving the torch downwards, Rudd shone it onto the gun that was lying on the boards.

"A 1910 Mauser automatic—6.35 millimetre, takes a rimless ammunition," Boyce said with the quick but deliberately off-hand knowledge of the expert. He fancied himself as something of a specialist in guns, those macho symbols of the phallus, the strong, thrusting extension of the body that ejaculated death. "Probably brought back by someone who'd served in the First World War as booty captured off a prisoner. It's a German officer's sidearm. But how the hell did he get himself here?"

It was the same question that Nina had asked and this time Rudd offered an explanation.

"Nina helped him downstairs as he couldn't make it alone. She had no idea, of course, what was in his mind. After he'd sent her out on the pretext of buying a bottle of wine, he must have got himself into the wheelchair which he could have managed on his own. Nina Gifford told me at the start of the investigation that he could walk a few steps by himself if he'd got something to hold on to. Besides, it's incredible what physical strength even a cripple can produce if he has to. My guess is that he propelled himself as far as the edge of the lawn and then pushed the chair from there, using it as a support. He couldn't have got it across the rough grass in any other way. And don't forget, he'd already done much the same with Quinn's body."

Earlier that evening, Rudd had already gone over that part of the theory with Boyce—how Quinn, having arrived at Althorpe House, had gone upstairs to find Max, as arranged, and had helped him down to the kitchen where Max had killed him. At the time, Rudd had not known what weapon had been used but Max Gifford's letter had now made that clear. The flatiron was not only to hand but was also the right shape with its blunted edge. And it was heavy enough to crack anybody's spine.

What happened after that had been, in effect, a dummy run for his own subsequent suicide. The body had been lifted into the wheelchair and Max Gifford, clinging to its handle, had pushed it across the yard to the outbuilding, not daring to leave it in the kitchen, If he had, suspicion would almost certainly have been directed immediately towards him for he could not have failed to be aware of a murder taking place inside the house. As Rudd had pointed out to Boyce, the fact that the murderer had obliterated the marks on the washhouse floor should have put him on to Max Gifford much earlier. It wasn't footprints that he had been so anxious to get rid of but the telltale double line of grooves where the wheels of the chair had run across the dust.

How the hell he had got himself upstairs again, Rudd could only guess. It must have taken a superhuman effort to drag himself from one tread to the next. It was no wonder that it had been three days before he had recovered from the exhaustion and that when Rudd had interviewed him he had appeared an old, sick man.

Rudd was, however, in no doubt that Max Gifford had planned the murder as carefully as his own suicide. On both occasions, he had made sure that Nina was out of the house, sent away on some pretext: on the first, to fetch medicine from the doctor's; on the second, a bottle of wine. The only mistake he had made was to mention that Quinn had spoken of a partner, thus leading Rudd eventually to the fact of Gifford's guilt, although Rudd was half inclined to believe that Gifford might have deliberately let fall that one, small, significant piece of information. An attempt, perhaps, to hint at the truth or even to give Rudd a sporting chance of discovering it?

Out loud, he said, "Well, there's nothing more we can do here, Tom. Get on the car radio and call up McCullum and Pardoe. We'll need an ambulance, too, and a couple of DCs to give a hand generally. Kyle and Marsh will do." Suddenly he changed his mind. "No, make that Kyle and Cunningham. It's about time that young recruit had a taste of violent death. And while you're at it, arrange for a car to bring Danny Webb over here. We've got no reason to hold him any longer and Nina Gifford's going to need someone to be with her."

"Will do," Boyce replied. "Where'll you be? Here?"

"No. I don't think Max Gifford will be needing my company. I'll be at the house with her."

She had been crying, he realised, when he reentered the kitchen. Her face had the swollen, blotched look of someone who had recently wept and her movements were heavy and languid. But pride, or perhaps having no more tears to shed, prevented her from breaking down again in front of him.

"I'll stay with you until Danny arrives," he offered. "That is, if you'd like me to."

"Please. Will it take long?"

He knew she did not mean just Danny's arrival but also of the police who were to take Max's body away.

"About an hour," he told her. "Possibly less. Is there anything I can do in the meantime?"

She answered so quickly that he guessed she had thought it out already.

"Yes, there is. Could you help me take down the picture over Max's bed? It's too heavy for me to manage on my own."

"Of course."

He followed her upstairs, wondering what she planned to do with it but, when he had manhandled it down from the wall, all she said was, "Turn it round, please, so I can't see it."

He propped it up under the window so that the canvas back was showing, permitting himself only the briefest of glances at it as he did so. Not that he could see much at such close quarters. The portrait was reduced to a mere chiaroscuro of swirls and daubs of colour, pink, red, black, flesh-tinted, the pigment standing out proud in places above the flat surface like a contour map of the body, following the landscape of the flesh.

After he had moved it into position, he drew the curtains across the window. That way, she would not see his men about their task when they arrived.

"What will you do now?" he asked her later when they had returned to the kitchen. They were drinking tea again which she had made this time, with an abstracted air as if only half her mind was on the task.

"I don't really know. I really haven't thought about it except I shan't stay here. I couldn't bear it. I suppose I shall sell the place and move back to London, although I can't imagine it will fetch much."

"Oh, I don't know," Rudd put in. "The land alone must be worth quite a bit."

"But the house needs a lot of spending on it."

"Could be," he agreed vaguely.

She made no further comment although Rudd could have added the ending to that particular story. She would buy, or possibly lease, a flat in London and Danny would move in with her. It had, he thought wryly, the inevitability of a fairy story. "And they lived happily ever after."

God help her!

Danny arrived before the ambulance. Rudd heard the car draw up in the yard and guessed, by the impatient slamming of its door, who it was who had come.

Getting up, he crossed the kitchen. Nina had guessed, too. She had risen to her feet in order to be ready to greet him, her arms already lifted in a gesture of welcome, her face transfigured, and, as he passed Danny on the doorstep, he heard her cry out loud,

"Danny! Oh, thank God you're here!"

Supervising the photographing and the removal of Max Gifford's body kept his mind busy and it was only when he returned to the yard, following the men who were carrying the stretcher to the waiting ambulance, that he allowed himself to think of her again.

Pausing in the yard, he glanced across at the lighted kitchen window, its curtains drawn against the outside world, and thought there would be no more homecomings for Max Gifford. Nor, come to that, for himself.

JUNE THOMSON was brought up in an Essex village, in a background very much like the setting of her novels. She was educated at London University. She makes her living as a teacher, and in her spare time has written the nine Inspector Rudd novels which have brought her a wide following in England and in the United States. Her most recent novels are *Shadow of a Doubt, Alibi in Time, The Habit of Loving,* and *A Question of Identity.* She lives in Hertfordshire with her two sons.